D0891818

Books by Thomas Williams

Ceremony of Love
Town Burning
The Night of Trees
A High New House
Whipple's Castle
The Hair of Harold Roux

THE HAIR OF HAROLD ROUX

THOMAS WILLIAMS

THE HAIR OF HAROLD ROUX

RANDOM HOUSE

NEW YORK

FIRST EDITION

 Published in the United States by Random House, Inc., New York, and simultaneously in Canada by Random House of Canada Limited, Toronto.

Library of Congress Cataloging in Publication Data

Williams, Thomas, 1926–
The hair of Harold Roux.

I. Title.
PZ4.W7275Hai [PS3573.I456] 813'.5'4 73–20583
ISBN 0–394–48988–8

Pages 76–91 and 223–228 originally appeared, in slightly different form, in *Esquire* Magazine.

Manufactured in the United States of America
24689753

First Edition

I would like to thank the Rockefeller Foundation
for a generous grant which helped give
me time to write this book.

Koi sureba abata mo ekubo.
(If there is love, smallpox scars seem as pretty as dimples.)
—Old Japanese saying

Men do not sham convulsion,
Nor simulate a throe.
—Emily Dickinson

When a man tries himself the verdict is in his favor.

As easy as lying.

THE HAIR OF HAROLD ROUX

Aaron Benham sits at his desk hearing the wrong voices. The human race he has been doomed to celebrate seems to be trying to prove to him that nothing is worthwhile, nothing at all. He sits in his small study surrounded by the interesting, haphazard fragments of the business of his life—books, stacks of old galley proofs, knives, pencils, pens, typewriter, dictionaries, shelves of old and new quarterly magazines, catalogs, incunabula. A wooden filing cabinet is filled to its drawer tops with stacks of papers, letters and manuscript pages as if each drawer were a bushelbasket. His one firm label in this area seems to be "miscellaneous." And yet it is his work to seek meaning and order. On the shelf just above his desk are his five books in their various editions and translations, each full of words he has painfully arranged in order.

But right now it seems to him that his world, with perhaps a temporary remission now and then, is departing upon a long slide away from any sort of rational middle, like a psychotic plunging toward his bleak end. Nobody is listening to anybody else. He wonders where he stands between chaos and that other order, the order of death—wonders if there is still a place to stand. Throughout the world he cannot leave, all of those in power seem corrupt, dimwitted or insanely committed to false assumptions. Children are being starved to death by the millions, yet twice as many more are being born into starvation and despair. The Prince of Peace has revealed himself to be in thrall to a legalistic code suited to the ages of plague. The tide of fascism he once observed from the shore now seems to have risen to the foundations of his house.

He leans over his notebook, feeling the ghosts of words in his fingers, but instead of words he draws a human torso. It is the body of a woman, slim-waisted, and now he draws, below the weakness, the vulnerability of the slim center, the hips' heartbreaking generosity, then the delicate bulge of belly implying all the inner complexities of life, passion, creation. He feels that this drawing has been called up by a certain episode in his past that has now turned dreamlike, bittersweet. In the sudden, sinking aura of memory he scribbles over the drawing, tears out the page and crumples it. Perhaps there is no longer enough time in his life to go back and illuminate to himself that dark episode; one never knows until the search is under way. He can think about it, try to explain it, but mere words of definition bore him because they are too simple, too full of lies. They can never be responsible for the exact quality of light that slants across his desk now, or through the pines of years ago; for the deep complexities of those undiscovered metaphors. But why go on, why describe, why search for the metaphor that would touch the scene with life? Because exercise begets energy, life begets life, rest is illness, paradox is all.

"Paradox," he says out loud, surely startling all his mute possessions. Against the pain of memory he holds the word. Para, parasol, parachute, parabellum. Dox, doxy, doxology—paradoxology. Remember that actual events are seductively plausible and contain meaningless emotion, like dreams; false importance, like dreams. If he can only begin, perhaps the realities of this unborn fiction will compel him forward out of the rigid past, away from a present that seems to deserve either tears or hysterical laughter, into the world of meaning.

But that world is, as always, contingent upon this real one, this small globe with its thin skin of air the gods of money and pride are so busily destroying, this world hermetically sealed by blackness of absolute zero.

So celebrate the race, celebrant. He hears cold cheers, ancient voices full of cracked glee, the voices of the dead.

It is 11:30 A.M., the sun just coming out again, now just missing the edge of his desk. Fire along the carpet. His wife should be home soon from the supermarket, the trunk of the car full of bags of groceries, bags within bags within life-proof plastic—at least fifty or sixty dollars' worth. The children are at school. He is supposed to call the septic tank man. He is supposed to make an appointment to have the car headlights adjusted because they point too high now that the snow tires have been changed. There are several other things he is afraid he has forgotten.

It is spring, and many of the birds are back. Across the road in the dying elms grackles and starlings jabber and creak, a strange descending tonality in their voices, like distant arguments in Italian.

Now the telephone in the front hall begins to ring, its smug, brainless imperative repeating, seeming to listen, repeating with impatience, even anger. He has to go to it.

"Hello?" he says into its network of infinite possibilities.

"Professor Benham?" A woman's ragged voice.

"Yes?" he says, fear waiting.

"Professor Benham? This is Louise Rasmussen, Mark Rasmussen's mother?"

Whenever he is confronted by emotional disintegration his spirit immediately capitulates, his heart beats erratically, his palms grow damp.

"Yes, Mark Rasmussen," he says, thinking that he would never use a telephone to convey anything but cool information. He tries to hold on to this calm thought.

"Professor Benham, he's disappeared! He's left school again and we don't know where he's gone! He hasn't been to any classes for three weeks and his roommates—the people he lives with—won't tell us anything! They say they don't know where he is!"

First he thinks of Mark's homely, intelligent face, upon which the ironies of despair constantly flicker as he suppresses one inexpressible joke after another—a gnomelike, grayish young face above its tangled beard. It is a face that allows laughter only. Mark would never blat out his feelings this way.

"Have you talked to the dean?" Aaron's fraudulently calm voice enters the telephone's electronic diaphragms and filters. Her voice continues, too intimately near his unprotected brain. He can feel her breath that really isn't there, as if she might at any moment insert her hot ravaged tongue in his ear. He shudders for Mark. Who wouldn't want to flee this swampy intensity?

"Yes! He told us about Mark not going to any classes and that's how we found out that you were Mark's adviser and how you might have some idea . . ."

She stops, demanding by her silence that he take over her sentence, her problems. But after a moment she takes hold again, her voice weeping and demanding, and he thinks good God he can *see* this woman he's never seen who's lost her whelp, her offspring she never understood under all that creepy weirdo hippie hair anyway. But Mark is her child, isn't he? He came from her womb.

"We don't even *know* any of his friends! We don't even know what they look like he wouldn't bring them home after what happened last fall . . . what awful drugs he's taking or what! *Mir, mir, mir,*" she utters, weeping those syllables.

He can see her, the granulated skin of her soft cheeks, her eyes ugly from crying. She is probably not much older than he is, but Mark seems much more his contemporary than this damp maternal force. He resents the tears of pity that have got in the way of his vision.

"I'm on leave this year," he says, "so Mark has another adviser . . ."

"Yes. Professor Parker. We know! But he only signed

Mark's schedule, that's all he knows about Mark at all! That's all he knows about Mark!"

"I'll see what I can find out for you."

"Oh, thank you! Thank you! We thought you might know some of his friends. He must have friends. Students. We just don't even know who his friends *are*, Professor Benham!"

"Well," he says, still amazed by his falsely steady voice, "I knew who some of them were last spring. Let me have your telephone number so I can let you know if I find out anything."

She gives him a number in the town of Somerville, a depressed little mill town fifteen miles or so from the university. But Louise Rasmussen wants to talk further, to try to explain now that her original question has been answered. She sounds as though explanation is more her forte, and Aaron remembers that Mark once told him she used to be a grammar school teacher. Yes, she e–nun–ci–ates. Guilt and self-justification: "What did we do wrong? We've given Mark everything, Professor Benham! Everything!"

He wants to tell her that she probably didn't do anything wrong, but of course that's no answer because it isn't much of a reason for all that hair and those raggedy clothes and that funny smell of burning rope. He wonders if the Rasmussens wouldn't have preferred some other variety of freak—a mongoloid, perhaps.

"What did we do wrong? What did we do wrong?" How many times has he heard that self-defeating cry? He is irritated now, because God! these women with their middle-aged quirky crazy desperation hung out like the raw flesh of a wound!

"I'll see what I can do, Mrs. Rasmussen," says the benevolent, paternal voice of the professor.

"We'll be eternally grateful! We love Mark so much! Thank you! Thank you!"

And again he is betrayed into tears by her worry and grief. She finally hangs up and he howls to his empty house with the ear-popping intensity of a tortured baboon.

When he is through howling, Aaron stands at the kitchen stove listening to the tiny whines the coffeepot emits while it is heating. A cigarette hangs dry in his lips. Yes, he'll probably be able to locate Mark, and he'll do it because he said he would, and because Mark was once one of his most talented students. Presumably Mark is still talented, but Aaron has learned not to become overexcited by any sort of potential. It is as if a specific solvent for talent has been introduced into the national diet. Perhaps it is a new symptom of ecological poisoning.

With a heavy, soggish feeling, he realizes that soon he'll have to go back to teaching. For every student with Mark's iron in him, there are so many others. Unused talent can break your heart, but the others deaden the soul. So many times in the last ten years he has so patiently explained that self-indulgence is not art, that in spite of all temporal evidence to the contrary what is gained is earned. How many thousand more poems must he read beginning thus:

Kaleidoscope of the City
comes
neonpulsing
the I Ching
opens
leaves
silhouettes
upon
the
burning
we
ecstaticly
Revitalyse!

Or thus:

Violets vibrating
My pad

You rhyme me
Warm asleep
Hare
Hare
Hare Krishna
Hare
Hare
Hare Krishna
Strung
Out
Beautiful
Hare
Hare
Hare Krishna

How many thousand more times must he with sweet reason convey the information that he is neither pleased nor dismayed by *any* statement of belief or of feeling or by any object supposedly disgusting or supposedly beautiful unless it is made so by the poet. And heaviest of all is the knowledge that he will always search until he finds something, some small, possibly accidental voltage engendered here or there between a word and a word or a phrase and a phrase, and, in mentioning this, store up somewhere in his psyche another dangerously explosive charge, until . . .

But not Aaron Benham, that kindly sufferer of fools.

And then there is still poor Mark, whom he has known now for at least seven years and who has been through most of the major storms and awakenings of his times, beginning with sit-ins in the South, with SNCC, jail, a beating that left him with a broken hand, and on up the twisted years of the late sixties and into the seventies. Chicago, Washington; after the Cambodia–Kent State–Jackson State spring he disappeared for more than a year and came back sad, cynical, allowing that maybe he'd try to write again. Aaron hasn't seen him for a month or more, but then Mark knows he is on leave and trying to work, and beyond Mark's usual brashness is a perhaps inordinate respect for those who are working.

Aaron is back at his desk, his bitter coffee in hand. Suddenly he puts the coffee cup down, walks to the corner of his study and picks up a rifle, black cold metal embraced by the organic walnut of its stock, the long bolt silvered by the locking slides of the fifty and more years of its existence. It was manufactured in January 1918 for a quaint war now passed out of all but a few living memories. The rifle in his arms becomes part of him, part of his humanity. Why else has it evolved to fit shoulder and arms and eye with such perfection, even comfort? His heritage over the generations, slowly evolved from matchlock and harquebus into this smooth instrument of his culture.

His, indeed. He can not imagine how he has come to be a professor. Aaron Benham, professor of sweet reason? Hysterical laughter in the background. Don't list your beliefs because they are all, essentially, lies. You are not the sweet rational person whose face they know. One click over that line and murder steams in your heart. You have always been armed. You have always swung your shoulders like a typical arrogant American, and enjoyed the ice of confrontation. Christ! If he could only have some friends, some enemies he is not constrained to understand. He is sick of reason, sick of convincing. The professor is sick to death of *explaining.*

He puts his rifle back in its niche; it seems to have given strength to his arm and at the same time to have robbed his brain. He wants to think only of the rifle's purity of function, which cleans his mind of all the paradoxical complications of having to be a member of his race.

THE HAIR OF HAROLD ROUX

his notebook says to him. But that is only a title. The rest of his creation fades back across a long plain into mist and darkness. He has always thought of a novel, before it has taken on its first, tentative structure, as a scene on this dark plain, the characters standing around a small fire which warmly etches the edges of their faces. Distant mountains are turning moon-cold and blue as the last light fades as if forever. It is that small fire he must constantly re-create or these last warm lives will cease to live, will never have lived even to fear the immensities of coldness and indifference around them. Absolute Zero is waiting, always. In Paradoxology that is perhaps the name of God.

He has a poem he wants to write, called "To an Ice Tick." Unfinished lines haunt him.

> *. . . the synapse*
> *Must contain in small the conception*
> *Of the conception of warmth*
> *Here in its always small increments*
> *A dry and an ice age hence.*

Compared to Zero the tiny exoskeletal mite, protected from our inevitable stupidity by the mile-thick icecap of Greenland, is our warm ancestor, our only hope for a re-creation of humor, grace and love. When one cannot look back and find even one incident in the sad history of the race in which vanity was not more important, even, than survival, one tends to search desperately for a friend. Perhaps he will presume to instruct the ice tick in the possibilities of selective evolution toward a consciousness of its own mortality—that dark knowledge from which all gaiety and humor arises.

But then again he might not. He thinks of stabbing his pencil straight down into his notebook to see how many pages the graphite point will pierce, when the telephone rings.

No. He will not answer it. He will not answer it, he silently declares as his various traitorous appendages move him away from his desk toward the front hall where the mad thing squats and screams.

"Aaron?" Another worried voice not far from tears, but this time it is Helga Buck, his friend, the wife of his friend. "Aaron, I know you're working . . ." Her voice is deep, breathy as the voice of a singer of the fifties whose name he can't recall.

"What's the matter, Helga?"

"It's George," she says.

She seems to have lost her breath, and he compulsively offers his. "What's the matter with him?"

"He's out in the garden. He's got the blues something awful, Aaron. I was just wondering if maybe you couldn't just drop by or something. I mean I know you're working and I think it's a dumb thing to ask. I mean maybe beg. Christ, I don't know . . ."

"Sure, Helga."

"I mean at breakfast I just mentioned something or other—maybe it was the Corps of Engineers—and he went into the bathroom and I think he vomited."

"Okay, I'll try to cheer him up," Aaron says. "You know me. I'm just a bundle of joy."

He gets her to laugh a little, anyway. "Aaron, don't tell him I called you, huh?"

"Okay, Helga, sure. Of course not."

"And thanks, Aaron. Thank you." She is grateful, almost cheerful as she hangs up, which makes him feel noble, or something. He isn't able to think of a word for his feelings because for one thing he is exasperated by George Buck. George won't finish his Ph.D. dissertation. He's been given a deadline by the dean and the department; he has to have it passed by his adviser at Brown by the end of August or next year will be his last. If he doesn't get the thing finished he will have to take his wife and his bright seven-year old son Edward and go somewhere else to teach, and jobs at decent places are almost impossible to find. Aaron finds this procrastination hard to understand. A little, yes; maybe even a lot. He is no stranger to sloth himself—but not at the certain, documented expense of his job and his home. In the Bucks' case their home, their beloved old house, has become important far beyond material considerations. George and Helga have taken a sill-rotted, almost hopelessly warped and sunken eighteenth-century farmhouse and by their own sweat and patience made it square and sound. From the sodden, foundering hulk that it had been they have erased time and made it light and crisp upon its green lawns again, as true as its loving builders crafted and squared it in A.D. 1749. Aaron knows that the house is deeply—scarily, in fact—part of George's continuing life. George uses it the way some people use drugs or alcohol; sometimes in the middle of a conversation Aaron can see George's eyes as he looks for calmness and satisfaction, measuring his ancient hand-hewn beams, counting whatever blessings are left in the midst of so much cold knowledge.

But during the four years they've labored to restore the old house George has put off his dissertation—a time bomb he must have known would destroy all their work.

But does George really know this, or not? The rationalizations of the highly intelligent can grow subtle beyond human understanding.

"God *damn* it!" Aaron yells as he goes back to his desk to write a note to his wife. In his unhinged state he finds himself writing something flippant.

> Dear Agnes,
>
> SOS from Helga, so out to comfort George. Yippee! I don't have to write! Also, I am definitely insane, but not to worry: Heaven protects a fool.
>
> Mossy buckets
> of concupiscence,
> A.

From the hall closet he takes a nylon windbreaker and his white crash helmet, goes to the garage and straddles his black and silver Honda. As he pulls the crash helmet down over his ears its warm, foamy cushioning reminds him of the interior of a Greyhound bus—too plushy and humid. State law says he has to wear the thing, so he must thank the state for protecting him from himself.

The machine changes him in ways he finds interesting and somewhat frightening—frightening in retrospect, at least. It is similar to the effect his rifle has on him, in that they both tend to purify and somehow heighten him as an animal. He cannot ride this gleaming power slowly or hesitantly.

Now he chokes the machine, opens the fuel-cutoff valve, finds the green dash light signifying neutral and kicks down the starter. It has its own authoritative cold life, and he lets the engine warm itself—low, businesslike revolving beats smoothing toward power. It is not a big machine but it is meant for racing, and the short throws of gearshift, clutch and throttle are for quickness and precision. It will take him into the wind, where he will lean through the curves.

He rides out through his graveled driveway, feeling a hardly perceptible, yet precisely perceptible, sliding out of the rear wheel. Every motion of this machine *means*, under pain of instant violence to his body. On the asphalt he finds a steadier traction and increases his speed. Soon he is going sixty miles an hour, his tender bones inches from the road, and he asks himself what he is doing here. Isn't this stupid? some part of his brain insists upon quietly asking. If his chain breaks, or if any one of a number of little possibilities occur, he will instantly become a basket case. The answer is that when this ride is over, he will be safe; nothing exists to force him to ride so dangerously again. And after the next ride, he will be perfectly safe.

Five miles later, with a few bugs splashed against his glasses, a few more in his teeth (a peculiar, acidy taste, something like fresh tomato), with memories, as if he's been drunk, of trees leaning, fields tilting, cars about to do threateningly irresponsible things, he turns into the Bucks' driveway and stops next to their barn. He finds neutral and with a sigh of transition turns off his engine. When he pulls off the thick helmet, his head feels light, giddy. He walks on tingling delicate feet to the kitchen door, where Helga meets him. She has been described to him as homely, something he will never be able to understand; she is a small, intense girl, a little skinny, with unfortunate hair the color of tarnished copper, but her smallness is not cute, her intensity is not demanding or aggressive, and when Aaron talks to her he sometimes finds himself abstracted by daydreams of Helga's vivid little body naked beside his. Learned hesitancies or not, this vision sometimes intrudes, but there is no guilt attached; if he took the time to feel guilty about all the things he thinks of doing, rather than what he actually does, he wouldn't function very well in this world. But here he goes again, her slim thighs flickering in the muted, strobic light of his fantasies. To him she is always, for some reason, green—a delicate mint green that reminds him of those perfectly formed people in Flash Gordon, from the planet Mongo.

"He's out in the garden," Helga says in her deep voice, a voice that always reveals the breath that is so vital to life. He notices that the fingers holding her constant cigarette are stained browner than usual, and that her large eyes are a little smudgy, the gray irises bleached.

"You do look a little sad, Helga," he says.

She tries to smile, but it turns into a little self-deprecating quirk of the lips. "Well, you know I'm worried," she says.

He puts his hand around her arm above the elbow, feeling the bone surrounded by its delicate warmth of flesh. "Where's the patient?" he asks.

"In the garden. Come on."

Together they walk around the corner of the old gray barn and stop to observe George, who sits among the pepper plants playing listless mumbledypeg with a garden trowel. He wears dungarees and an old gray sweatshirt so full of holes it looks as though it has been sprayed with acid. In faded blue letters, BOWDOIN can still be made out across his slumped back.

"George?" Helga calls. "Look who's here!"

George turns his head, smiles and jumps up. He immediately goes down again, then gets up smiling ruefully and massaging his left calf. "Leg went to sleep!" he says, limping toward them. "God, it feels like a bag of nails!"

"How's it going?" Aaron asks, thinking not only of the general but of the specific, meaning George's dissertation, which concerns the verse of one Henry Troy, 1548–1610, brewer, wool factor and occasional, lousy, poet.

"Pretty good. Pretty good," George says. "Not bad. Can't complain." His wide honest blue eyes seem never to indicate that they reflect any previous knowledge or opinion, but that whatever they gaze upon is new and fascinating, even quite wonderful. George is thirty-one, Helga twenty-nine. She turns away, looking at the dark earth of the garden.

"Hmm," Aaron says.

George is looking at him; is there a gleam of resentment somewhere in that innocent blue? George decides to smile. "Well," he says. "Well. I'm a liar, yes. Things aren't really too good." He suffers a spasm of the lips, turns away, turns back shrugging apologetically.

A cloud passes across the sun, making them look up. More are coming; dark anvils grow in the west above the wooded hills. A gust of wind turns the field hay dull silver in swathes.

"I'd better put my motorcycle in the barn for the moment," Aaron says. George hurries ahead to open the barn door. When the machine is safe inside the barn they go back to the house and join Helga in the low, beamed living room George loves so much. Little light comes through the narrow old windows, less as the dark cumuli move over the house. Helga turns on two warm table lamps and it might be night.

"How about a beer?" Helga says. "Aaron?" She looks to him, a little gleam of conspiracy in her eyes, and he answers correctly. She brings them beer and glasses on a black stenciled tray, and they ceremonially, silently, pour.

"It's going to *storm,*" Helga says.

"I guess I'm letting things get me down," George says.

"Who can blame you?" Aaron says.

"I mean, what we're doing to the world. I can't believe it, Aaron. Sometimes I forget it for a few minutes and when it all comes back it's worse. It's like remembering at four in the morning that you're going to die, only it's worse than just you dying. Christ, it's everybody, everything!"

"I have the same hallucinations."

"But you still get your work done!" George says, meaning that it must not bother you *enough.*

It is two-thirty, and now the storm surrounds them. The electricity goes off with none of the fading, brightening, fading that predicts only a temporary failure. It goes off as though God's hand has pulled all the wires like hair, in snarled handfuls. They sit in the white flashes, the narrow old windows printing their framed lights intact upon the optic nerves. Aaron wonders if George welcomes these moments of blackout as he himself does—these moments free of guilt about his work. Right now he cannot work, and though he enjoys this feeling of lightness it also shows him how constant and heavy is the burden of his work.

"I love storms," Helga says. "I love anything powerful that isn't caused by man."

Hmm, Aaron thinks.

As yet there has been only distant thunder, but now it comes rolling across the hills toward them, sharp breaking sounds within softer rumbles. The only metaphor Aaron can think of has to do with some game or other of man's. Barrage, etc.

"Wouldn't it be nice to be scared of thunder again!" Helga says.

"Yes," Aaron says. "Wouldn't it be nice to be scared of God."

"Instead of some nasty little men," Helga says.

"Christ, yes," George says. He gets up; in the lightning flashes each movement is frozen, framed like a still camera shot. Soon he comes back from the kitchen carrying a lighted oil lamp and puts it on the table. Its truly yellow light brings out their faces, seems to hang them like glowing portraits against the darkness. Warm, ice-blue, warm, ice, as the lightning arcs across its polarities. When the wind and rain begin, the old house creaks and releases its secret mustiness into the air, cool breath from ancient interior spaces.

"So nice to be under this old roof," George says dreamily.

George's dreamy impracticality exasperates Aaron. He knows better than to grab George by the arm and talk straight to him. For one thing, he's done just that before, and he knows his words will be greeted with hysteria in one form or another—sullenness, partial deafness, a counter-lecture about the evils of The System. But here is George Buck, after having spent ten years of his life preparing himself for one profession, and he still won't let himself believe in its simplest technicality: that the advanced degree is necessary for promotion. And the plain simple hardfast rule, printed clearly in the Staff Handbook—surely the language is clear enough for a teacher of English to decipher—states that without promotion no contract will be renewed after the fifth year. Aaron wants to shout, *Look, George! This is incredible! You've been told over and over again! Believe it!* But what good will that do? Aaron does have some understanding of George's beautiful baroque set of rationalizations. George works so hard, he teaches so hard, he is so close to his students and so necessary to them that he has to believe that somehow he is above such crassly technical considerations.

As the intensity of the storm grows, George's dreamy mood changes into excitement. He goes from window to window to stare at the wildness outside. "Beautiful! God *damn*, look at that!" Beside the house their four-foot avocado tree, set out for the summer, writhes frantically in the rain and wind, flashes rich green, bows nearly flat, then comes partially back upright, its leaves like hands in religious ecstasy. "Shee-*it*, man! There goes a limb off that white pine!" He turns joyfully, his hand strongly caressing the thick boards of the window frame. "This old house knows how to roll with it, by God! Strong! I know how bloody strong!"

A bolt hits so near it really scares them all—its tearing *crack* felt in the fingertips, and then the slightly delayed knowledge that they are still alive.

"Wow!" George yells gleefully. "That one hit the transformer on the pole! I saw it!"

The faint smell of ozone breathes through the house.

"I must admit I've had just about enough of this storm," Helga says, a little shakily. The oil lamp flickers, though there is no obvious draft.

Aaron is slightly nervous, too, so his tone becomes as nearly pedantic as it ever does. "But you love this power, Helga. This primeval energy that belittles nasty man."

"Well, I don't like it when it belittles us *too* much," she says.

"Oh, come on," Aaron says. "We need something we're too scared to enjoy. Anyway, something up there that isn't controlled from Houston. The Furies—that's what we need, or we can't even enjoy a good old roof."

CRACK! BLAM! says the storm.

"*Jesus!*" George answers.

After a time of slightly less apocalyptic explosions and gusts, they realize that the storm's salvos are just perceptibly diminishing.

"I wonder if it's safe to go into the kitchen yet," George says. "Sometimes we get these little fireballs zapping around between the stove and the water heater." As the storm subsides into rain and mist, he grows quiet and sad. "Well, it looks like it's over. As dear old Henry Troy once sang,

> *'The Furious Surge hath sped away;*
> *Soft smiles now galeth all the pretty day . . .'*

or some such immortal couplet."

"So how is it coming?" Aaron rather carefully asks.

"Okay. It's shaping up, little by little." And George jumps up to get some more beer.

Aaron looks at Helga in the lamplight. She seems to have lost her vernal green, and stares, loyally, away from his eyes. "I've told him," she says in her whispery voice. "I've done all I can. Aaron, he just can't believe it. He prepares harder and harder for his classes. . . ."

"Christ," Aaron says, keeping his voice low, "I don't even think he knows I'm a senior member and have to vote on his case—because you know there were a couple of exceptions, a long time ago, and even if it's only theoretical we're still supposed to have the power to break the rules—only we don't in this case because it's really up to the dean, and we know what he'll say, and the president and the trustees. But mainly I don't think George *knows* what sort of machinery gets set in motion. What do you think?"

"I don't think he thinks about it at all, Aaron. I mean, he knows but he won't consider it for a minute. He'd rather think pleasanter thoughts, like about pollution, the military-industrial complex, racism, overpopulation and the cobalt bomb."

Usually Helga does not mix irony with her worries, and Aaron looks at her carefully. She becomes unbearably important to him because he is devastated by this change in her that sounds like despair. For the moment she is the only other person in the world and he becomes her, feels his nerves leading to all her muscles and glands and tendons; even her small bones seem to shiver with a kind of ticklish pain beside his own, inside his flesh. He is a man with a woman inside him, and he seems to feel and understand her womanness, the vulnerability of something like incompleteness, of empty womb, empty everything—though here he begins to doubt his evaluation of female helplessness and tries to shiver off this excruciating union.

George comes back with the beer, a flashlight held in his armpit. For a while they talk, deliberately, about storms, those great natural explosions, their mostly benevolent power of sustenance and change.

This storm, sending its farewell rumbles back from the east, moves on, and the narrow windows lighten again toward day. "It's clearing," George says.

The sun comes out for a moment, printing a window upon the varnished pine floor. "I wonder if there's a rainbow," Helga says.

They go out onto the front lawn, where the evenly trimmed wet grass seems to grow greener by the second. Part of a rainbow in the northeast, pale pastels, can be seen against a black bank of cloud. The sun comes across the house again, just as a gleaming yellow school bus, tires dripping, red lights flashing, stops at the mailbox. Its front door opens to the cries of children, and out comes Edward Buck, a second-grader, with his tin lunch box and green book bag. He looks like his mother—a little green man from Mongo. The children on the bus wave their arms behind the glass, but Edward pays no attention to them, or to their now muted screams. With dignity he comes up the front walk, book bag over his shoulder, lunch box in his hand.

"I didn't eat my pickle," he tells his mother. "It was a dill pickle."

"Oh, I'm sorry," Helga says. "I thought I put in a sweet pickle. I must have got the jars mixed up."

The bus departs with its lively cargo. "I don't like that driver," Edward says. "He won't make them shut up. It's enough to break your eardrums. Mrs. Bailey is better because she lets them talk in a normal voice, but they can't yell all the time."

Edward is bright. Soon he will be skipping grades and taking advanced courses taught by university faculty. George looks at him now, his expression pure and serene.

"Hello, Aaron," Edward says, now that the business of the pickle and the bus have been dealt with.

"Hi, Ed," Aaron says.

Edward turns to his father. "Billy Davis got his foot caught under the merry-go-round and nearly broke it, so they took it away."

"The foot?" George says, his eyes wide in mock wonder.

Edward laughs. "No, the stupid merry-go-round." Smiling, he shakes his head resignedly.

"Well, that's what you get for a vague antecedent," George says.

"All our antecedents are vague," Helga says, "but we're here."

In the fresh sunlight, mist steams from the gray clapboards of the old house. Aaron watches this young family standing in its own place. With a surge of possibility he wonders if he might somehow write George's dissertation for him. For a moment it seems perfectly possible: George will show him his notes, his drafts, tell him the central idea, and Aaron will sit down and write the damned thing. Sure.

"I guess I'd better be going," he says. In the back of his mind a wisp of memory bothers him, but he decides it is merely guilt because he isn't working.

"Oh, don't go, Aaron! Helga says. There's plenty more beer."

"It'll keep," he says. "Anyway, the motorcycle doesn't run too good on beer. It thinks it does, but afterwards it has nightmares about running up the sides of trees."

"Stay a little longer. It's only three-thirty or so."

Why does she want him to stay so badly? They have their perfect triangle. Why a fourth? He looks at George, whose humorous serenity concerning his loved child has changed. Darkness has crossed his face again, his mouth has fallen, his eyes stare at some non-place in the middle of the grass. As if she knows what to do in this case, Helga takes Edward, a hand lightly on his shoulder, into the house. George stares on, not seeming to notice their departure.

"Hey," Aaron says. He stands firmly on the sod, feeling strong, capable, even generous. A whisper in his innards scoffs at this self-estimation, but faintly. He examines his unhappy friend, daring to look for anything, however dark.

"I think," George says carefully, "that I may be going off my nut, and I don't like it, Aaron." His eyes are still unfocused. "I mean I can't shake it. It's like my head's in a vice and all the assholes of the world are turning the goddam handle. We haven't learned lesson number one. Maybe we don't even know what it is. But we're killing the world, Aaron. We know what we're doing and we keep right on doing it. That's psychotic, man, and I think I've caught it and what's the use? How can you *not think* about something? Christ! Nerve gas, radioactive wastes that have to be kept refrigerated for eight generations or else, not to mention being located in earthquake zones. Television fucking outright lies, brain rot, money worship, rivers in hell that catch on fire. Or forget all that, don't think about it and just listen to our great leaders off the record talking about kikes and niggers, man, or go down to gasoline alley to get your oil changed and hear the same murderous arrogant shit. What the hell? And meanwhile it's one holy war after another. And the whole stinking race is born of rape. Screw fuck bang jab nail hump shag score—we've got our metaphors, Aaron, don't we? Oh Christ, I know you know all this and I'm sorry."

"So why bother finishing your dissertation?"

"Oh, that. I don't mean that. I don't know, maybe so. But everything is dying so what does anything matter?"

"I don't know, George. I've never understood how we ever began to cope with the idea of death. No other animal seems to be cursed with that bit of knowledge."

"But, Aaron! We're deliberately killing ourselves!"

"I am the asphalt; let me work."

"Yeah."

"Get your dissertation done and then worry about all that."

"Shit," George says, weakly, as though he's out of breath.

"It's pretty around here, anyway," Aaron says.

George looks around at the tall pine and maple trees, the green lawn, the smooth hayfield backed by pine woods—all fresh and gleaming after the wind and rain.

"That only makes it worse!" he says.

So every time Edward comes home from school, that probably makes it worse, and every time George makes love to his warm green wife, that probably makes it worse. And George won't finish his dissertation so he'll have to sell his house and move away from all this pretty stuff that makes it worse.

"I used to think I could do something about it," George says. "I was involved, man. You know all that. But now I know better, Aaron. They're all a bunch of murderers. The murderers always take over in the end. On both sides. I'm telling you, Aaron, I think I hate the whole *fucking human race!*" His voice breaks, tries to seem angry, but what happens is really a sob.

Evidently those wondering, wonder-filled blue eyes have been betrayed too often, because they are now glassy with tears. Aaron puts his hands on George's thin shoulders. As for himself, he feels healthier and morally inferior—a condition he seems to remember having been in most of his life. But now he realizes that for his own stability he must get back to his desk and his notebook. Back there is where he has to be. The hair of Harold Roux—something about Harold's hair makes his own scalp prickle about the ears. Whatever the discovery is, it's probably not pleasant, but it is a discovery, not one of the items on George's list of boring known stupidities, and it is back there at his desk.

George says wearily, "I don't know. I don't know."

"In any case, I think it would be dumb to go off your nut," Aaron says, squeezing George's thin drooping shoulders, shaking him until his neck stiffens a little. George looks up with a hopeless smile.

"Thanks for the advice, anyway," George says.

After Aaron has wheeled his motorcycle out of the barn and George has rolled the big door shut, Aaron remembers the call from Mark Rasmussen's mother.

"You know Mark Rasmussen, don't you?" he asks.

"Mark! Yes!" As George's face clears with pleasure, his blue eyes open again to wonder and care.

"He seems to have disappeared again—at least out of his parents' ken. His mother called me this morning, me having been his adviser last year. Not that he ever asked me for any advice."

"Damn him!" George says excitedly. "He's brilliant, but he's lazy! He ought to have his ass kicked around the block. Anyway, I think I can find out where he is. Yes, I think I know someone who'll know."

"Give me a call if you do. His mother was off *her* nut, I'll tell you that. But we ought to ask Mark if he wants to be found. I mean, in between kicking his ass around the block. After all, he's 'of age,' as they say."

"Of course!" George says. "Of course!"

He leaves George standing there by the barn, the general expression of his spine and shoulders lively again—for the moment. As he goes up through the gears, air hissing past his helmet, he takes one backward glance. George waves, so he risks a moment of control to wave back, then bores on through the narrow permissible tunnel of wind and motion a motorcycle must so precisely follow. He leaves George and Helga behind—George and Helga Buck, sadly and inevitably bound to their real lives. Now he is free but he must watch everything ahead, see and understand every single thing. Dogs, mailboxes, stones, children, potholes; the deepest intentions of all drivers, moving or parked; old ladies, their brittle senilities of motion; raccoons, chipmunks, sand, cats, fallen branches, leaves, acorns. The way must have traction and be free, or else his life will instantly and drastically change, and his huddled people, motionless there on the cold plain before the small fire, will never grow into their own dangers and intensities.

He is flying, a projectile governed by the brutal judgments of velocity, but also directed by the thin precision of control. His right wrist twists the throttle farther, as far as it will turn. It is madness, but this danger is of his making; he alone creates it. Wind shrieks by him, the whole earth tilts through a long bend, black trees flash past, every one a death, but it is his own wrist, no matter its fragility, that holds the throttle turned. Fear speaks to his nerves, whispers, subsides, shrills to him. He is at the mercy of each spoke of his wheels, each blurred rivet of his chain, the few pounds of entrapped air in his narrow tires, but he is also the controlling force whose skill may successfully complete this journey. It is merely a simpler journey, with a simpler conclusion, than the longer one he hurtles toward.

The five miles pass and he does make it back safely to his

driveway, to the smooth cement floor of his garage. The relief, though post-foolhardy, is deserved, except that he is the only one who has put himself in such needless danger. No one asked him to live this way, just as no one asked him to live or die with those waiting souls on the cold, metaphoric plain. But he is here, he has made it, and in small he feels the completeness, the symmetry of having made something out of chaos. It is the shadow of his expectations about his book, and now he must get back to his work.

As he enters his house he feels the wrongness, the prophetic stillness of the air. Agnes and the children should be home, but the car, he remembers, is not here either. On the kitchen counter in a square of harsh sunlight is a note from his wife:

> We have gone to Wellesley. I write the name down because you probably wouldn't remember that, either.

That is what has been at the back of his mind, wanting out. Now it is all there with horrible clarity; they were supposed to go to Agnes' parents' overnight because it is her parents' fortieth wedding anniversary. The reception is this afternoon; the kids weren't in school, they were with Agnes getting clothes for the occasion. They must have returned and left just about the time he buzzed blithely off on his Honda.

The depth of his depression amazes him. He hears himself groan; his hands tremble. Black wings hover over his life. Why hadn't she called the Bucks? Because the telephone was undoubtedly out along with the electricity, or, more likely, she was justifiably infuriated.

She has written her short message over the one he left her:

> Dear Agnes,
>
> SOS from Helga, so out to comfort George. Yippee! I

don't have to write! Also, I am definitely insane, but not to worry: Heaven protects a fool.

Mossy buckets
of concupiscence,
A.

The words are unforgivably asinine, and in this context not only flippant but cruel. How can he have forgotten? then her reality; she loves and serves to a fault, and she would never, never commit this particular crime. Thus her icy intolerance. And her parents will really be hurt that he hasn't come. But he is not going to buzz in, four or five hours late, on his motorcycle. He hasn't the energy left today to ride a hundred miles. No, it is bravery rather than energy he lacks, and his resentment of his just reward enervates him still further, knocks out his strength. What he has done is unforgivable. He groans again, frightening himself badly with that unpremeditated sound. He cannot stand this. "*God damn it!*" he yells at the house empty of his noisy family. The accusing answer doesn't come.

He walks up and down the kitchen. Sunlight vibrates on the sills.

So he forgot! Everybody forgets things once in a while! Yes, but what things, Aaron?

He'll make himself a drink. After he opens the refrigerator door he is so rattled that he drops the ice-cube tray on the cat, who gives a breathless grunt and runs away. Cats are always prepared for betrayal; all she wants is some Calo and the bastard drops a brick on her.

Of course his note to Agnes might have been even stupider, even more degradingly flip. He might have written words that would now torture him even more, and he indulges his quivering mind for a moment in a fit of self-hatred; ah, how (is this, and in what way, coldly interesting?) the inventive brain lacerates the soul:

Dear Agonous,

Motorsickle in crotch, go I in mercy to a sick psyche.

Carnally yours,
A.

Dear Agonist,

Sick psychward on motorpsychle Samaritanwise fly I.

Airily,
Aileron

No, he still doesn't have it right. He could have degraded himself even more. God, what a genius for cruelty Agnes has when he, in his usual fashion, hurts her. And he's got to call her and receive more of it. But it's only his preoccupation, his necessary concentration, isn't it, that makes him seem cruelly indifferent? Then why the bottomless, anxious shame he suffers now?

The bourbon is tasteless. The liquid is brown and real, but his body signals nothing, not a shiver. Desperately needing something to hold on to, something with even the smallest hope of a future, he goes to his study and looks down at his notebook.

THE HAIR OF HAROLD ROUX

his notebook says. It speaks to him tonelessly, from an impossible distance. The words form a cryptic message from a stranger whose dark, complicated intellect is far beyond his simple understanding. And yet the handwriting is ominously familiar. That pretentious hand is his, and it tells him that his imagination is bankrupt, that this project is far beyond his powers. The passion, the energy subside; senility enters on stunning little cat feet.

THE HAIR OF HAROLD ROUX

As he reads the words again he finds almost against his will that he is peering, straining to see as if through a thin wall of ice the far plain, cold as the moon, the small fire that is the one warm spark upon its immense uncreated emptiness, and there his people wait. Mary, Harold and the rest are waiting and will wait forever if he cannot separate himself from all the needful vampires of this life—Agnes, his children, his friends, those beloved drinkers of his blood (oh, paradox!)—whose remorseless realities place him here, in this world, now, at his desk.

He is at his desk but he is thinking of Mark Rasmussen, the strange authority of that young intelligence. One time Mark came by his office at school while Aaron was talking to a nervous girl, one of his advisees, about a course she was probably going to get a D in. It seemed she just couldn't get along with that particular professor; no matter what she wrote for him he didn't like it and made sarcastic remarks in the margins. She was a large-boned, husky girl, with a wide, heavy face full of desperate earnestness and all the raw or half-healed wounds young flesh is heir to. Her great hams, stippled with irregular indentations where the muscles were not in stress, filled the chair.

Mark, although he didn't know the girl, entered freely into the discussion. "You can't beat it," he said. "Drop the course."

"But I need the course," she said. "It satisfies the humanities requirement!"

Her eyes had begun to glisten and Mark put his thin arm around her muscular shoulders. "Come on," he said. "It's all bullshit, but so you get a D or something. It still takes care of the requirement."

"But I've never gotten a D in my life!"

"Oh hell, what's a D?" Mark said lightly. "Professor Benham here gave me a D once, didn't you, Aaron?"

"It was a gift," Aaron said, and Mark smiled like a grinning dog, his lips pulling back from naked teeth and gums. The girl, whose name was Jackie, didn't know how to react to Mark's affection. He continued to squeeze her gently and to pat her hands, and Aaron could see the great mixed desperation in her rigid trunk and burning face. While Mark's feeling for her was no doubt genuine, Aaron couldn't help think that his gesture contained more than a small amount of rape. She blushed, she tried to smile, she was pleased and terrified.

But when she left she seemed calmer, as though those moments of high emotion had somehow let her transcend her apprehension about the prospective D.

"Do you know her?" Aaron asked when Jackie had gone.

"No. What's her name?"

"Jacqueline Tobia Blum, but she signs her name 'Jackie.' "

"I'll look her up," Mark said.

"You find her attractive?"

"The poor chick's so hung up. That's interesting. Kind of pitiful. Yes."

"You mean you just want to mess around with her hang-ups?"

"Ah, Aaron! You disapprove!" Mark laughed his sibilant laugh, "*See see shoo shoo!*" his long, gnomish face turned nearly to the ceiling. Mark was a strange case; he looked like those boys whose almost freakish homeliness make them awkward and shy, and he came from a small New Hampshire mill town, which might have compounded any feelings of inferiority. But Mark was as un-shy as anyone could be; he looked at the world with constantly judging eyes.

"Well," Aaron said. "Aside from my disapproval—pardon the aesthetics of another age or something—do you find poor Jackie physically attractive?"

"All girls are physically attractive if they're in reasonable health," Mark said.

"That sounds lovely, if slightly patronizing," Aaron said. "It's just that one of her healthy young legs probably weighs more than my whole wife. I can't help it. I mean I'd feel like

I was doing something a little too monumental."

Mark laughed tolerantly. What he had come for was to ask Aaron if he would like to go as crew for a day on a fishing boat run by a friend—a party boat. Mark thought it would be interesting, and that Aaron ought to get out of his ivory tower for a day and see how the other half lived. "You know," he said, "the real guys."

"You think I need that?" Aaron said.

"Sure, man. There's another world out there, you know, where nearly everybody gets a D nearly all the time, but they don't know it. Anyway, the fish are pretty. How about it?"

So early that Saturday, a warm blue morning in May, Mark picked up Aaron at home and they drove toward the ocean. Mark's car, a Volkswagen so old it had a little oblong porthole for a back window, went along with at least nothing too urgent about its wheezings and raspings.

"You'll find it entertaining," Mark said, grinning his con grin. "Billy—that's the captain—sent out this SOS for a crew on Monday. By the way, you can swim, I hope."

"I can swim. The only thing is I *won't* swim in the Atlantic Ocean in these latitudes in May. Is that clear?"

Mark laughed and laughed. He'd gotten what he wanted—the faint odor of apprehension. He went on to explain that the group Billy was taking out today came from Revere, Massachusetts, and that they had been blackballed by the other fishing boat operators. They called themselves the Joe's Spa Troops because they spent all their evenings in a bar called Joe's Spa. Each trooper put a dollar a week into a kitty, and after twenty weeks or so they would rent a boat for a day and have their big blast. Billy needed the money to pay for a baby his wife had just had, or he wouldn't have taken on the Joe's Spa Troops either.

"Wait'll you see them, Aaron. I know you think you're in the middle of what it's all about and all that, but you're not. You're surrounded by high IQ's all the time. Christ, you think somebody's dumb if he doesn't know the difference between 'disinterested' and 'uninterested,' or 'imply' and 'infer.' "

"Listen, Mark. I was in the army for three years."

"That was a long time ago, Dad."

"You think I'm going to find out something I don't know?"

"Maybe," Mark said.

They came into the little town of East Cove, its gasoline alley paved from foundation to foundation with asphalt, the enameled service stations and their gaudy signs rising out of the black. A few years ago the town had observable limits that Aaron could recognize. Houses and streets ended where fields and trees began. But now the buildings, the summer-only hot dog stands, the new streets, the trailer parks, the split-level garrisons and aluminum-sided salt-boxes—all had spread out to meet the same progress coming from the nearby towns and the city to the south. The prime color of this metastases was that putty-pink, somewhat the tone of pancake make-up, that was the color of a certain kind of asbestos siding.

The broad salt-marshes to the north were in danger, as was all the temperate life of the cove, because of a proposed atomic power plant that would raise the water temperature an estimated ten degrees.

"It's funny how pretty it gets once you're out on the ocean," Mark said.

They came to some delapidated-looking wharves, finally, with shacks, houses and house trailers set behind them above the high-tide mark. In the cove were lobster boats, skiffs, dories with rusty outboard motors, and several larger fishing boats. Lobster buoys bobbed here and there among them. Along the shore were old boxes, piles of lobster traps, beer cans, signs, flotsam: the whole place was junky, cluttered—a familiar American scene, revealing that no one had a way of looking at anything whole. One of the fishing boat operators had built his house here, and amid rocks, kelp-strewn sand, odd fifty-five-gallon drums and piles of clamshells being picked over by gulls, was his little quarter-acre featuring the square pink box of a house and a bit of lawn with a white plastic goose leading her white plastic goslings across it. Thus we re-create our beloved and magic nature in plastic. As usual, cars were everywhere, operable and inoperable. Beyond the point was the real blue ocean.

They parked and walked down to one of the wharves where a white boat, about thirty feet long, rose and fell gently, rubbing its burlap fenders against the pilings. Mark explained that Billy had bought the hull from the Navy and remade the boat himself. It didn't look like a sport-fishing boat at all, but more like a thin tugboat.

As they came nearer, Aaron read its name from the side of the wheelhouse.

FRODO B.
EAST COVE

"Dear old Frodo," Mark said. Aaron had read the Tolkien books a few years before, mainly out of self-defense (he didn't care much for fantasy), but he'd found himself dreaming along with Frodo Baggins toward "Mordor where the shadows lie" with nearly as much fascination as his students. The experience had startled him, and given him some somber thoughts about literature, about its power and purpose. Tolkien's prose was so banal, yet a broader, deeper metaphor had rung its dark tones there in the somewhat silly volumes, and he came away from them haunted by life. To see Frodo's name now, so carefully painted on the white boat, seemed almost a violation, the theft of something from its proper element.

"Orcs and goblins," Mark said. "Balrogs, gollums and nazguls. Wait till you see the Joe's Spa Troops."

"Why should I want to see them?"

"To use one of your favorite expressions, Professor, 'the fascination of the abomination.' "

"The abomination is all around me and I'm sick of it. I'm up to my ass in the abomination. I get the abomination delivered every morning before breakfast. I don't have to go looking for the abomination."

"Ah, but you do, Aaron. Frodo had to go to Mount Doom, and you have to go to the abomination." Mark thought this was extremely funny, and he was still hissing and percussing with his strange laughter when a tall blond boy came out of the wheelhouse of the *Frodo B.* Mark explained, as soon as he could speak, that this was Captain Billy. Captain Billy, somehow immensely calm, smiled and said hello. He wore faded dungarees, sneakers and a yachting cap—all of these items cured down to the basic weave. His shoulder-length blond hair actually seemed to glimmer, and Aaron was reminded of the illustrations in a book he'd had as a child: *Hans Brinker: Or, the Silver Skates.* Was that it, or was it the Dutch boy on the paint can, with his blond bangs and cap? But there was a feeling of purity about Captain Billy, of simplicity and strength, a fantasy in which handsomeness equaled goodness, as in Tolkien.

"His real name, of course, is Aragorn," Mark said. "And, as you know, I am Gandalf the Gray."

Captain Billy gazed seriously down at Mark. "I always thought of you as more of a Hobbit," he said. His pale blue eyes caught the light and seemed for a moment hollow, like cerulean-tinted spheres of glass.

Mark laughed, while Captain Billy continued to gaze at him seriously.

They went on board the *Frodo B.*, where Captain Billy explained their probable duties. The Joe's Spa Troops would, no doubt, quickly entangle all their handlines, and when they gave up trying to untangle them they would sneakily throw them overboard and come to get new ones. Each handline, with its hook, leader, sinker and wooden stretcher, was worth over a dollar, so this was to be discouraged as much as possible. And in general they were to keep an eye on things. If one of the Joe's Spa Troops was about to fall overboard, for instance, they were to make him sit down. Fights should be discouraged, as should various kinds of monkey business that might occur. They should play it by ear.

The three of them sat on the *Frodo B.*'s thick-painted gray benches in the sun, waiting—Aaron with more than a little anxiety—for the Joe's Spa Troops' chartered bus. The boat moved gently beneath them, and the smell of the cove was powerful: that salty compound of life and rot, chemical, natural, speaking of the dense life of the sea. Through the fathom of water below the boat Aaron could see clamshells on the mud bottom, and crabs moving sideways over white strings of fish parts someone had thrown out. This deep window was only in the shadow of the boat; beyond the shadow the water turned a bright reflecting blue again.

When the bus finally came, it was three-quarters of an hour late, having had a flat tire, and the troops had obviously been at the booze. They filed slowly out the front door, a little too careful of the steps. Some carried spinning rods and tackle, but most carried, with many grunts and deep breaths, cases of beer, plastic coolers, and cardboard boxes of food. The logistics of the operation were complicated. Aaron, Mark and Captain Billy soon took over the stowage not only of the supplies but of several of the troops, who would never have been able to come down the short gangplank on their own.

They were men from their late twenties to early fifties, but all their faces, beneath their sporty hats or long-billed caps, were equally blasted, the younger haunted by the finalities of the older. Except for the starved, thin bodies of the burnt-out, gut-trouble types, most were soft-bellied. Though thin elsewhere, they carried a feminine roll over the hips, and navels or pale hairy mounds of flesh were visible between T-shirts and low-slung belts, or between the gaps of printed sport shirts. Perhaps the younger were quieter. Flesh colors were tones of gray; they must all have worked indoors, and in their evenings at Joe's Spa (all their evenings) the television set above the bar must have chrome-tanned them into its own metallic tones. There were shades of green, or of bruised blue—all on the side of the spectrum away from blood and life, toward the dank, the enclosed.

They were laughing and yelling jokes to each other, these wraiths, these gross phantoms, and if Aaron didn't listen to the words it did seem that they were laughing and tossing jokes back and forth. But at a dreadful click of the attention the jokes were not funny, were unstructured, referenceless. The words didn't matter.

"Hey, Ooligah!"

"Bafundam! Yuk! Yuk!"

"Hornish gaw unner a seat!"

—Screams of virile raggedness.

"Bustis fuckin' head!"

"Watcher language, Meathead.' "

"Hey, Ollie! Hey, *Ollie!*"

God, Aaron thought. These poor, deprived organisms. Given so little in the first place, what had they done to themselves? How could a man of approximately thirty have abused himself into such cretinous shape as that one, whose left eye had migrated too far toward his nose, like a flounder's, whose very expression of dangerous toughness seemed to have caused that evil drift?

Mark caught Aaron's eye, and grinned. Among these goblins Mark was suddenly strong, even handsome, and Captain Billy was certainly part Elven, a reflection of God's true aspirations for the evil race. Aaron caught the Joe's Spa Troops looking at Mark's and Captain Billy's hair, and smirking, the little secret of their opinions of course unkept.

Some of them were strangely lethargic, and took their positions at the rail with dull, unexpectant stares. Later these would spend much of their time afloat picking helplessly and hopelessly at their snarled handlines. Their apparent leader, or the organizer of the outing, was a recognizably more intelligent man of fifty or so. Toward them all he seemed to have much affection. "They're all good boys," he said often in the face of much evidence to the contrary, even when, later, one of his boys vomited on the poop, where a plain sign said no one except crew should go. Vomited his thin beer-puke on the curved poop so that it dripped on the people below, then slid, half-conscious, in his own lubrication into the blue sea, from which he was rescued by means of a gaff in the waist band of his slacks.

"See?" the leader said. "No fights. They're good boys."

But this came later. When everyone was aboard, Captain Billy started the big engines and steered them through the channel, past the point, into the heaves of the sea where a great bell buoy clanged them toward the immensities. Far out to the northeast were the Isles of Shoals, gray rocks low on the horizon; to the west the continent receded slowly under its yellowish pastel pall. They rode the swells into the clean blue, leaving in their wake a trail of beer cans, sandwich wrappers, aluminum foil and cigarette butts. White gulls scouted them from the horizons, soared low to examine their trash, and moved on, one or two staying always within sight. Later they would have their feast.

After an hour's run from the land, Captain Billy circled for a while until, with the aid of his fathometer, he found the underwater ledges he wanted. Mark and Aaron dropped the anchor on its swiftly uncoiling hemp line; when it caught, the *Frodo B.* swung with the deep tide. Captain Billy ground some sand eels for chum in a kitchen meat grinder that was screwed to the deckhouse, and poured the thin gruel over the side.

"Bait up," he said. Mark and Aaron distributed cans of sand eels to the troops, helping the more fastidious bait their hooks.

Soon they began to pull in cod, the smooth, lippy, innocent faces staring from the washtub in the middle of the afterdeck. When the tub was full, the plump, yellowish fish flopped on the deck in slime and spilled beer. There were periods without crisis when Aaron and Mark had little to do, but after a while a burnt-thin man in his late forties chose Aaron for his confidant. He had several bottles of ginger brandy in his tackle box, and insisted that Aaron try it. It was made, Aaron read from the label, in Detroit.

"I was in on the invasion of Germany," the man said. He was at first not obviously drunk. "Invasion of Germany—

most fortified country in the world." He shook his head. "Most fortified country in the world."

Aaron thought he had missed the reference, but soon he found that, as with the jokes of the day, there was none. The thin, stringy, banty-like man, whose name—from an embossed tape glued to his tackle box—was Harry Remers, cast occasionally with his expensive and new-looking spinning outfit. He used a stainless-steel jig, disdaining cod and pollack. He wanted only mackerel.

"Left my wife ten years ago," he said, his reddish eyes peering sincerely into Aaron's. "Went back to her in six months. Who wants a mess of fucking cod?" He cast again, and slowly retrieved his jig. "Have a drink of this ginger brandy. It's good."

Aaron did.

"Let me tell you something. If a woman just lets you rub it around on the outside, it's no good. Said it hurt all the time."

Having retrieved his jig, he had a good slug of ginger brandy, then offered the bottle to Aaron, who had another medicinal, or anesthetic, slug of it himself.

"I was in on it, all right. Germany, most fortified country in the world." He lit a cigarette with his Zippo, and tossed the lighter expertly back into his shirt pocket. "Good woman. Don't complain. Stays home all the time. You follow me?"

Aaron nodded.

"I tell her I'm the only guy I know been married twenty-years to a virgin and she says don't I let you rub it on me? Left her ten years ago. Went back in six months."

The two gulls, on quivering, correcting wings, came back to check on the boat, their heads moving, one eye and then the other turned to scan. Someone at the stern threw a sand eel into the air, and both gulls watched it carefully but let it fall to the surface before they landed and squabbled briefly over it.

"You follow me?" Harry Remers said.

Aaron was suddenly dizzy. "I've got to go check the inlet ports," he said, moving away.

"Hey!" Harry Remers called to him. "That was January 21, 1944! That's a date to remember!"

"That's right," Aaron said. He went into the head to find the thirty-gallon galvanized can full and even sloshing over as the boat rolled. The stench pushed him back. He could see no drain or apparatus to remedy this, and it was nightmarish; the boat would soon be running scupper to scupper with these liquids and solids. He retched a little, fumes of Detroit ginger brandy scalding his nostrils, shut the door and went to Captain Billy.

"Jesus," he said to the tall, calm captain. "The can in there's sloshing over." Captain Billy merely nodded, and went to take care of it. Soon he returned, his hands and clothes unsoiled, and Aaron never did find out how the job was done.

One of the troops had caught a skate about two feet in diameter. Lying flat on the deck, its brown eyes observed from the little pilothouse above its wings. Several of the troops looked at it with wonder and then did what was expected—furiously stabbed and stomped it to death until its eyes were squashed and its tough white flesh winked through gashes and tears in its blue-black skin. "Stingray! Stingray!" they yelled. Skate blood, red as a man's, smeared the gray deck. One of the troops gaffed it and tossed the corpse back into the sea.

At Aaron's elbow a pale, plump man in a straw fedora whispered fiercely to him. "See that guy over there?" he said, pointing guardedly at Harry Remers. "I want to tell you he's the meanest, filthiest son of a bitch alive. The biggest prick-bastard alive." Squinting, nodding, having made the point to his satisfaction, he staggered with righteous dignity toward the bow.

Down the line the man with the drifting eye vomited with the noise of a flushed toilet, and with nearly the volume, then slowly leaned back from the rail, slid from the bench and lay on his back in the bilge.

The troops were using their knives on the fish, some filleting, some gutting, throwing the guts to the gulls who had mysteriously multiplied into dozens. The gulls cried, soared, deftly caught food from the air, landed gracefully on the water to examine parts too large to swallow—but not the trooper who at this point slid in vomit from the poop and fell eight feet into the sea. As he drifted slowly alongside, most of the troopers observed him as if he were another kind of strange, natural phenomenon, and only one or two thought it anything out of the ordinary. At the stern Aaron gaffed him by his waist band, and he and Mark hauled him out. None of the troops helped pull him over the rail, but as he lay passed out among the fish, fish parts, blood and beer, one of his fellows, to great hoarse shrieks of appreciative laughter, unzipped his fly and stuffed a small, violated cod into his crotch.

Aaron looked away, at the sunlight on the undulant blue sea, the white gulls planing against the sky. He looked down again to see a balled, tangled handline drift by out of reach.

The leader of the troops, perhaps showing some disappointment, said, "They're good boys. They're good boys. No fights. No fights."

Again Aaron looked away, examining his own emotions with what seemed to be infinite care. What was he doing here? He felt that he shouldn't have to be here, and with this came an accusation of self-indulgence. There was, though, the danger that in truth he couldn't stand it much longer. Never in his life had he enjoyed the abomination, or been a pure observer. There was the danger that he might enter as an actor here. The Detroit ginger brandy had been a mistake. He didn't want to turn away from the blue elements, back toward mankind as collective slob, back toward these goblin exaggerations of himself. Finally he did turn back, because he had to, but the sight of the blood and gore, these humans having fun disemboweling fish, gave him traitorous thoughts: he could see them all dead; he was on the side of the fish. Yes, he was on the side of the fish, not just now but in a deeper and more despairing way. *Animal bipes implume,* the two-legged animal without feathers. He was sick of being one of them.

When he turned back he found that they had discovered a new game. Gulls are not stupid, but three of them had been caught before the others realized that some of the fish guts contained hooks. Great shouts of encouragement rewarded those troopers who had their living kites on strings, the gulls crying, flapping, suddenly awkward in the air.

As Aaron proceeded toward the first kite-flier he heard Captain Billy's shout of astonishment and disapproval. The first kite-flier was a young man who responded to Aaron's presence by his side with a pleased grin, as though he expected only approbation. His face was smeared over with vagueness, however, and as he jerked the string to show his control and possession of the gull his bleared eyes didn't quite focus. He couldn't understand why Aaron wanted to take the string himself. At first he pushed Aaron's hand away with some good nature, meaning to say in his gestures and laughing, garbled words that Aaron should go get his own bird. Finally becoming irritated, he blinked and scowled as though someone were shaking him awake in the middle of the night.

"Wha' you doing!" he said, his expression caught at dead low tide as it struggled through the change from pleasure to danger. In it was disappointment, almost a pout at this loss of pleasure, and then with effort it began to signal sternness and anger. The young man cocked his right arm, upon which a stenciled anchor shone bluely through thick reddish hair.

Later Aaron would wonder why this action lifted from him the weight of despair: he needed that aggressive response, and in his own sudden change of metabolism he lost years, ascending as he did toward a purer definition of himself. Never having known much moderation once it came to rage, he did have time to fear his own dangerousness before he knocked the young man down on the bloody deck. Strange how time seemed to slow; rage had always heightened perception in him until he could observe himself and the world as if in slow motion. He had time to choose a blow he hadn't thought of for years—one he'd seen an MP use on a black soldier, in which the forearm is at the last moment of the arc drawn quickly back toward the chest and the law of conservation of momentum increases the elbow's velocity so that it hits with stunning force.

The young man lay on the filthy deck gasping and hugging his chest. A shout, half moan, arose from those troopers still conscious enough to have witnessed it. Their collective disapproval began to form itself into aggression and the determination to exact revenge. Aaron could read this very clearly in the changes of flexed arms, sucked-in bellies, the stance of feet and legs. In response, his voice listed in their own language their canon of unforgivable definitions—those meaninglessly shameful epithets that are so powerful.

Captain Billy and Mark, he noticed, had put themselves between him and the troopers, so he pulled on the line that led upward to the crying gull. One of the other gulls flapped away dragging its whole line, wooden reel and all. Trying to be gentle, but of course not able to communicate his intent to the gull, he pulled it down from the sky. As it came nearer its great wings beat in an arc as wide as his spread arms, and it stared at him and fought desperately, its tail spreading and angling for control. The wind of its wings blew into his eyes. He saw that it had swallowed the hook and there was nothing he could do but unsheathe his knife and cut the line as close to the beak as possible. Perhaps it would live. He cut the line and the gull rose powerfully in a swift spiral and was gone, as were all the other gulls from this nemesis of a boat.

It was very quiet now; Captain Billy was talking to them. Aaron wondered as to how he was not present in his own body, which he seemed to observe as a system of weapons. His knife resheathed itself, his prisms scanned, his bipod adjusted upon itself its marvelous complications of balance. He was at that point of readiness, of purity of intent, in which the body and mind are most nearly one.

But of course the Joe's Spa Troops never did rally, their cause being rather doubtful even to them. Their grumbling, in fact, degenerated still further into something like a collective whine. Aaron, out of sudden and devastating embarrassment, retired to the bow. Soon Mark came to help him haul in the anchor, and the *Frodo B.*, as bloody as if it had fought boarders, cutlass and pistol across its decks, turned with the blue swells and churned toward home.

After the subdued troopers had been helped onto their bus and the bus departed, the crew hosed the gore off decks and railings and retrieved those handlines that weren't snarled beyond all reason. They filled two GI cans with bottles, cans and other trash that the troopers hadn't had the energy to throw to the innocent sea. The dead fish were, according to their kind and condition, relegated to lobster bait or saved for food. After two hours or more, when the *Frodo B.* rode clean again at its moorings, Captain Billy brought out a six-pack the troopers had abandoned and they sat in the slanting afternoon sun, each with a warm beer.

Mark began to laugh. Between his high, mirthful wheezings, he glanced at Aaron, and finally held up his beer. "Here's to nonviolence," he said. "Oh, *my! See see shoo shoo!*"

"I'm sorry," Aaron said to Captain Billy. He was terribly ashamed and depressed—emotions he had tried to hold at bay while he almost frantically helped clean and scour the *Frodo B.* "It was none of my business. I acted like an idiot."

Captain Billy just smiled, seeming to encompass within his youth not only the proper answer but a patience and tolerance that made Aaron's violence seem even more undignified and juvenile. This made him conscious of his age; he could have been the father of these men. He thought of the blow that had decked the trooper with such efficiency, and how in his time it would have been admired. Now, in their eyes, it must seem merely stupid, which it was—the usual betrayal his generation managed whenever it had the inclination.

"I'm an asshole," he muttered. "You ought to put us animals in the brig."

Mark put his arm around the old professor's shoulders and shook him. "Shit, Dad," Mark said. "You're not used to it, that's all."

"Patronize me at your own risk," Aaron said.

Mark laughed and laughed.

Aaron finds that he has been suffering; it is as if he has just awakened from anesthesia, aware all at once of vast traumatic manipulations of his body that must have happened while he was asleep. "God!" he cries out, hearing himself with the critical ear of an actor, hearing the cry as a simulation of despair. If one is to die, why not now? That question has never been properly answered.

He goes to his study, where all his books and toys sit looking almost as they did this morning when they interested him, yet now devoid of life, dimmed out. On the other side of the room from his desk are his fly rods, his pack frames, his light ax, squash rackets leaning in the corner. Maybe they will never interest him again, but will hang there and sit there dusty and dim forever.

There on the shelf above his desk are his books—his own, the ones he has written. They have been too often seen, too often examined and remembered for the ancient passion he once felt for each of them. Now they are faded other worlds, dim, yellowing.

He would like to leave this place. He would also like to leave this time, but of course that is impossible, and without a movement backward in time he cannot recover energy and cannot cut those connections of use and love and custom that hold him here. No, he must, from this ancient base, work.

Part of that work is memory, but memory is not always trustworthy, because here he is remembering one spring night, walking alone through the crowds of tattered people in Tokyo Station. He smells again the faintly acrid air of the great city. The spring wind is warm. All across the city in its rubble thousands of hibachi fires are burning, rice and delicately pungent foods are cooking. In his memory of Tokyo he is always hungry, nineteen, conscious of his resiliency and strength. He thinks all Japanese are tough, spare and beautiful. An old woman with sturdy legs carries on her back a gigantic bundle of fagots that must weigh a hundred pounds, her trim feet grayish in her *geta,* the taut cloth band of her tumpline shining across her forehead. The fagots themselves seem shaped by art, drawn in their delicate black twists by a fine brush. But he does not want memory to take him off into nostalgic moments of the past like this. Tokyo has nothing to do with the work at hand. Nothing. Nor has Paris, London or Rome, towns he knew in his early twenties when they seemed so ancient and he so modern. A small university town in New England is closer to his real present, his work now, than all those dreaming old cities. He must go back to that little town, feeling bad about it, not wanting to go there, having huge doubts that he has the will or the energy to make that journey back in time.

On a clean page in his notebook he writes in block letters:

THE HAIR OF HAROLD ROUX

Staring at the words he feels something like despair. He's got to disengage himself from people so he can get to work. He's got to stop killing himself in various ways, large and small. Smoking and drinking, just for a start. Sure. *The Hair of Harold Roux:* he must begin quite simply, muster those facts that he knows, and build, arrange, populate that barren plain with trees and names. Allard Benson, Mary Tolliver, Harold Roux, Naomi Goldman, Boom Maloumian . . . There is a world there, partly of the past, that must sustain itself. All right.

Our rather thinly disguised hero is one Allard Benson, and the story (a simple story of seduction, rape, madness and murder—the usual human preoccupations) seems to begin when he has reached the age of twenty-one. A veteran, though no war hero, his combat has consisted of earnest attempts to maim his fellow soldiers rather than the enemy. He doesn't really approve of violence, and rather believes that he is always having to defend himself; his theory is that he is not so large that he overawes potential aggressors, nor so small that they might overlook him. There is some truth in most theories. There is also the theory that he wants to kill the world for girls like Mary Tolliver, and a certain raw look upon the faces of large, aggressive men suggests to him the causes of her unhappiness. Let us say that he believes that one human being should not cause pain in another, and that whenever he himself sins against this catchall bit of orthodoxy he is clearly aware of it; whatever it is that he has done is printed coldly and permanently upon his soul. This is Allard Benson's voice, of course, masking certain things in an unfortunate flippancy.

And then there is Harold Roux. Poor Harold. What visions did he have of college? The war was over at last, and no longer would this pale, thin, sensitive young man have to experience the crudity, the vulgarity, the sheer horror of barracks life. He must have thought longingly of ivy-covered walls in the bright autumn light, of formal elegance and wit, the life of the mind, of dignified professors in tweeds, of long, serious discussions of great issues in places like "Commons." Also of the talented and beautiful girl who would be his companion. Allard always wondered if Harold got any further with this last dream than holding hands, perhaps, or a chaste kiss. Because on the day after his discharge from Fort Dix, New Jersey, Harold went to New York and made a strange decision, a magical decision which, like all choices in magic, contained its own dark laughter and the necessity of the third and last wish, the one that always erases the damage done by the first two. Harold made this Midas choice; he later paid and paid again the price that magic exacts from mortals.

While in the army Harold had gone bald. It was nothing pathological, just an inevitable shedding of his top hair—first a tonsure, then the lenghthening of the forehead, then the shiny top of the skull bare from brow to where the cowlick once grew and beyond, the whole process complete at the age of twenty-three. And in Manhattan he happened to pass the doors of an establishment whose necromancers claimed the undetectable restoration of Harold's loss. He hesitated, he smiled, he began to walk on, he hesitated again. He looked through the display windows at pictures of men of forty (before) suddenly transformed (after) into dashing young men of thirty surrounded by luscious, though rather witless-looking girls. As far as Harold was concerned, they could keep that type of girl, but still . . .

Allard brooded often upon Harold's need, the desperate wishfulness that led him to enter. "Abandon all candor, ye who enter here." Harold could never successfully deceive, never. But once he entered that place, the world and all its former values changed. He entered the place of believers, and for a while believed.

Allard once knew an Arthur Murray dance instructor, and for minutes after talking with him felt himself shedding an odd feeling of the importance of the man's gigolo enthusiasms. At one time in the army he had felt at home in a group of men whose enthusiasm was for the kill. He thought he understood Harold's conversion. He had known people whose clothes preoccupied them, or whose automobiles, old bottles, or muscles, became central to their lives. Harold in his need was no match for the spell the hairmakers wove. But they wove their spell better than their hair; Harold could pass at a certain distance, yet the intimate distance, the one he had beautified himself to attain, betrayed his secret. Midas' wish. He was afraid to bend over, and kept his shoulders level as though balancing a book on his head. Twenty-three, and he couldn't run, jump, somersault, bend very far from the waist. Once he came to college and was seen and known, it was too late to take the last wish and wish with all his heart that the wig (or toupee, or hairpiece) had never happened.

Harold was born in Berlin, New Hampshire, a northern town set among blue-green mountains covered with white birch, spruce, pine, beech and ash—great rolling forests of these and other noble trees. Into Berlin flows a beautiful river, graced with rapids, called the Androscoggin, a river hospitable to rainbow trout and salmon, those quicksilvery fish of clear cold waters. When the Androscoggin flows out of Berlin it is the color of lead, its surface frothed from bank to bank with puslike yellowish strings and globs of filth, a river so far beyond mere death its carrion stench takes the paint off houses. The great red brick paper mills of the Brown Company are here, towering out of the river gorges, their tall chimneys pushing out such volumes of smoke it seems the explosive density of the brown and gray billows could never have been contained in vents even as monstrous as these. At ground level huge conduits vomit whole rivers of sulfite wastes down ancient ledge into the Androscoggin. The massive heights and complications of the industrial fortresses, pulsing smoke and steam, gushing torrents of raw poison, awaken myths of the dark sulfurous glories of hell.

Unsuspecting travelers who drive down from the mountains into this charnel reek have been known to accuse each other of unbearable flatulence; then, as they frantically crank down the car windows, the full force of Berlin's miasma flows over them in all its claustrophobic power. It is a sweet stench, so nearly tangible one fears nausea and asphyxiation. It is said that the natives of Berlin and the towns downriver get used to it, but at what price, the traveler wonders, to the delicate senses through which life reveals itself and is judged?

Aaron Benham hears his heart's labor in his chest. Would Harold Roux use those sonorities, those ganged superlatives, he wonders. No, and he'd never mention farts. That voice is Allard Benson's—one of his voices, for he is a chameleon of voices.

Berlin's pride is to call itself "Hockeytown, U.S.A." It is a somber place of drab, mostly wooden buildings made to fit odd levels and corners. To the west a sheer granite cliff rises above the town, as if to crowd it down closer toward the sewer it has made of its river. And it was here, in August of 1923, Harold Roux was born. He grew up living above a small grocery store, where the crooked, soiled back windows of the apartment looked across the water to the cloacal bases of the mills.

Harold had four older sisters—actually three sisters and a half sister, the child of his mother's first marriage. That first husband had died beneath an avalanche of pulp logs. Harold's father also worked for the Brown Company. A minor demon, he presided over a vast, jiggling tank of chemicals he was responsible for stirring and cooking properly. He was a borderline alcoholic, one of those who, though a terror at home, managed to keep his job. Quite often he beat upon his wife; random blows sometimes made it dangerous for everyone. Harold's mother worked in the grocery store below, which belonged to her sister and brother-in-law, Tante Louise and Oncle Hébert. It was his mother who mainly supported the family; his father mainly supported his habit. With the precision of young surviving animals, all the children knew that beer was not too bad, but wine was dangerous and whiskey a disaster. Harold remembered something the youngest of his sisters once said when asked what sort of man she would like someday to marry: "I want to marry a man who won't be drunk when I come home from work." She was quite serious about that.

When Harold was twelve his father disappeared. Much later his mother told him the story—not an uncommon one in its basic details. Somehow, it seemed, Harold's father and his stepdaughter had been left alone in the apartment on a Sunday afternoon. Yvonne was sixteen, a sulky, rather stupid, buxom girl who had already left school. Harold's mother came back long before she was expected to find them naked on the conjugal bed. Tante Louise came in then, too, and they both got a good look at the pale-skinned, wrinkle-necked man atop the spread-eagled sixteen-year-old. The two women just stood there for a moment. Allard clearly saw Harold's mother staring at the naked buttocks of the man she'd slept with for twenty years, seeing them, white and hairy, driving with their goatish jerks that other thing into her own daughter. What licks of shame and hellfire must have singed her pious soul in those few seconds! And legally this was incest, statutory rape and what-all. Tante Louise had the presence of mind to grab an iron bridge lamp and bring it down across the man's bare back. "*Monstre! Animal! Va-t'en!*" She got him a few more good ones before he made his escape. Yvonne, though scared, gave the two women a superior, languorous shrug and began to put on her panties and bra with the sang-froid of a whore. They gave her a few good lumps, a black eye and a split lip, but she never gave them back a sniffle or a tear.

But when did Harold's mother, whose life was composed of work and prayer and the avoidance of candor in such matters, tell Harold at least some of these details? Later, much later, when Harold was out of the army. They were both adults then, and he found that she had not, for instance, slept with the man every night for twenty years out of sheer duty. It was Harold who was shocked by her rueful humor concerning those ancient events.

Of course Harold didn't tell the story quite like this to

Allard. There would be little crudeness, and not even a hint of the chill of irony. Allard was the first friend Harold had ever considered close enough, trustworthy enough, to reveal any of it to, and he spoke of these things as if he used an unfamiliar language.

Harold and his sisters were told that their father had gotten a job in Manchester. Yvonne stuck around for nearly a year, though her mother would not speak a word to her and didn't care whether she came or went. Harold thought she got married, but he wasn't sure. He was surprised to find out later that his three sisters had known all about Yvonne, and that her bad reputation had commenced to grow when she was at least as young as seven.

The store was barely profitable but Tante Louise and Oncle Hébert let them live in the building for very little rent. Harold's mother worked nights as a waitress, as well as in the store. She was a saint, Harold said, always trying to raise her children up in the world, while she herself went to church more and more often. He remembered an encyclopedia she bought for them—later repossessed, but this was because of fine print in the contract and a smooth salesman. She fed them, she washed, she sewed, she prayed upon her rosary. Harold was good in school, perhaps because he had no friends —no *real* friends, he said, meaning real like Allard—and with his mother's devout and nearly frantic aid he entered the seminary at seventeen. He was not quite sure when, or why, it became obvious to him and to his teachers that he had no vocation as a priest. In 1943, to his mother's sorrow and despair, he left the seminary and was drafted into the army.

Though still devout—his doubts were of his own character, never of the Church—he had thought to make a complete break with the things of the seminary, but after basic training he was assigned as an assistant to the Catholic chaplain of the 3rd Infantry Replacement Training Command, where he spent the rest of the war. In 1946 he was discharged as a technician third-class.

One fine spring day of sharp borders, when the trees

were yellow-green against an unmoving, enameled blue sky, Allard, Mary Tolliver and Harold Roux sat on the grassy bank overlooking the tennis courts, where girls sweatily chased white fluffy new balls, laughing at their own awkwardness. Allard was talking about a play he was writing, called *The End.* And he was writing it, of course, back to front.

The day was so warm and benevolent Harold had actually removed his coat and tie. The long white points of his shirt collar, unused to such informality, still held themselves together. The sunlight seemed to disappear into his pale skin, and his immaculate wig (or toupee, or hairpiece) rode too perfectly his smooth forehead.

Mary wore a white tennis blouse and shorts. Tiny golden hairs gleamed along her slim thighs; the slightest dew was on her upper lip. Her hair gleamed light gold, though her eyes were a startling dark brown, dark and soft to look into. In the brown radiations of her left iris was set the smallest shard of green, like a splinter of jade. She had been decorated at birth with this surprising little jewel. Now, she expressed her happiness in each limb, each motion. Even the wrinkles and folds of her clothes seemed to draw smoothly toward excitement and contentment. It was so obvious that of all the places and times of the world, here and now was where she most wanted to be, and was. Allard watched her, thinking how each cell of her body must be operating in harmony with that happiness. She was eighteen; she would be nineteen in the fall.

While she and Harold listened, Allard explained that in his play the last scene would take place in a restaurant with booths all along the back and sides of the stage. On each table was a lamp containing several bare flash bulbs. Just before the final curtain, all lights would dim into total darkness long enough for the audience's retinas to open to maximum diameter. Then all the bulbs would go off at once. In the ensuing stunned mass blindness, the actors would run down the aisles sobbing and screaming that they were in agony, blind and dying. The end. For the curtain call (after the audience had regained its sight, and whether or not there was any applause), the curtain would open not upon the happy actors arm in arm, but upon a huge movie screen on which was projected in full color the blinded, ravaged, pus-laden face of a victim of Hiroshima or Nagasaki. Silence. The audience could stay or leave. No actors or attendants would be visible in the theater.

"Whew!" Harold said in admiration.

"I wonder what the audience would do." Mary said.

"Lynch the author?" Harold suggested.

"No," Allard said. "They'd be masochists or they wouldn't have come to the play in the first place."

"But maybe it would be a little cruel," Harold said.

"Cruel?" Allard said. As if in answer, he leaned over and bit Mary lightly above the knee, her skin sun-warm and salty to his tongue. Laughing, she took him by the ears and shook his head. Harold smiled painfully.

"You taste good. You're edible," Allard said. "I knew you were edible." As he turned onto his back she blushed, but let his head down in her lap and lightly held it there. He looked up at her breasts and chin against the clear blue, the tall college elms framing her. As she looked down at him her hair fell around her face, sunlight seeming to be inside it, and her expression was suddenly private, the two of them alone within the arbor of her hair. A straight, grave look, her eyes wide, said that he was the one. He knew that.

Harold wanted to be with them, they knew, so she let his head go and he sat up, the three of them again facing each other, now including Harold, who had introduced Allard to Mary a week before. He was a companion, good company, almost an official observer of their relationship. He was also something of a confessor, like the priest he might have been. When he looked at Mary it seemed to hurt his eyes, and he quickly looked away at the green campus. They sat there, the three of them, Indian fashion, the cool moisture from the grass meeting the hot sunlight.

* * *

The telephone in the hall rings, and rings again. It demands him before he can gather his objections together. It rings again. "No!" he says. Let it ring. He will not face Agnes and her wounded wrath. His shame is too deep to have been caused only by that forgetfulness.

Except that he must answer it; never has he been able to ignore any question. When he picks the live black thing out of its screaming cradle it is only George.

"Hey, Aaron?"

He is grateful, immensely relieved that he can now share some of this with George. The possibility hadn't occurred to him, and he wonders what he has come to, that he didn't think of a friend. George has been talking excitedly, and though Aaron half hears him he is immersed in the depressing consideration that perhaps he has come to think of himself almost as an institution—older, successful (at least to George), perhaps he can no longer afford to admit to anything.

"I don't know exactly why we got so worried about you," George is saying. "Anyway, you were going like a scalded cat when you went out of sight. Hey, man?"

"Yeah, George."

"You all right, Aaron?"

"I guess so. Except that . . ." Here, with gratitude and a full breath, he explains, each word subtly lifting the more intense pangs from whatever morbid combination of emotions has him down. "Thus have I again betrayed my family, lost the love and trust of my children, revealed my cold monstrous egocentrism . . ." It is almost a pleasure.

"Wow. I'll bet you've got a fist full of bourbon," George says.

Aaron thinks of malt and Milton, or mash and Milton, but decides that he won't say that (is this choice, too, the finicky hesitation of age?).

"Are you going down there?" George says. "Hey, you want to borrow my car?"

"No, I can't go down there now. A hundred miles. I can't

even see straight. I'll call and tell them I broke a leg. No, I'll tell them I'm terribly confused, which isn't much of a lie . . ." He began by trying to be funny, and now he stops. He will call Cynthia, Agnes' mother—at least that will solve the problem of having to speak to Agnes.

"Come out and have supper with us then, huh? No sense sitting around getting smashed all by yourself. I'll come and pick you up. Leave the motorcycle alone. I'm scared of it. It hasn't got enough wheels on it."

"I don't know, George . . ."

"Listen. Helga's made son-of-a-bitch stew. You've got to try it. It's fantastic. An old recipe from her grandmother in New Mexico. Among the ingredients is the lining of the second stomach of a calf. Helga just told me that would appeal to you."

"She's right, George. She's always right."

"Okay, it's all settled. I'll be right over."

"Wait a minute," Aaron starts to say, not necessarily to refuse, but George deliberately hangs up. George must really be worried about him, because hanging up is simply not characteristic of George unless he has developed some theory of terrible need, in which case the end justifies the means.

Ah, well. And now Aaron must deliberately use the telephone. He must pick it up and dial. No, wait, he wants to call person-to-person, so he's got to converse with an operator, a voice through the opaque tunnel of all those wires and switches, diodes, rectifiers, solenoids—all those words for functions he doesn't want to understand. He'll get himself another drink.

He comes back and studies the first several pages of the telephone book in order to find out how to call person-to-person long distance. The pages are full of open spaces and huge typographical devices earnestly designed to make the finding of this information simple, but as usual the information comes into his tricky brain full of connotations not meant for it. "Directory Assistance," for instance: exactly why did someone take the old word, "Information," and change it to "Directory Assistance"? He has theories. A directory is a telephone book. They want you to look in the book. They don't want you to be a helpless slob who can't read the book and asks for help. So some English major figured that the term for information ought to *all inside itself* serve to make you stop bothering the telephone company and look in the book.

Then he is reading: *Whoever willfully and wantonly or maliciously uses a telephone facility to transmit to another any comment, request, suggestion or proposal which is obscene, lewd, lascivious or indecent . . .*

Wait a minute! He has to call; he simply cannot think about this language. He cannot, for instance, make up a sentence to which all of these words exactly apply. The subtle difference between "obscene" and "lewd," for instance . . .

He dials the operator and begins to explain to her his inability to read the telephone book, but she, it seems, is the one he needs after all, and he reads the number from the back cover of the book where Agnes has written it down.

Actually it is his father-in-law, John Campbell, who first answers the phone. He would just as soon speak to John, but the operator insists upon Cynthia, who finally comes to the phone and says "Hello?" with a worried little quirk in her voice.

"It's me—Aaron," he says.

"Are you all right?" Cynthia's young-sounding voice is really asking why he is calling her person-to-person, and they like each other because both of them are tolerant enough to answer implied questions.

"Naturally Agnes is highly pissed off at me," he says, "and I didn't want to talk to her. And if feeling like a shit is all right, I'm all right."

"That's what I thought."

"Whatever Agnes told you was probably for your own benefit," Aaron says.

"I'm sure you had a reason, Aaron. Both John and I would find it impossible to believe you didn't want to see us.

It would take too much reinterpretation of former conduct."

"How well you put it, Cynthia! God damn, I really dig your mind! How do you put words together like that?" He feels the sliding of the whiskey. "You could cheer me up on the scaffold, you and John both. Let me put it this way, Cynthia: I had a reason for forgetting, an opportunity to feel somewhat noble, and my desire for that nobility overrode memory. Hell, *anything* can override my memory. Also, you've got to admit it isn't exactly a pleasant drive from here to there, and that may have helped blank it out. I do wish with all my heart I was there with you now, toasting your nobility and lasting dignity and wit and love and care. In fact, in my right hand is a noble drink, as my rhetoric has no doubt already informed you, and I now toast you, Cynthia. May you and John be there forever and ever; if I didn't believe that were somehow possible I would despair. Half of what I do seeks your approval. More than half, and I wish I were there with you right now, sober and hearty and above all—innocent."

She laughs, and then says seriously, "Don't go riding your motorcycle, Aaron. You hear?"

"Okay. And so you won't worry I'll tell you that George Buck, a colleague, is picking me up and taking me to his house for supper. Tell Agnes that, if she seems at all inquisitive. And give her my wretched love, and John, and the kids. Tell them Daddy's done wrong but someday we'll all make a new life together."

"You're funny but you make me sad too, Aaron."

"I don't mean to do that."

"Cheer up. We'll see you soon."

"Thanks, Cynthia. Really I do appreciate it. I'm not really drunk, either."

"I know that."

They are both silent for a moment. He sees Cynthia Campbell, nee Holloway, his mother-in-law, standing, probably, in the kitchen, her bony hip leaning against the Formica counter, the yellow Princess telephone in the soft flesh of her neck. As she grows older, near her seventies, she is fading out of her light clothes, and her skin is somehow like wheat moving in the wind. There has always been an intimacy between them that goes just so far. Then his younger brashness goes beyond the pale and she begins not to hear him quite as well. If he were to ask her now "Are you happy? What are you wearing? Is your daughter the kind of person you wanted her to be? Am I the sort of man you wanted her to marry?"—if he should do this and continue to do it, she would smile vaguely and have something else to do. And she would be right to hear the patronization, as though he were stating that the old people were no more real than history, a merely ornamental frame surrounding what is real.

"I'm sure Agnes will forget it, Aaron," she says.

"Yes," he says. "We can't ever forgive, but thank God we can at least partly forget."

"Aaron, I'm sure it isn't that bad."

"Yes, yes," he says. "Think of all the things I *haven't* done."

"That's right. You'll both get over it." After a pause in which he thinks she wants him to say goodbye, she says, "Goodbye, Aaron." She is fading out, fading away now.

"Goodbye, Cynthia." They both gently hang up.

In one way he feels a little better, but somehow the conversation has gone too far. He thinks maybe he has blabbed too much, and a little worm of shame appears—not from his original forgetting but from the conversation itself. Christ, when is this sort of progression going to stop? His hands are shaky. They seem as weak as leaves.

His wife and children. They are his, the three people who have gone away from him because his memory abandoned them.

Once, before a fire on a winter evening, snow falling outside the warm house, he sat on the sofa with Janie on one side of him, Billy on the other. Billy had his feet up and was leaning back against the arm. Both were in their pajamas, washed and lively and ready for bed. Agnes sat in the easy chair next to the fireplace, a cone of yellow light from a lamp illuminating her head and shoulders and the book she had stopped reading, outlining in dark gold the now passively content, loving woman who had given him these children and also the stillness or gravity that had let him stay in one place and build this house among the trees in the small university town. It was an island not necessarily reflecting his deepest needs, but he had grown into it and here he was. Janie was six, Billy eight. Was it before Christmas, or after? And what year? No matter, it was a winter evening with the snow closing the warmth of his house within itself, the walks and driveway and the streets muffled up and blanketed away until there was no departing, even in the imagination, from this comfort. It was now all love and expectation, the bright, washed children having lost their jealous edges, softly uniformed for sleep but insisting that the last hour of wakefulness not be wasted.

Janie held his arm in both her hands, her round face turned up toward his. "Tell the story about the old lady that smelled," she said. Her eagerness to be enthralled by the old story gave him a power he hesitated to use. Billy said, "And the little boy! And the little girl," he added as if to be completely fair.

"I always forget it," Aaron said.

"I'll tell you when you forget!" Janie said.

"But if you know it better than me, why don't you tell it?"

"No! You tell it! Come on, Daddy!" Janie was kind and forgiving, except at times toward her brother, but the idea that she might have to tell the story she wanted to hear was bad, teasing, beyond toleration. Anger and frustration darkened her eyes.

"Yeah," Billy said, kicking him in the leg. "It's your story and you tell it. Come on, Dad. 'Once upon a time there was a family named Hemlock . . .' Come on!"

"Who lived either before or after . . ." Janie said.

"In a log cabin on the side of the Mountain," Billy said.

"Mount Gloam," Aaron said. "The darkest mountain of all."

"That's right!" They both settled in, having primed him, the big presence moving their way, the one who could at times be weary, bored, illogical, asleep or gone. They must feel, he thought, the wonder of their occasional control of one of those dark, mountainous adults who had so much arbitrary power. But it was the power their attention gave him that he used with fear and care, hardly daring to look at their faces as he told the story. A phrase, a deepening of his voice, even a single word could cause in them real sorrow, anxiety or joy, and when he saw that he had caused such deep emotion he would feel the story with their reality and lose his voice.

Perhaps it was the past (he began), but if so it was a different past. Perhaps it will be, but then how do we know the story? All we know is that once upon a time there was a family named Hemlock, who lived either before or after, in a log cabin on the side of the Mountain, Mount Gloam, the darkest mountain of all. Eugenia was the mother, Tim the father, Janie and Billy the children. No other people lived in houses for a hundred miles of forests and meadows and swamps, lakes and rivers blue and unnamed where the swift animals lived in their ways, running and flying, and the slow animals blinked away their long years.

Tim Hemlock was a hunter, a maker of things, and a farmer; his two small fields were the only ones cultivated for a hundred miles around. He was a silent, thoughtful man, kind to his family and to his animals, though at times he seemed to hear voices that made him sad and stern. He watched and listened most of the time, as a hunter must.

In the Hemlocks' log cabin, Janie, who was six, was helping her mother with the big wooden butter churn, spelling her mother while the clabber was new and the crank easy to turn. Billy, who was eight, was out in the cold-storage cave that was dug into the hill behind the cabin, helping his father cut the venison jerky that they would dry in long strips in the short-lived October sun. For it was fall, the time before the cold storms would come with the white hiss of snow over Gloam Mountain, and they must prepare for the long dark season when the days were short and the wind like frozen iron, when their cow, Oka, and their ox, Brin, and the three goats and the pig would barely heat the small barn with their bodies, and in the cabin the fireplace would burn by day and ember by night, eating the precious cords of hardwood Billy and his father had stacked under the long eaves after Brin had hauled them from the woods on the iron-shod sledge.

In the kitchen Eugenia was singing, her long brown hair in braids Janie had woven, her blue eyes as clear as the October sky. She sang the butter song. Sometimes Janie sang along with her, but sometimes she just listened to her mother's sweet voice as she sang.

> *"Out of night comes daylight,*
> *Out of thin comes thick.*
> *Oka knows how butter grows*
> *So turn the paddles quick."*

In the storage cave, on the thick maple table by the door, Billy's knife sliced the dark red venison into the thinnest ribbons. His father was quicker and his ribbons of meat thinner and longer, but his father told him he was doing well.

"You must be quick and careful with the gift the deer have given us," he said. "Remember, we do nothing for the deer as we do for Oka and Brin, the pig and the goats. The deer feed themselves and nearly starve every winter, and we don't help them at all, so their flesh is a gift to us."

"Like the salmon in the river," Billy said.

Now, the Hemlocks were all expecting the Traveler, who came once a year in his long canoe. Every once in a while Billy or Janie would stop what they were doing and look down into the valley to the river, wondering with excitement if they could see the Traveler's canoe in the distance as he poled his way up the rapids to the last landing of all. Every October he brought them lead ingots for rifle balls; saltpeter and sulfur for making black powder; salt, oil, steel, iron strapping, needles and flint. If Tim Hemlock had a good year of hunting and trapping and a good winter at the forge beside the barn, and if Eugenia and Janie had a good winter making the beautiful deerskin moccasins decorated with porcupine quills they cut into beads and strung on thread (I forgot to say that Billy pumped the bellows for his father!), there would be skins and fur, the Tim Hemlock knives of steel and deer horn that couldn't be duplicated anywhere, the most beautiful moccasins in the world to trade, and the Traveler would return to his canoe and bring them licorice, powdered chocolate, tea, tobacco and other things they enjoyed but didn't really need . . .

"They didn't need the tobacco," Billy Benham said.

"You forgot the colored ribbons," Janie Benham added.

And colored ribbons. So it happened that Janie, having taken her turn at the butter churn, went to the cabin door thinking she might be the first to see the Traveler's canoe on the blue river. As she opened the door . . .

"There was the old lady!" Janie Benham said. Her hands kneaded his arm, their small strength great in her excitement. Her blue eyes were wide in anticipation, the whites showing all around, pure as the whitest milk. She breathed fast, waiting with an intense expectation for what she knew was coming. Billy, too, though a little cooler, stared at him, at the scene, waiting.

. . . As she opened the door she jumped back with a cry, for standing there, absolutely still, was a person, a small person all in brown, her brown deerskin dress touching the ground. It was an old, old woman, her hair thin and white, her old face as brown as her deerskin clothes. She didn't speak or change her expression, just stood there with her bright old eyes staring at Janie. Her face was covered with wrinkles so deep, crisscrossing like the cracks in the mud of a dried pond, that her face looked like it could have been taken apart like a jigsaw puzzle. Between the wrinkles her skin was as smooth and shiny as shoe polish. In her hands she held a basket made of water reeds.

Janie's mother had heard her cry and came quickly to the door. She was startled, too, because the Hemlocks hadn't had a visitor other than the Traveler for many years.

"Who are you?" Eugenia asked, but the old woman didn't move or say a word. Only her brilliant old eyes moved from Janie to Eugenia, then into the open door of the cabin as if she were looking for someone else.

"Go tell your father," Eugenia said to Janie, who made a wide circle around the old woman and ran to the storage cave.

"There's an old brown woman!" Janie said. She felt like crying as she tried to tell her father and Billy, she was so excited and upset. "At the door! She scared me!"

Quickly they all went to the cabin, and the children, who soon looked to their father, saw a strange expression on his face when he spoke to the old woman.

"Who are you?" he asked, yet his face was puzzled, as though he shouldn't have had to ask the question at all. He seemed to be trying to remember.

When the old woman saw him she moved for the first time, nodding her head, then holding out her basket to him. He took the basket, still puzzled, and nodded his head three times. The old woman, her face as unchanging as wood, nodded three times in answer. And from that time forward, Tim Hemlock never again tried to say words to the old woman. He handed the reed basket to Eugenia, then pointed to the cabin, made his hands into the shape of a roof, pointed to his heart, then to the old woman, and moved his hand in a slow sweep toward the door, bidding her to enter. She did, walking so smoothly it seemed she had no feet but glided over the ground. She went straight to the bench beside the fireplace and sat down, her worn and ragged deerskin skirt still covering her feet. Her hands were knobby; the brown fingers seemed to bend at the wrong places, the joints swollen and painful-looking. But with smooth motions she seemed to be speaking with them just the same. She cupped her two hands, pointed to the basket Eugenia held, then made one hand act as the cover of the basket and opened this hand as she nodded. They all knew that Eugenia was to open the basket.

The children came up close to look. Inside the basket were various small objects, each wrapped carefully in a basswood leaf. First there were mushrooms, on top because they are fragile. Corals, pink, white and light blue. Morels, that look like brown sponges. Puffballs of pure white, that when sliced and fried taste like delicious meat. Beefsteak mushrooms, that look like their name. Oysters, because that is how they look. And then there were some strangely beautiful orange and yellow mushrooms the Hemlocks had never seen before and wouldn't have dared to try if they had.

Beneath the mushrooms were perfect little birch-bark boxes fitting side by side. Eugenia took them out one by one and put them on the big oak table. On the top of each box was a picture of a plant cut into the birch bark, and inside of each box was a different colored powder, fine as flour. Billy, who liked to collect wild food, thought he recognized some of the plants in the pictures. There was goosefoot, arrowhead, roseroot, kinnikinnick, glasswort, purslane and dock. But many of the plants he couldn't recognize. One box, full of a fine brown powder, had on its cover a picture of a gracefully drooping human hand.

"She says they're a gift for us," Tim Hemlock said.

"But what are all those powders?" Eugenia asked.

"I don't know, but they're a gift, so we'll put them on the shelf," Tim Hemlock said, and they did. They put the little boxes on the shelf over the fireplace, where they would stay dry. The old woman never moved or said a word, but her eyes were bright. In the following days they ate the mushrooms they knew were good to eat, but left the orange and yellow ones in their leaves on the shelf.

Time passed, and the old woman sat on the bench by the fireplace. She sat quietly, hardly moving, all day long. During the early morning hours before dawn and just after, she was gone, but she returned sometime in the early morning to glide quietly to her place on the wooden bench. She ate very little and was no trouble, but after a week or more Eugenia began to get a little upset. She and Janie were out by the watering trough where Tim Hemlock and Billy were working, and she asked Tim Hemlock how long the old woman was going to stay.

"It isn't that she's a bother, but she looks at me all the time and it makes me nervous," Eugenia said.

"And she smells funny," Janie said. "She smells like sometimes when you're taking a walk in the woods and there's a warm sort of animal wave of air you don't know where it came from but it's different."

"If I could only *talk* to her." Eugenia said. "Who is she? What is she doing here?"

Eugenia asked because sometimes Tim Hemlock and the old woman did talk, with their hands, and no one else could follow their meanings beyond something simple like "Would you like some more soup?" which was easy enough to understand.

"I'm not sure who she is," Tim Hemlock said slowly, the puzzled look on his face. "But I know we must let her stay."

Later, when he and Billy were in the barn feeding the animals, Billy said, "How do you know how to talk to her, Dad?"

"I don't know," his father said. "My grandfather—your great-grandfather—could talk that way. Once when I was a boy, when I was about your age and one of the Old People came by, my father told me that. But he couldn't do it. I don't know how I know how to do it."

"Is the old lady one of the Old People?"

"She must be the last one, if she is," Tim Hemlock said.

"Were the Old People always old like her?"

"No. It's that they were here before us."

"And they're all gone?"

"Men have thought so for many years," Tim Hemlock

said, and Billy, seeing his father's doubts and maybe even fears, said nothing more.

One evening, a cold, late November evening when the winter had snapped down hard and all the small cabin windows were furry with frost, Tim Hemlock said, "The Traveler isn't coming this year. It's too late. The ice is forming on the river."

They had all been thinking this, but it was too important to talk about. Now they all sat in silence, for without powder and ball, and oil, salt and steel and flint, the winter would be long and hard at best, and at the worst they might starve. Janie saw the fear in her mother's blue eyes and went to her, to stand between her mother's knees and look up into her beautiful eyes that had turned dark, like the blue of a storm cloud you think is sky until you see it is really part of a dark cloud. Janie put her head against her mother to feel the warmth.

Billy was silent, too, because he knew how little powder and ball his father had left. Each year the Traveler could bring just so much of everything, because of the long hard journey up the river, so in the fall they were always short of supplies. He looked up at the long flintlock rifle that hung on its deerfoot racks on the log wall, at its full stock of bird's-eye maple and at its brass fittings engraved with animals and plants. From its tang hung his father's beaded leather possibles bag, and the small priming horn and the large powder horn, now only half full of black powder.

The old woman sat more still than all the rest, but now her bright eyes were upon Tim Hemlock, and she began to speak to him with her hands. He replied, and soon their hands moved swiftly, seeming to dance in the air, Tim Hemlock's great horny working hands and the old woman's small bent brown ones, gleaming in the firelight.

After watching this for a while Eugenia cried out, "What are you saying? What are you saying?" She was close to tears. Tim Hemlock and the old woman stopped moving their hands, and Tim Hemlock turned to Eugenia.

"She says the Month of the Iron Ice will be the worst," he said. "I can't quite understand all she wants to tell me."

"It's not right!" Eugenia cried. "Why can't she talk?"

"She doesn't know our language." He saw how unhappy Eugenia was, so he went to her and put his arm around her. There was nothing he could say to reassure her, other than a lie, so he said nothing at all.

The children looked at the old woman who sat as still as wood, the orange flickerings of the fire reflecting from her dark face.

It was Janie who first thought she saw something stranger and deeper in the eye hollows of the old woman than any of them had ever noticed before. She said nothing about it, because even though the old woman wasn't supposed to know their language she couldn't talk about her right in front of her as if she weren't there.

But late that night, after everyone was asleep, Janie woke up with a strange question on her mind, as though something had called her awake. The children slept on the loft at one end of the cabin, where it was warmest. Janie got up and put her quilt around her shoulders, for the fire had burned down low, and even on the loft it was bitter cold. She went around the log partition that separated her bed from Billy's. It was dark, with only an occasional spark of flame from the fireplace that would dimly light the rafters and die down again.

"Billy," she whispered. She had to feel for him, and found the very top of his head, which was the only part of him that wasn't bundled up in his quilts and blankets. "Billy!" she whispered again. "Wake up!" She patted him on the top of his head.

"Umph grumph," he mumbled.

"Wake up!" she whispered.

"Wha'?"

"Shhh!"

"Wha' matta?"

"Wake up!"

Then he did wake up all the way. "What's the matter?"

he whispered. "It must be the middle of the night."

"It is. But there's something very peculiar we've got to find out about."

"In the middle of the night?"

"Yes, because she's asleep."

"Who's asleep?"

"The old lady. She goes sound asleep. I've watched her. She sits there just like always, but she goes sound asleep. And there's something we've got to find out. I don't know why. But it's her eyes. There's something funny about them."

"I know that," Billy whispered back.

"But this is really strange. I'm scared to go down and look by myself, so you've got to come with me."

"I don't like the idea."

"I don't either, exactly, but it's something we've got to do."

"You want to look at her *eyes?* How can you do that if she's asleep? And suppose she wakes up?"

"We've got to take that chance. We've got to, Billy. I don't know why, but we've got to."

Billy could tell that she meant it. His little sister was only six, but when she made up her mind it was made up. And he was curious, too, even though he was scared. So they fumbled around on the loft in the dark, finding clothes and putting them on, and Janie followed Billy down the ladder.

In the dying flickers of the fire they could see, across the room on her bench, the upright figure of the old woman sitting as straight as if she were awake. But they also heard the long, even breaths of sleep. Slowly, as quietly as they could, they crossed the room. The smooth breaths continued. They were both trembling with fear, yet they had to go toward the shadowy old woman who sat so stiffly upright in her sleep. What were they doing? They both thought this, but something seemed to make them move quietly, in stockinged feet, toward the very presence they feared.

"We've got to have a candle," Janie whispered into Billy's ear. "We've got to be able to see her face."

Though it seemed even more dangerous, Billy took the candle from the table and lit it noiselessly from a small flame in the fireplace.

Nearer, the old woman's smell grew stronger. To Billy it was like the first puff of air from the paunch of a deer as his father's long knife freed the tripas from the body, or the way the very leaves could hold and keep the news of a black bear's passage through them, so the hairs on the back of your neck stiffened almost before you could remember what the smell meant, and then when you knew, and looked around quickly for your father, it seemed that your stiffening hairs and not your nose were what had told you. To Janie it was the smell of small animals just after being born, a vixen licking her still damp kits deep in a moist cave. She had smelled it in the early spring when it came in a warm wave of air.

Closer and closer they came, the old woman's body never moving at all, just the regular, even breaths. They had thought they were getting used to the old woman's presence in the cabin, but now, at night, when everything was asleep, on this strange quest they knew must be guilty because they were so quiet about it, she seemed to loom above them.

Billy held the candle up before the ancient sleeping face. If the eyes had opened at that moment, Billy was sure he would have died of fright. But the eyes didn't open. The wrinkled face shone, brown as polished wood, shining squares and diamond shapes and triangles cut by the deep cracks. The old woman's mouth was closed, her lips folded and collapsed at the outer edges. Gray hairs curled and straggled from a black mole on her sunken chin.

And then as if in a dream Janie found her own shy arm reaching out toward that face. She came closer, closer, till she felt the warm, rich air of the old woman's breath on her hand. She reached toward the brown, wrinkled eyelid and lifted it up from the sunken eye.

What they both saw then was so strange that in their wonder they almost forgot to be afraid, for in the eye was no pupil or iris but a clear lighted glasslike globe in which they could see with the clarity of a bright winter day green spruce trees and a great crystal waterfall, and behind the wildly flashing water a dark mountain. Over its gray rock, black clouds rolled and climbed against a clear blue sky.

When they had seen the waterfall, the mountain and the clouds just long enough so they would never forget them, ever in their lives, Janie let the old skin of the eyelid settle once again over the clear globe. With a long glance at each other, but not a word, they crept back from the old woman, put the candle out, and climbed back to the loft, each to his own bed, where they slept, each one, a sleep full of dreams of the ominous beauty of a mountain, surging clouds and falling water . . .

"And now it's late and both of you have to go to school tomorrow," Aaron said.

"No! No!" Janie Benham said. "Tell about the winter and when Oka gets lost and the little girl!" She trembled, blinking, unable to leave the lonely log cabin in that wilderness.

"When they didn't have enough to eat!" Billy said. "And the boy remembers the birch-bark boxes!"

"No. Some other time, kiddoes. It's late. Come on, now, no fuss."

"No! Dad, please?"

But the forceful noise of their objections was bringing them back to here and now. "I don't want to go to bed in my old bed," Janie said.

"It's a great old bed," Aaron said. "What's the matter with your old bed?"

"I want to hear about what happens!"

Agnes had gotten up, making come-now noises, and they began to see the inevitability of this evening's events, futureless and doubtful and ordinary as they were. Not a story, but the usual, the usual. He kissed them good night and Agnes went upstairs with them. He went to the kitchen and opened a beer, then went to his study to look down at whatever he was working on then. After a while Agnes came up behind him and put her arms lightly around his waist. It was nice, and they would, barring possible drastic changes of mood, make love. But like an alien to such domestic probabilities he felt just the smallest, the most remote sense of irritability that she should translate his hour with the children into affection toward him. How women loved their domesticated beasts. Control, control. Horses, lions, wolves, meek and gentle. But her presence pressed against him, this strong, real woman, and even though he knew the old story of the two of them he turned toward her, tensely willing to find it out all over again.

George Buck arrives, nervous and upset about something that is obviously new, a new consideration since their telephone conversation. He comes down the front hall yelling "It's me!" and comes striding or stumbling through the house to Aaron's study, where Aaron has been staring down at his notebooks.

"Jesus, Aaron! Jesus H. Christ!" George says, and stands, waiting for the question.

"What's the matter?"

"Well . . ." George looks away, suddenly evasive. "It begins with Irv Lebowitz. You know him? A graduate student. I just found out he got busted last night in Litchwood."

Litchwood is four miles from the university, another depressed little mill town where rents in the old mill tenements are cheap.

"Begins?" Aaron says. "What was he busted for?"

"Just grass, as far as I know, but we can't get him loose on account of other things. They're being really difficult about it. One thing was—this cop was examining his rectum. Did you know they did that? For evidence, I guess. And if you know Irv, of course he couldn't resist. The situation wouldn't seem too funny to most people, but Irv . . . Anyway, he's supposed to have said, 'Tell me when you're through, honey,' among other things. They didn't take it too well. Plus asking them all sorts of rather personal psychological-sociological questions. Bill Zinner says they would have killed him if they thought they could have gotten away with it, they were that mad. Irv sort of got on this track, like the cops were his patients. He's amazing when he gets going, funny as hell. But you can imagine the local cops. All that *hair!* Irv wasn't even at the party they were suspicious about, but when he heard all the ruckus he came out in the hall and they took one look at him and that was it. They collected all the whiffle dust out of his pockets and his bellybutton lint and everything else. Man, I mean I think long hair's a pain in the ass, myself, but all this shit makes you ashamed to go near a barbershop." His hands busy under his raggedy Bowdoin sweatshirt, he scratches the blond fuzz on his slim but rather slack belly. "I don't know, Aaron. It's all a bloody plot or something."

"You said it 'began' with Irv Lebowitz," Aaron says, a little apprehensive. George obviously has something else he finds hard to go on with.

"Well, it's a favor I'd like to ask, and it isn't fair, really, so you can certainly say no and it's my own goddam fault I got in such a bind anyway, but this is it. Irv was going to read a paper tonight to my senior seminar I have at my house and now Irv won't be able to make it and I'm about totally unstrung. Listen, none of this occurred to me when I asked you out for supper. You've got to believe that, Aaron, but I thought you could just possibly stay for the class and answer questions or something. Just rap about the literary situation, or read something. Anything. They're bright kids. It's a great class, really. They all talk and argue and there's not one real asshole in the bunch. It's that kind of class—they *like* each other. You know."

Of course he can't refuse. He has never been able to refuse this sort of request. He thinks of the handsome supply of bourbon left in the half-gallon bottle of Beam, but drinking always turns bad except right after some kind of triumph, meaning the completion of something, and he hasn't completed anything for months. He is, after all, supposed to be a teacher, though often in the middle of a class he wonders why he is there. How did all those faces come to be looking at him? In his real dreams he is usually an uncommitted odd-job man, an aspiring artist of some kind, about twenty-six years old, and what he really wants to be is a student gleaning knowledge from some older, established person, a master. He wants to be *potential.* He wants to want to be known, not to be known. He wants to want to show them, not to have shown them.

"All right," he says to George, who, suddenly relieved and happy, thanks him over and over again.

Back at the old farm, the beloved old house, George and Helga listen sympathetically to his further compulsive discussion of his having forgotten Agnes' parents' fortieth-anniversary reception. After a while he detects in George's smooth young face, and in Helga's friendly, toothy one, the sort of care one tenders to the ill. With that he leaves off his twisted, self-mocking jokes and they talk of other things.

Dinner, with red wine and candlelight from candles set in old pewter candlesticks, is mainly a very fine beef stew. Helga is a serious cook—a follower of Joyce Chen and Julia Child on educational television, the TV set hidden upstairs some place—and in her kitchen things are always marinating in twist-top jars of various sizes. Herbs hang drying from the beams, festoons of garlic gleam. When they go to Boston she always visits ethnic grocery stores. Edward disapproves of most of her best efforts, but tonight he doesn't mind the stew, even the pearly sections of tripe. A while after dinner, when the students begin to arrive, Edward wants to stay. It is hard to explain to him how his mere youth might inhibit discussion. "Not that any of us feel that way," George says.

"It's stupid," Edward says resignedly, and he and his mother go upstairs. For too much of his life he will have to suffer living in too young a body.

Aaron knows several of the students who arrange themselves on chairs and wicker stools, and on the floor around the chair that has evidently been saved for him. Linda Einsperger is a tall, blond, caustic-voiced girl whose incredibly long thighs—alabaster columns descending for what seem yards below her skirt—always remind him of the legs of a giraffe. When she moves, she has that same ungainly grace. John Periault is a hockey player who comes from a Canadian border town. He is still on the hockey team, but in his senior year he has undergone a fairly common intellectual change of life and as one symptom has let his hair grow even longer than is fashionable these days. On the rink, from beneath his headguard, a wide black cape of hair flows over his neck and shoulders. A scar over his left eye bisects his eyebrow, and his nose points somewhat to the right. In class discussions, unlike his savage behavior on the rink, he is reasonable, self-deprecating and rather gentle. Frank Hawkes, whose tawny hair shoots out for nearly a foot from all over his head as though his brain constantly generates twenty thousand volts, is a former Maoist—or perhaps he still is one—who has recently returned to school after two years' disappearance. His smile is fierce; he knows, it proclaims, what is not known by any of the others. Bradford Wilkins is a Black, watchful and arrogant, who is handicapped by having to make a definite predecision before he speaks: *Will this answer compromise me?* It is almost like thinking in one language and speaking in another. In moments of indecision he forsakes the general language of the class and speaks jive, man, y'know? I mean, y'know, this dude come along, y'know. I mean what that got t'do thit? I mean what's all this *shit*, man? Bradford is dressed in blue jeans and T-shirt, and on his head blooms an Afro of such extraordinary dimensions his neck seems too thin to support it. A silver comb handle sticks out of the side of that dense black cloud like something prosthetic.

There are ten students in all, the others not quite as exotic, including a slender woman of sixty or so who seems to carry her age into this young group with self-conscious bravery. Obviously an okay member of the class, she is included in the others' conversation. Aaron hears one girl call her Gladys.

Except for Bradford Wilkins, those he knows smile briefly at him as he takes the official chair. Wilkins gives him a curt nod. It is always a strangely unfocused moment when he first becomes the center of everyone's attention this way. He wonders, thinking back to his own merely potential time, about the quality of their expectation and curiosity. And resentment, too; that is always there, waiting, possible—the resentment toward someone who has done something along the lines of what you would like to do someday, only you will do it better, much better. And now this person has the gall to appear before you looking merely human and vulnerable, but seeming to act upon the supposition that he deserves your attention, even your regard.

George explains that Irv Lebowitz can't make it tonight because he has been busted in Litchwood, but Aaron Benham has kindly agreed to come at the last minute even though he is on leave this year. With that, George sits down on the rug beside Linda Einsperger. One of her long arms is across her knees, and she seems to be chinning herself on this arm while she stares at Aaron with pale blue eyes. She has slipped out of her sandals, and her bony toes seem as long and articulate as fingers.

Aaron decided, easily, before he left his house, that he would read them a story. He knows that it is imperfect in many ways, but like many stories one reads these days it has an interesting middle and a certain intensity of tone here and there. He knows enough to keep all this to himself; without telling them more than that it is a story in progress, he reads.

My name is Allard Benson and I am a writer of fiction, a college professor, and an unwilling collector of paranoiacs. Perhaps I am no more surrounded by paranoiacs than anyone else, but sometimes I wonder. Like those who fear dogs only to excite in all dogs an immediate, aggressive affection, I seem doomed to be the chosen confessor of those who have systematized their delusions. I wonder if they know how much they frighten me.

Long ago I used to try to explain to them that the world was mainly plotless, chaotic, random. I used to have that warmth and time. In spite of their eyes that are always bright beyond mere alertness, as bright beyond the tender depths of protoplasm as polished gemstones, I once, in my surfeit of time, brought them home for a drink and tried to explain. That was before I knew how short life was, how long it takes to learn the craft I am apprenticed to.

This morning I have just finished a short novel written by G., a student. At three this afternoon, in my office at school, we will have a conference. I ought immediately to tell him that he has no ear for dialogue, that his few metaphors consistently violate his intent, and finally that his chief motive for writing, so clearly revealed in his novel, is not the creation of art but an attempt to create legitimate targets for vengeance. His villains are carefully prepared and set up for their deserved reward, and his hero is armed and ready. Armed, in this case, with a weapon G. actually carries himself; he once proudly showed me the knife he carries in his boot—a vicious little dagger he calls an "Arkansas toothpick."

In the last conference I had with G., a week ago, he chose not to discuss the short story he had written, but to tell me about the universal cheating in courses where multiple-choice tests are given. At other times he has revealed to me the blatant callousness, cynicism, laziness, senility, dope addiction and suspected perversions of my colleagues. In his revelatory stance he is more than a little threatening. He leans his shoulders toward me, smiling the bitter yet triumphant smile of one who knows all, and demands that I enter his world. I, too, should find in the discovery of evil the joy that keeps his eyes so icy bright.

You can see why I'm not looking forward to the three o'clock conference with G. His intimidating attitude causes me to be dishonest with him, and in that sense he is right; his psychosis is not all fantasy. It is the encompassing magnitude of his "delusional system" that disheartens me, that diminishes my soul and makes me evade my responsibilities toward him. He excludes the world until there is only he and I, and in that small, cold cell I am lonely and apprehensive. So I nod, or shake my head in feigned wonder, and wait for the hour to pass.

And while I wait rather tensely here in my study for the hour when I'll have to go to my office to meet G., I remember other confrontations with delusion. Perhaps there is an order to them, not in time but in another way. In fiction one plays a strange game with ugliness and fear.

F., an occasional handyman and jack-of-all-trades in our town came up to me in the general store and told me that he had been seeing several deer, including a large buck that would go at least eight points and two-hundred pounds, in the orchard behind his house. The deer nearly always came into the orchard at dusk, he said, and why didn't I come out and see if I could "connect"?

F. was a rugged, dark little man, about thirty-five years old. He always wore the laborer's uniform of our region, which in all seasons is basically green chino work pants and shirt, and leather boots. At this time, since it was November and getting cold, he had added to this basic outfit a greasy red wool hunting cap with his hunting license pinned to the crown, and a faded red sweatshirt. He had been sitting with the others on the benches in front of the store in the morning sun when I came to get the Sunday papers, and I was surprised when he followed me into the store, touched my arm and offered me a chance at his deer. I hadn't shot a deer for two years in a row, and the offer excited me perhaps beyond my better judgment, because I knew that F. was a tense and unusual character, a man involved in many complicated, interlocking local feuds. Some of these involved work that he had contracted to do and never finished, some were over damages he had claimed for one reason or another, some were with the selectmen and road agent concerning the plowing or grading of the gravel road that led to his place. He was quite a verbally clever man, and his voice was heard often in town meetings. He was generally considered to be a good workman, too—if you could get him to do the work. He could blast ledge, fix nearly anything mechanical, paint, paper, shingle, glaze, wire, do stonemasonry that was widely admired by other professionals, and so on. At times, however, he wouldn't do anything for months on end except sit on the benches of the general store, or drive around in his old pickup truck drinking beer and tossing the empty cans with an expert backhand flip out the window of the cab into the truck bed. Or he wouldn't be seen at all for weeks.

His hand, still on my arm, was a cracked red instrument of scars and calluses, the ridged brown fingernails packed smoothly with hardened black.

"You git your gun and come on out 'bout three-thirty—'bout an hour 'fore dark. You know the way."

I thanked him for the chance at the deer, and said that I knew approximately where he lived but I'd never been there and wasn't sure I could find the place after I left the blacktop.

He feigned surprise, or I thought he did—all of F.'s publicly displayed emotions seemed exaggerated, meant for effect. Then he laughed loudly, his hard little eyes, as always, watching through the mask, and gave me closer directions.

"You familiar with the back road to Cascom?" he said, and continued with the directions, smiling as if the whole thing were a needless hypocrisy and of course I knew the way exactly. At the time, partly, I suppose, because of my greed for venison, I took this to be only another of F.'s peculiarities. The reason for the gift, I thought, was that I had recently published a book. This event had been mentioned in our local newspaper, and I thought F.'s gesture was a manifestation of the intense interest that even the smallest amount of celebrity seems to evoke.

That afternoon at three-thirty I found F.'s place, a run-down farm typical of our region. The small unpainted house was fairly level upon its foundations, but the barn sagged, a wooden silo had spun down upon itself like pick-up sticks, and the connecting outbuildings and sheds had all begun to lean heavily upon one another, doors sprung, roofs mostly stripped by wind and ice of their ancient tar paper.

Nailed to a tree in the ragged front yard was a sign, uneven black letters on a white-painted board:

THELMA'S BEAUTY SHOP

The house had been well banked with sawdust, but the sawdust was old, reddened by age, probably put there winters ago and left by someone who didn't care enough that the house would rot at its footings.

I didn't see F.'s truck anywhere, but thought it might be around in back or in one of the leaning sheds. The front door to the house was obviously never used; it seemed as permanently fused into its frame as the gray subsurface of an old wound in a tree. I left my rifle in the car and followed the worn track to the kitchen door, feeling that I was being observed. I knocked, and after a suitable amount of time the door was opened by a young woman in her late twenties. She seemed frightened, but asked me, without the usual belligerence that emotion causes, what I wanted. I said F. had asked me to come out this afternoon to see if the deer would come into the orchard.

"You mean he asked you to come here?" she said.

"Yes."

She seemed puzzled and cautious. After some worried thought she asked me to come in and sit down. I sat at the table in the large, crowded kitchen. The implements of the beauty shop stood among the domestic paraphernalia like a double exposure, dominated by what I took to be a hair drier —a huge, battered, chromed bell on a stand.

"You're Thelma?" I asked, and she nodded, smiling quickly.

She knew who I was; she told me that her cousin had been a student of mine several years before, and that the cousin had pointed me out to her once. "I don't get to town much, though," she added.

She wanted to be friendly, but it was so obvious her friendliness was undercut by fear. I watched her as she prepared coffee, thinking even then how one might document this unfortunate woman, who seemed in her unhappiness typical, common, yet sharply her own living self. Her hair was a dull, lusterless brown that no surface beautification would ever bring to life, her face was smooth and well boned, yet dark, wasted by the forces of poverty and unhappiness. That look, which is common among oppressed children and women, has deeper causes than poor diet and lack of sunlight. She seemed a woman of another kind of shadow, a prisoner of this prideless house. It took a startled second look to see that she was pretty, that beneath her faded print dress she still carried her light burden of woman's flesh with grace. When we smiled at each other, we both grew tense and shy, as if appalled by a vague and secret understanding.

F. came in then, banging the door open. He stood in the doorway, arms akimbo, a look of mock anger on his face. "Well!" he said fiercely, looking from Thelma to me, then back to Thelma. "So you come after all!" He laughed, to indicate that his fierceness was only put on, but we were not all that reassured. "Come on," he said, and took his Winchester from a wall rack made of cocked deer hooves.

Until dark, F. and I sat beside a granite boulder where we could overlook the small orchard, but the deer didn't come that evening. Their one great talent is, of course, survival. When it became so dark we couldn't see our front sights, F. got up, saying, "Tomorrow. Sure as hell they'll be coming back one of these nights. Let's give her a try tomorrow."

We walked back to the house in the dark, coming upon its warm windowlights. In the kitchen we sat at the table and had a cup of the coffee Thelma had made earlier.

F. sat across from me, grinning like a wise cat. "I don't know what's going on these days up to the college," he said, his expression belying his words. "Some of them coeds, they wear their skirts any higher they going to have two new cheeks to powder!"

Thelma was over at the oil stove, her back to us, and F. pretended she couldn't hear. His hand rose to the side of his mouth—one of the stage devices he used to superpose his own artifices upon reality. "It must git you all hot and bothered, having to look at it all day long." He laughed and pounded the table. When this timed paroxysm was over, he wiped his eyes. "And you a writer, too," he added, shaking his head.

I grew weary at the thought of trying to plead anything before the court of F.'s prejudices. "Sometimes it's not easy," I said.

"'Course I suppose you git caught with your eyeballs hanging out they'd throw your ass out of there."

"No," I said recklessly. "We can look all we want."

He seemed taken aback. "That so?" He expressed exaggerated surprise. Even his thick black hair seemed to stiffen as his eyes stared at me. "Well, you never know!"

I began to wonder just what I'd said to cause such a reaction, but of course it mattered little what I'd said; F.'s drama coexisted with real life. Finally he did drop this subject and we talked for a while of the deer—a subject as rigidly classical in its turns and counterturns as Oriental theater.

When I left, I promised to come back the next afternoon.

Again when I arrived at the small farmhouse F. wasn't there, but a rusted-out Chevrolet was parked next to the kitchen. Thelma opened the door for me without my having to knock. I saw immediately that she had prettied herself up. She wore red lipstick, and her hair was fluffed out. A customer was just leaving, a pale woman in her forties who, below the convolutions of her freshly baked hair, wore a man's old mackinaw over a polka-dot dress, her milk-white legs descending into unbuckled galoshes. As Thelma explained carefully that I had come to hunt with F., the woman's steady eyes judged this information upon its own merits.

After the door closed, Thelma busied herself putting away the various objects of her profession. In the air, competing with the domestic odors of the kitchen, was the odor that always reminds me of burnt feathers, or burnt glue—the chemical that sets the hair. As I watched her putting away the jars of goo, the racks of curlers and other torture devices that women think powerful enough to do magic, I knew by the delicacy of Thelma's movements that she knew I was watching her. For me she kept her back straight, calculated the cant of her pelvis as she knelt to a cupboard, the profile of her breasts as she rose on tiptoe to reach another. It was all innocent and pretty, and I felt considerably more than pity for her.

Now, I am a man whose mere daydreams do not excite guilt. In my fiction I am constantly haunted by adultery, murder, cruelty and betrayal, but that is another world, and in it I will enter any darkness, leaving whatever loyalties I have back in the real world. So if I began to consider then, even in the most vivid detail, how I would take F.'s young wife to a motel on the highway to the city, ease her of all the sickness of her ugly marriage (in bed, she trembles as I gently touch her pink, childless nipple, etc., etc.), I felt no guilt. Thoughts are merely thoughts.

And I was here to kill a deer. A knife at my belt, my

accurate Marlin in the car, I was prepared only for that kind of reality.

F. came in then. He stood in the open doorway looking at us, not speaking. Toward him Thelma turned the wasted look of apprehension.

"My!" he began in a high falsetto. "Ain't we all gussied up! What's the occasion, as if I didn't know." He turned to me. "Ain't she something, though? You kind of like her sweet little ass, don't you, Professor."

He strode forward and hit her in the mouth. She nearly fell down but held on to the counter, one hand over the lower part of her face.

"Hey!" I said.

He turned to me, his hands held low in front of him, as though he expected, or welcomed, an attack. "You think I'm so bone-dumb I don't know what's going on? I knowed for a long time."

Without looking at her he hit her with the back of his hand, and her head hit the cabinet like a piece of wood. A canister set rattled on the counter. Quickly he took his rifle from the deer-hoof rack and levered a shell into the chamber. The rifle pointed at my belly, where I felt its ghostly power in the form of ice.

"You want to stay and watch," he said, "or you want to git the hell out of here?"

I heard Thelma bawling as I left. At first I was going to call the police, and I drove fast down the gravel road in the cool light of dusk. But by the time I got back to town I had gone through in my imagination what that summons would entail in this world, where actions beget actions. I considered my wife, my family, but mostly my work, the symmetries and balances I pursue, and my dwindling reservoir of imagination and time.

I don't have to look for trouble in this world; it comes to me. For instance, there is a little man I've seen three times over the last few years. I find him waiting for me in the hall in front of my office door. I don't remember his name, but I remember him so well that after not seeing him for a year or more I am aware of the increasing gray in his brush-cut black hair. He is wiry, big-handed, a factory worker, as quick in his movements as a squirrel that finds itself a little too far from the nearest tree. As I come up to my office door I see him, and keep my eyes away from his as I unlock the door. After I've entered the office he stands peering at my name in the little card slot on the door, then at me with alert, avaricious eyes. He asks if I am Professor Benson, and during our subsequent interview makes absolutely no reference to ever having seen me before.

Something is wrong, he says, with what's going on in the White House, and he needs my advice.

Should I agree that things are going wrong? Things are going wrong indeed, and I could go on intemperately for an hour, for two hours, for a marathon, a filibuster, a teach-in. The difference between his delusional system and mine is that mine is not encapsulated, and my despair at the vain and vicious actions of men can be documented at all levels. Something is going wrong in the White House, in the Kremlin, in Peking, in Cairo, in Athens, in Tel Aviv, in the Vatican, in your living room and mine. Something is going wrong and it always has the symptoms of the incurable psychosis he has brought to me with such excitement that I know he believes it to be a precious gift.

He has a letter from the Office of the President, an answer to a letter he has previously sent. He has studied this answer very carefully, as you can imagine, and in its bland, perfectly trite, noncommittal platitudes he has found a code in the form of an anagram. If you take the first letter of the first word, the second letter of the second word, the third letter of the third word (at this point his smile is sure and hard, for even the most skeptical dolt would have to be convinced by now), you will see that these letters, slightly rearranged (according to an arithmetical formula he won't go into now), spell DEATH U.S. The President is surrounded by Communists, but how to let the President know? And there is one other little problem—he wants to be rewarded for submitting this vital information to the President. He wants to be paid, and paid well.

I am not a snake-poker. I am afraid of this man and of the multitudes he represents. The things I might tell him, however, rush through my mind like the horrible thoughts one can't thrust away at four in the morning.

I might close the door and turn toward him slowly, a grim smile on my face, and say, "So you know. It is very unfortunate for you, sir, that you have such an inquiring mind. But you haven't gone quite far enough, and I can tell you this because you will never get out of this building alive: the President is in no danger, *for he is one of us!*"

I think with awe of the perfect ecstasy these words would evoke in him. What glorious, heroic justification! How terrible it is of me to deprive him of this gift.

But I don't want to enter his system in such an active role; he has, of course, already enlisted me in the secret armies of his fantasy, and I want to resign my commission, please, thank you. I do not want to be caught again. So in order to get away I must lie with great subtlety, treat his madness with respect and even sympathy, yet beg to disagree with certain of his conclusions—when all the time my violent apprehension screams from below: *Kill him, don't let him get out of this building alive.*

I look around me and observe how reality and our common paranoid tendencies reinforce each other. For instance, I believe that H., a radical student, was framed on a marijuana charge by the police in a nearby town. He is a militant who has a pure, messianic contempt for drugs, alcohol, or any other distraction that might lessen his usefulness to the cause he so fanatically serves. I have known him for three years, and at first we were quite close. Now, I no longer question to his face the elaborate system he has devised in order to find, over and over again, evidence that there is a deep, revolutionary alliance between his faction and great masses of the exploited workers of America. I wonder how much longer he will even speak to me.

He may be mad, dangerously infected by one idea, but he did not keep marijuana in the bottle marked "Oregano" on the shelf above his stove. In their raid upon his apartment the police triumphantly confiscated his posters of Che Guevara and Mao Tse-tung, and also informed the newspapers that "human excrement" was found on his floors. He and his wife had recently adopted an unhousebroken puppy.

Where does delusion end and reality begin as our various delusions start to mesh? The connection is made, and madness, as always, seems dominant.

And now another incident comes to mind, one that happened many years ago, when I was a young soldier. In Phenix City, Alabama, was a second-story beer joint frequented by paratroopers from nearby Fort Benning, Georgia. Perhaps Phenix City has changed, and the second-story place, along with all the other squalid clip joints, has disappeared, but in those days the town, with its air of small-time graft, was a study in degradation, in which the varied possibilities of humanity seemed to have been reduced to nothing but a vicious strut.

The second-story bar was called Club Geronimo, after the fierce Apache chief whose name had been adopted by the Airborne as its battle cry. One entered the place by way of a wooden outside staircase. Inside the club were mismatched wooden and metal tables, chairs, a linoleum floor always damp with spilled beer and booze, and several young but used-looking waitresses who changed off during any evening because of accepted propositions or the results of slugging the dregs of too many drinks. On the musty papered walls were calendar pictures of streamlined blondes in shorts and halters. Hamburgers and other simple foods were served, but these were not highly recommended.

If a paratrooper left Club Geronimo with a girl it was proper for him to use the stairs, but otherwise he had to jump off the balcony—a descent of some twelve feet—onto the hard dirt alley below. Because of previous broken ankles, collarbones and wrists, this practice was frowned upon by the MP's, and if they caught you at it you would receive "company punishment" for two weeks. But the punishment by the members of your own company for breaking tradition was rather harsh, too. So, while drinking in Club Geronimo, you always had ahead of you this scary little choice of exit. Somehow this awaiting test made the atmosphere of the club a little more edgy than it ordinarily would have been even among paratroopers, who had already, by volunteering for such duty, indicated their physical narcissism.

But this is a story of madness in the context of madness, about the actions of Corporal E., who couldn't seem to leave me alone. He came from Pennsylvania, where he had grown up on a farm. Though he was solidly built, I always thought of his broad muscles as lacking in tone, like an animal raised too quickly for slaughter, transformed at the end into its proper increments of protein and fat, something less than animal. He carried no extra fat, of course, but to me his strength seemed dumb, badly organized. He was always ordering me to do push-ups, and because he was cadre I had to do them. It seemed to perplex him that I did push-ups as easily as I did, and I could see in his eyes a deep yearning for some more satisfying way to utilize me. At the time, surrounded as I was by the army's irrationality, I didn't consider his constant need of me to indicate any namable psychosis, but now I think I can put a name to it, and the name is erotic delusion. He was always winking at me, and bumping into me, his expression indicating collusion between us. It was only after my usual cold or exasperated response that he would have me do the push-ups.

This night, he'd been watching me for a while, and when I was coming back from the head he deliberately bumped me into a table. When I didn't respond the way his delusion predicted, he pointed to the wet linoleum and told me to get down there and give him twenty. I examined the cruddy floor and my clean, creased chinos and told him to go fuck himself.

I won't reproduce the usual ceremonial posturings and banal insults that followed. Suffice to say that at a certain point he hit me on the left cheek hard enough to hurt like hell and cause me to taste blood. I won't indulge here in the usual modest protestations of inadequacy, either. What happened next was that I hurt Corporal E. very badly—so badly, evidently, that he was reduced to a strange, childish panic. He managed to grab my left hand and clamp his teeth over my bent forefinger. Once his jaws were set, the rest of him turned passive and still. In considerable pain, I found myself standing there with the corporal more or less on the end of my left arm.

A strange feeling. His eyes were open, and seemed to stare into mine. I requested that he let go. When he didn't comply, I made the mistake of hitting him in the nose. The pain became unbearable, as if the blow had turned the bolt in a lock. He didn't even blink, and blood from his nose mixed with blood from my finger. I had to get away from him. I felt that I was becoming my own finger, as though he had all of me in his jaws. I continued to argue with his unwavering gaze.

"Let go or I'll have to hit you with this bottle," I said reasonably, pressing a beer bottle tentatively along his head above his ear. "Let go and I won't hit you any more, okay?" Maybe he had won after all, I thought. I couldn't believe, had never known before, how one small member of my body could generate so much pain. I became afraid of all wounds, as tender as a child. Even the twelve-foot jump from the balcony now loomed before me like an impossible cliff. The pain was so intense I couldn't hit him with the bottle for fear of causing such pain in him.

My friends had gathered around us. They argued with him, too, and offered me helpful suggestions I could barely hear through the vibrating, screenlike immediacy of my pain. They told me to hit him, to gouge out his eyes. One tried to pry open the jaws with a spoon, another by pressing the joints of the jawbone with his thumbs, another by strangulation. Nothing worked. I began to faint, and had to put my head down for a moment until the drab colors of the linoleum resumed their proper tones. I tapped his head with the bottle, a tender, tentative little blow that failed to register in his bright eyes. The others discussed where on his head would be the best spot to sap him. No one wanted to kill him, really, but all could see that the situation was intolerable. Corporal E.'s right canine, in particular, was half sunk into my finger, surely grating upon white bone.

"Maybe they got a crowbar," I heard someone say.

The pain flowed up my forearm and scorched my elbow, played about with my upper arm, sometimes on the surface, then again like the thrust of a huge needle down into the clefts between the muscles themselves. My arm felt flayed, then drawn, as though it were being stripped, layer by gleaming layer. I had no idea what was going on in Club Geronimo then, I just spoke to the corporal's steadfast madness. I had a steel table fork at his throat, the dull tines pressing into the complications of his neck. "I'll kill you," I told him. "I'll have to. I'm going to shove this fork clean through your neck. I'll twist it. Let go. Listen, do you hear me? I can't stand this. I'll have to kill you. Let go. Let go of my finger. Let go."

My earnestness had reduced me to plain language. I called him no names, accused him and his mother of no perversions. It was as though we were alone, made one by this terrible connection, bone to bone. When I touched the fork to his neck the pain thrust my own consciousness askew. It was just his head that had me, like the severed head of a snapping turtle clenched upon a stick, the stick you hold out, dreamlike, as a substitute for your hand.

The pain increased. It never reached a plateau where I might confront it, know it, and negotiate some kind of treaty with it. But it was the sight of his teeth deep in my flesh, and the fear of amputation, that finally made me act. I took the bottle again and began to tap above his ear. With each small blow my whole left side was seared by fire. I felt like a man having to amputate his own limb. Still operating, I think, was a deep rule against murder, but this was true desperation and I began to tap his head harder, faster, the soft ring of the bottle on his skull growing harder until the tympanic hollows below his bones answered, and finally his black pupils widened. With a slow, even, peaceful elevation of his gaze the pigmented parts of his eyes moved up into his forehead. His jaws slowly opened upon a gush of my blood and I was free, singular; it was like being born again.

A human bite is considered dangerous, and my crushed and torn finger was treated by the medics in radical fashion. After the Novocaine, the cleaning, the stitches, the tetanus and penicillin shots, I felt as I know Corporal E. did the next morning—that something much more climactic than a saloon fight had occurred. Within a week he had arranged to have himself transferred out of the regiment.

Soon I will have to go to my office to have the conference with G. about his frightening novel, and I find myself in anxiety, yearning again for that sudden clear freedom, the clamped homunculus gone from my flesh forever.

Did I say that one of the fictional objects G. has set up for vengeance is a college professor whose open, rather shy demeanor hides the most calculating, malicious intent, and whose initials are the same as mine? This character in G.'s novel is called Albert Bamberger, and in the end, when Bamberger is found out, degraded and subjected to public contumely, G.'s lack of narrative and descriptive talent is transcended by a kind of gleeful energy. At the most dramatic point, Albert Bamberger, attempting to escape, is brought down by a knife thrown by the hero.

Am I right in believing that Albert Bamberger, who gets the "Arkansas toothpick" between his shoulder blades, is me, or am I just another madly alert animal in a world of imagined conspiracy? G. will no doubt watch me slyly as we discuss his novel, because I won't bring this matter of identification into the open. That is what he will be waiting for, but I won't do it. I know he wants me to admit it, to have to feel that fictional blade, that ghostly steel, in my back.

We use each other, the materials of reality, our experiences, everything at all in our "encapsulated delusional systems." Even in my apprehension I sense my kinship with G., and cannot wholly condemn his mad attempt to make his own satisfying order out of chaos. I, too, am driven by a similar *horror vacui.* Though I would call my work by another name, I will use G. and all the rest for my own purposes, use them coldly and without mercy, more coldly than their own warm needful selves could ever understand.

He looks up into the vacuum left by his stilled voice. Helga is there in the shadows; he hadn't seen her return. There are, after a moment, murmurs of approbation. Laughter has occurred in the right places. He has revealed something of himself and his work, and he feels the shivery apprehension and then the acceptance of responsibility. The water is not so bad once you get your whole body wet, but you are still swimming toward a shore that may or may not be receding. Linda Einsperger wants to know how autobiographical the story is, and he answers that it is too autobiographical, that it makes him self-conscious, and who wants to write about or read about a professor who is a writer who is writing about writing. It is all incestuous and even narcissistic. Yes, for instance, the corporal, who was really a private and somewhat smaller, did bite his finger. Here are the scars, and much of the sense of touch is gone from the pad of that finger. And Thelma, poor Thelma. That is a longer story altogether, in which he was guilty of more than daydreams, but he doesn't tell them this. John Periault asks, If the story isn't finished, what is he going to do to finish it? He replies, now safely into a familiar, literate, honest glibness, that the beauty shop section seems to him to outweigh the other parts. Something is wrong with the balance of memory, with the story's symmetry. What the hell does it have to be *symmetrical* for? Frank Hawkes asks. Having found his issue, he will now defend the story against this sterile academician. No, that is overstated in this instance, but it is true of Frank's positions on most matters. Aaron goes on, perversely, he thinks, in order to gain the initiative, to say that the story is told by a rather pompous, rather rhetoric-conscious person. Witness all those balanced, somber, periodic sentences. The narrator is being characterized by his tones, and there is in his narration the further defining necessity for what he (the narrator) might call meteness, and in his case this must be reflected in symmetry. That dude is sick, man, he just as sick as anybody *in* there, Bradford Wilkins observes, to which Aaron answers, Yes, that's the problem, isn't it? Some agree, some do not. Gladys, the sixty-year-old, leans forward into the light, her gray hair pulled back from her face in almost painful tension as though she strains against a tether. She moves her arms and hands tentatively, with the dimming grace (it seems to Aaron) of a woman who has once been extraordinarily beautiful. In the way she holds her head and shoulders she displays some gallantry in the losing battle against gravity and age. She says that the story, as Professor Benham said before, is about writing fiction, isn't it? Linda Einsperger grows excited, her pale eyes flash; the A student has begun to perceive the answer. Yes! Yes! she says, but does not elaborate. She knows, almost. If she could write it down, she would know. Now she looks at Aaron with the excited admiration of one who discerns beneath an interesting surface a puzzle to solve—a puzzle with a legitimate solution one can grasp as a neat reward for thought. But they all have a horror of vacuums, Gladys says. I know the feeling. Frank Hawkes says that it isn't necessary to be paranoid these days. Everybody breaks the law. Like he's got a joint in his pocket, so what? The law's after everybody's ass. You ought to really know that, Bradford Wilkins says, implying that the white boy can't really know, which causes Frank Hawkes to part his electric hair at the top of his head and offer to show Bradford Wilkins a view of some scars.

George decides that the conversation is getting away from the story and asks if it's possible that all the various characters are at least somewhat justified in their varieties of clinical paranoia. Both Bradford Wilkins and Frank Hawkes give him disgusted but essentially tolerant glances; George has to do his professor thing. Well, John Periault says, F. is right in a way because Allard Benson does consider balling his wife, even if he's too chicken to try it. Frank Hawkes suggests that maybe it's those who can, do, and those who can't, write about it. Aaron thinks this is interesting, but can you really write about something if you couldn't possibly do it, and be at all true. Imagine it, man, Bradford Wilkins says. Are any of the other people in the story real? Gladys asks. Aaron says they're all somewhat real, but changed for the purposes of the story. Not changed deliberately, but as they come on they change the meaning of the story, and it changes them, as the story changes meaning in the writer's mind—as he begins to find out what it's really about. Linda Einsperger says that it's really about people making order out of chaos and that's what fiction does, so maybe by comparing fiction to paranoia the writer learns something about fiction. Yes, Gladys says. But what has he learned about fiction? That it doesn't always work, Aaron says, earning a few doubtful looks for his facetiousness. No, I'm still not sure what I wanted to find out. One girl who hasn't yet spoken suggests that the writer is colder than the paranoiacs because he manipulates them deliberately, while they actually believe in and fear their fantasies. Aaron notices that this formerly silent girl is admired by the talkers for her theory. Yes, they nod, well put. George says that the difference is that the writer produces, at his best, art, which is good, while the paranoiacs cause danger and even, possibly, murder. Oswald, Sirhan, Beckwith, Ray, for instance. Who's Beckwith? Frank Hawkes asks, and is informed by Bradford Wilkins that Beckwith is the white mother now walking around free that shot Medgar Evers in the back. Well, Linda Einsperger says, does the end justify the means—with a writer, that is. Only in art, maybe, George says. Frank Hawkes says belligerently that he likes the goddam story anyway, no matter what anybody thinks about it. So what's wrong with thinking once in a while, Linda Einsperger inquires, an edge in her voice that reminds Aaron that she and Frank used to live together. You can sit around and stink and think all you want, Frank says, meaning that some people are out on the barricades where they ought to be. Well, Linda replies, I haven't had a populist prefrontal lobotomy like some people I know. George does his professor thing again.

Helga serves coffee, Cokes, cheese, crackers and cookies, and after a half-hour in which Aaron, the formerly silent girl and Gladys talk about the writer's intentions, who he writes for (himself, Aaron says, but that's too simple maybe), with Helga sitting nearby listening, the class is over and people begin to leave. George brings Frank and Bradford over to Aaron and asks them if they know Mark Rasmussen's whereabouts, and what he's doing these days.

Frank looks up into his head, showing the whites of his eyes—an imitation of unconsciousness. Bradford shakes his head. Standing there together in their wild rigid hair they look like two varieties of the same exotic flower.

"So I take it the news is not good," George says.

"The news is bad news," Bradford says.

"Mark's on a long, bad trip, I'm afraid," Frank says.

"Listen, man," Bradford says. "That boy'd shoot cat piss if he thought it was a kick. I mean he's shooting stuff nobody can *pro*-nounce."

"Do you know where he is?"

"Last seen in Cambridge," Frank says, going on to explain that when last seen Mark was sitting on a mattress with a variety of freaks, all holding hands. Frank isn't sure what kind of high, exactly, they were on, but they were seriously, *seriously*, discussing the possibility of getting plastic tubing so they could attach each one's bloodstream to the next, through maybe the femoral artery. Then they would all have exactly the same high, a kind of super-togetherness, the ultimate circle-jerk.

"That is *dumb,*" Bradford says.

Frank says he thinks he can find out where Mark is, and Aaron gives him some money for telephone calls.

"I can get a message to him—if he's receiving," Frank says. "He's pretty down, you know. On all of us. On the people. He doesn't hope for anything much."

Aaron looks at Frank, startled by this tone which is so unlike Frank's usual militant certainty. Aaron wonders if he will ever get over being surprised and touched whenever another person escapes, if even for a moment, the raw simplicities of his ideology.

When the students have left, Aaron, George and Helga sit in the living room that is now large and quiet in its emptiness.

"God, that sounds awful about Mark," George says. "I keep wondering if there's any hope at all for him. And after all the *causes* and everything like that he's been through. He was always so idealistic. I just don't know much about drugs, except what I read, and I know half of that is probably bullshit. But Mark's too old for all that now. You know he's twenty-six? I mean all I know is about pot and maybe bennies and Dexedrine and that old stuff. But Mark went through LSD and all *that* crap years ago. I mean this must be something else . . ." He stares bleakly at Aaron, his pale blue eyes filmy. "If we could just find him, Aaron, we could get him back here and . . ."

And what, Aaron thinks. Make him stop killing himself? Make him able to get along with his history and ours? Change him somehow with our love and care so that he'll do the equivalent of getting his dissertation done? George is now silent and morose, and finally he yawns, his eyes shiny as if with tears.

After a while Helga says, "That was a weird story, Aaron."

"Maybe it said too much, Aaron," George says. "I mean it might reveal too much. No secrets left, or something."

"I thought just the opposite," Helga says.

"Me too," Aaron says, being quite serious about it. They both look at him and see this. "In some ways it's a shitty story."

"What do you mean?" George asks somewhat defensively.

"I mean it's so easy to be insincere."

"But we know everything the narrator thinks," George says. "Everything."

"Everything he chooses to tell," Helga says.

George, evidently deciding that he doesn't want to go along with this, says, "They really liked it. I think it was a good class, Aaron, and I'm awfully grateful you bailed me out like that." He yawns again, then unsuccessfully tries to suppress a whole series of yawns. Aaron suggests he'd better be going home but it is soon decided that he should spend the night, and Helga gets the guest room, which is the old "birthing" room off the kitchen, ready for him.

When George goes upstairs Helga stays behind, giving his departure a quick look, quick as the wing of a bird. "Aaron, what can we do?" she says. "If I even mention the dissertation he sulks."

"I don't know," Aaron says. At first he is angry at George for making her have to go down with this sinking ship; never has he put a woman in such a position. He couldn't think of doing such a thing. What the hell is wrong with George? Yes, but he himself has put women in other positions maybe as unhappy. For instance, is Agnes happy? It seems irrelevant, somehow, though it shouldn't. He would like to take Helga to bed. If Agnes is unhappy sometimes it is usually because of something he's done, or forgotten to do—never because he is passive or lazy. Somehow this seems a better basis for a marriage. This is ridiculously egotistical; suddenly he feels completely inadequate. How can he comfort Helga? A person whose own life is stupidly messed up, whose work is in bits and pieces. He feels that during the evening he has falsely posed as a person who is objective, mild and sincere. He has compromised himself by playing that role.

Helga puts her hands to her face, her shoulders hunched over. Then she stands straighter—almost a jaunty stance—and wipes her eyes with the palms of her hands, like a child. "I'm sorry," she says.

"Why?" For some reason he thinks of a sweet, hard yellow apple.

"I shouldn't break down. George is in bad enough shape. Would you like a nightcap, Aaron? I'll have one with you."

He says he would, and follows her to the kitchen. His legs seem to have too much strength, as though they might spring him painfully against the low ceilings.

"He loves this place so much," she says. "Not just the house, but everything. He can't think of going anywhere else. And it would be so good for Eddie to stay in school here. He knows that, too."

"I've tried about everything," he says. "For a while I thought that official letter would wake him up . . ."

"Oh, dear!" she says. She puts the two glasses on the shelf and her hands on her face again. His arms go around her and she leans against him, her face against his chest.

The shock of pity does not lessen the shock of desire. He holds her against him very carefully, his hands frozen into the act of comfort. Pity, love, lust—they all reinforce each other until he knows he must stop touching her right now. His hand, tender, sliding, falsely innocent, caresses her slender neck just once, just once a little bit too shapedly, too unpattingly. Her lovely muscles have defined themselves too clearly beneath his hand.

"Have a drink," he says, and they turn away from each other to reach for their glasses.

He follows her into the living room, the little sheathed levers and fulcrums of her bones moving against his nerves.

They sit across from each other in the lamplight and have their drink. He says he will talk to George again in the morning. As he speaks his eyes mist a little, though firmly forbidden to do so, from love and sympathy for George and Helga.

"I'll force something out of him, Helga." He wants to help them both, but there is no way to make a man do work that has to be done inside the head. But why are they so concerned about this George, this other fellow, anyway? Who needs a third party here? You ass! he thinks. You *idiot!* But he didn't cause George to procrastinate away his opportunities, damn it! What he knows, and this is always delicately and precisely known, and will never, ever be made more specific by Helga, is that his fantasies do not have to remain fantasies. Beyond her love for George and Edward and her present life is the inclination, one she hardly lets herself consider possible, to blow up in one recklessly sensual, guilty, even partly revengeful affair with the older, more aggressive man who is looking at her now. The signals are so sweet, so dimly frightening, so minute that, not acted upon, they have the perfect right never to have existed at all.

When they finish their drinks they say good night, sadly and with tenderness. Helga remembers that he hasn't a towel, and gets one for him before she goes upstairs.

Aaron lies in the strange bed, in the fresh crisp sheets that smell just slightly and foreignly different from fresh sheets at home. The pillow is more bulky, the old bed sags in the middle. This and the quilt's small sewn squares beneath his fingers remind him of his childhood, the hard body of the child alone, always alone in bed surrounded as if by an elaborate canopy with possibilities, scenes, futures.

Through the open door to the kitchen he feels the long room's strange spacial vibrations. In a far corner the black wood stove stands on wide iron feet, an ancestor of the modern white enameled stove against the south wall. When the refrigerator comes on, its real hum pushes the other voices back, but they are still there. The sink breathes water, the wooden cupboards are silent, but inside them the hanging copper-bottomed pans wait to clatter and gong when disturbed. Upstairs a board creaks as Helga slips into the ancient fourposter beside her sleeping husband, his boyish face slack around the long breaths of sleep. If only she were slipping, smooth and tender and cool, into this bed. No, he should be with Agnes, the good firm body of his wife, his calves her stirrups. Or with Mary, or Naomi, and so on. Or with Thelma, for that matter, though her name wasn't Thelma. A girl—was it Mary?—once told him, long ago, that he considered every girl in the world to be, secretly, his property; that deep down inside him he really believed this, and that all other men were not quite adequate substitutes for him. That would have to have been long ago on a warm May night in College Woods, in the real past that has moved away from him, some years faster than others but all dimming now, moving away like a planet in space, its warmth surrounded by absolute zero as it grows smaller and dimmer on its long path toward infinity. He can pull it back, slowly, little by little, fragment by fragment, but it is all changed then. Changed but still true. True, but he doesn't know what that truth will be.

He has a brief glimpse, a telescope's field, a clear view of the receding planet. My God, it's Earth, so where is he? There are the waiting figures on the cold plain, lighted warmly by the small fire. They are there, but he must build whole nations and cities around them, and buildings, trees, weather, breath, sweat, the sweet funkiness of mortality, and apprehension, fear—the seen object growing toward the eye as though alive. And love, the lovely vacuum, the lovely oil. The task is impossible, and he groans with fatigue.

George carried the black kitchen stool out into the garden, saying he knew the damn legs would sink down into the dirt. He stood at the garden's edge studying the rows of pale green lettuce and peas and beans. "There's a good place. Good as any, I guess," he said. He was right about the legs; when he sat on the stool, the legs sank down several inches into the moist black loam. "It's okay, though, I guess," he said. "There's a hoe I left out. Would you toss it over on the grass, Aaron?" Now his pale young face was calm. "Okay," he said. "I think the best place would be just behind the ear. What do you think?"

"All right," Aaron said. He lifted his 8mm. Nambu and shot into the thick blond hair just behind the ear. George's head moved and some blood came to the surface where the hair was scorched.

"That didn't do it," George said. "Jesus, it sure stung, though. Try the temple, okay?"

Aaron put the Nambu to George's pale temple and fired; the pistol jumped and a blue hole with some soot around it appeared in the tender flesh.

"Wow!" George said. One of his eyes rolled out of synch. "Ouch! Ouch! Aaron? Find a better place, huh?"

He put the Nambu to George's forehead. George shut the one eye he still controlled, and again the pistol pushed back against Aaron's hand. The blue hole yielded a thick drop of blackish blood.

"Jesus, Aaron, I wish you'd get it over with. It hurts like hell!"

"Maybe I ought to shoot you in the heart, George."

"Yeah! Yeah! Any place. Come on!"

He shot George in the heart. The process was irreversible, of course, by now, even though Aaron had grave doubts about what they were doing. George seemed to go out of himself, to become almost somnolent, yet he still lived. Aaron fired again and again, hurrying now.

Aaron awakes, tangled in legal possibilities as well as the not yet flown justifications for what he has done. George was the one who wanted it done, but maybe Aaron was too agreeable. Now the idea comes that the whole thing was not done, that it was only a dream, and there is loss as if it were loss of any past action. It was *not* done. He is in bed in George's house, it is still black night, and he is shuddering and twisting away from the dream.

He stares at the blackness. He cannot in his life remember being so unhappy. He must be in hell; it must be all over and here he is in hell. Angst. It is angst that slides icily over his belly and up his ribs, taking his breath. The nausea of the soul. Everything is wrong, though if only he could look calmly at everything, everything is not wrong. He should be able to discount his mistakes, count his blessings. He could so easily be worse off than he is in this world. He could be poor George, who can't make himself do the work he knows he has to do. He could be poor Mark. He could be without a job. He could work at a job for which he is barely inadequate. There could be illness or some other tragedy in his family. But his family is, in fact, amazingly all right. Agnes will forgive his lapse of memory—all that will pass.

His book is a shambles, but every book is a shambles, or a potential shambles; that is the risk. His trouble is that it is bothering him in a strangely new way. Is he already dead? The thought of death makes him reach for a cigarette, death's ally. Of course, like any death-preoccupied creature, he's left his cigarettes and an ashtray handily on the chair beside his sepulcher.

The match lights up the room, a moment of warm color and sanity against the black. With that glimpse of homey perspectives he feels some comfort. So he takes a long, lethal drag of smoke into his lungs. Immediately all the capillaries in his legs tingle. What shall he think of? The other day he received a letter from one of his readers.

99 Crescent View Terrace
Plumville, Ohio

Mr. Benham!

Little did I know when I borrowed your book from our Library what obscene filth it was! I have notified the librarian and the *Chief* of *Police!*

But why, why, Mr. Benham, must you bring forth this worthless dirt, in our World, where everything—hippies, lawlessness, riots, communist agitators, students, are all around us! Think, Mr. Benham, *think!* It is people like you who will be the first to go when we clean it all up!

Mrs. Robert H. Ferranos

What does Mrs. Ferranos mean by "first to go"? Does the dear creature want him liquidated, eliminated, deactivated, shot? Perhaps Mrs. Ferranos' husband Robert, after finishing off his legal quota of hippies, students, and other nasty types, will come to Aaron's door with authorization in hand.

He's never answered such letters, which are usually unsigned anyway, but why not?

Dear Mrs. Ferranos,

I have forwarded Xerox copies of your threat on my life to the Postmaster General, the FBI, and your local Police Department. Initial legal advice informs me that you have broken U.S. Postal Statutes 148–b (1914), 291–f (1960), and 395–g (1970), all of which constitute felonies. I trust my books won't be found in your prison library.

Yours for Law and Order,

How long can games keep him sane? It is three-thirty in the morning; the black window leans in on him like death. Death makes him think of Boom Maloumian—one species of death, at least. Boom Maloumian is dead, that once brutal force. Aaron remembers, suddenly, one of Boom Maloumian's jokes, one of thousands: It seems this old maid and old bachelor get married. On their honeymoon, in a hotel, she gets stuck on the toilet, stark-naked, and can't get loose. Finally, in desperation, she calls her husband. What will we do? What will we do? Call the plumber! But before the plumber comes the husband puts his bowler hat, for modesty's sake, on her lap. When the plumber arrives he takes one look and says, "I can save the woman, but the man's a goner!"

The principle of risibility involved here, students, is the shock of the change in visual conception from a mere bowler hat on a lap to a whole man somehow fed down the mysterious convolutions of a commode, coupled with the intellectual shock of the change of manners from prudery to the plumber's immediate hedonistic toleration of whatever weird, probably sexual play got the two toilet-bound people in their fix. That, however, is only a very superficial reading of this remarkable story. It encompasses psychological overtones, symbolic insights, comments upon the whole paradoxical maze of the human condition. If I list, even in haphazard fashion, a few of these possibilities, I'm sure you will find among them, or preferably beyond them, a subject for your theme. You may be as fanciful as you like, but you must still be honest.

1. Bowler hats and the Velveteen Age
2. Toilets and sex

    a. "The throne of love is firmly mounted in the sewer."—Swinburne
    b. Freud on same
    c. Dr. Spock on same
    d. Your parents on same
3. Toilets and humor
    a. Child folk humor, such as "Milk, milk, lemonade,/Around the corner fudge is made."
4. Death and humor
    a. The ultimate put-down
    b. Hysteria
5. The Plumber as ultimate authority
    a. Charon, Gabriel, Yorick, etc.
    b. Plumbers make over $5.00 per hour
    c. Value of function in our society
        1. Input, or fresh-water function
        2. Outtake, or sewerage function
    d. Why aren't you going to plumber school?
6. Form and style
    a. Reflection of a universal linguistic pattern
    b. Patterns of expectation (invoke transformational grammar at your own risk)
    c. Genius
        1. The pleasure of being encompassed
        2. The pleasure of being fooled
7. Can prudery be sincere?
    a. Write a letter to Mrs. Robert H. Ferranos, 99 Crescent View Terrace, Plumville, Ohio, in which you gently but thoroughly convince her that Aaron Benham has never written a dirty book.

Enough. But who was the anonymous genius who structured that joke, that perfect fiction? How it ends so completely, having told everything! Economy and perfection. But it is not envy of that perfection that makes him feel weak now. He shudders again, thinks he might and then decides not to go get himself some whiskey from the kitchen. No, he will just ride out this anxiety. While flying on commercial airplanes he has a constant, quite similar anxiety all the time. For a minute or two a magazine or a movie might take his thoughts away from his insane speed and altitude, but the shock of return is worse than the constant awareness, so he has decided that on airplanes the best thing to do is to sit there and fly. But how can you just sit here and fly this planet with its disappearing thin skin of atmosphere? There is no destination where you will be able to relax. When the cabin depressurizes, no yellow oxygen mask will pop out in front of your face. There will be no emergency procedures. You have to forget for longer periods or you won't get your work done. Not that it matters in the long run whether you get your work done or not. When the sun turns super-nova your work reverts to hydrogen atoms, anyway. But in the short run, if you have been cursed by art, you have to do your work or you die before you stop breathing. And in the short run you can't fend off the darkness for a lovely hour with your friend's wife. The reasons are simple, but there are quite a few of them, each vectoring in on its own course toward unhappiness, of which there is too much already.

It would be nice if he could go to sleep. He wishes he had a pill of some kind, but pills are one of the few vices he's never taken up. Instead he will try to go back through the years, several wars back. Sometimes he thinks of the Earth as the repository of all the pain it has ever been host to, as if somewhere all pain must be registered, on a great dial, or column, shimmering and exploding to new heights, like those explosions reaching out from the corona of the sun. Each agony must be somewhere recorded—each chipmunk ever tortured to death by a cat, the bellowings of ancient reptiles sinking in tar, each burned or dismembered child. But if he might find his way back even a few years, then the volume is by an infinitesimal fraction smaller, a little more manageable perhaps.

So he thinks of Harold Roux and Mary Tolliver, young and alive on that green campus.

Harold, because of the delicate thing on the top of his

head, had to have a single room in his dormitory. And because single rooms were available only to proctors, he had to be a proctor. Perhaps it was this semiofficial, rather doubtful position that first brought him into the gleeful or baleful notice of Boom Maloumian, The Mean Armenian, who lived a few doors down the hall in a three-man room. One of Maloumian's roommates was a strange poet named Gordon Robert Westinghouse, and the other was Short Round, a small, battered-looking person whose real name was Paul Hickett and who was Maloumian's minion, or even slave. Short Round was the one usually delegated to assault Harold's peace. At times Maloumian was implacable, but at other times he could be deceptively friendly, as though he had slight remissions of his sadism. It must have been worse, even, than the army for Harold. There, he had expected to be among savages, but here, amid these ivy-covered walls!

Once, in the middle of the night, Short Round poured Energine lighter fluid under Harold's door, screamed "Fire! Fire!" and pounded on the door, then lit the fluid so that Harold awoke nearly surrounded by billowing orange flames. The dormitory was of fairly fireproof cement block and terrazzo construction, and the flames were easily beaten out with a blanket, but even so Harold was terribly upset.

Once, when Allard was visiting Harold, water began to come in under the door. Allard opened the door and caught Short Round in the act of pouring it from a wastebasket. Short Round, unused to any confrontation by Harold, shocked by Allard's sudden presence, was paralyzed; his gray face and even the scraggly tufts of his sparse blond hair seemed to grow paler. His green army fatigue jacket, in fact, seemed to be losing air, like a leaking balloon. Allard turned the wastebasket over Short Round's head, jammed it down, turned him around in the direction of his room and more or less threw him down the hall. Afterwards Allard remembered that his anger was chiefly because he, Allard Benson, had been subjected to this irritation, not that his friend Harold Roux was. He even said a few words to this effect as he dealt with Short Round, who then landed in front of Boom Maloumian himself, two hundred pounds of naked Boom Maloumian, brown burnished muscle and fat and glossy areas of black pelt, his laughter booming down the halls, down the stairs, surely filling all the floors and rooms of Parker Hall, flooding obscenely through the housemother's tidy apartment and washing out over half the campus. "Short Round! Short Round!" he said when he could. "Oh, Short Round! Didn't you get it!" Then what seemed like ropes, chains and hawsers of immense laughter began again when Short Round managed to get the metal wastebasket off his head. The towel over Boom Maloumian's shoulder seemed much too small to have dried all that fur and flesh.

But when Allard and Short Round next met, such was Paul Hickett's half-cringing adjustment to the world that one would think it had never happened. A flick of the wary, calculating eye, and Short Round was prepared again to be tolerated and patronized. They had just left Knuck Gillis, one of Allard's roommates, who in the war had seen all the officers of his company and ninety percent of its enlisted men killed in the volcanic ash of Iwo Jima. "You know," Short Round said to Allard, "that guy's seen more combat than you and me put together!" Allard, who hadn't been in combat, knew that Short Round hadn't either, and Short Round knew he knew. Allard was struck silent by this statement. What an interesting contract Short Round was offering him! What a gross, yet almost tempting lie to bind them together in this pact of dishonesty! They could tell each other all kinds of battle tales. He wondered if Short Round made many, or even all, of his alliances this way. And of course Allard thought about himself, too. Perhaps his own social lies and assumptions were merely a little more credible. Afterwards he thought about this quite often.

A few days after the wastebasket incident Allard stopped by Harold's room an hour or so before Commons opened for supper, and Harold, with grave pleasure, brought out his Bristol Cream sherry and two immaculate wineglasses. He arranged these on a paisley cloth on his special little round table and poured, his grave joy reminding Allard of the formality of the Japanese tea ceremony. This was more Harold's idea of the dignity of college life.

Harold's room was neat, his books evenly aligned on the shelves above the small, built-in desk. Harold himself was frail, white and orderly, yet his constant seriousness gave him a kind of strength. Unlike Harold, Allard had always, it seemed to him, entered any new situation, such as the army or college or whatever it might be, with an instinctive eye for farce, even though he didn't always want to. Maybe college ought to be everything Harold expected it to be. Harold craved the life of the mind—or at least he wanted the life of the mind to dignify all human relationships here. So Allard tried, knowing Harold's feelings, to be serious. But it was hard. For one thing, Harold did not want to talk, ever, about Boom Maloumian or any of Maloumian's crude friends, even when those gargantuan noises and appetites intruded, through doors and walls, upon his seriousness. This did not conform to Allard's idea of reality.

So Allard drank Harold's expensive wine and they spoke, now, about Edward Arlington Robinson.

" 'He may go forward like a stoic Roman/Where pangs and terrors in his pathway lie—/Or, seizing the swift logic of a woman,/Curse God and die,' " Harold quoted admiringly.

A bellow of gigantic laughter could be heard down the corridor, but Harold seemed not to notice. Neither had he ever complained about Maloumian to Allard and his two roommates, Knuck Gillis and Nathan Weinstein, even though Allard, Knuck and Nathan were considered to be Harold's friends.

More laughter, brutally energetic now, as though something was being amusingly destroyed. Allard knew that Maloumian and several of his jock friends from Kappa Sigma—O'Brien, Harorba, Whalen and that bunch, were having a case or two of beer prior to going to Litchwood tonight.

"Pangs and terrors is right," Allard said, nodding toward the sounds.

Harold frowned slightly and shook his head as if to forbid any mention of that subject.

"Anyway," Allard said, "aren't there other alternatives to being a stoic Roman or a woman? How about he just beats a strategic retreat? In fact he could run like hell."

"Allard, I don't want to talk about those savages at all. Please."

"Well, what pangs and terrors did you have in mind, then?" He heard in his own voice the facetiousness he really didn't want to use with Harold.

"I meant life and death. Deeper realities." Harold poured Allard more wine. "I meant important things. Choices. What to make of your life. Things like love, and morality, philosophy, art."

"Okay."

"I'm writing a novel," Harold said shyly.

The voices and laughter from the hall had increased, then moved like a rattling train along the hall to the stairs and down, muted, finally, by distance.

"That's ambitious," Allard said, knowing Harold would like that word. He had been making notes for a novel himself, but Harold's sounded much more possible, more concrete than his own vague jottings and cravings, because Harold always did what he said he would.

"I just wondered if you'd read the first chapter sometime, Allard, when you get the chance."

"Sure. How about right now?"

"Now? Oh, I don't know." Harold was startled by the immediacy. "Right now?" Startled and shy. "Well, I guess, if you want to." He was for the moment flustered and shaky, but then he composed himself and handed Allard a sheaf of typed pages so evenly stacked they might have just come out of the original box.

Glitter and Gold Harold's novel was titled, and it opened

high in the towers of Manhattan in a richly decorated modern penthouse suite. Across the crowded living room, where all the clever, scintillating talk and noise of a cocktail party seem nervous and inane, a boy and a girl suddenly see each other. Both, their look seems to say, are rather bored by the glitter and the triviality of their glamorous surroundings. He crosses to her and offers her a cigarette and an ironic comment, to which she replies with modest but delightful wit. Her hair is the color of honey, her complexion creamy, her eyes deep brown except for a fascinating green glint in the iris of one, her arms and hands aristocratically tapered; he thinks he might fall in love with this girl, just as she thinks somehow that she might fall in love with this man. He is well built, of middle height, with thick dark hair and a strong jaw—a face of dark secrets, rugged, yet with the flash of humor about the eyes. He is dressed in dark slacks and a casual Harris tweed jacket of ancient lineage. His name is Francis Ravendon, hers Allyson Turnbridge. She wears a plaid skirt—her mother's family (Ferguson) hunting plaid, closed at the thigh with a solid gold safety pin—and a white silken blouse that reveals the warm roundness yet proud uptilt of her nubile breasts. He lights her cigarette with a gold lighter decorated with a strange device. Curious, she lightly holds his wrist as he explains that the device is the Ravendon crest—nonsense, of course, in these enlightened days, but his Uncle Alfred gave the lighter to him, and, after all, it is useful. After some more light conversation—yet strangely intimate, as though they have known each other since childhood—he suggests, since they can hardly hear each other over the babble, that they get out of here. It's a beautiful afternoon and he has his open car. Why not drive out of the city to Long Island and perhaps have dinner in an excellent little French restaurant he knows? She hesitates; she really doesn't know him at all, and he seems so masculine, so sure of himself. In spite of his charm there is something dark and dangerous in this handsome man. But he is so kind, gentle, humorous and reassuring, she finally relents. Without bidding their hosts goodbye (host and hostess seem so involved in conversation and, well, so rather drunk), Allyson and Francis descend in the elevator to the street, where they find Francis' Lincoln Continental phaeton gleaming in the slanting light amid the hectic hustle and bustle of Manhattan. Soon the phaeton's smooth power has taken them away, across the long bridges, past the teeming tenements of the poor, and at dusk they are on a country road lined with beautiful tall trees, the muted lights of great estates shining down across wide landscaped greenswards.

"You seem so, somehow, *right* sitting here beside me," he says. She can think of no answer. The car hums steadily along the smooth, winding old road. He is an excellent driver. "But we know absolutely nothing about each other," he muses. Then, after a pause, in a low, almost startled voice, as though he speaks to himself, "Except, perhaps, the most important things of all." He turns his head and smiles at her in the warm light of the dusk and the dashboard instruments, and even as she smiles back she cannot help but feel a warning of danger, for never has she felt this way about a man. Though she works as a junior editor for a sophisticated national magazine, she has never, among all that cleverness and affluence, known a man who gave the impression of such depth and, yes, even sadness, behind his surface charm. She wants terribly to know all about him, but something keeps her from asking.

The little French restaurant is quaint and charming; the proprietor himself comes to wait upon them *(Ah, Monsieur Ravendon! C'est . . . depuis quand? Un an? Mais c'est merveilleux!).* They go on, Allyson's high school and one year of college French not quite up to the occasion. They both consult her in English. And the meal is delicious, the wine light and clean on the tongue. At their intimate, candlelit table they do speak of each other's past and present. She tells him of her upbringing in a small Vermont town of white houses and towering green elms—her father a scholar and teacher of modest means, her mother having died when she was a little girl. They are both editors, it seems, he an associate editor in a famous publishing house in Manhattan. He is twenty-six, and (his face darkens, he speaks slowly, painfully) a widower, his wife of two years' marriage having been killed in an airplane accident a year ago, in Switzerland. There were no children. "I've never talked to anyone about it before," he says wonderingly. "That's strange. In fact I haven't talked to anyone very much, except on business, for nearly a year—until tonight." Suddenly he seems shy, then looks up into her eyes with a grave, considering expression. "When we finish our brandy I'd like to take you to meet my father. He lives just down the road. Will you . . . Allyson?" It is the first time he has used her name. "Allyson," he says again, softly, as if trying out her name to see how it sounds.

She agrees, though she is hesitant. She has only known him for a few hours! Somehow it seems much longer, even though the time has passed so swiftly. And there are depths to this handsome, square-chinned, yet so sensitive man that she cannot plumb.

They drive a mile or so down a country road and enter, between old, ivy-grown stone portals, a long winding driveway. Finally they come to a huge stone mansion set into its trees. The moonlight glimmers upon formal hedges and gardens. At the massive front door they are greeted by a tall, imperious-looking butler.

"Master Francis!" he says, in spite of himself letting his pleasure show through.

"Clifford, this is Miss Turnbridge. Is my father home?"

Clifford's eyes widen a little and he bows slightly toward Allyson, his face cold. In his clipped British accent he says, "Your father is in the library, Master Francis."

As they pass beneath the high, ornate ceiling of a long hall lined with family portraits, Francis smiles and says that to Clifford he is still, evidently, the little boy he once was.

The library is a high, wide room of dark wainscoting. Books rise in tiers to the ceiling, and at one end of the room beside a cheery fire, beneath one of the softly glowing table lamps that make cozy islands in the room, sits a silver-haired man. "Father," Francis says, and the man, Horace Ravendon, gets quickly to his feet and removes his reading glasses. Beaming his welcome, he strides toward them on long, patrician legs.

"Francis! How wonderful!" He spies Allyson, and his bushy silver eyebrows rise over his kindly blue eyes. "And my! How doubly wonderful!"

Francis introduces them.

"My dear, you are lovely, lovely! You have no idea how happy it makes me to see Francis with a lovely girl. He's been . . ." Horace Ravendon stops, thinking he's said too much, but Francis smiles and reassures him.

"It's all right, Father, I've told her about Sheila."

"Oh, well. That's a sad subject, my dear. But my, you are . . ." He looks for a second or two into Allyson's face, and seems a little confused. "Smashing, really! Now, how about some sherry or something? And come and sit down by the fire!"

While Horace Ravendon pours sherry into crystal glasses, Allyson looks around the room. Above the mantel is an oil portrait of a dashing young officer in Air Force uniform, his silver wings shining above his colorful ribbons, two silver bars on each shoulder. Then she realizes that it is a portrait of Francis. She looks to him in surprise, and, having been watching her, he nods, smiling. "Yes, Father insists upon celebrating my late, unpleasant occupation."

"But," she says hesitantly, "I mean, my uncle is an army officer, and so I think I know . . . Isn't that a Purple Heart, and that one . . . the Distinguished Flying Cross?"

"Yes, Father made certain the artist got all the fruit salad into the picture," Francis says, smiling fondly at the old man.

Horace Ravendon hands them sparkling crystal glasses of sherry. "Never used to wear his decorations. Never could understand it. Distinguished record in the war. Well, *I'm* proud of it and I'm not going to let it be forgotten in this house!"

As they sip their sherry, Allyson sees on the end table near her a novel in its bright dust jacket. *Never the Sad March* is its title, by F. H. Ravendon. She has read it and was greatly moved by this dark, powerful story of war and love . . . and suddenly the name, Ravendon. "Are you related to this Ravendon?" she asks, picking up the book. "I've read it and I was . . . still am! . . . deeply moved by it."

"Well, yes, my dear," Horace Ravendon says, smiling an enigmatic smile. "You might say that, yes!" He is trying to keep from laughing, she can see. And then she reads the name again. F. H. Ravendon. *Francis?* She looks at him, knowing how her admiration must be shining in her eyes.

"Yes, I admit to that novel," Francis says.

"How I've wanted to talk to the author!" she says. "How wonderful! I'm afraid I'm gushing or something, and I'm sorry but I can't help it!"

"That is my reward for writing it," Francis says. She looks at him, and he is quite serious.

And they do talk, long into the evening, later still after Horace Ravendon bids them good night, saying, "You must stay over, my dear children. Clifford will fix you up, Allyson, in the blue guest room. No, I won't hear about you two driving into the city at this highly improbable hour. Dangerous. Tiring. Now! I'll see you in the morning. Good night."

It is one in the morning before they know it, the hours having flown by as if they were minutes, seconds. They both have to work in the morning, so Francis takes her up to her room off the balcony, and at the door he looks steadily down into her eyes. "Allyson, you don't know how much this evening—all of it—has meant to me. At that silly party I was so tense, so . . . But I won't go on as if I really were one of the spoiled *jeunesse dorée* my father would turn me into. Yet I am so grateful. You've been a spring breeze. Promising . . ." He stops, perhaps embarrassed. "Sleep well, Allyson . . . my dear!" He kisses her quickly on the forehead. "Sleep well!" And he is gone.

It is later, hours later, when she wakes in the strange room. The moon is down and the tall windows are pitch-black. Has she heard a noise—a scraping noise? Her heart pounding, she reaches for the bedside lamp, finally finds it and turns it on. No one is in the room. But she *did* hear a noise. Quietly she dons the old-fashioned dressing gown Clifford laid out for her and goes to the door, opens it a crack and listens intently. Yes, there is a sound. Is it a deep breath from somewhere down the curving staircase, or a quickly stifled sob? Curious beyond fear, she goes out into the hall and down the thickly carpeted stairs, her hand on the railing of the cold marble banister. There is a light from a room on the left, a door that had been closed when she first came into the hall, and she creeps softly to the open door. A man stands, his back to her, looking up at an oil portrait of a young woman with raven-black hair and blue eyes. Allyson has never seen such graceful, bewitching beauty, such a glowing face of wit and intelligence, yet with a hint of patrician superiority. Such glowing irrepressible life! The young woman seems to be looking straight at her, her half-smile knowing all, her ice-blue eyes staring into her very soul.

Involuntarily she gasps, and the man quickly turns. It is Francis, and his eyes are cold, remote. "Well. And do you see the resemblance? Father did. Clifford did."

"Resemblance?" she manages to say. She is frightened by his coldness, his terse statement, his cruel voice.

"Look into the mirror. Dark and light. Raven and gold. The other side of the coin."

And suddenly, with terror and anguish in her heart, she does see that but for the raven hair and blue eyes her own likeness stares icily down at her from the wall.

Allard put down the manuscript and reached for his glass of sherry. "Hmmm," he said. "Well, you've got some good details in there, Harold." Now, was this the time for honesty, or not? No doubt, in spite of everything Harold had ever read, to him the purposes of this story were the very purposes of literature. And there was energy and emotion in this wishful fantasy. Work had gone into it. The pages were neatly typed, the paper crisp, expensive, rag-content watermarked bond; other drafts had been agonized over, words no doubt looked up in the dictionary and thesaurus. Was it the same faith in magic, the same mistaken sort of effort that had led Harold into the clutches of the hair people? Why not say so? How important was this creation to Harold? Why not tell him to take off the goddamn toupee, throw it in the garbage and take his medicine, because if he wanted Mary, or whatever it was he wanted, he must learn the difference between fantasy and reality. Suppose Allard were to tell him all this, to say right out, "Look, Harold, this is jerking off, buddy. This stuff is like being alone in your room at two in the afternoon with the door locked, beating your meat. Wouldn't you rather be involved in what's real? Why not write about Berlin, New Hampshire, about growing up above a poor grocery store as a French-Canadian kid in a New Hampshire slum with a drunken father and a retarded half sister and a mother who saw you as a priest? How about all that? And the army, and growing bald at twenty-three in a civilization that worships its follicles . . ."

Harold sat there in his desk chair, turned toward Allard, silent and a little apprehensive because he wanted his friend to admire the sophistication of his story's setting, the intelligent conversation, the mood, the tone. His sports jacket was just a little too thin in the nap to go with the striped regimental tie that was knotted too tightly and led down to his silver belt buckle, the kind that was solid and you fed the leather through it to the right place where it was held by some kind of inner roll-lock, and you bought it with an initial stamped on the outside of it, *R* for Russell, or Reade or Richardson or Ravendon or Roux, and your gabardine slacks were pleated at the waist and too much of a light blue and your socks were machine-knit cotton argyles and the soles of your too shiny, too pointed black shoes were too thin. Harold, Harold, of all the people in the world you should be the last to labor to deceive.

And you, Allard Benson, having another glass of Harold's Bristol Cream and feeling it in the back of your head, if you took on the job of changing Harold Roux into what he wanted to be, would you do it out of care? Would you really give a shit? Would you do it because you understand the sweetness and gentleness of this fellow creature who, compared to you, is practically a saint?

About then it was probably time to go to Commons for supper, where they would meet Mary and her roommate, Naomi Goldman, who was a communist, and whom Allard called Yetta Samovar.

But that is another story, and now Aaron Benham is lying in a strange bed in the cool vast gray light of predawn. A cock crows from a neighboring farm, a clear, mindlessly too early, machistic, bullying yodel.

Aaron can just make out his cigarettes and matches on the chair beside his bed. As he lights a cigarette the inevitable sermon against this form of suicide runs its boring, desperate course through his head. He holds the match up to the matchbook the better to read about La Salle Extension University of Chicago, which will change you into an accountant, artist, high school graduate, night club manager, diesel mechanic, and more—if you are smart enough not to mail the matches along with the cover.

One drag on the cigarette tells his capillaries what death's soothing syrup feels like, and he puts it out. But deep in his body he feels a sea change. Certain glands have closed, and his heart is running well, almost without effort. His muscles and joints are full now of sweet fatigue, and he believes that he can sleep. He must sleep, but he never desires that nothingness and never really wants it to happen. That suicide in small—he has never understood it, never remembered how it came to him when it came. He has watched others fall asleep and it was almost as if they willfully died before his eyes. And yet he loves to dream; he loves that emotion so encompassing it destroys all the concerns of the other world and makes something so great out of nothing. But to die in order to hope for a dream?

No dream; there is that small single room in Parker Hall again, and Harold Roux, having by his writing revealed something of himself to Allard Benson, sat smoking a Parliament cigarette and carefully tapping the ash into a shining glass tray. His legs neatly crossed at the knee, his pale face calm, he vibrated on a frequency the eye could not quite discern.

Allard glanced quickly, guiltily, at the line across Harold's forehead where the dark neat cloud of hair had settled upon the flesh. "Well," he said. "It's really a fantasy, isn't it? I mean, you'd like to be Francis Ravendon, and have Allyson look at you like that."

Harold nodded, smiling. "Yes, I guess so."

"But, Harold . . ." How was he to say to Harold what was so obvious? "It's not really the truth."

"The truth?" Harold said. "Isn't it the truth if you believe it? Fiction isn't the truth, is it?" Though terribly disappointed by Allard's reactions so far, Harold would consent to discuss theory, which hadn't such a personal claim on him. Allard didn't want to destroy him, and he didn't want to mention Mary, either—to say, for instance, that Allyson Turnbridge was obviously, from more evidence than the shard of jade in her brown iris, Mary Tolliver. Though he had, almost as a matter of predestined right, taken over Mary as soon as Harold introduced her to him, he still wondered why Harold wasn't angry with him. Here was a real, live, warm girl, after all, not a fantasy.

"Wouldn't you rather . . ." he began tentatively, but then felt himself change; irritation, exasperation, and possibly a feeling of his essential benevolence toward Harold made him reckless and a little brutal. For one thing, he believed that if it weren't for him and his two roommates, who were known to be Harold's friends, Boom Maloumian and Short Round would by now have beaten Harold naked through the halls, painted his balls and bare skull blue and crucified him. So maybe he did have a right to speak straight. "Wouldn't you rather have Mary than dream all this moonlight and roses? Damn it, Harold. I mean, wouldn't you rather even *write* about what it's really like?"

"I don't particularly like what it's really like," Harold said. "Why should I write about that? I know what Mary is like. Perfection, that's what she's like."

"Oh Christ, I don't know. You're a strange case, Harold."

"You mean because I . . . All right, I'm not ashamed of it. I love Mary. I think she's the most beautiful, sensitive, kind, wonderful girl in the world. I do love her."

"Okay, I agree that she's damn near all those things, Harold, but wouldn't you want to take what you love? Wouldn't you want to have all of her, not just the ideal? Wouldn't you rather . . . I mean, well, fuck her, Harold?"

"I wouldn't use that or any other dirty word in connection with Mary."

"If you were in connection with Mary, what *would* you be doing to her then?"

"I don't think that's funny!" Harold's voice was rather shrill; usually he tolerated Allard's lapses into vulgarity with a shake of his head, but now his disapproval was nearly outrage. "Mary is a virgin and will remain a virgin until marriage. She's a good Catholic, too, or hadn't you noticed that? No, I'm not worried at all about Mary in that way. I think she's fascinated at the moment by you. You're very sophisticated and all that, but she's not going to let anything bad happen. She's too moral and too honest with herself. I know her very well because we see each other and talk for hours when you're not around—when you're giving Naomi Goldman rides on your motorcycle or something."

"What do you mean by 'or something'?" Allard said, wanting to laugh, although outright laughter would do more violence than he wanted to do to Harold's seriousness.

"You take her out to the reservoir or to College Woods

and neck with her. I've seen you come in with pine needles all over you."

"She also likes to be bitten high up on the insides of her thighs," Allard said.

"Cut it out! I don't believe that or anything else you say!" Harold was near tears; he was also horrified to be talking to his best friend this way, Allard could tell. Harold thought he had put himself in grave danger of losing Allard's friendship by this show of real anger. Allard stood up. My God, he thought, I've not removed my friendship from people who've smashed me in the mouth. What a delicate world Harold inhabits. He slapped Harold lightly on the shoulder of his padded jacket. Because of some fear that he might dislodge the toupee, the slap was gentle indeed.

"Come on, Harold, old chap. I do believe Commons is open, and shall we dine?"

Partly pacified, at least, and certainly relieved, Harold smiled as he tidied up his room. Of course he still held to his arguments. A certain grimness of jaw indicated that. They walked down the stairs and across the green campus to Commons.

Actually Harold's ordered world appealed to Allard a great deal. How wonderful all that honor and virginity and sacredness would be, in a way. The immense sacred value of Mary's lovely body until such momentous dark acts were sanctified by a Higher Being; meaning beyond mere fleshly considerations! It was a world he'd once believed in too—back, say, in grammar school, when a girl's very glance might give him palpitations. Now he had chosen not to dream but to be there in the flesh, and in acting on that choice he had to admit to a vague feeling of sadness and loss; perhaps those childhood intensities could never again be recaptured.

Aaron hears, above the clamor of birds, Helga moving around in the kitchen. Dishes and silver tinkle and clank softly, water is about to boil and is making its squeezed complaint—the sounds of a domestic morning. He squints one eye at his watch, which tells him it is seven o'clock. Helga must have shut the door between the birthing room and the kitchen so he could sleep a little longer. But he is only a guest here, an alien to the clink and clatter, the soft voices—Helga's and Edward's—that form this *kleine Morgenmusik.* He must get up, so he does. Through the birthing room's other door is the downstairs bathroom, in which the real ceramic tiles, glassed-in shower, plumbing, cabinets and all had been lovingly assembled by George the craftsman —instead of crafting his dissertation. Each tile must have told him in a small voice, even as it fit so perfectly in place, *Loss, waste. If you do us and not the other thing, you will have to leave us.* All the while he made this beautiful house, in order to keep his family warm and safe, he was doing just the opposite. It was not a matter of improving the place and getting equity in it in order to sell it. No, this is love.

George is a teacher. Teaching is what he has been chosen to do. Everyone in the department agrees on this point, and certainly this is the only point in the world upon which they all agree. George's students expect him never to fake or lie. They expect from him generosity, but in the matter of work and marks they expect firmness, because he cares about what they learn. He is an enthusiast of his subject, which is literature in English. But if his contract is not renewed he will simply have to go elsewhere—to a two-year college, to one of the new small colleges of somewhat doubtful standards and aims, to a secondary school somewhere, or even to another job altogether, because in these hard days teaching jobs of any kind are scarce. The one certainty is that it will have to be somewhere else, away from his beloved home. Neither George nor Helga have any other source of money, so they can't simply continue to live here, the way some failed scholars and teachers have. The property taxes on their house and acres are nearly confiscatory now, and will of course get worse.

Aaron examines his ageless, always unfamiliar face in George's mirror. "*Glah,*" says the face. "And who are you, anyway?" Aaron asks as the face cleverly imitates the words.

Men do not sham convulsion
Nor simulate a throe

"*Ulgh!*" says the face. Emily Dickinson is wrong. "*Ullsh!*" the face says, simulating a throe.

Nothing is funnier than simulated agony. A man's head sticking out of a commode, Boom Maloumian laughing at a world that always lives up to his expectations. But maybe Emily Dickinson is right after all, and the deepest causes for our imitating throes, gags, convulsions, spastics, drunks, babbling idiots and stunned drooling mongoloids are the real causes. We only think we are doing imitations.

Aaron washes whatever invisible stuff is supposed to be washed from that face, from among those morning bristles, borrows a handy comb and combs his hair.

Morning sunlight turns the kitchen bright and dark, changes Edward's hair from Helga-colored to gold. Edward bends over his bowl, netting the last grains of Crunchy Granola from the milk. "Good morning, Aaron," he says.

"Good morning, Ed."

Helga looks just a little puffy about the eyes, as though she's been awake too long in the night.

"Bacon and eggs?" she says cheerfully. "This is George's day to gorge himself on breakfast, but you can order what you like."

"That sounds fine. We'll gorge together," he says. "I'll gorge with George."

She laughs as she skillfully separates the bacon strips with a spatula and arranges them side by side in a big iron skillet. Sunlight brushes the down on her upper lip and flashes on her flowered housecoat as she moves across the light. To Aaron's strange eye she seems as green and graceful as a young tree.

George comes in humming and smiling. "Beautiful day! Beautiful day! Hear all the goddam lovely birds screaming! Everything they say means life, procreation, plenty of tasty bugs to eat!"

"Tasty!" Edward says, laughing over his bowl.

"I have a great class this morning," George says. "I won the freshman lottery with this class. They are all merely beautiful people."

Aaron meets Helga's eyes. It's as if George has a terminal disease and is unaware of it. How easily they can keep the secret from him.

At seven forty-five he and George drive toward town, leaving Edward with his lunch box and green book bag to wait for his bus, which comes by around eight. George hums happily as they drive along, and Aaron argues with himself about bringing up the dissertation, that nest of snakes. Should he destroy such obvious contentment? George is, in a sense, killing himself with this self-deception. What good is a friend if he can't grab his friend before he leaps? But not now, not on this spring morning that is so bright each border of tree, house and hill imprints itself almost painfully, nervously, on the brain. And maybe George *is* really happy; maybe no small voices speak to him at all. Aaron, to whom small voices constantly scream and babble in tongues, in code and in clear, finds this hard to believe, yet he does know something about lying to oneself and God knows it might be true.

Of course, George might rationalize his laziness through criticism of the system itself—a system that can sacrifice teachers of George's sensitivity, knowledge and care, sometimes in favor of idiots. But that is too simple; how can you find out if a scholar is still alive in his discipline if you can't read his words? "Where are thy fine wondrous works,/ And where are they to read?" Lecturing itself is a kind of publication, and if your ideas are worth giving to your students, are they not then good enough to be written for your peers everywhere? This, after all, is a university, not a trade school. Here you are supposed to be on the cutting edge of knowledge, not merely teaching known skills. George can fill up all the hours of his days teaching, caring for his students, getting them out of jail, helping them with the problems of addiction, pregnancy, madness, vicious or cold parents, faulty logic, fanaticism, dull complacency, misinformation, but that is not his only job. The system is also meant to give him time to write, to produce that solid thing: a book. The general class or contact load is six to nine hours a week. There is an old story about a businessman and a professor. Businessman: "How many hours do you teach?" Professor: "Nine." Businessman: "Well, that *is* a long day . . . but it's easy work." Another, even more ancient story, about two men talking below the cross upon which Christ is crucified. "He was a great teacher," says one, and the other says, "Yes, but he didn't publish."

George hums and drums happily upon the wheel with his fingers as they drive along. He doesn't seem to have a care. Smiling cheerfully, he drops Aaron at his house and drives off to his eight o'clock class of freshmen, those beautiful people.

Aaron stands in his driveway in the warm sun, not wanting to go into his house. He anticipates the feel of the doorknob, the sound of the heavy door pulling out of its weather stripping as it swings open, the sound of his own feet in the hallway and across the kitchen floor. On the desk in his study will lie his manuscript. In the silent air will hang his various anticipations of Agnes' behavior when she returns this evening, and his rehearsals of his own cold or warm guilty responses. He shivers, even out here in the sun. There in the garage is his Honda, silver and black, everything upon it functional and clean-lined. It seems such an easy toy, but it contains thousands of design choices, subtleties of torque and friction, electrical circuits of staggering complexity. Alternating current is changed to direct through the mysteries of selenium, that mineral with a selective mind of its own. Gasoline is vaporized and fed in minutely precise amounts into an engine whose reciprocating and revolving parts can whirl and valve more than eight thousand times per minute, over one hundred and thirty-three times each second. And the complications of suspension, balance and control: he despairs of ever understanding. He cannot contemplate such brilliant competence.

He goes into the house. After only one night unoccupied it smells a little close, the air too still, as if the house feels and resents its abandonment. The cat comes in with him at his ankles, all forgiveness, which means it is hungry. He spoons some of its gray, fish-smelling glop into its dish and goes on into his study, where his manuscript lies perversely unchanged, exactly as he left it, not a word added.

Last night he dreamed that with George's aid and advice he shot George several times in the head and heart. The pale face looms, the weeping bullet holes hardly affecting George's earnest reasonableness. He unlocks the desk drawer and takes out his black Nambu, unlatches the slide a crack to see if it is loaded, which he knows it is, and puts it back. Those fingerprints on the oily metal are his own. He is an adult; he makes his decisions in private, on his own, with only himself for counsel. He can live, obviously, with paradox, guilt, ambivalence. It may not be the clear golden life of the dedicated or the faithful, but it has its occasional rewards. It is not rewarding him at the moment, however.

Once he went toward his pleasures with near arrogance, believing not only in his strength but that no matter what debacle of nature or of emotion or even of machinery occurred he would, by agility and luck, survive. He dreamed of being in a high tower as it toppled, and as it came through high trees he coolly stepped off onto a branch and let the tower fall past to its destruction. In another recurring dream he, a corporal, is being taken by speeding staff car with military motorcycle escort down the dark roads of a combat zone. Colonels and generals ride with him, but he is the center of things because he carries a message of high importance. Sirens screaming, they come to an airfield, and out on the field under harsh lights a trim and dangerous silver jet fighter plane is in readiness for him. It is a single-place airplane, and suddenly he realizes that he doesn't know how to fly it, that the only flying he's ever done is holding the controls of a Piper Cub for a few minutes in the air. So a little debate goes on in his head, but finally he decides what the hell, he'll give it a try. The dream ends there, but with some disappointment that it does end there, because he always wants to find out how he did with the jet.

He has had so many close calls in his life, big and small, from mere inconvenience to the threat of death. Whatever fate or magic gets him into these situations usually gets him out. The odds seem to favor him; something seems to be on his side, and he has at times consciously counted on this. Once, broke and hungry in a miserably cold gray Chicago dawn, after a bad run of luck at poker, he was walking back to his room when, across from the university bookstore, he heard a scratchy, ticking sound from a barberry hedge; impaled on a thorn was a crisp ten-dollar bill. Twenty years ago an odd ridge on an otherwise smooth cement highway caused his sliding motorcycle to jump vertical just before he hit the car that had turned in front of him, so that he hit the soft door panel with his side and crash bar, and wasn't hurt at all. A septic-tank hole in wet sandy earth collapsed just before he was to be lowered into it to dig. A hunting bullet seared his leg and gave him nothing more than a burn. Congress passed a law, just before he was to go to the battle of Okinawa, saying that he was too young to fight without a full six months of training. While dozing next to Norman Winebaum as they drove to New York, he awoke just in time to see that Norman was going to keep to the right of a car parked facing them on their side of the road. When he and twenty other soldiers were lined up to bail out of a C-47 over suburban Los Angeles, the copilot came running back to find out why the plane was so tail-heavy and told them that the plane was not going to crash—the pilot was losing altitude, circling and wagging his wings as a greeting to his wife below. His reserve enlistment ran out twenty-eight days before the Korean War began. He got the mortgage on this house a week before the rate jumped a whole percentage point. It is almost frightening to go on listing his luck. In Tokyo, one summer evening, two Kanakas had him cornered and were in the process of deciding to throw him out a fourth-floor window of the Nihon Yusen Kaisha building when help arrived in the form of Iwashita and Ohara, members of his squad and also Kanakas, thus as fierce as the first two. The cold sweat of that balmy night can still be felt. He shouldn't go on; luck is luck, and should never be listed. Do not think of it. His children are intelligent and handsome . . .

But what has now happened to the Prince of Luck? Has the long-deserved comeuppance begun? Here on his desk lies his work. In the morning light it seems to him dry, starved, flippant, even somewhat nasty. And there is always, in any moment of stasis in his work, the temptation to think about what is currently fashionable, which is a disaster and the death of energy, the death of sincerity. Unless a man has given away his brains to one of a thousand current Salvation Armies, he is alone, judging himself. He wants to congratulate no one. He doesn't want to shock anyone, either. He doesn't want to shock anyone's Aunt Mabel, or Mrs. Robert H. Ferranos, of 99 Crescent View Terrace, Plumville, Ohio. That is not his purpose. She is human, is she not? Are you not human, Mrs. Ferranos, once an open and delightfully sentient young animal running and jumping over the daisies? He did want her to hear his voice, and he failed.

Mrs. Robert H. Ferranos
99 Crescent View Terrace
Plumville, Ohio

Dear Mrs. Ferranos,

I was hurt by your letter, not so much by its judgment of my book, but because I caused you to write to me in anger. How can I tell you that I respect you, and that no matter where I take you, I don't want to hurt you? I don't want to shock you in the way I've shocked you. I may call upon you to witness terrible things at times, but I am not upon the side of terror. There are those who would want to shock you, of course, but I don't think I have their rather infantile needs. Maybe you and I have different, but respectable, ideas about what literature should do. You object, I think, not to the violence in my book but to the occasional (but not random) sex without love, the recognition of the gross mechanics of our needs, the stinks and emissions of the human animal. These would not be part of your literature, which would have as its purpose entertainment and moral instruction—both good things . . .

Boom Maloumian ruled his room, an exotic despot sitting in state and dominating his roommates, visitors and anyone within hearing by exuberance and the sheer intensities of his needs, demands, his constant blast of anecdote. To be near him at all caused in Allard a change of style. He resented this influence because in his moral center he despised Boom Maloumian, but after hearing the flow of that huge voice for a while he detected in his own voice some of those rhythms and even assumptions. In Boom Maloumian's presence this force was stunning. Sitting majestically on his sagging bed, two hundred pounds of shining brown hairy flesh, sweat always gleaming on him, he celebrated his adventures: how he tupped a humpbacked hooker in Toledo, diddled a ripe banana-titted jigaboo in Big D. There was always something odd or freakish about his women, and they always paid for their sins. He told at length how he rolled queers one season in Beantown, the things he or his outfit did to jigs shines spades inks spooks shades coons dinges smokes coals zulus tarpots jazzbos fuzzies darkies shinnies boos nigs boogies. He was an encyclopedia of racial, ethnic and sexual derogations. When his troopship docked in Sydney two men were missing, both fairies. "Official report was, they flew away!"

He looked you in the eyes, beginning one of his tales, daring you, beginning softly like a huge engine idling. Allard had the feeling that if he tried to get away from that fierce, possessive regard he would not quite make it to the door; almost, with the last fearful optimism of a mouse, but not quite. Boom Maloumian threatened always some last horrifying burst of potential you didn't ever want to see activated, even against someone else. You were afraid even to witness it. He had the rare quality—at least rare to Allard, who was no stranger to violence—that caused your bones to feel thinner, and when you are conscious of your bones as sticks you are intimidated. This is when the logistical section of your brain calculates that he outweighs you by forty pounds of living tissue, that in the cold regions of his intent he is much less ambivalent toward murder.

Although Boom Maloumian must have had some kind of reconnaissance going, because he was never caught, he seemed to pay no attention whatsoever to any rule or law. He was a constant, almost casual thief, shoplifter, scrounger. His towels and shoes came from the athletic department; one sweatshirt improbably claimed itself to belong to STATE POLICE, TROOP C. You would find your possessions in plain sight in his room. Allard and his roommates would, without comment, take their things back, but others didn't dare.

He roasted a whole lamb in a pit Short Round dug behind the dormitory, made Short Round eat one of the hot green tomatoes from the five-gallon crock he kept beside his bed to clean the shish from the kebabs. Short Round ran down the hall screaming "Water! Water!" which only made it worse, while Boom Maloumian whooped and bellowed, swaggering down the hall naked, scratching his moss-grown balls. The housemother stayed carefully downstairs in her enclave, and Harold Roux, as floor proctor, was by this time making frantic efforts to find another place to live. Boom Maloumian and Short Round would line up in front of their door as Harold walked past to the showers. "Now," Boom said in ponderous baby talk, "Evybody who beweeves in faywies cwap dey itto hands!" And they softly clapped Harold down the hall.

Maloumian was often in the company of others who

resembled him, who had the same sort of nickname: Mung Harorba, Flash McLeod, Engine Whalen (who had worked on the Mt. Washington Cog Railway), Snake Morrow, Prop Gilman (also called Flieger because he had been a pilot). Their noises when together were always raucous and challenging, but Maloumian was the loudest of all.

When he wanted to, or when his inner balances were in equilibrium, Boom Maloumian could be generous with his booze and food, and he could be funny, if in sometimes horrifying ways. In this mood his stories changed, and the central intelligence responsible professed a somewhat rational wonder at the craziness of the world. But he could change back the next moment, the pale cast of civilization fading from the big face, the red mouth, the teeth like pearls, too clean and bluish, as though polished by the hot flush of his breath. When a certain depth of meanness appeared, he seemed to be viciously biting his own cheek and blaming someone else for the pain, his face screwed to port, his small black eyes lost in the thick flesh that was muscled even at the temples.

Allard quickly read these changes, and he resented in himself the tinge of fear that made him so sensitive. He was also ashamed to be amused at Short Round's willing degradation. He would find Short Round sitting on the floor outside the closed door, reading. "Boom's jerking off and he wants privacy," Short Round would say.

It was strange that of the ten or twelve Armenians Allard had known, Maloumian was the only one he hadn't felt to be somehow more gentle than other men. Armenians: an orphan race with a history of persecution by their neighbors. Arabs, Romans, Turks, Georgians, Mongols, Byzantines, Persians and again the Turks. Starvation and massacre. Once a Turk had taught Allard some Turkish curses, saying, "If you say this to an Armenian, run!" *Eschék! Pezze venk sen e meshú! Sen gurt dúrn ful lama sinis!* The last meant "You were born out of your mother's asshole." Occasionally Allard wondered if Maloumian did know these words, and felt them at the back of his tongue like dangerous little bombs.

Maloumian's other roommate, Gordon Robert Westinghouse, spent most of his time in a small enclosure deep in the stacks of the library. But even so, he had to come back to the room, and here he had a strange immunity, probably because Boom Maloumian was, at least for the time being, awed by real dottiness. Gordon Robert Westinghouse was one of the few nonveterans in the dormitory and it was easy to see why he'd been 4-F in the war. Quite often he wasn't really there —or perhaps he was there but you weren't. He had days when he didn't look at other people at all. Another of his peculiarities, widely discussed as indicative of a strange upbringing, was that in front of a urinal he didn't use his fly but slowly and carefully undid everything and urinated with his pants and underwear down at his feet. Sometimes, after days of ambulation inside himself, he would appear in Allard's room, his grayish ankles showing below pants that were six inches too short for him, his socks having mostly worked down into his sneakers, and talk, usually about his poetry. He gave the impression of feverish dankness; his joints all seemed to articulate at about forty-five degrees off-center. Because he looked so mournful and sick, at first Allard felt sorry for him. This was before Allard discovered the true depths of the man's unctuous egomania. He listened to no one, ever, and could not be kept from explaining, in utter detail, things generally known.

"Your standard-sized birds," Gordon would begin in his hard, inflectionless voice. He gave you the cold, helpless feeling you get from a recorded message. "Your standard-sized birds are your robin and your chicken. Smaller birds are compared with your robin . . ."

"Hey, poet," Knuck Gillis said, "you leave my goddam robin out of it."

". . . larger-sized birds are compared with your chicken."

While Nathan Weinstein's oogah laugh reverberated around the room. "Oogah! Oogah! Oogah hyuka-hyuk!"

Gordon Robert Westinghouse heard none of this. He was

going to be a famous, immortal poet. He would reverently place a piece of wilted paper on Allard's desk.

Lady of the night
Slide gently down the orbiting moon

"I worked twelve hours on those two lines. Twelve hours and fifteen minutes before I got them exactly right. I didn't eat, I didn't take a drink of water, I didn't go to the bathroom." That was why he was going to be a famous poet. If he could work more hours on each line than anyone else, he couldn't fail. It was a matter of work, of concentration. "Remember well," he said over and over again. "You knew me here, before I was famous. You must keep careful notes." Did you see Shelley plain? "Your observations and *mémoires* will be extremely valuable someday."

Evidently Boom Maloumian found him more valuable to observe than to exploit, or maybe, as in the case of Harold's toupee, he would settle for nothing but perfection. Maloumian would wait for inspiration; he was an artist at torment, a genius at giving pains.

Allard and his two roommates would occasionally wonder at their own heterogeneity, but they were not quite as mismatched as those in the Maloumian enclave down the hall. Nathan Weinstein was short, skinny and dapper, and considered himself a man of the world with a brilliant future ahead of him in business and/or law and diplomacy. Knuck Gillis was a large, abnormally pale ex-Marine who was captain of the defensive unit of the football team—this unit called the Kamikaze squad. His ambition was to have a professional football career and to be, eventually, a head coach. The friendship between the three of them fascinated Maloumian, and in one of his more rational moods, one day, he invited them to his room for a few beers.

Paul Hickett, representing the tradition of cowards, traitors, liars and fawners who are cruel in power and abject before power, was also there. He wore an Ike jacket obviously not his because where the chevrons of a staff sergeant had once been sewn on the sleeves, the cut stitches still carefully revealed this shadow rank. He had actually been a Pfc. Harold Roux wouldn't have been there anyway, but as it was he was busy in his room trying to remove bubble gum from his best pants and jacket; earlier Short Round had chewed up gobs of it and strung fine webs back and forth across Harold's doorframe for him to walk through.

"I was a cook, just assigned to this outfit outside of Yokohama," Boom Maloumian said. "Don't ask me what the outfit did. They ate, is all I know. Supposed to have something to do with Military Government, but far as I could see they spent all their time trying to keep from getting the clap. Commanding officer was Colonel Koons, bird colonel, craziest son of a bitch I ever saw in my life. Spent all his time with his Leica and floods and flash bulbs and what-all taking pictures of whores' crotches. I wouldn't bullshit you, word of God! Bein' a new man in the outfit I had to take his personal tour of his artwork, with a lecture how not to get the clap, and of course the Old Joe, which was worse 'cause penicillin didn't work as good on the Old Joe as it did in the beginning. Anyway, Koons was a spit-and-polish man—even wore his marksmanship medals. Looked pretty professional till you found what it was the only thing he was interested in. Anyway, here we go to the latrine, first off, and by God above every pisser, where you fuckin' had to look at it, was this life-size blowup of a whole whore's crotch with pus and lesions drippin' all over it, some of 'em all the way asshole to bellybutton. You had to stand there shakin' it with this globbed up snatch starin' at you like some great motherin' Cyclops!"

His big face twisted into startled curiosity and disgust before he laughed. "All over the goddamn billet you run up against these murals. Needless to say nobody in that outfit thought much about anything *but* pussy. Short-arm every morning, man, and it better be clean. Colonel Koons' outfit maybe didn't have much else to do, but he was gonna have the *ichi ban* record in Japan for low incidence of V.D. Any man come down with the drip, he was busted right *now*, right down to buck-ass private, it didn't matter how many stripes you had, time in service, Regular Army, medals, campaigns, top-three-grader, nothing! And you should of seen those short-arms! Fifty men lined up bare-assed in the halls, covered all over with goose pimples, it didn't matter how fuckin' cold it was, and here he comes, Old Eagle-eye. He'd get right down there and *examine* each and every pork like he was going to have it for breakfast. I mean you really had to milk it down for Old Bright-eyes. You had to pull it back four or five times, anyways—I mean, once more and it would of been technical masturbation—and milk it down slow and e–e–easy. Following behind was the First Sergeant—fifteen years in the motherin' army, you should of seen the expression on his face—and a sweet young thing of a medic, a Pfc., queer as a three-dollar bill, pushin' along this friggin' tray with slides and needles and all. Man, he was in paradise. But if one half a friggin' *drop* come onto the end of your wang that medic had a smear before you could blink an eye. He loved his work, man. He was not only quick, he was *rapid!*

"Now all the boys in that outfit was a little crazy, who could blame them? Nervous? There was a run on flashlights at the Eighth Army PX, everybody had one. At night it looked like fireflies all the way into town—in the fields, in the alleys, beside the goddamn road, it was these nervous bastards with their flashlights, examining cunts. It got so you couldn't say *kom ban wa?* to a hooker within ten miles of that place she wouldn't flop on her back, pull up her kimono and spread, waiting for a clinical exam! Must of been startling to strangers.

"But to get back to when the shit hit the fan was when the First Sergeant himself come down with the syph. As if he wasn't tear-assed enough—it's no joke to latch onto the Old Joe—this little flit medic ratted on him to the Chicken! Fifteen years in the army, RA, Bronze Star. Purple Hearts up the gink, master sergeant, he shouldn't of even been in the outfit, he was just waiting for orders to the repple-depple at Zama and transportation back to the States. And this chickenshit colonel busts him! You know what that means? He's gonna have to go home by slow boat and do K.P.! He's thirty-eight years old, been in rank four years! Jesus H. Christ!

"Anyway, next morning after short-arm I'm in the kitchen about ready to dish up Colonel Koons' breakfast when in comes Toppy with no stripes, he's a yardbird private. 'This his plate?' he says. 'Yup,' I says, and he whips out his prong, calomel ointment, pus and what-all smeared all over it, and rubs it up and down and all over the Colonel's plate. I dish up a pile of scrambled eggs on it, and he says, 'Okay, take that in to the muff-divin' son of a bitch!' Which I do. Man, I made it to the officers' mess and back, I don't know how, but when I got back I never laughed so hard in my life! I nearly split a gut!"

While Allard was willing to concede that this tale might have a moral, he was not so certain that its author was responsible for its moral value. Other tales, told with equal relish, also had to do with the humiliation of women, and finally one reduced Allard to a state similar to the aftermath of rage—weakness and shame. It concerned a First Cavalry unit's revenge on a Japanese neighborhood that was hospitable to a nearby Negro quartermaster battalion, especially what was done to women who were found with niggers jigs shines spades dinges coons, etc. When the story came to this part, Allard's memory presented him with a Japanese girl he had once known, with her delicate grace, and it was her hair cut off roughly with a K-bar knife. He got up to go.

"Where you going, Benson?" Boom Maloumian smiled, but the thick neck cords moved, slowly swiveling the turret of his head toward diminishing Allard. The black holes of the periscope slits slid half shut.

"Out," Allard said.

"What you say, boy?" The voice came from somewhere down inside, a muted loudspeaker from the center of control.

But Allard left, the rare mouse who managed to beat the claws to the crack beneath the door. Escape was not his way and he was humiliated, so when he found a hockey stick tied across Harold's door, roped to the knob so that Harold was imprisoned inside, he broke it in several places and threw it and the clothesline down the hall. He remembered then that Short Round had been out of the room for a few minutes.

"It's me. Allard," he called to the door. By this time Harold wouldn't open his door without positive identification. "You in there, Harold?"

The door opened. Harold stood there all dressed up in the clothes from which he had painstakingly removed the bubble gum. His eyes were shiny, a little evasive, and his face was gray, even grayer than its usual sunless clerk's pallor. He moved his lips but at first he couldn't speak. "I was supposed to meet Mary at the Youth Center. The church. It's all over now."

"Why didn't you pound on the door? Or maybe you could've broken it open. It was only a hockey stick. Somebody would've let you out, Harold, for Christ's sake."

"I pretended I wasn't in here."

"You what?"

"I didn't want them to know I was in here." Harold went back into the room and sat down at his desk. His hands trembled as he carefully put them flat against his cheeks. "I don't know, Allard. I thought I could just study, and live and let live. I don't know why they hate me so much. What have I done to make them do these things to me?"

"That fucking Maloumian can't leave anybody alone."

Harold winced a little at the bad word. He drew a Kleenex from a drawer and blew his nose lightly—probably not hard enough, Allard thought. Harold would consider that noise in bad taste. He had been crying, or nearly crying. Allard considered telling him that Boom Maloumian didn't hate him at all, any more that a cat hates a ball of yarn or a mouse, but decided not to.

At this moment, making raucous but not really dangerous noises, Boom Maloumian, Knuck, Nathan and Short Round came laughing into the room. Maloumian had what was left of a case of beer under his arm, the cans clunking together in their cardboard box. "Hey, hey!" he said. "Drink up!" He dropped the box on Harold's neatly arranged desk and with much spray opened the remaining cans with his church key. "Here, Mr. Proctor man, chugalug this mother! This crazy little Hebrew here has volunteered to drive us all to Litchwood so we can get ourselves fried to the ass!"

In Litchwood was Sarge's Café, an incredibly squalid bar that was so dark, so filthy, so loud and odorous, so far beyond the pale it had become popular with the students.

Boom Maloumian took one of Harold's thin hands and wrapped it around a beer can. "You're a good sport, anyway," he said. He put his big arm around Harold's delicate shoulders and squeezed him; then, with a sneaky, evil little smirk that didn't seem to belong to the width and breadth of his face, patted Harold once, delicately, with one effeminately arched finger, on the very top of his head.

Harold gave out a little squeak, dropped the beer on the floor and ran out of the room with both hands on his head. Boom Maloumian roared. "I guess I must of pushed his button!" On the floor the beer frothed over Harold's braided rug.

"Why don't you lay off?" Allard heard his own voice enunciate these unbelievably clear words. Yes, that was what he had just said.

Boom Maloumian was suddenly calm, interested in Allard. "What you say, boy?"

"You heard me." Again his voice betrayed his frail body. "Why don't you play your little games with somebody your own size?" Now, this was a foolish and inaccurate thing to say, because Allard wasn't Boom Maloumian's size at all.

"You want to play some little games, Benson?"

"You're a bully, Maloumian." The inadequate word came from childhood, where at least one part of Allard felt itself to be at that moment. Or would have preferred to be.

At this point Nathan Weinstein entered into the situation. Allard was extremely grateful, though he hadn't much hope. "Hey!" Nathan said. "If I'm going to drive you assholes to Litchwood let's go!"

"Yeah, let's go," Knuck Gillis said. Nathan, like the little banty rooster Knuck called him, pushed between Allard and Boom Maloumian, ostensibly to get a fresh beer, and the ceremonial strutting was disrupted just enough. After a little more urging, Boom Maloumian went with Knuck, Nathan and Short Round.

Weak and shaking, Allard went to the latrine, where he found Harold, identified by his shoes, sitting in a locked booth. "Come on out, Harold. They've left. Come on and I'll help you mop up the beer."

"I don't see why I have to live this way," Harold said without moving. "I'm leaving, Allard. I can't stand it here any more."

"Well, come on out. I'm telling you it's safe now."

"I can't stand it any more."

"Come on out and we'll clean up your room and go see Mary."

"I was supposed to meet her and Father Desmond at two, and now it's four."

"Shit, Harold, that's all right. We'll explain what happened."

"Can't anybody ever say anything but *sh't?*" Harold said. Somehow he couldn't quite pronounce the word. "Is that everything anybody ever says? Is it?"

"It does get kind of monotonous, I suppose," Allard said.

"For three years in the army all I thought about was getting away from those animals and coming to college."

"Yeah, I know. And now you've got the same animals only with slightly higher IQ's."

"I'm twenty-four years old and I was in the service for three years and two months. I didn't see combat but that wasn't my fault. I admit I wouldn't have liked it, but I never raised even a finger to keep out of it. I have an honorable discharge and I don't think I deserve this."

"Well, come on out anyway, Harold."

"I thought college would be dignified and intellectual. I never thought I'd be hiding in a toilet."

"Well, *stop* hiding in a toilet. They've all gone now."

"I could go live at a place out of town but I don't want to. I want to live here at college. That's what college is for, really. That ambience. Like a community of scholars." He explained in a still-tearful voice that some friends of his aunt and uncle owned a group of cabins called the Lilliputown Motor Inn about five miles north of town and he could stay there, clerking for room and board. "But it would be lonesome, I know it."

Finally he unlatched the door and came out, wiping his eyes with toilet paper. He was angry—a pouty anger that seemed hard and real, yet unpracticed. He turned back to throw the toilet paper in the toilet and fastidiously flushed it away, watching as it went.

"I've been thinking of quitting school, or transferring to some other place, and I don't *want* to," he said, his voice turning plaintive.

Allard thought, Yes and if Harold could manage to lose the toupee en route, in a strong wind, it might be a good idea to transfer. Here, again, he wanted to deal directly with Harold in this matter, but found that he simply couldn't mention that piece of hair. It was as if by even mentioning it he would brutally tear it from Harold's head. What would stand revealed then but some skin? No, something unmentionable and horrible might happen, like the whole top of Harold's skull coming raggedly off with it, revealing the gray-pink of his squirming brain. But Allard knew this wouldn't happen. He wondered, though, if the thing were glued down. His eyes sneaked guiltily at its edges and away.

After they cleaned up the beer and spray from Harold's room, Allard suggested again that they go see Mary, thinking that this might cheer Harold up a little, but Harold refused, somewhat curtly. "No, I don't think I want to," he said.

"I thought it might cheer you up."

"Allard, don't you understand that it doesn't exactly give me pleasure to see Mary look at you like you were some . . . *idol* or something?"

"I wondered about that."

"Well, now you know. I can see why, superficially, she'd prefer you. You're fairly good-looking and I look more or less like Donald Meek. I know that. And you're clever and even sort of crudely witty at times. Much as I like you, I don't trust your feelings about Mary. I'm six years older than Mary and I feel very protective toward her, and now, if I have to go away . . ." Harold gave him a deeply serious look. "Allard, you won't hurt her, will you?"

"Oh for Christ's sake, Harold, you sound like a character in your novel."

"I'm being serious. I'm being deadly serious."

"Then I feel obliged to inform you that my relationship with Mary Tolliver is, as you might say, 'strictly platonic.' " Then the worm of truth, or perhaps sadism, stirred in him and he added, "So far."

Harold looked at him. "It's true. You can be unkind. You can be cruel."

"Anyway," Allard said, pleased by this attribution to him of power and danger, "you said once that Mary was too good a girl and too good a Catholic to fall for my cheap, facile, crudely obvious wiles."

"I think that's absolutely true!"

"But maybe you'd better stay here and keep an eye on her anyway."

"Maybe I'd better!" Harold said angrily, then had to smile, painfully, and resented it.

Aaron Benham comes slowly out from the middle of his head into a bright spring morning. Will there have to be a chapter entitled "The Seduction of Mary Tolliver," which will deal with her background, how her mother died six years ago when she was twelve, and how close she is to her younger brother and especially to her father, who isn't well? Will she have to shed bitter tears, tears of betrayal made even more bitter because betrayal has not destroyed her destroyer, which is love? Tune in next week.

Of course this is an old story, and loss of innocence usually doesn't kill, after all. But each time it happens it is new to the one it happens to, fresh and terrible both in what remains and in what has been washed away. There is still the desire to possess forever, yet part of the mystery's awesomeness and power has been washed away forever, all in the same act, an act which, on one level, can be described in rather crudely mechanical terms. A girl (Winifred Cott) once told Aaron that if a girl wore tin pants, he'd have a can opener—an earthy, kitchen metaphor, definitely revealing the demise of awe. But we won't do it that way. And with Mary there are those terrifying beliefs she will never be able to exercise, those that come from her childhood, from retreats in which nuns and priests have limned the wages of sin, which always seemed to be sexual, and told of torments, of hellhounds eating the flesh of the unabsolved. She has told Allard something of this, he sitting there incredulous, safe within the bland memories of his own benevolent, even gooey Protestantism.

He and Mary are sitting in the wide living room, or lounge, of her dormitory. The room is all shades of dusty, worn brown, and all around against the walls are davenports, with single, empty easy chairs here and there. Upon most of the davenports are couples who don't have an available car, or whose relationships haven't got that far yet, or who perhaps enjoy necking in public. Do you know there is a *written* house rule that one's feet must touch the floor? Allard will not put his arm around Mary, much less kiss her, in such a ridiculous place. All around the room the other couples are exacerbating themselves in excruciating stop-motion. Later will come the silent howls to the moon as all the frustrated studs' seminal vesicles unsnarl themselves from bowlines, half hitches and sheet bends.

"I've got another one," Mary said. " 'Tack factory.' There actually is one in my town." She was fond of collecting such phrases. Another she had discovered concerned heels that, upon the sidewalk, "metrically clicked."

"Met–trick–click–clicked," she said. "Isn't that interesting?"

"Did you know there are African languages called Click languages?" Allard said. "I bet that means something to a Bushman in the Kalahari, or wherever one would find a Bushman."

"I wonder," Mary said. "It sounds sort of like a warning."

"Maybe it means 'What a nice afternoon for a motorcycle ride.' "

Mary shook her head, smiling. The green glint in her brown iris caught the light from the floor lamp (always on, day and night) that stood over them on its ponderous pedestal like a watchful housemother.

"I told you I promised my father I wouldn't ride on your motorcycle," she said. "He was so worried about it I just had to promise."

"You shouldn't have told him about it."

"Why not? I mean I really had to. He asked me if I was seeing any boys down here, so I told him about you. He's worried, you know. He thinks this is a pretty sinful place."

"Did you also tell him I'm some kind of a godless atheist?"

"No." Her face darkened; he put his hand on her cheek and felt the warmth of blood. "I don't know why he didn't ask." She hated even a lie of omission. This quality did awe him considerably.

He looked at her steadily as she continued to blush. What a pretty, high-cheekboned face, now full of ambivalent excitement, with all that fresh young blood careening around at the slightest command of emotion. She continued blushing because of his cool appraisal. She was such a complete living thing, but all humans had to be just slightly defective in some physical way or other, except possibly those rare, statistically certified idols of the movies. Was Mary's neck a centimeter too short for perfection, or her little-girl hips a centimeter too narrow? What cold, inhuman standards this uncrowned prince demanded as the price of adoration.

He had been stunned by beauty in the past, but Mary didn't do this to him, and he couldn't find the principle behind her vulnerability. Right now she was excited rather than bored by his silent examination of her. He had the feeling they could sit next to each other for hours on end, saying nothing at all, and to Mary each second would be all intensity and life. Out of the ordinary qualities of Allard Benson what a paragon of excitement and glamor she must have created. This bothered him a little, as though he had the opportunity to take advantage of someone who was under the influence of drugs, or of magical delusions. He could not imagine what he had done to deserve the look she gave him. This thought registered itself and quickly began to fade in importance. But it did register.

His coolness impressed her; he was not trembling worshipful Harold Roux, nor was he Hilary David Edward St. George—another of her calf-eyed infatuates, whose debility in her presence was the inability to stop talking about everything in the world except what he wanted to talk about.

"Anyway, you can always take Naomi for a ride on your motorcycle," Mary said, imitating jealousy—pretending to imitate jealousy. When Allard first asked her if she would like a ride, she declined, but her roommate, Naomi Goldman, said she would, so he took Naomi. She and Mary were improbable roommates, brought together by chance and the housing office.

"And Naomi and I could talk politics," Allard said.

"Is that what you talk about?"

Oh, oh. A bit of edge there, though deprecated by a smile.

He wondered if she had seen, or been told of, other times he had taken Naomi for rides on his motorcycle.

"We'd discuss the finer nuances of *Das Kapital*, or perhaps sing anthems in praise of Stalin," he said, thinking that there was some truth in this but very much aware that the conditional tense was a pure lie.

The first time he took Naomi for a ride (seemingly with Mary's approbation) they rode around the campus for a while, Naomi talking constantly into his left ear. She wanted him to take part in a symposium on the Marshall Plan—as the politically illiterate opposition to her position—at the next meeting of the Liberal Club. He was deliberately noncommittal about this project because he could feel her long high jumper's legs squeezing him as if he were a horse she rode, and her hard, melonlike breasts seemed to burn great holes in his back. She was a tall, coppery girl—copper and rose, with black hair, a noble Roman nose and a jet-black bar of eyebrow that came across unbroken above her eyes, which were robin's-egg blue and at first glance seemed cold and doll-like. Naomi was serious; humor was flippancy, irony facetiousness. The world must be fixed. But she knew as well as any middle-class girl the precise language of touch. When her arms slid down to his waist they clearly indicated that they were feeling the torso of a man, so without a single word on this subject he turned across the railroad tracks and took the bridle path into College Woods to a place he knew, a little alcove in the pines where the sun warmed the long needles and there were no signs at all of human traffic.

"After the war," Naomi said as they sat on the soft tawny needles, "there were eight million more people in Europe than before the war. How does your theory of economic ruin account for that?" Naturally she was against the Marshall Plan.

"That's very interesting. I didn't know that," he said, scouting for possible roots beneath the needles before he pulled her (a signal touch, not an actual pull) down beside him. Her arms hadn't lied to him on the motorcycle; when she arched her back to let him slide her Levis under her it was a pleasant, mild shock to find that she wore nothing under them. His throat contained a large bubble. Olive tones shimmered beneath her copper and rose; her blue eyes, almost as strange as Mary's green-flecked assymetrical ones, watched him undress, seemed to approve of the equality of nakedness. He was not used to unshaven armpits and legs, but the tight shimmery gleam of her flesh shone as though she had been anointed. Myrrh? She smelled vaguely of salt and sand. The dry carpet of needles seemed to undulate as her comradely body received him.

Afterwards her long fingers encircled his buttocks. "Wait a minute. Don't go away yet," she said. "Stay inside me. I suppose we should have used something, but I've just had my period so it's not the most fertile time in my estrual cycle." She stared into his eyes. "You know, it's strange you didn't suck on my nipples. Maybe you're not infantile in that sense."

"Did you want me to?" He was heavily aware now of the sky open above them and the breeze that signified that they were, after all, outdoors and could be discovered. He slid out of her and she reluctantly let him sit up.

"I want you to do whatever you want to do, providing it doesn't hurt. Hurt too much, I mean, or in the wrong way. I'm kind of a masochist, in a mild way, and I'm not ashamed of it. If it feels good to both partners it's good, don't you think?"

He hastened to agree.

"What I don't like are rubbers. It just seems wrong to have a layer of rubber between a man's penis and my sheath. Anyway, if we do this again I'll know how it will turn out and I'll wear my diaphragm."

"Do you think about all that during intercourse?" he asked. Although she hadn't spoken recognizable words during those minutes, she had made little yelping and purring noises.

"No," she said seriously, "I can't remember thinking at all then."

She lay there naked, open to him, her doll-blue eyes wide open, too, and with her last words a wave of fondness for her, maybe love, nearly drowned him. Came from somewhere behind him with no warning, and suddenly he was in its element and couldn't breathe. He got over her on his hands and knees and kissed her. "You're beautiful," he said.

"You're ready again already?" she said, surprised, her hands competently checking him out.

That was the first time he took Naomi for a ride on his motorcycle. Later it became fairly regular. She might call him at his dormitory but he didn't call her at hers because Mary might answer the floor telephone. He could usually get her at Herbert Smythe's apartment downtown. She had only recently been promoted by Herbert from mimeograph girl to a more or less vocally respectable comrade. The Marshall Plan symposium (which Allard attended but did not participate in) was her first assignment in this new rank, and she carried it off quite well.

They spoke of Mary occasionally. Naomi was quite fond of her. "She's such a little bourgeoise," Naomi said. "But she's sweet. She has a sweet nature. And she's your nice little small-town 'girl friend,' which I think is stupid but quaint."

He searched her ice-blue eyes for some humor, but couldn't find any. Or jealousy, either.

He could detect both in Mary, however. She looked at him and said, "Naomi's really quite an attractive girl, don't you think?"

"I like blondes with one brown and one green eye," he said. "I know it's a fetish, but I can't help it." He leaned over until their noses touched and looked into her left eye where the glittering green and dark brown turned kaleidoscopic. Her breath was as sweet as cool water. "When the sexy secretary from the tack factory trotted, her heels metrically clicked," he said.

She laughed and pushed him away. "Everything you say, practically, has 'sex' in it somewhere." She thought it quite sophisticated and daring even to say the word.

"All I do is take cold showers," he said.

She blushed.

"Let's go for a walk or something," he said, looking around the room at all the Laocoon groups of two in their saddle shoes and loafers. "There're enough sex spores floating around here to give asthma to a Buick."

"You *are* funny, Allard," she said. She had to go fix herself up before going for a walk. While he waited he watched one couple across the room. They were immobile. Their mouths had grown together. She wore his sport coat over her shoulders so that his hand, hidden by the cloth, could fondle her breast through her pastel blue cashmere sweater and her brassiere. The boy was the one who was sweating, however. His glasses lay neatly on the table next to the davenport, as did her pink ones. His legs were crossed in order to hide his erection, which meant that his back, because he had to keep his foot on the floor, must be in terrible pain. Her scuffed saddle shoes were primly, solidly and legally planted on the rug. Their tongues must be tired. Just then the girl opened one eye, looked at Allard and shut the eye again. That was all. Their locked immobility was, he thought, reptilian.

When Mary finally returned she was wearing a silk blouse, a cardigan sweater and one of the plaid skirts she made herself, pinned together at the thigh with a gold safety pin. She also wore knee-length knitted stockings and the kind of shoes usually called "stout brogans." She was always dressed up in some sort of ensemble, and inside and out she wore all the complicated rigging dressed-up girls were supposed to wear. Boom Maloumian nudged him one time and said, leering at Mary, "That's eatin' stuff, Benson," smacking his wet lips. Mary certainly heard this, but said nothing. Allard wondered about it, but thought, finally, that it sounded not nice and was probably screened out of her mind somewhere between issuance and reception.

They walked down the sidewalk among the students, many of the men wearing parts of military clothing—especially those whose jackets were decorated with stenciled bombs or other informative devices. No one would go as far as to wear decorations, but any other sort of visible bragging seemed to be considered all right.

Down Main Street in front of the Student Union, people were gathering on the lawn near where garbled yelps and static came from a sound truck. Allard and Mary drifted over with the others, two hundred or more, most of whom were at this moment between classes. Next to the sidewalk was a big granite boulder. Herbert Smythe and Naomi stood on the boulder and several of their supporters stood rather quietly and nervously around it. The sound truck was parked next to it in the street. Herbert, a slender young man whom Allard instinctively pitied and despised, affected a uniform consisting of a cheap blue pin-stripe suit, GI boots and a white shirt worn with the collars spread over the lapels of the suit coat. To him this was the costume of the poor workingman, the embattled but unbowed organizer of the people. Unfortunately his head, appearing on top of a thin neck above a satisfactory, Lincolnesque Adam's apple, was all wrong. It was a nice-boy head, a mama's-boy or divinity-school head, too young and somehow evasively not shy but embarrassed, as though it wondered, without daring to look, if his fly was open. His oratorical gestures were classic, learned, out of the last century, and now, in the giant cone of force of the amplifiers, his shrill voice blared and squealed. The oratorical gestures were just out of synch with the voice, and of course the voice was completely out of synch with the audience, who at first wondered what in the world this fellow was so instantly hysterical about. But soon they got his drift. A few phrases such as *Triumph of the proletariat!* and *Capitalist running dogs!* sorted themselves out of the blast. Actually Herbert was protesting a movie that was to be shown that night at the local theater. The movie was an old one, *Ninotchka,* in which Greta Garbo plays a humorless (at first) Soviet agent who is seduced and converted by an American capitalist (Melvyn Douglas). Soon the crowd, sensing a common target and buffoon, and angered by his seriousness, began to howl Herbert down.

Herbert responded by howling, with the advantage of electronics, back at them.

"*Fascisti! Fascisti! Fascisti! Fascisti!*" Herbert madly screamed, and just then none other than Short Round ran up to the boulder shaking a quart bottle of beer and squirted foam all over Herbert and Naomi. Boom Maloumian roared in the crowd, the crowd roared, and the man in the sound truck turned Herbert off with a gigantic click. Herbert's mouth continued to open and shut for an evidently hilarious few moments, and the sound came on again, this time carrying another voice which explained that the views of the previous speaker were not those of Acme Sound Services, Incorporated. Cheering and laughing, the crowd began to disperse.

Allard and Mary continued down toward the Coffee Shop. "*Fascisti*, for Christ's sake," Allard said. He had seen *Ninotchka*, and though he'd enjoyed it he knew that its basic assumptions were simple-minded and that it sucked up to its audience's self-satisfaction. Some truth was perhaps revealed in it, and for Herbert and Naomi to get so exercised over this bit of froth merely reinforced its message. When Short Round squirted beer all over Naomi, however, Allard's first instinct was to attack. He was very fond of her as a creature whose crannies, pleasures and quirks he knew in intimate detail. And Short Round, that utter creep, had the gall to squirt beer all over Allard's nice animal.

He and Mary were having their coffee in one of the cramped wooden booths of the Coffee Shop when Herbert and his troops came in, back from the barricades, their eyes illuminated by Righteousness Embattled. They sat at a corner table, eight or nine of them, including Naomi. One of the group, a small, deprived-looking boy wearing steel-rimmed GI spectacles, sang in a low, emotion-wavered voice:

"*Die Heimat ist weit,*
Doch wir sind bereit.
Wir kämpfen und siegen für dich:
Freiheit!"

Sitting glumly with Herbert's friends was Ilse Haendler, a rather nice, sad, blonde German girl whose parents, it was said, had died as political prisoners in a concentration camp. Allard couldn't understand why she hung around with Herbert. She did, however, have the firmly superior, kindly look of those who are dedicated to some transcendent ideal or other, and that benevolent, understanding firmness could at times be highly irritating. He caught her eye, raised his left fist and said, "*Hoch die rote Fahne!*"

She frowned. Naomi had seen this, too, and she spoke quickly to Ilse, who then got up and came over.

"Won't you sit down?" Allard said, rising. Against part of his will he made a joke of his politeness.

"Hello," Ilse said to Mary, and sat down. With no change in her stern, forgiving face she said to Allard, "Why are you so aggressive toward us?" She had almost no accent at all.

"I thought Herbert's performance out there was ridiculous and stupid," he said. "The fellow is an ass."

She frowned, perplexed. "But what has that to do with it?"

"Those people aren't '*fascisti*,' they're just boneheads, and for that matter hardly any of them are even Italian."

Ilse struggled not to be offended, and won. "It's too bad. I hope one day you can try to understand." She got up, saying abstractedly that she had a class she ought to attend. They said goodbye, rather distantly.

As Ilse walked away on her healthy German legs, Allard felt just the slightest pang of loss. It was partly the impermeability of her opinions, like a soft, erotic irritation.

Perhaps it was then, not later in College Woods, that Mary accused him of believing that every pretty girl in the world really belonged to him. She often surprised him by reading his mind—a startling little side effect of the intensity of her regard.

"Are they really communists?" Mary asked. "Naomi thinks I'm so naïve about politics we don't talk about it any more."

"I don't know," Allard said. "I suppose you are if you think you are, but I don't know how official it all is." Naomi's politics seemed to him an undisciplined mixture of the Freudian doxology of her middle-class parents and those parts of radical thought that justified what she wanted to do. As for Herbert Smythe, he seemed hardly real at all. When Allard asked Naomi if she'd ever made love (his euphemism) with Herbert, she made a disloyal grimace and said that even if he wasn't exactly her sex image, she put her hand on him once and he just froze, so they both pretended it had never happened. Herbert, she said, was dedicated.

"But how do you know so much about all this political stuff?" Mary said. "Like that German—*hoch die,* whatever it was."

"Well, I've heard those songs before," he said.

He'd come by his mishmash of left-of-center beliefs through inheritance, which in some not quite logical way seemed to make them more legitimate. Perhaps they had been legitimized in Japan. He'd been doing the work of an officer, and his commanding officer suggested that he apply for a commission. He was nineteen, and there was an arrangement where he could go to a quick officer training school and come back to his job. He passed the exams, the physical, the OCS board and all the rest, only to be told a month later that his eyes weren't good enough. Because this made him worry about his eyes he got them tested by another army optometrist, at St. Luke's Hospital in Tokyo, and aside from a permissably mild myopia they were all right. Then it occurred to him that the army of his country, the whole huge apparatus whose uniform he had been actually proud to wear, had conspired to make that little lie. Because of certain left-wing connections in his family he would never be trusted enough to assume any real authority. It was a quick and very interesting education for that American. Amazing how many myths were lost all at once in that Tokyo summer; the void they left in his assumptions proved that he had believed a good deal. He'd been thinking of staying in Japan another year, but when his hitch was over he came home. Home? Back to the States, his only country, from which he'd innocently, apolitically sprung.

He never mentioned his new knowledge to any of his family. They had all settled into their businesses and professions, those few who had been radicals having been tumbled and buffeted by the Moscow trials, Trotsky's assassination, the invasion of Finland, the Moscow-Berlin alliance, until they had retreated back toward positions of respectable Democratic leftishness. They tended their own business, raised their children and sent them to college. He was the oldest of all his cousins, the only one old enough to get in on the tail end of the war against fascism. Later a cousin would die in the First Marines near the Changjin Reservoir in a war generally approved of by most of the family.

It is noon in Aaron's lonesome house. The house belongs to Agnes—its heart does. Just look anywhere and you'll see antiques, which make him nervous because he doesn't want to break or stain them or burn long brown cigarette grooves in them. He likes to look at that lean, delicate Shaker chair, but he won't sit in it. In his study he has a ragged Morris chair he found at the town dump, and his desk is a solid-core birch door on sawhorses; if he ruins this side he can just sand it down or turn it over. Everything he owns is cracked, burned, dented, faded, flawed in some way, small or large, but everything works. The ejector-holding spring, for instance, on his 30–06 came from something as unmilitary as a ball-point pen, but it works as well as the original flat spring, which tended to break. The rubber footrests on his Honda are cracked, now held on with elastic bands made from an old inner tube. The left bow of his glasses is mended with masking tape.

He is having a beer for lunch. As far as the writing is concerned, this is like cutting his throat. After lunch he will have another beer for desert. *Finito.* No words will appear, only chaotic thoughts, memories, nostalgic scenes. How

Mary cried. The taste of her tears, like the warm unsaline seas of the Eocene. She would have liked that phrase. He would like to drink her tears again.

That evening, when Allard and Mary went to see *Ninotchka*, they had to pass a picket line of Herbert Smythe's friends, including Naomi, who pretended not to see them. In the semi-dark before the screen, they held hands. Mary squeezed his hand, signals in a little code it was not necessary to decipher. He had crude thoughts. He had tender thoughts. The tender thoughts combined with the crude thoughts to give him what Boom Maloumian would call a blue-steeler. Throughout the film he was urgently aware of the delicate organism beside him who held his hand, nerves touching at fingertips. He could feel her happiness. She had a talent for shimmering happiness he had never known before in anyone. Yet it was not demanding or cloying; it seemed always that he owned her, not the other way around. Near the end of the movie he was desperately trying to think his erection down. He had various ways to do this, gathered over the years. His motorcycle needed a new front tire; but that didn't work because the new tire was suddenly installed and he was taking Mary out to his hidden place in College Woods. Arithmetic didn't work; it had no power over the current flowing through her touch. She moans as her first man gently but enormously enters her. Garbo laughed. Melvyn Douglas smiled. Allard Benson grimaced at the extruded frozen fire the whole middle part of his body seemed to feed. Fetch the baggy tweeds and we'll smuggle it into London, said the Duke to his valet—courtesy Boom Maloumian. All life, even the shadow people on the screen, inflamed him, bade him erotic welcome. He could think of nothing that was not sweet help and welcome. Since puberty this desperate situation had lain in wait for his dignity. High school had been hell. How in God's name to make this willful monstrosity desist? The bell will ring, he'll have to stand up, and he'll look like a triangle.

But so what? God knew what; for some unarguable reason he could not let himself be observed in public in the rut. Ah, but alone with Mary! He decided, at the last moment, that he would visit her family this weekend. Either that resolve, or the usual end-game desperation, enabled the mindless, mind-proof member to partly disengorge, and they left the theater looking more or less like the other people.

They stopped at the College Pharm and had a sundae, chocolate fudge with crushed nuts. Crushed nuts? asked the soda jerk of the trembling man. No, shell shock, was the reply —courtesy B. Maloumian.

They sat in a narrow booth, facing each other, Mary's neat lips at her sweet spoon. She was so pretty, so perfectly immaculate, that she had the power all at once to turn him into the perfect date for her. America, innocent honest sweet America, the girl next-door, the wonder of growing up. And with most of his real, or dark, desires wafted away before this American idol, or ideal, or idyll, he fell in love with her, or it, as though he were the kind of person (boy) whose fondest dream was to possess this sweet clean intelligent American girl, meet her family, take instruction in her religion, marry her in church—she in taffeta, lace and veil, an untouched virgin until her sacred wedding night. How God and all the authorities, heavenly and civil, would smile upon the pretty young couple! How all would approve!

He told her he'd changed his mind and would like to go home with her for the weekend.

Her happiness deepened, sobered into deeper places. "If you come to mass on Sunday, I'll have to show you how to genuflect."

Holding hands, they walked back to her dorm. In a shadowed place beside an arborvitae he unbuttoned her jacket and put his arms around her, his hands on the silken warmth of her blouse. She trembled as they kissed. Her mouth was sweet, not sugary but the deeper sweet of her health, giving him a feeling of his own rough unworthiness.

"I think I love you, Allard," she said, breathless mystery

and bravery in these words. "I know I love you. I couldn't feel anything stronger than this."

"I think I love you, too," he said.

"You," she said. "You won't . . ."

"Won't what?"

"Oh, I don't know. I can hardly breathe. I'm all confused." She turned her face away. "It's nearly eleven, I've got to sign in." Her ear was hot to his lips and she trembled so much a buzzer seemed to be going off inside her somewhere. She turned back and kissed him awkwardly, as though in reckless desperation, then stepped away from him. He held her hand and pulled her back.

"We've got a full thirty seconds," he said.

When he kissed her again she seemed to be committing a sweet but mortal sin. "I love you," he said.

"I love you. I've never felt anything like this. I love you."

How beautiful to say that, to say something with no reservations, with nothing at all left unsaid.

Gravely blushing, with her face averted as though she were ashamed of what must be too apparent upon it, she ran up the steps to the dorm entrance and inside.

He walked, dazedly, back to Parker Hall, dreaming upon the sweet simplicities of love. The trees leaned, sweet green, benevolently above him. Orange windows were gentle depths, each with its meaningful life inside. A lamp seen glowing on a student's desk must surely illuminate a calm, important volume explaining the beauty of existence. Mary seemed now all perfect and whole, gleaming silver and gold. He could worship her heel, idolize the pit of her knee. No part of her could displease him, nothing. He was unworthy of her body yet protectively superior to her mind, to her strength. She was his to tenderly break, yet honorably, honorably.

But of course he would then bring her into his own world—as soon as he achieved it. For instance, he was not about to become a Roman Catholic. He had nothing against its pomp and ceremony, but he would always view it as interesting theater. Their children could have their choice. With the thought of their children a fearful shiver of pleasure quaked his loins; they were good protoplasm, he and Mary. To enter and become part of her body in another! It awed him, that sweet mortal union. Its particulars, its biological miraculousness awed him. My God, there was a deep complex inside her body made to welcome part of his body. Little live parts of him would then swim up into her, there to meet and combine with her in that blood darkness. Life, continuation. No miracle conceived by man could compare to the one made actual by protoplasm itself.

Dreaming upon these sweet and dangerous possibilities, he returned to Parker Hall. He wanted to talk to Nathan, who would, in his fashion, take him seriously. It seemed necessary to Nathan to consider him naïve in those worldly affairs having to do with money, or the Great American Game of Con, and perhaps also, on a less important level, fashions in clothes. Allard's genius, as Nathan seemed to need to have it, was in art and in love. All Nathan's friends had to have their spheres and be great in them. Allard believed that as audience for this confession of love and future, Nathan would be properly and seriously correct. Harold Roux would have suspected his motivations and quizzed him sharply—too sharply—on the practicality of it all, but Nathan would never doubt the romantic importance of this crisis.

Allard knew all this but without any diminution of enthrallment. Our self-importance raises the importance of our friends, our loves, our world. To be truly involved while observing our skill at the scene itself is not really dishonest. Does he cry at the beauty of his sorrow or joy (both of which are real)? Does he love the beauty of his vision of love?

Back at the room he found Nathan studying. Knuck was snoring, his gray-white head as insensible to its own signals as a buoy rocking upon the sea.

"Ho!" Nathan said. "The lover returns." He looked at Allard, the large dark eyes in his bony little head holding, after the first glance, seeing what Allard wanted them to see.

"What's the serious bit?" Nathan asked.

"I think, my friend, I am under the influence of love."

"Mary?"

"Mary. I'm having a crisis about marrying her, Nate."

"Whew! Ooee! That *is* serious." Nathan's face turned properly grave at the wonder of this life-important decision. "That's a big step, Allard. A big step."

"In fact, I'm going home with her this weekend and meet her father and little brother."

"And go to Mass on Sunday?" Nathan asked shrewdly.

"I suppose so."

"That's sort of like getting engaged, you know." Nathan, who was a Unitarian himself, made it a point to know about the protocols of various Christian sects. "I mean, are you going to turn R.C.?"

"Impossible."

"Mary is going to turn whatever you are? What are you, anyway, come to think of it."

Allard couldn't think what he was, and realized nervously that this question would certainly be asked. A non-Protestant? A paradoxologist? "I don't know what the hell I am, Nate."

"You better think of something before ol' Dad lays his cold eye on you, boy. You're the crummy crud who's going to violate his sweet virgin daughter."

"How true."

"You haven't touched her yet, though, have you."

"No."

"Maybe you *are* in love, Allard." Then Nathan's avuncular side began to function. "You're only twenty-one, right?"

"Yeah, but I've been around. Maybe I'd like to settle down." He felt that he had important work to do, and maybe all this dating and screwing around was what kept him from it.

"Are you sure you're ready, Allard? I mean it costs money, and then come the babies. You want to tie yourself down to a nine-to-five?"

"I've got the GI Bill for about four more years."

"Slim pickin's. What does Mary think about birth control?"

"We haven't discussed it. But I know what I think about it. Mary doesn't know much about the whole subject of sex, as a matter of fact."

"Sometimes they know more than you suspect."

"The way Mary was educated it was a sin even to have any curiosity about the subject. I asked her what she was going to confession and confessing to all the time and she blushed."

"Goddam. With Mary I kind of believe it," Nathan said. "But how about Naomi? She could give Mary a course in the rough mechanics, from what you've told me." Allard had told Nathan about Naomi, though with some reservations and a serious pledge of secrecy. He considered it a rather juvenile need, but he'd had to tell somebody. He wondered if he'd told Nathan because he and Naomi were both Jewish, and then had complicated feelings indeed about his motivations. Nathan hadn't seemed to have any proprietary feelings about Naomi, but then, of course, he was Unitarian.

"Naomi concurs about Mary's fairly total innocence."

"Amazing. Amazing," Nathan said. "But Mary knows you take Naomi out to the woods and jab her, doesn't she?"

"I doubt it. I really think she doesn't know what we do out there. I don't think she can get her mind around it."

"Now, that is what's called *purity,*" Nathan said, with an oogah muted so as not to awaken Knuck. Then, in deep seriousness: "But Allard, I have to say that Mary Tolliver is the sweetest, loveliest girl I've ever laid these old eyes on." Nathan was twenty-two. "Yes, you've got some kind of a queen, there, Allard. There's nobility there. I mean it. And a sense of humor, intelligence. Yes, Mary is one in a million. You're one lucky fellow."

They were both quiet, musing upon their mutually accepted high seriousness. How dramatic it was; they could almost hear sacred music.

Allard lay back on his bed. What a decision he could

make. It would be so sweet, life with Mary. They would move into one of the small, one-room apartments built for married veterans with no children. How right, how companionable it would be to study together in the evenings. Her wonder at their legal, sanctified status, her wonder at the powerful dark postures of love, her ecstasy at having the one she loved passionately at work upon her shy yet eager body and mind. He would perhaps do more studying for his classes than the minimal amount he did now, but mainly he would have the calm, the time, to write his play and his novel, to create, and thus to deserve the life he would bring lovely Mary toward. She would of course leave her Catholicism gradually behind, and he would become famous. Not famous, really. What he wanted was more a solid, respected reputation as a man of art. In that life they would be surrounded by people of wit and accomplishment. They would have a future uncloying, always new and good. And Mary would be there to relieve his pressures—to, in fact, worship at the altar of their union. Well, not quite like that. Of course it would all be mutual. What gave pleasure to one would give pleasure to the other. In the haze of these idyllic thoughts, her own, more immediate, dimensions and textures came to mind and he began to gather toward thickness. A strange golden light gleamed into, or out of, his eyes and he was falling, absolutely sure of what he was going to do.

Though Boom Maloumian got the last word that evening, it was to Allard merely a passing grossness, a minor interruption. Short Round was the first to come into the room. Laughing, giggling, wary, dingy around the eyes, he was followed by a contentedly roaring Boom Maloumian.

"What? What?" Knuck said, convulsively waking into speech.

"Boom, you got to tell them!" Short Round said. "The one about the mud!"

"Well, now," Boom Maloumian said. "It seem you got to heah 'bout Rastus. Rastus, he a stud. I mean, he a *stud!* Rastus got a whang on him drive them nigguh gals plumb crazy.

Speshly this little ol' gal Mandy. She think she sumpthin', too, snatch fulla honey, she a powerful lovin' gal. Anyways, she finely git Rastus away fum them other gals an' man, they bofe in a hurry! Onliest place handy is down by de levee in de nice soft Mis'sippi mud. Purty soon they goin' at it hammuh an' tongs. Atter a while Rastus, he ask, 'Is it in, Mandy?' Mandy, she say, 'No, Rastus, it in de mud.' 'Put it back in, Mandy.' Little latuh on Rastus ask, 'Is it in, Mandy?' 'No, Rastus, it in de mud.' 'Put it back in, Mandy.' Little while latuh Rastus ask, 'Is it in, Mandy?' 'Yes, Rastus, it in.' 'Mandy, put it back in de mud.' "

Short Round's screeches of laughter followed Boom Maloumian's deep rumble down the hall.

"Put it back in de mud!" Knuck Gillis said. "That's rich. My God! Put it back in the *mud?*"

The telephone rings, surprising him. Who wants him now? He feels guilty, violated, defensive. If he could only let the thing ring. He could let it go on and on until it lost its breath and quit. But it insists; its shrill, self-confident yowl demands him, and so he goes to it and picks up the black bar, the crooked Bakelite dumbbell, and puts it to the side of his head. "Hello," he says in his always receptive, neutral telephone voice.

"Hello, Aaron? Hey, man?" It is Mark Rasmussen, his voice high and accelerated, coming from a long way off as if through a conduit.

"Mark!"

"*See see shoo shoo!*" Mark laughs. "Aaron, now! Wee green pinkadoolic voices tell me you've been inquiring after me, man. Very paternal, responsible. Brother's keeper, like. I mean, pardon me, just mean to say it's all fine, okay, so don't worry about anything. Okay?"

"George and I want to help you, if you want us to. Where are you, Mark?"

"You're both sweeties. Indeed you are. Appreciate it oh so much but never mind, huh? I mean, forget it? It's such a bummer, the whole bit. Bummer bummer bummer, as we used to say. But I'm all right. Strictly in control. Right on top of things, so just wanted to ease your mind, give you a friendly ring on the telephone. Mean it. No, wait a minute. Didn't mean to sound so bad. Why do I always give the wrong impression like that? I mean Aaron you're perfectly well away—aware—of what a stupendous bummer it all is and I don't mean to confuse the issue. It's merely the consensus of opinion, so don't worry about a thing. Not a thing. Right? Anyway, I've got a busy schedule, so I'll be saying ta ta and cheerio now, okay?"

"Mark! Don't hang up!"

"Hang up! Hang up!" Mark says, sliding into his sissing laugh again. "Oh, I mean! *See see see see!*"

"Where are you?"

"Aaron, I hate to tell you, but I'm on *earth!* Same place you are, and I'm looking out of this teeny-tiny crack. Did I happen to mention what a bummer? Sad. But don't worry, now, Aaron. Everything under absolute control. Don't mean to sound so shall we say bitter about it. Giving wrong impression again, I can tell. Really very calm. Calm acceptance. If I had an udder I'd give five gallons of rich cream. No shit."

"Mark, damn it!"

"Just thought you ought to be the first to know Federal Government ran out of good trips. Inside information." Mark laughed for a while, too long a while, then sighed. "Sorry. Strictly unimpeachable source. High up in Pentagon. Unimpeachable! No fun even burning babies any more. Up to the ass in cooked babies. Oh dear, here I go again, giving the wrong impression. Don't mean a word of it. Scout's honor."

"Where are you, Mark?"

"Oh me, I can see I'm not making my point again. Where I am is in this box, smelling slightly of piss, with teeny-tiny cracks in it. Or did I mention that before. But Aaron, are you there? Lately people tend to go away, don't know why. Giving absolutely wrong impression again, but anyway I'm in this box with heretoforementioned teeny-weeny cracks. But Aaron, in the glass—right in the middle of the glass is this pretty silver wire. How the hell did they get it *in* there? I mean it kind of makes you proud just thinking about it. I'd like to just spend the rest of the day looking at it and feeling proud, but I've got a date, you know, and now I really do have to run."

"Frank Hawkes told me you were down on all of us," Aaron says.

"Shit, I'm surrounded. Cute little pissers, full of warped love, which is why they want to kill, but they don't. No alternatives, right? Even that ol' boy deputy sheriff broke my hand way back in the ancient age, the old times, man, when there wasn't any black and white. Remember? Salt and pepper then. Now spade cats I was in jail with won't shake my hand. Fucking honky. I understand. Understand perfectly. Ta, ta, comrade. Perfectly all right."

"Mark, please tell me where you are."

"Broken record, dad. Broken record. You ought to hear yourself. Where are you Mark where are you Mark where are you Mark where are you Mark. On and on like that. Lack of communication. Ill of our times."

"Okay, but you don't sound exactly normal either."

"Oh well now. Let's not get insulting about it. Not worth it, you know. Shall I say that I rather sense that I'm a little *quick?* Yes, I'm very *quick* at the moment. Very quick. Got to slow down a little. Got to see the elevator man. Genius. Control. Up and down. A little down will fix me up. Down, up, right? Dichotomy, paradox, Professor? Oh shit, there I go again, giving the wrong impression. Communications failure. Short circuit in the intercommunication complex. Absolute flop. Just terrible."

"Mark, how can we help you?"

"You're awfully slow, Aaron, or shall we say that you're a real pile of goo? Shit, I mean you're a perfect sweetie, a perfect marshmallow. We'll keep in touch, huh? I mean, don't call me, I'll call you." Suddenly the hornlike voice turns hard and angry. "And in any case, Aaron, fuck off, will you?"

A woman's flat, businesslike voice says, though with a certain institutional breeziness, "Deposit sixty-five cents for three more minutes, please."

"I haven't got the change, honey," Mark says.

"Mark, give me the number. Let me call you back."

"I told this guy to fuck off, operator. What do I do now?"

Then silence. Far off in the the ether, women's voices chat busily, just below the level of understanding.

Suddenly Aaron remembers another dream he had last night. First comes its heavy mood—horror at a lack of horror. Deep calm. It was on a lake with an Indian name—Minnetonka, Iduhapi, Pasquaney—a calm, clear lake surrounded by forest, with only a few cabins on its shores, and those were old dark cabins made of logs or rough lumber some time in the teens of the century. In those cabins would be found mounted antlers, beaded doorway curtains, hand-operated pumps in the kitchen sinks, blue enameled tin dishes and cups, bare pine studding dark orange with age, stone fireplaces with half-log mantels, owl's-head andirons, kerosene lamps. In the dream Aaron stood up to his waist in the cool water, near the end of the dock, tying the mooring line of his small sailing dory. It was dusk, the sky darkening into an orange the color of oak leaves in the fall—that rich subdued orange-umber that seems so warm. Several yards away, on the float, Agnes sat, gleaming from her swim, touched on smooth shoulders and arms by the sky's orange light. He did not speak to her, nor she to him, but she watched him carefully, levelly. Her hair, darkened and flattened by the water, covered her head like a hood. The evening wind, barely felt, was warm. His feet were down in darkness, in the slightly risky other-world of water things, but he could look down his body past chest, sternum, ribs, into the darkness. Currents of delicately changing temperature passed his thighs. Upon the float, Agnes, still watching him, pulled her legs up to sit with her arms around her knees. It did not seem startling that the Negro body floated next to him, impassive black face up. It was the body of a husky man. The dead eyes were open, showing a brown stain in the whites. Bluegum, he thought, the blackest of the black. The body nudged him, and he pushed it slowly away, his hand white against the thick, shiny hair on its head. Another body floated near the dock, just the back of the woolly head and onyx shoulders above the water. Out in the lake, several more naked black bodies, men and women, floated low in the calm water. It did not occur to him to wonder what event had caused these well-formed black bodies to be here, floating with stern calm in the evening water. The fact signified its own inevitability. Someone would have to remove the bodies from the lake, but he did not feel immediately responsible. It would be taken care of later. Perhaps he would write about it, but it didn't fit into his plans for the next morning's work, nor would it interfere with this evening's calm enjoyment. Perhaps there was a slight doubt; it seemed sadly ominous that the bodies were here. Of course if they weren't removed for several days they would begin to pollute the lake. When he had finished tying the dory for the night he looked deep into the water and saw the buoy anchor line going down, down, fading into that other element. He then felt some fear. Agnes slipped without a splash into the water and slid toward him as if propelled by fins. Briefly their cool mouths touched, and they walked, pushing the weight of the water aside, to the shore. Here, the one white body, that of an older man with shaggy gray hair and beard, lay in the shallows, his mouth wide open, torn-looking, as though he had died in the midst of a scream.

He has been holding on to the telephone, and now he puts it back into its cradle. He is still stunned and bemused by those dignified bodies, and by his attitude in the dream of calm acceptance. "In dreams we are other people," he says out loud, his voice startling him as though someone has sneaked up behind him and spoken into his ear.

But in dreams we are really, truly ourselves, aren't we? Except that in dreams all is supposed to be in code. Nothing is what it seems.

He wanders into the kitchen. He's just had two beers. If he doesn't drink any more at all he can at least *think* coherently about the hair of Harold Roux. He ought to call Mark's mother, but he can't stand the idea. Maybe he'll send her a post card, but what can he tell her? That Mark called and said not to worry in a voice that obviously had the heebie-jeebies. "Mark's fine, Mrs. Rasmussen, he's just a hair strung out, is all. On his uppers, you might say. Can't get off E (Empty), but I don't believe he's on H . . ." But what the hell does he know about it? He'll have a drink; he knows about addiction, all right. It's right now, reaching for the half-gallon of Beam, not wanting it but having to have it. Or watching a student who takes whole minutes to find a ragged manuscript in his book bag, moving so slowly, so slowly. That's heroin, probably. Or is it Seconal? In the recent past they have written him stories and poems about all the stages along the way, about smack and a one and one nosin', and a two and two, about so and so's OD'd and he's dead so they leave him. He's *dead*, so what can they do? Heavy, man. Heavy.

The chemicals stain the ice cubes. C_2H_5OH: ethyl, or ethanol. He knows that language. He's smoked pot occasionally over the years, too, but there's that mean, nasty business of the law hanging over it, and like it or not he's got too much to lose; he's got insurance policies, a mortgage, a profession, children to feed and doctor and educate. But the state's own commission hustles the booze, so that's okay. He drinks. Blagh. The dope goes down and assaults his pyloric valve. It's a depressant, for Christ's sake, and who needs to be depressed? He lights a cigarette, another kind of dope with its grinning skull of blue smoke, gray after his lungs efficiently filter it. He swings his hand through the hemorrhage of smoke, roiling it madly.

With his drink expertly in hand he is, as always, drawn back to his study, to the scene of the crime. Commission or omission.

The dormitory room, its bland maple furniture, its putty-colored cement block walls, on a spring afternoon. Outside it is raining and has been misting and dripping all day.

Nathan Weinstein, at this time, was having a very short infatuation with sparkling burgundy. He didn't really like whiskey or beer; he wanted his drinking to be fancy and ceremonial, the way it would someday be when he was important, suave, consorting with the influential of the earth. So he'd bought a case of sparkling burgundy, a thirty-five-pound block of ice, a washtub, a set of six champagne glasses with hollow stems, a box of fancy unsalted crackers, and several jars of salmon and whitefish caviar. Knuck Gillis busily chipped the ice with the bayonet from his souvenir Arisaka rifle. Before they thought to lock the door against thirsty visitors, Hilary David Edward St. George ambled amiably in, so they invited him to stay.

"Oh, I say!" Hilary said. "My! You fellows are preparing to have a bash, what?"

Hilary had come over to give Allard a set of photographs of Mary. He often followed the two of them around, snapping pictures, preferably of Mary alone. At the Student Union or downtown they'd see him, waiting for them, following them, or sitting across a room mooning at Mary. It made her genuinely upset and sad to see this, but it didn't bother Allard. If bloody Christopher Robin wanted to shadow them, it was no harm, which was strange because Allard didn't like to be followed at all. He was the hunter; if any stalking was to be done he would do it. So what it meant was that Hilary David

Edward St. George hadn't the force, or the presence, to irritate him that way. Yet Hilary was a legitimate hero, a former RAF flight sergeant who had flown "Hurries," as he called the Hawker Hurricane fighter. He'd shot down an Me 109e, a Henschel 127, and (he laughed deprecatingly about this) a Feiseler Storch. Allard had seen the documents and the gun camera series that confirmed these victories. It was true, all of it, and what a lark it had been for Hilary. A tall, gangly boy of twenty-seven, he looked fifteen, with his thick black hair standing up from his head like a busby, his cheerful, vacuous smile and constant chatter. His father was English, his mother from a somewhat Brahmin family in Boston. Hilary's accent was somewhere in between. He made model airplanes in his room, charmingly confessed that what he really enjoyed was to sit in his bath and squeeze little whiteheads from his scrotum, so he missed his mother's house in Boston where they had wizard great tubs. He had asked Mary to marry him and taken her down to meet his mother. ("Hilary's mother is awful—both meanings of the word," Mary had said afterwards. "And how could I marry someone I always want to pat on the head?") One of Hilary's stories was about a time he'd gone, just for a lark, as a gunner on a Lancaster flown by his friend, a four-engine type named Bunny Berkhamstead. Good old Bunny! On the way home over the Channel the bomb-bay doors were jammed open and the navigator, silly clot, forgot and stepped out. No parachute. They all got to giggling so hard Bunny almost lost his way back to Blighty. Funniest thing that ever happened. "Oh, that clot, that silly, silly *clot!* They were all laughing so hard Bunny could hardly bring the aircraft down, nearly forgot to lower his undercart!"

Allard was fascinated by all this. Christopher Robin at ten thousand feet in his Hurricane, being shot at by real guns, with real bullets. He couldn't get over it. He'd think, My God, was the war fought by children? Hilary was like one of his own double exposures: Allard could accept the official certification of Hilary's combat, and he could accept charming, candid, living Hilary, but how to believe the two together?

Hilary spread the photographs out on Allard's desk. "See this one. It's got part of your motorbike in it, there on the left, but *tant mieux* it's a lovely shot of Mary. Lovely! And here's a smashing close-up of the two of you looking at each other. No, *you're* looking at something over the top of her head. I wonder what? It's simply impossible, Benson, to snap a poor picture of Mary. I thought you'd like to have them!"

Allard thanked him, wonderingly. He also thought, but didn't say, Hilary, old chap, I have *Mary;* what do I need a flock of photographs *for?*

"Hey, you bloody lime-juicer!" Knuck Gillis said. "Pass the mucking bubbly!" Knuck drank, his big pinky carefully cocked. "Pip pip, cheers and a jolly good show, what?"

"Absolutely! First-rate!" Hilary said.

In Knuck's eyes the last pale shade of blue seemed about to fade away. He was all pale—his hair, his skin, his fingernails. Bloodless force. Nathan once wondered aloud if there could be such a thing as a partial albino. "I'm a white man," Knuck informed him.

Knuck had other strangenesses. Nathan and Allard studied him. He made little nests of soiled clothes on his desk and on his bed. His face would go dim, go away somewhere while his hands arranged the circular piles of cloth. His face assumed the faraway, instinctive, compelled expression of a beagle who turns around several times before lying down, even though the ancient grass has been a thousand generations gone. The big hands patted, changed, rearranged a jockstrap, a sock, a T-shirt, a pair of shorts until something deep inside said, Yes, that's the proper order, now it's all right.

While Allard and Nathan studied him, Knuck was amazed that he lived among these strange new friends. He was a member of Kappa Sigma, a fraternity even more jock, then, than most, but he chose to live in a dormitory and have for friends a small Jew, a bewigged, flitty (probably) mackerel-snapper, and an intellectual-type English lit. major. He couldn't get over it, because he knew who he was, and what he was just didn't go with such types. The School of Hard

Knocks was his college; he was a phys. ed. major. He couldn't get over it. It was miraculous; it added another dimension to his life. "I *like* this little Jew here, for Christ's sake! I even like that skinny pansy with the hair piece!"

"I don't think Harold's queer," Nathan said.

"Pass the bubbly. Maybe not, but he surely does walk like a man with a paper ass."

"He's afraid his hair'll fall off," Allard said.

"I'd never noticed it until Mary told me," Hilary said. "Pass the beluga, old chap. That's a good fellow!"

Nathan laughed his reverberating oogah. Other octaves, changes, tonal depths issued from his voice box. He seemed too frail an instrument to contain his sounds—a ukelele producing the deep tones of a cello. Later, as he vomited away his infatuation with sparkling burgundy, they would hear his voiced throes resonate throughout the whole floor, as though a Wurlitzer had been installed in the latrine.

Meanwhile they were all getting drunk, Knuck more than the rest. He had a liver ailment contracted by drinking what he called "Jesus purple" in the Marines. He hadn't known the difference between ethyl and methyl alcohol, and while on a hospital ship had nearly died of this error. He said he had the liver of a sixty-year-old lush and he could get drunk just by smelling his shaving lotion. Now, as he proceeded to drink the sparkling burgundy, an ominous theme began to be apparent in the few remarks he made between brooding silences. He plucked at a nest of laundry on his bed; his eyes had turned a sanguine pink around their wash of arctic blue.

"Ruinin' his life," he muttered. "Makes him walk like a goddamn Powers model. No wonder the poor bastard can't get him a broad."

"I think he even takes showers with the thing on," Nathan said. "He's probably got weevils under it." Then his strange laugh.

"What's a friend for, by God?" Knuck asked himself. "I don't know why, but I *like* that poor, pansyfied little bastard. Oughta do it, by God."

"Do what?" Allard asked, his receptor of danger not quite dulled by the wine.

"Snatch that poor fuck bald, that's what," Knuck said. "Get rid of it."

None of the rest of them was drunk enough not to be disturbed by the violence of this solution.

"A toast!" Nathan cried. "Gentlemen, to the future!"

"Snatch that goddam piece of mattress stuffing right off his fuckin' head, flush it down the toilet."

"I say," Hilary said. "Pretty drastic, don't you know? No end of psychological ramifications, eh?"

"You bet your sweet limey *ass* it's drastic!" Knuck said, getting up from his bed.

"Now, Knuck," Nathan said. "Let's think this over, huh?"

Knuck pretended to confront Harold at the door of Harold's room. With his left hand he grasped an imaginary thin neck. With his right hand he slowly, carefully unscrewed the top of an imaginary jar. The top removed, he carried it to the wastebasket and at arm's length let it fall.

"Now I'm going!" he shouted and ran for the door. Little Nathan Weinstein tackled him, fortunately just as Knuck's drunken balance was off-center. He actually went down and slid into the doorframe with percussive, crunching jock noises. "Hup! Hup!" he said. Nathan held one of Knuck's legs with his whole body, like a frog in amplexus, knowing that one of Knuck's big legs was about as much of that halfback he could even attempt to immobilize.

"Help! Help! Allard!" Nathan screamed.

Allard jumped on the struggling bodies. Knuck kept saying, "Jesus, what's *on* me. Jesus, what's *on* me." Allard tried to get a full nelson on Knuck but it was like getting a full nelson on an oak tree. His arms couldn't make Knuck's arms move. He and Nathan could change the direction of Knuck's slow contractions, but they couldn't stop them. Knuck would begin to get a knee under him, or an arm, and at just the right moment they could manage to collapse him to the floor, whereupon the great slow heaves began again. "Jesus, what's *on* me," Knuck kept saying. Allard and Nathan were beyond speech—with them it was all desperate breathing and a few small cries. Knuck's giant muscles couldn't quite break him loose. This slow struggle went on too long for Nathan, who crawled away and vomited first in the wastebasket on the imaginary toupee and then on the way to and in the latrine. Hilary came back to say that Harold wasn't in his room anyway. And then Allard remembered that they all knew Harold wasn't there. If he had been, of course Nathan would have invited him to the party. So Knuck had known all the time, too. Allard lay gasping on his bed while Hilary observed these savages and Knuck continued to drink the wine. Nathan's brash, wracking throes could be heard down the hall—strangled coughing amid bronze gongs.

"Jesus," Knuck said. "Is that poor little Nate?"

"Nathan is tossing his cookies," Allard said.

"He better hope nothing green comes out," Knuck said. "There ain't a long-handled spoon in the house."

After a while Nathan came back into the room, talc-white, staggering weakly. "My God! Help me! I'm *hemorrhaging!*"

"You're a goner, Nate," Knuck said. "I can tell. Seen it too many times." But it was only the burgundy, of course. Knuck drank a whole glass of it in one draught, which sent Nathan groping back to the latrine, moaning in despair. They kept an eye on him, though, and when he was empty of all but colorless strings of bile they carried him back to his bed, where the dry heaves shook and bounced him. They all decided they had never heard more mournful sounds.

"Was it him that tackled me? That little banty rooster?" Knuck said admiringly. "How d'you like that balsy little fuck? God *damn!*"

"You knew Harold wasn't in his room," Allard said.

"Heh heh."

"Sheer madness," Hilary said. "Sheer lunacy."

Knuck counted the remaining bottles of burgundy. "I got

an idea where a body could buy six bottles of this rotgut dirt-cheap," he said, looking over at poor Nathan.

Nathan moaned and something inside him went off like a released bowstring. They could almost hear the twang. "Oh, *God!*" he said.

"The head looks like a goddam massacree. So don't the hall," Knuck observed. "I guess none of us make it any easier for Harold. Specially those salmon eggs all over the place."

But later on, after Hilary had gone, Harold knocked softly on the door. When it opened he slipped furtively into the room and shut the door himself. He wore a trench coat with elaborate shoulder loops, rain flaps and Sam Browne belt accessories. "They've gone to supper," he said. "Will you help me get out of here? Allard? Nathan? Knuck?" He was so upset he could hardly whisper.

Nathan came to life a little bit. "Whaa?" he said.

"I'm leaving. I can't stand it any more and I'm leaving." Harold's eyes were full of tears, brimming with small ridges that sloshed and spilled as he moved his head. "I'm at the end of my rope," he said. "I'm sorry!"

Then they were all full of concern. Nathan was too weak to help much, so he kept watch. They weren't exactly certain whether Harold wanted to evade Boom Maloumian, the housemother, the police, or what, but in their assumption of this common concern for Harold they would go along with whatever fears he thought he had. Soon they'd loaded Nathan's 1941 Ford with everything but Harold's chintz reading chair, which they put in a far corner of the downstairs lounge to be retrieved later. Nathan considered Knuck and Allard far too drunk to drive, and himself too sick, so Harold drove. Allard and Knuck sat in the back seat with Harold's rolled rug across their knees, boxes between them and under their feet. They drove north, out of town altogether. As they hissed pleasantly along through the rain, Allard and Knuck passed a bottle of sparkling burgundy back and forth over a box of Harold's precious books. It was cozy in the car, smooth and nice to travel through the rainy day with the trees in their fresh new leaves passing like green globes in the mist. He was a separate warm life, unique, independent of all this, yet moving along.

Nathan had slumped down out of sight, and Knuck was elsewhere, only appearing to be present when the bottle was offered, the big white hand gently taking it and carefully giving it back.

"Hey, Harold?" Allard said, not really caring. "Where we going, to Berlin?" He calculated that trip to be over a hundred miles, but he didn't care. The bottle, however, was getting low and he was nearly out of cigarettes.

"No," Harold said. "We'll be there any minute."

That was too fast, too quick. He liked it in the moving car, seeing the trees go by so smoothly, the wine smoothing out everything. To move and not care was what he liked.

They were about to arrive at Lilliputown Motor Inn, owned by friends of Oncle Hébert and Tante Louise. It had been arranged that Harold would live there and help take care of the place—the model town with its church, saloon, barbershop, library, jail, etc., which was more of a compulsion on the part of its owners than a commercial proposition. While one could rent, for instance, "The Little Brown Church in the Vale" and within its sanctified walls fornicate, one must not presume to be part of the real population of Lilliputown, because the real population of Lilliputown was imaginary. Its people walked its fictional streets to church on Sunday mornings, went about their lives within a rapt fog of creation.

On that first visit to Lilliputown all Allard saw was the Railroad Station and the Town Hall. They didn't stay longer because all the while they were taking Harold's possessions over to the station platform, where they would be out of the rain, poor Nathan lay across the front seat of his car uttering sharp sounds like the breaking of sticks. The owners of Lilliputown were in Boston for the day, Harold said.

The Town Hall was a Doric-columned edifice of some grandeur, even when a giant human figure passed before it and reduced its scale. The columns across the front of the building were only a little taller than a man, and the main doorway seemed in all its paneled elegance about two feet square until, as Allard later found, its real dimensions turned out to be much larger, containing first- and second-story windows and expanses of wall. He saw at once that Lilliputown was no mere gimmick to lure tourists who liked that sort of cuteness, but a labor of real craft and care. Across from the Town Hall was the Railroad Station, the only other building visible from the parking area. From this marvel of nineteenth-century architectural mixes a single narrow-gauge railroad track led through a wall of Lombardy poplars into the rest of Lilliputown. The station itself was painted dark red—cupolas, Gothic and Romanesque arches, spreading eaves over an asphalted platform containing an iron bench, a metal-wheeled baggage cart of varnished wood, a mailbox, a miniature circus poster in its frame against the station wall. As though it had been especially airbrushed on, over everything not recently polished was a real railroad station's patina of coal dust, along with the familiar sooty, peppery odor. The platform gritted slightly under Allard's shoes, reminding him of all the days and miles trains had taken him. Switches, signals, polished steel rails—there had to be a train, too, somewhere, with a black engine leaking steam along its flanks where the bright steel of its pistons and rods slowly flashed and plunged. Along the deserted tracks' crushed cinders and spiked crossties was the expectation of that energy.

Yet everything was small. He felt like a giant, a freak; the details here had that power. Even the grass along the roadbed seemed to be narrow in its blades, and short, as if it too had come under the influence of Lilliput. He stood for a moment trying to blink away the mirage of scale, then walked back to the giant automobile and his huge friends.

Nathan's agony made them hurry. They decided to take him back to the university and deposit him at Brock House, the infirmary, where Knuck claimed they'd have something to calm his forlorn and desperate nausea.

As they left, Allard looked back at the Railroad Station,

its gilt-lettered signs on the station eaves saying LILLIPUTOWN with such believable authority. The two buildings, so complete in their setting before the living green wall of the Lombardy poplars, seemed to recede in finer focus than the surrounding landscape, as though he watched them through a fine lens. When they were out of sight he leaned forward toward Harold's neat, upright head, its sober verticality so different from Nathan's and Knuck's that he and Harold seemed alone in the car.

"Is the rest of the place like that?" he said.

"Maybe even more so. It's a very strange place."

"Who'd make such a thing?"

"Colonel Immingham. He's quite a person, Allard. I've told him about you and he wants to meet you."

"Why me?" Allard said quickly, surprised by his defensive response. "I mean, what the hell would you tell him about me?"

"I don't know. We just got to talking about the university and who I knew there, and from what I said about you he thought you might be interesting, that's all."

Just for a second Allard had the feeling of dread, of being hurried, manipulated. Harold's opinion of him did not seem based upon valid evidence.

Aaron sits at his desk remembering, changing what he remembers, picking and choosing. But nothing stays, nothing is written. Here he is, at the place where he was once able to do his work. He can remember when his hours here, at this desk, were the most vivid of his life, when all that generous energy was there.

But how intolerant we are of people who won't do what we are certain they could do if they only *tried.* Hasn't he told George Buck that he must finish his dissertation? It seems such a mechanical task, as easy as adding a downstairs bathroom. And the fatal thing, the hellish thing about all this is that he is right. He is absolutely right and therefore can't sympathize with George at all. But he does recognize George's immobility. He recognizes it in himself, right now. Lately, whenever he is asked for advice, especially when he is in fact *paid* to give advice, he has wanted to avert his face and mumble, "I don't know."

"I don't know," he says, trying it out. It's so relaxing. But there should be a certain uncaring lilt to the phrase that he can't quite manage to get into it. He can't quite get it right, so he should get himself together and simply tell George to do his work or get out, and tell Mark Rasmussen that his despair is the hurt ego of a self-indulgent little boy, that the system of our planet is rape and murder, not love and reason, that he is a fool weeping for Eden.

Aaron belches and his own brimstone fumes from his body, from his mouth and nose. He doesn't believe anything, not a word about anything. Can't remember what he thinks from one moment to the next. The only thing that might be true is paradox and he is sick to death of all these dramatic simplifications, these sanctimonious fictions. Everyone's. Nothing can stop a lie whose fashion has come, so why bother to try?

Upstairs in a small room is a functioning television set. He knows that in five minutes a baseball game between the Boston Red Sox and the New York Yankees will begin. He is not much of a follower of the game, but he played it all through his youth and knows its rules, dangers, sweats and moments of frantic grace. There is no one to tell him he can't spend the rest of the afternoon watching that perfect drama, that classically framed and disciplined story, unfold again before his eyes. The rigid form of the game is its art. There is always an outcome, always a total end, and the characters suffer humiliation or triumph, each moment of action framed by anxious immobility. This folk-created simplification is bound as if by steel within its rules, and its rules are known.

But Aaron Benham is not created to observe. It is his body and mind he must manipulate against the movement of time. He must make and dominate. If he listens and observes he is, at best, biding and using. If he is in action he is alive.

NOTES ON MARY TOLLIVER

is written on the page before him.

She has a funny smile. Not totally wide perfectly adjusted Pepsodent American Girl. No, a trace of self-mockery there, a small wry bit of self-consciousness. After all, she is New England, and also of the Irish-haunted Catholic Church, the foe of the flesh.

Her green eye-fleck catches the light, so you look at its jade glitter, specifically at it, and the rest of her fades yet grows—the impression of wide, present warmth. Then look carefully at her face. The muscles of her jaw constrict her lips, so that they are precise, almost as if carved, convexly firm, yet the effect when they move is one of generosity, as though her sweetness triumphs over her face's tension.

Her feet smell cleanly of walking, of shoes, of the faint and touching human vinegar of foot.

Her legs are slim, her knees as small as is, probably, functionally possible, yet when she (somewhat awkwardly) swings at a tennis ball a line of delineation appears in the muscle of her upper leg, running from hip to knee—a reminder of animal necessity. Power there.

Her calves delicately surround bone, saying inside is ivory, or gleaming pearl.

She is pampered by soaps and lotions which, combined with the faintest acridity of life, constitute her perfume.

So long ago.

His study closes in upon him. He remembers with a chill how he was once free to go wherever he wanted, whenever he wanted. He cannot leave right now and go to Paris. He cannot leave his possessions and those who possess him. But he could. Anxious despair flows through his lower body, seeming to dissolve his hips. He sees himself somehow crawling out to his motorcycle, trying to start it, his children crying, fading away from him.

*   *   *

Allard awoke that Friday morning before his visit to Mary's home with a quickly identified dread. He had met fathers before and those times had always been haunted by a tense semi-dishonesty in which he'd let his Jack Armstrongish clean-cut look of youth do most of the lying for him. Fathers always gave him a sort of mental blood test which he always passed—with reservations. There had been the hearty fathers with a detective glint in the oblique glance, the upstaging fathers who implied that real men weren't minted any more, the chummy fathers who implied that all women, including their daughters, were inferior (though precious), and so on. From what Mary had told him, she and her father were very close, which of course intensified his dread. As a free agent, why had he gotten himself into such a boringly anxious situation?

He had two classes that morning. The first was in psychology, which mainly concerned, because of the instructor's specialty and Allard's bad luck, the testing of the efficiency of industrial workers. This he sat through in a semi-torpor intruded upon occasionally by apprehension. The second was English, and concerned the much crisper minds of the eighteenth century:

> *Eve's tempter thus the rabbins have expressed,*
> *A cherub's face, a reptile all the rest;*
> *Beauty that shocks you, parts that none will trust,*
> *Wit that can creep, and pride that licks the dust.*

None would trust except Eve, that is. Or perhaps trust wasn't the right emotion at all.

Mary had a ride home that morning with a girl in her dormitory, and he would leave on his motorcycle that afternoon in time to get there for dinner, which Mary would prepare. To show how good a homemaker she was? He shivered with something like pity. He couldn't tolerate certain rituals, even those of his own class. Or especially those of his own class. Here was Mary, acting the part of the little mother to her family. Sad and embarrassing that she must peel potatoes and bake a chicken or whatever. Sad that she wanted to please by her domestic skills, and even sadder that she wanted her brother and father to like her boyfriend, her near-*fiancé* (that word offended especially), Allard Benson. Wit that can creep, and pride that licks the dust. As he left the class building he shivered in the cool spring air.

He met Nathan and his girl at the Student Union. Nathan's girl, Angela Fitzgibbon, at twenty was a handsome giantess with the natural presence of a duchess. Tall, broad and stately, she represented to Nathan all of the high-class values he admired. With her healthy skin, solid, confident haunches, husky shoulders and patrician jaw, she moved upon the earth as if she owned it. She was really a nice girl who had been born to gleam expensively, no doubt to be the consort of a rich and handsome giant. "Thighs like a wild mare," Nathan said admiringly (Nathan had just read *Darkness at Noon*). Allard had a vision of Nathan submerging into all that golden flesh like a wiry ferret. Angela outweighed Nathan by at least thirty pounds, but they were thirty pounds of solid value. She watched Nathan with fascinated admiration as he strutted and vibrated around her. Knuck Gillis admired Nathan's presumption, too. "Nate," he'd said, "you got to have balls as big as grapefruit."

Allard came up to their table with his coffee and Angela moved her coat to another chair so he could sit down.

"So today you're going to meet the family," Nathan said.

"Don't rub it in."

"Just be sure to use the right fork for the soup," Nathan said.

Allard said to Angela, "Have you exhibited Nathan to your family?"

"My fatha," Angela said in her high-class accent, "would take one *look* at Nathan and gew tewtally ewt of his mind."

"We're trying to think of ways to prepare them for the shock," Nathan said.

"For instance," Angela said, "we thought of hinting to them that I'm having a liaison with a Negro. After that they might even be *relieved* to settle for Nathan. Actually, once poor fatha got over Nathan's ratha classical Semitic characteristics and diminutive stature, I know they'd hit it off quate well."

"But he's a *big* bastard, Angela tells me," Nathan said. "He could eat me up in one bite. I mean, at least, Allard, you look like one of Mary's kind, even if you're not a Catholic."

"Fatha, I'm afraid, has always been ratha specific about tall men, preferably Scots."

"You could get Nathan kilts and some elevator shoes."

"Yeah," Nathan said, "the Weinstein plaid and ten-inch heels." He uttered a discouraged groan.

"When I was a *very* little gull," Angela said, "I had a little dog I deahly loved, a whippet. I've often wondered if deah little Samson hadn't something to do with my preference for vibrant, ambitious, possessive little men like Nathan."

"You don't have to be quite that brutally frank, Angela!" Nathan said, laughing his strange laugh.

Allard left those well-matched lovers at eleven in order to meet Harold Roux, who had to buy a secondhand car and needed advice. Harold had in mind a 1936 DeSoto for sale by a speech instructor, who wanted $300 for it.

"I thought I could hitchhike back and forth," Harold said, "but I don't think I have the temperament for it. I put out my thumb and most people just look right through me. It's awfully embarrassing for both of us."

So Harold had to cash in some of the war bonds he'd saved in the army. They stood in front of the library waiting for the speech instructor's class to get out. Allard, out of nervousness, he supposed, told Harold he was going to spend the weekend at Mary's home in Concord.

"Her father's been very ill, you know, Allard."

The implied warning—all such wearisome moral warnings—was irritating. "Evidently Mary thinks he can stand the shock."

"I wonder if Mary is thinking lately at all."

"Oh, for Christ's sake. Are you my spiritual adviser or something?"

"Maybe I should be."

"Well, go ahead. Advise, advise."

"For a start, don't say 'For Christ's sake' in front of Mr. Tolliver."

"Cross yourself, Harold. You just blasphemed."

"I wouldn't think it was funny if I did."

"Come on, now. Aren't you losing your faith, little by little? Consorting with all these godless intellectuals around here?"

"I find I need it more and more."

Allard leaned back against a sun-warmed fence of decorative ironwork. Harold, beside him, never quite leaned. A girl passed, a plain girl in saddle shoes, bobbysocks and a long tweed skirt. Her pink cashmere cardigan, part of the uniform, accentuated the nervous ungivingness of her face. Soft pink against the heavy strain of defense. She refused to catch Allard's eye, but as she walked on by, hugging her books, her whole body became so tensely centripetal she seemed to have difficulty walking in a straight line.

"An act of aggression," Harold said.

"What? For Christ's sake (pardon me), Harold, all I did was look at the girl. I wasn't going to goose her or anything."

"She knew what you were thinking."

"What I was thinking? I can't remember what I was thinking. This is unbelievable!"

And yet, in spite of his exasperation, he found pleasure in the intensity of Harold's disapproving regard. He hadn't told Harold that he was thinking of marrying Mary. The omission seemed logical and sadly ominous. This frail authority, this moral force who wore something like a crown of thorns—invisible thorns.

Finally the flattish bell in the Ad Building tower struck once, for eleven-thirty, a sound that might have been made by a tire iron on a wheel rim. Shortly after that, threading his way through the students, against the current, came the speech instructor. "Foreman, Geoffrey," he said, putting a large, firm hand into Allard's. He was an ordinary-sized man with large appendages, including a large square head made even more rectilinear by a squared off bow tie and a shaped black crew cut.

"Allard Benson," Allard said.

"Good to meet you, Mr. Allard!" The voice was also large, basso, reverberant, a developed voice handled with obvious pleasure. Harold was about to correct Foreman, Geoffrey, but Allard caught his eye and shook his head slightly. Harold frowned, but accepted.

"I am reminded of the poem 'O what is so rare as a day in Spring!' " Foreman, Geoffrey, said, slowly raising both arms in tribute to the sun, his face sternly, yet inspirationally, immobile. "But of course you want to see Matilda." The voice admitted business, virile business, into the poetic day. He laughed, the sounds of his laughter cradled, shaped, almost caressed by the wonderful instrument in the throat. "I call my car 'Matilda'!"

"Waltzing Matilda?" Allard asked, and received a totally blank look. Nothing. The instructor's systems had all turned off. But then the machine began humming, gathering strength until it could again define the moment.

"If you two men would be so good as to accompany me, I will take you to Matilda, whereupon you may effect the closest of inspections!" His laugh fascinated Allard; it reminded him, in spite of its ludicrously formal booms and transitional runs, of the memory of fear. Something from childhood—a radio program like *Inner Sanctum*, or *The Shadow*. Was a deliberate laugh a laugh at all? Nathan Weinstein had a very peculiar laugh, but was certainly unaware of it. If one even *heard* one's own laugh, was that laughter real? He couldn't think what his own laughter sounded like. In fact the very idea of laughter seemed so ridiculous he could easily believe that the human race never laughed at all. To make garbled, coughing, stuttering sounds just because you were amused was unbelievable. Crying, however, that other unmorphemed noise, seemed perfectly memorable in its sounds and logical in its purposes.

They reached the parking lot and Matilda, who though fairly unrusted about the scuppers was a little dowdy and scruffy in her old age. She seemed, without having been in an obvious wreck, to have lost her symmetry. Her old eyes were somewhat rheumy and unfocused. Allard, posing as the expert consultant, inspected her surfaces and peered into her orifices. Finally, in his gynecological, or perhaps urological, guise, he looked up her exhaust pipe. By the color, she used a little oil. Her odometer admitted to sixty thousand miles, but her engine ticked along in an easy, tappety yet contented way that indicated she would continue to run for a while. Harold drove Matilda up the highway for a mile or so, then back to the parking lot; Matilda was not overheated by the exercise. She even had a radio that worked, and her spare tire, Allard had noted, was nearly new.

"A little long in the tooth but a nice old soul," Allard said. "Why do you want to sell her?"

"Indeed, I hate to have to sell Matilda, but I am going to Europe directly following commencement, you see, and to keep Matilda would necessitate the procurement of storage facilities."

"That sounds reasonable." Allard looked over at Harold, who waited trustingly for his verdict. "I'd say she's worth all of two hundred," he said.

"Ah. It was three hundred," said Foreman, Geoffrey, from the back seat.

"She burns oil," Allard said sternly.

"A minuscule consumption of oil," Foreman, Geoffrey, said defensively. "Specifically, one quart of No. 30, SAE, per thousand miles. But shall we say, in order to effect an amicable compromise, two seventy-five?"

Matilda cooled creakily.

"Harold," Allard said. "Harold . . ." He laughed, noting the strange, breathless sound, also noting that he was devoid of anxiousness in this affair. Usually he could not bargain because he could not imply that a stranger was not telling the whole truth. But it must be easier to imply mendaciousness, avarice, or whatever it was, to someone whose very instrument of communication had been self-dehumanized. And then there was Harold's head of lush, false hair. Matilda, surrounding these actors with her worn plush, was the most honest party to the transaction.

Gravely they got out of Matilda in order to view her again from the outside. They examined her thoughtfully.

"Harold, I'd find it against my conscience to recommend that you pay more than two twenty-five for this friendly but spavined old creature." He patted Matilda on her hinged bonnet.

Foreman, Geoffrey, was again stopped, disarmed, as if he sensed Allard's powerful distance from involvement. Helpless for those moments without his voice, he looked pitifully inert, like a cutout silhouette. Then, with a shrug that was uncalculated, he accepted the implied final price of two fifty.

Harold's voice failed as he agreed. He looked fearfully at Matilda, obviously shaken at the prospect of owning all of her. But, bravely, he would join his fate with hers; he and Foreman, Geoffrey, went off to find a notary public.

Allard, feeling somewhat soiled by the ways of the world and at the same time shamefully proud of himself, proceeded to the student parking lot where he'd left his motorcycle.

Naomi was sitting on it, sidesaddle, reading a book. Her long black hair shaded her face from the sun but spread apart when she looked up at him, as though her face came out from dark curtains. She was good news to him, fresh air compared to the nervous inevitable business of visiting Mary's home.

"Have you had lunch?" she said. She was all dressed up, for her, in a dark green skirt of shiny material and a white peasant blouse with puffed sleeves. Though her arms were dark and smooth against the starched white, legitimately old-worldish and peasantlike, she looked very young in the outfit.

"What's the occasion?" he asked, indicating her clothes.

"I have to appear before the dormitory disciplinary firing squad this afternoon, which means I have to wear the enemy's uniform. Bunch of starved little cunts."

"Oh-oh."

"Lest I get evicted and lose my room rent, which the filthy fascists made my parents pay against my will in the first place."

"Oh my, Naomi! What did you do?"

"I stayed out too late a couple of times. Past the devirginizing hour, evidently. I also walked down the third-floor hall to the showers stark-naked, not to mention back to the room. I called the housemother a sneaky fink bitch, to a sneaky fink bitch. There is also the pretty rumor that I'm a lesbian. And I *am* a communist. I suppose it could be worse. Nobody's accused me of being an arsonist or a kleptomaniac—yet."

Though Allard laughed, Naomi wouldn't even smile. She swung her long leg over the motorcycle and tucked her skirt beneath her so it wouldn't catch in the spokes, waited while he put their books in the saddlebags and then straightened her leg so he could kick down the starter. The machine seemed hers, or theirs; it had taken them off to so many comradely hours—comradely after their immediate forces diffused within each other. She held him lightly, her hands on his ribs.

"You would laugh," she said. "You're so disgustingly apolitical."

He swung the machine away and they curved, leaning, out of the parking lot to the street, then went down the long hill to the business area, not trying to speak over the wind and the engine. With the engine stopped again he said, "But everything isn't political."

"It depends on how you look at it. How aware you are. I can't understand how you can accept, even *laugh*, at a system that's so viciously exploitive."

"One that doesn't want you to walk down the halls naked?"

"That's part of it. That really is part of it. It's sick, rotten to the core. I mean there really *are* those poor bitches who've been driven out of their fragile little minds by what they've been told, and they do go hysterical when they see me naked. Can you imagine how sick they are? And I'm supposed to be the lesbian. Jesus Christ!"

"Well, maybe deep down inside you are a great wild bull dyke, Naomi." He laughed, and to irritate her still more took her hand to help her off the motorcycle.

"I think *you're* hysterical," she said, pulling her hand away. "I don't know why I spend any time at all with you. You're not serious." They went into the varnished wooden interior of the Coffee Shop, found an empty booth and sat down, their elbows careful among the damp plates, cups, spills and ashes of its previous occupants. Allard took the side of the booth where he could see an always amazing wall panel of marquetry, its wood veneers depicting in warm tones a castle, clouds and mountains in Bavaria, probably—Schloss Wittgenstein or something. The grains of the various woods so precisely gave clouds, meadows and forested hills their reality. The truest precision here was random, accidental. When he looked closely at those lines made by the jigsaw they were not good at all; the perspectives were crude, the human choices bad. But he felt almost inside that wooden world, feeling its heights and depths in his centers of balance.

"I've been asked why I spend so much time with you," Naomi said. "It's been discussed."

He knew why she did. It was the simplest thing in the world—they loved each other. When they looked at each other strange things happened in their middles. It was simple. Only he was going to marry Mary. But that didn't sound exactly right because then he couldn't make love to Naomi when he wanted to and she wanted to. Perhaps he was insane. Polygamy was the obvious answer but that was somewhat illegal, which was bothersome. It was all bothersome and took time away from his work, so-called. Maybe the only thing he was truly good at was making women want him around. The term for that occupation was gigolo.

"Is love political?" he said.

"Love, phooey," she said. "If you want love get on your motorcycle and go see Mary. She's sick with it."

"Well, there're different kinds of love, aren't there?"

Naomi waited while the student waitress cleared off the dirty dishes. Then she said, "Love is a euphemism, in our case, for sexual gratification."

"I'll bet it isn't."

"You make me sick!" She seemed quite angry, and her real anger made him apprehensive, as though something real might be in danger.

In spite of his apprehension he couldn't stop. "Is anger political?" he asked.

"Phooey!"

"Is phooey political?"

"Herbert's right! You're worthless! You're a waste of time!" She got up, tall, neat and furious. People were looking at them. Her eyes glittered. He appreciated her lean waist, the firm dark muscles of her neck. She had a little red pimple on her temple, with another, embryonic one below it. Lustrous black hair grew out of her head. She was alive, this functioning organism. What force and presence she had! She. That word wasn't powerful enough for Naomi. From her skin came invisible moisture, scent, living gross precious effluvia. This complex, feeling animal was part of the atmosphere he breathed. She left. Of course he was worthless. Insane, insane.

He ran out and caught up with her down the street just as she was about to go up the stairs to Herbert Smythe's apartment. He grabbed her from behind and held her in a bear hug so hard she couldn't struggle loose. People stopped to watch.

"Are you alive?" he said into her black hair.

She wouldn't answer so he turned her around and picked her up in an undignified fashion, his arm through her crotch, and carried her upstairs. "I'm real," he said in the dentist's-office-smelling upstairs hallway. He kicked Herbert's door open and carried her inside. Herbert and several of his troops, including the deprived boy in GI spectacles, and Ilse Haendler, looked up from pamphlets, a purple-ink-spattered mimeograph machine, chairs, tables, coffee cups, earnestness palpable as putty. Overflowing wastebaskets. Naomi was hitting him on the head with her fists, which was mildly confusing, but he had something he wanted to say. He held her tightly in the same undignified but secure, right-feeling way, his right arm between her legs, his hand firmly spread across her spine.

"I have brought Naomi," he began. The deprived boy in GI spectacles attacked him, but he paid no obvious (he thought) attention, merely turning so that Naomi's back protected him from the deprived boy's sharp little knuckles.

"I have brought Naomi in order to recover Naomi's brain. I will not leave until you return Naomi's brain! Do you hear? I will pull off your heads, one by one, as I have done to rabbits, until Naomi's brain is returned!"

"You son of a bitch! Put me down!"

"Ladies and gentlemen! Distinguished guests! *Kameraden!*" He wanted to tell them that, no, really, he was a man of peace, that he wanted to be reasonable, but then he had to kick the deprived boy in the shin just to keep him quiet so he could speak, and they were all overly impressed by this act of mere self-protection. The deprived boy fell down, moaning and holding his shin. Allard knew, finally, that their disapproval, reinforced as it was by every belief they held, precluded any communication at all. Herbert Smythe stared at him, disgusted and horrified.

"Herbert, it has been discussed in FBI circles why I spend so much time with Naomi. There are those who think it bad for my character, that it might jeopardize or soften my ideological discipline. Well, fuck them, Herbert, I say! I'm going to take Naomi away. Naomi is mine; I am Naomi's. You can have her brain. Keep it. She can grow another one. Goodbye!" He turned as if to leave.

"No! No! Don't take her!" Herbert shouted.

"Put me down, you bastard! You *shit!*"

Suddenly it was all real. He had no right to treat them

this way. He was brutal, he was a brutal shit, so he put Naomi on her feet—gently, he thought—and left. He skipped and slid down over the stairs as if he were skiing. The incident, left behind but with him, was so profoundly boring and shameful he decided not to think about it. He started the Indian Pony and rode recklessly around the little square, his footrest scraping and sparking on the pavement, then back to the dormitory, where he slewed around to a stop like a Harley-Davidson show-off.

He went into the dormitory, pushing open the institutional door that never closed tightly, its brass hardware evidently a compromise between strength and precision so that its thousands of violent openings and closings would neither break it nor close it firmly. No one cared about the door or the dormitory, or much about anything here. It was temporary to all of them. Knuck Gillis was thinking of going back into the Marines. Nathan wanted to get his degree and get the hell out into the real world. Most of Allard's classes seemed to be for someone else in the classroom, as though he were a slightly bored visitor who could attend or not attend as he wished. He read so he could pass examinations, and maybe he got something out of the reading.

He ran down the long corridor, cubicles of rooms on each side, up the grimy stairs where a banister rail had been pulled loose from the wall and gray cement dust sifted from the bolt holes. He had two hours before he would leave for Concord. With a pang of pity and revulsion he saw Mary at home getting everything nice for him, dusting, polishing the silver. The little wife-to-be at her domestic arts, her soul humming with innocent happiness. B. Maloumian: What's the difference between a woman coming out of church and a woman getting out of the bathtub? A woman coming out of church has a soul full of hope. Also, if a mechanical pump sucks and sucks and never fails, what does the Swiss Navy do?

No one was in the room. On Knuck's bed was one of his atavistic nests of soiled clothes. Nathan's desk was neat, his bed made, his sharp suits and jackets hung neatly in his third of the open closet, his polished shoes lined up neatly beneath, toes out. Allard went to his own footlocker, a sturdy, joined wooden box made for him by a Japanese cabinetmaker, and opened its combination padlock. At the bottom of the box was a bottle of Suntory whiskey with only a few drinks out of it. "Medicine for the fiancé," he said, and took a drink of it. It reminded him of Japan. That smooth bite of the demon brought back temples and torii, the land's misty promises, most of which it kept. Also a girl named Yoshiko Nakamura to whom he'd lied because he was only a soldier overseas and therefore did not exist in terms of permanence. Ancient history. But did he exist even here in terms of permanence? By now he could have had Mary near or over the cliff of damnation if he'd really wanted to. Perhaps he was kind and didn't want to hurt her. But how do you not hurt women?

He put the bottle of Suntory back, next to the dark leather holster of his Nambu pistol, then covered them both up with the GI suntans he'd been issued shortly before his discharge. He locked the footlocker, locked away all that, and got undressed to take a shower.

Short Round appeared. Maybe the door had been left open a crack. Here was Paul Hickett in his army clothes—field jacket and OD wool pants bloused over well-dubbined combat boots. The day was balmy; warm waves of air came through the open windows, but Short Round lived dryly within his heroic clothes, the texture of his skin a moistureless wrinkled gray.

"Man!" Short Round said. "Did you hear what Boom and me got going?"

Allard was gathering up towel, soap and other necessities, including one of Nathan's razor blades. "No. What Boom and you got going?" Allard said. One shouldn't treat even Short Round this way, especially because Short Round would never notice it.

"Don't tell anybody if I tell you, okay?"

First, there was a car, a Buick. Short Round spoke conspiratorily, his excited voice lowered a little. This brand-new

Buick had less than three hundred miles on it. It seemed this old man bought it and a week later had a heart attack and died in it, in his garage. He lived alone and they didn't discover him for a month. By that time he was so rotten they had to spoon him out of the car, and the car stank so much inside nobody could get near it, so there it was, brand-new, and they only wanted $150 for it. Short Round had put up $50, Boom had put up $50, and they needed one more shareholder. Boom's plan was to strip the whole inside of the car and fumigate everything, even if it took weeks, then put everything back—probably have to buy a new front seat—and they'd be in business.

"Have you seen the car?"

"No, it's down in Connecticut."

"Has Boom seen it?"

"Sure!"

Short Round could kiss his $50 goodbye, Allard decided, but at the same time decided not to tell him.

Short Round followed him to the showers. "Man, we can sell that Buick for two thousand bucks! What a deal! We'll make around six hundred apiece!"

"Why doesn't Boom buy the car all by himself?" Allard took his shower, Short Round hopping around the periphery of spray but not answering. This question evidently didn't interest him. Water gushed around Allard's ears for a while so he couldn't hear anything else. When he shut it off Short Round was still talking. "Six hundred bucks! And then we got this deal where we can buy war-surplus jeeps for one fifty apiece. Made by Ford, GM, hardly used. Some still in the cosmoline . . ."

He continued to speak of these great opportunities as Allard dried himself before the mirror over one of the wash basins. There he was, himself outside of himself, muscular and flesh-colored, an image that wasn't himself. And look at that face. Undistinguished but fashionably Anglo-Saxon, the face was flexible; people were always startled by the strange, violent expressions, or masks, it could instantly warp itself into. And yet it didn't smile easily. Behind his mirror image was one of Paul Hickett, who wanted to give the visual impression of a veteran-hero, or maybe now a hero of deals, profits, the man who was In. Paul had once tried to lure him into a strange sort of mutual lie about combat, and he wondered how naïve Paul was about new Buicks and surplus jeeps. Maybe this was the same kind of thing, but he thought not. No, this was belief.

Allard shaved his light beard, something he could never do without remembering what Nathan had said—that Nathan himself had a tough beard and tender skin, while Allard had a tender beard and tough skin. A tag of insistent memory he would never lose. Short Round didn't seem to have beard or skin. His skin looked like parchment, young but ancient, like the skin on a pickled human embryo. Still talking of his deals, Short Round followed him back to his room.

Just a few years ago, Allard thought, four or five fairly short years ago, he himself was a child playing at what he had to know were games. Short Round's schemes were so plainly games. Boom's weren't, but he needed Short Round's belief in fantasy in order to con him out of real money. The price of the Buick and the price of each jeep were deliberately the same. This was the joke; the con man always laughed because his game was so simple, belief so easily had.

He got his clothes together. For Mary's father he would wear a white shirt, a tie, and the light flannel suit he'd bought in Boston after his discharge. Such a neat, clean young man he'd seem. A cherub's face, a reptile all the rest. No, damn it, he had honorable intentions. Then why did this charade seem dishonest, and because dishonest, boring, deadly boring? He did not enjoy fooling people. From the con he got no joy at all.

Or maybe not at this particular moment. For instance, he would let Short Round go on believing because it would only hurt him to tell him that he was probably being taken, that the dead-man's-car story was so old it could probably be found in the Aramaic, referring to a sedan chair or a chariot.

But the old stories were the best, or they wouldn't have lasted so long. Stories were to be believed. Even when you didn't believe them you believed them because you knew how you wanted them to come out.

"Hey Paul, you got any beer?" he said.

Short Round was perfectly willing not only to be interrupted but to drop his games immediately. "Yeah, but it'll squirt all over the place. It's a squirty case, I don't know why. Nobody dropped it. Usually you can open Pabst warm okay, but this you got to watch or you'll get a bath."

"Go get me a couple," Allard said, handing him fifty cents. Pleased by the order, Short Round went to get the beer.

Allard would wear his suit, he decided, under army fatigues, so he could peel off the fatigues at Mary's house and enter formally. The motorcycle would unnerve Mr. Tolliver enough.

Short Round came back with three cans of beer—one for himself—and put them down gingerly on Allard's desk. "You got a church key?" he said. Allard had a church key. He took one of the cans and opened it at the window so the spray would go mostly outside, then capped the hole with his mouth and drank the pressured warm bitterness. When the pressure eased, he said, "I've got to ride the Red Wonderplane to Concord."

"To see Mary," Short Round said diffidently.

"Yeah. How did you know?"

"Oh, I don't know. Somebody mentioned it."

"Hmm." His eye was dangerous to Short Round, who looked away. But Short Round liked that danger. The world was full of exceedingly different pleasures.

He rode the old motorcycle toward Concord, the slow, long-stroking engine pulling him over the hills and through the valleys. Even though this trip brought him toward a confrontation he really didn't want to have, the riding was a pleasure. It still seemed miraculous to him that an engine and not his legs moved him across the land, down the curving highway at forty-five miles an hour. The rural state presented to him in passing so many pleasant vistas of green fields and the deeper green of pines and spruce, white houses and grayed barns, elms like benevolent high fountains of wood and leaves above stone walls, old maples with trunks like knotted muscles, arms of the earth. He passed through little towns consisting of a general store, a garage with gas pump, a town hall and church no bigger than houses. Into valleys, over small rivers, part of a lake blue and sparsely cabined, a bass fisherman casting from the highway beside his pickup truck. Onward steadily, easily, the engine's oily heat between his legs, the warm wind a receiving push his body parted firmly and smoothly, mile after mile.

The miles were more precious because of the destination that moved toward him as he moved across the state. Unless he turned around, or went on by, soon that destination would surround him with its particularities and demands.

He rode down the long hill from East Concord, the State House dome a small gold bubble across the river, then over the metal-grate bridge with its gruesome potential toward his flesh. Once into the small, rather dingy city, he turned north in heavier traffic, watching the intent of all drivers lest they be blind or mad. It was ominously, almost unfairly, easy to find the row of sooty duplex houses across the road from and above the mill they served. He drove up the short, steep driveway of Number 16b and parked his motorcycle, the rangy machine leaning raffishly on its kickstand beside the small garage made long ago for a Model T or a Model A. The dark houses crowded around him. It seemed a descent into other people's lives to intrude into the density of this place. Everything was dusty, brown. Even the grass, where it was allowed to survive within narrow borders, seemed to grow behind an iron gray filter. Stunted shrubs brushed the cement foundations of the houses. Down across the street next to the river the long, dark mill, once powered by water, smoked and steamed tiredly here and there along its length. Looking at the river now he couldn't imagine how it had ever been lively enough to power anything. A tepid brown, it puddled slowly about within its scum-enameled banks, barely able to carry off the mill's brownish foam. Brown. All the houses were painted brown, the wood deep within thick paint, a capitulation to the inevitable tones of the dim factory air. Yet this color, on the modest filigree of porch columns and banisters, seemed also to want to indicate dignity and permanence. A sad meticulousness in the choice of dark gray trim here and there, as on the frames of windows and the narrow doors, proved that someone was conscious of design. White lace curtains could be seen through clean glass, light keeping out light, inside a perpetual autumn. How different, as if this were a descent into the past, it all was from Allard's home in Leah, where crisp white houses were surrounded by grass so green it seemed to glow, even in the dusk, from within each blade.

Mary had been watching for him and came, vivid as a butterfly, from the old house. She wanted to kiss him, but before this intent became too obvious he was taking off the army fatigues he'd worn over his suit. She took them, cradling the soiled GI cloth in her bright arms. She wore a yellow dress so neatly held to her quick body at waist and bodice, so airily swirling at her legs, that she was made preciously delicate by it, as though she were brand-new and he'd never seen her before.

He took his army musette bag, which contained his toilet kit and a clean shirt, and Mary took his fatigues. These could just as well have been left in his saddlebags, but Mary wanted to take them, to hang them up in the closet of the guest room. She wanted to do this. They went up the steps to the front porch and opened the front door, its panes of glass jiggling in their frames. A brass-handled crank bell in the door tinkled once, flatly, though it hadn't been touched. In the vestibule upon a bureau was a religious statue, or doll, with a pinched, young-old doll's face. The figure stood a foot high and was dressed in an elaborate doll's dress edged with pearls and glinting jewels. One hand held a globe surmounted by a cross; the other, too tiny for the rest of the body, was raised, with fingers in the sign of a V. When he stopped to look more closely at this object, Mary said that it was the Infant of Praig, a special care of her dead mother, and in the bureau were drawers full of beautiful clothes for the doll. Her mother used to change the clothes according to the religious seasons. The clothes the doll wore now were dim with dust.

"The Infant of Praig?" he said, preparing, according to his own lights, to be properly, secularly interested.

"It's really Prague, like in Czechoslovakia," Mary said, "only it's always pronounced 'Praig.' I've never heard it called anything else."

But they couldn't dally; they had to proceed into the small living room, where stood a tall, stooped man of no more than fifty who seemed, though intensely there, smudged about the eyes. He seemed, Allard immediately thought, gone by. About his eyes was the hazed look of an abandoned store window.

"Daddy, this is Allard Benson!" Mary said as though highly pleased and surprised.

Allard took the pale hand in his square one. The hands detached themselves quickly, almost with haste.

"How do you do, sir," Allard said.

"Yes, and you, Mr. Benson?" The voice was weak, though tense. Again Allard saw in his mind the abandoned display window, old placards or posters inside covered with dust, curled at the edges, their information obsolete by years. Even the sun's light, if it entered here, would turn dull and sad. Mr. Tolliver's skin was yellow-brown, his glasses tinted sepia like an old rotogravure. The skin of his face and neck hung as though draped over his head and tacked here and there, at the corners of his eyes and where his ears were attached to his head.

"What are those?" he asked sternly, pointing to Allard's soiled fatigues.

"The old clothes Allard wore over his suit," Mary said. "I'll put them in his closet."

Mr. Tolliver didn't nod; evidently he disapproved of his daughter's carrying this man's dirty clothes. It must have seemed too domestic of her, as if she were closer to him, the young and healthy stranger, than Mr. Tolliver had been told.

"Won't you sit down, Mr. Benson?" he said.

A silence while Mary was gone with his musette bag and fatigues. Allard sat in an armchair, breath from its cushion rising slowly around him. Information Mary had given him intruded upon him. She had told him that her father was a minor white-collar person in the yarn mill. He had always been in the same niche; he had gone to junior college but had never risen in his job at all, just grown older. He had no tenure, no seniority, and even after all these years they could let him go any time they found it convenient. The mill itself was shaky, sometimes not running at all for a week at a time.

Mary's brother Robert came in, staring around into the corners of the room as if he were looking for something, said hello and shook hands distractedly. He was tall like his father, taller because at sixteen he hadn't yet begun to stoop. He was not interested in his sister's male friends. He was busy; he left for his mad-scientist electronics laboratory in the basement where among other things, Mary had told Allard, he generated great blue shredded clouds of electricity that destroyed all radio communication in the neighborhood.

"Mary tells me you're majoring in English, Mr. Benson," Mr. Tolliver said.

"Yes, so far."

"What would that prepare you to be?"

"I'm not sure—if anything," Allard said, smiling from habit at the self-deprecating statement he had made so many times. He smiled though he knew Mr. Tolliver would not respond. The man was ill, and probably had no time for any kind of frivolity. But Allard knew also that his statement had not been self-deprecatory at all—just the opposite; in his youthful arrogance he had no need for any dull profession, and he had said this to a sick man worried about his daughter's future. Mr. Tolliver's lips were too red, his eyelids too loose around his eyes. It was not really age, it was his illness that like a short circuit had drained away his powers.

"It's a hard world, Mr. Benson," Mr. Tolliver said.

Allard didn't care if it was. His world was a different one, anyway, not of this room or of the people who had furnished it, not even visible from here. That they wanted to live here among this furniture he knew, but it was still shocking to him that these choices had been made deliberately. Ocher and umber, cushion dust, varnish, draperies and curtains too heavy for the small room, the white lace at the windows nearly lost to view from the inside. He had been in such rooms before, but they had always seemed the former habitations of people long dead and gone. Glass-covered pictures hung on tasseled cords from the picture moldings. Photographs of relatives and ancestors, some in round or oval varnished frames, leaned out from the dull flowered print of the wallpaper. The pictures were of faded, formal people he knew were dead, their stern dim faces communicating nothing but mortality. The ornamental turnings of the legs of tables, the cast flutings on the columns of lamps, all calculated by someone to be in good taste, seemed only impoverished excess. Tassels on the arms of the sofa and its matching chair hung above the thick, bent legs. The carpet was vaguely Oriental; to examine in any detail its scrolls of ill-defined and exhausted flowers seemed wrong, so Allard took his eyes away from it.

Across from him, over Mr. Tolliver's thin shoulder, was a framed reproduction of a painting. Jesus Christ stood upon a greenish ball representing the earth, his tapered bare toes seeming to clasp it. Over his flowing white vestments he wore a pink robe open at the chest. On the white cloth that covered his chest was a strawberry-shaped heart he touched with the index finger of his rather effeminately posed left hand. His other hand, held toward the viewer, spurted a white spray from a slit in the palm. The back of his left hand also spurted a strange white fluid from its wound. Calm eyes gazed from the slightly tilted, handsome head that was surrounded by a sunburst halo. Behind the figure, evidently in space, was a pretty sunset or dawn. Allard looked again at the red heart, which was not a stylized valentine heart but something in between that and a real muscular valve. Small radiations, like flames, came from the top of it where it had a short stem, and above the flames was a gold cross.

"The Sacred Heart of Jesus," Mr. Tolliver said in his faded, stern voice. "The Sacred Heart of Jesus, Mr. Benson. 'Take My yoke upon you, and learn from Me, for I am meek and humble of heart; and you will find rest for your souls.' That is from Saint Matthew."

"Oh," Allard said. Mary had told him that her father was a convert to Catholicism, with a convert's intensity of belief.

"You understand that in this house we are all very devout Catholics."

"Yes," Allard said, nodding. His eyes slid away from the dim ones behind the sepia glasses. In front of the small brick fireplace, between two tall brass-headed andirons that would never have fit inside, was a vase of cut daffodils. It must have been Mary who had placed them there. She came back, then, and there were two bright things of yellow in the room. Lively, nervous and loving, she smiled at her father and at Allard, then sat lightly on a fringed ottoman beside her father's chair.

From the photographs Mary had showed him, her mother had been small, with Mary's delicate bones, but with an intense, tortured Irish face all calm had left as she grew older. What must once have been a pretty face had later become ragged, almost skinless. And it was in this room seven years ago that Mrs. Tolliver had breathed and trembled, knowing she was dying. He wondered if the Infant of Prague or the Sacred Heart of Jesus had comforted her then. A dense web of alien memories and terrors surrounded him. A rope portiere fringed the doorway to the dining room, lampshades were fringed with yellowed lace, a corner whatnot cabinet displayed in its gloom gilded dishes and glass bowls decorated with pea-sized glass lumps. The fancy veneered cabinet of the Atwater Kent radio bore a more modern Bakelite radio on its top. Wall sconces held up orange light bulbs in torch shapes.

On an end table a cast pot-metal model of a sailing ship revealed that perhaps its designer had never seen the sea.

The unmoving air smelled of stale chocolate. Medicinal.

In a narrow, glass-fronted bookcase were a few books: *A Daily Missal, Health and the Mind, A Map of Life, Johnny Tremaine, Gone with the Wind.* He would of course stay out his sentence here, where people were still living out their lives. What did it mean to Allard Benson except a temporary oppression of his spirit? But this was their home, filled with their valued possessions; the warm cubicles of these rooms were all that had protected them from the hard world outside, from that cold of absolute zero.

Mary seemed to glow against the umber tones of the room. She was so lithe, so . . . workable. She worked so perfectly, so easily in all her senses and systems. Her one strange flaw was magic, the fleck of jade green in the iris of her right eye. He could catch its glint now as she looked at him. It was dark magic that she had lived her life in this somber house. She was a creature of sunlight, a jewel to be removed from this dullness.

"Mr. Benson was . . ."

"Allard, Daddy."

"Um. Looking at your mother's favorite picture. Perhaps it seems a little garish to your sophisticated eye, Mr. Benson, but it was a great comfort to her. She was a little girl from south Boston who hadn't the advantage of a college education."

"Well, yes, as a picture . . . I mean as a painting . . ." Allard said, unable to decide what terms the sick man demanded.

"It's not by Leonardo, you mean," Mr. Tolliver went on. "It's sentimental, isn't it? The colors are those of the nursery, the figure of Our Savior is too pretty for your taste. Is that it, Mr. Benson?"

"*Allard,* Daddy. And stop being so antagonistic."

Mr. Tolliver smiled, or Allard thought he smiled; the bloodless gums showed for a moment. Yes, Mary and her father shared a joke he couldn't quite figure out. Was it her chiding of her father that made him give that quick grimace of a smile, or was it their mutual recognition of Mr. Tolliver's deadly sarcasm? Perhaps Mary's part was to tell him, each time he began to get too nasty, to be quiet. They were "close," she had said.

"I meant to make the point that beauty is in the eye of the beholder. Mary's mother was, in her way, a saint. She lived in the love of God; the life of Christ entered into her. Beside this mystery all else is trivial, Mr. Benson. One should never forget that." He looked at Mary, then directly at Allard. "Have you expressed an interest in the Church, Mr. Benson?"

"Daddy, this is ridiculous. It's embarrassing, and I want you to lay off," Mary said. "You get the message?"

Again the grimace, but the sick eyes behind the tinted lenses returned coldly to Allard.

"Yes, I'm interested in the Church," Allard said.

"You're curious, you mean."

"Yes, I suppose so."

"What do you believe in, Mr. Benson?"

"I'm not sure."

"You're not sure. Do you believe in God?"

"I'd like to, maybe, but I find it rather difficult."

"For what purpose were you put upon the earth?"

"God knows."

"I sense flippancy in your answer."

"Daddy," Mary said, "it's time for your nap. You're getting tired. Come on." She took his arm to help him up. "If you're going to feel good at dinner you've got to take one of your pills and have a rest."

Mr. Tolliver stood up, sighing. Allard rose, too, but though they stood facing each other Mr. Tolliver didn't look at him. Mary put her arm around her father's waist. "Come on, Daddy. I'll help you if you want." She looked up at her father, her hair light gold against the brindled cloth of his vest.

"Yes, I'm tired," Mr. Tolliver said wearily. "Forgive me,

but you're right. I don't feel too well." Mary helped him, her arm tightly around his waist as they went toward the vestibule and the front stairs.

Heaviness left the room, though it would be only a short respite. There would be dinner, and tomorrow the strange journey into alien rituals. With Mr. Tolliver's departure the painting of Jesus relented a bit too, becoming less of a presence and more of a curiosity. The Sacred Heart itself, painted in three dimensions, was a little too small for the size of Jesus' body—as strangely euphemistic as the paleness of the blood that sprayed so lightly from His nail wounds.

When Mary came back he went over and sat beside her on the sofa's fat cushions. She put her hand on his arm and smiled at him—her sweet, slightly self-deprecating smile, the smile with her lips closed. Sometimes when he kissed her he would feel this smile impressed against his own lips until with a tremor it would partly open, tender as a flower. Then he would feel that his mouth and tongue had destroyed it, turned it into a kind of agony.

"I'm sorry," Mary said, "but he's sick and worried, Allard. It's some kind of kidney or liver trouble the doctors can't figure out. You know? And his job, too. And just now he was looking down at your motorcycle. It does look wild and irresponsible the way it sort of leans over—as if it's about to fall but doesn't care."

"Well, he's probably right about that," Allard said.

Mary laughed and squeezed his arm. "Oh, he shouldn't worry so much about you and me."

He put his hand around her slim waist and signaled gently that she should lean toward him. Of course she moved consentingly the way he wanted her to, her eyes closing, her lips opening slightly. Her breath was sweet and warm, the moist tissues of her lips cool. Through his thumb he felt her pulse in the tender, taut skin of her throat. He always found himself holding her in ways that resembled the grips of violence. When they moved apart Mary sat shyly, her head down, her hands upturned in her lap.

"I'd like to put you on that rakehell motorcycle and take you out of here," he said.

"Is it that bad? I know it must be strange for you and I'm sorry Daddy's so sort of picky."

"It's all right. Don't worry about me," he said, feeling a little noble.

"Anyway, you know I promised not *ever* to ride on your motorcycle."

"You'll break that promise, Mary." He felt pity for Mr. Tolliver, knowing that all the history of love and care, family, shared sorrows, everything she might owe her father, would matter very little when his own need—this callow young stranger's supposed need—took what it wanted of her. He didn't have to exact promises or make demands, as her father did. It was not necessary to do anything, or to be anything but what, for better or worse, he was. But then he reminded himself that his intentions were in fact honorable.

She smiled and shook her head. "I never break promises," she said.

He believed it—in every case except his own. "Let's go for a walk or something," he said. "Have we got time before dinner?"

"Yes. I'll put the roast in now and we can go. I can show you where I went to school, if you're interested."

In the small, crowded kitchen he put his arms around her. She laughed and pushed him away so she could fiddle with the gas stove. The oven came on with a blue whoosh. She put the roast in the oven on its pan and turned the flames down, then opened the door to the cellar and called down to Robert, telling him the roast was on and to look at it once in a while. Allard couldn't hear Robert's answer. "He probably won't think of it, anyway," Mary said.

They went out of the dark house into the warm light. On the sidewalk Allard was conscious of being watched through the windows of other houses, of being considered Mary's suitor. At the corner a woman in black said hello to Mary while looking only at Allard, then crossed the street, walking with difficulty, as though her legs were partly fused where they came together.

They turned up the hill, away from the brown river, the mill and the row of duplexes.

"When Robert goes to M.I.T. next year, Daddy will be alone most of the time. He thinks of that a lot and it's sad, you know. He couldn't stand the idea of someone living in, like a housekeeper. He's so desperate and weak."

"How about his religion?" Allard said.

"It's no substitute for people."

"Isn't that kind of sacrilegious?"

"It's true, isn't it? Unless you have a vocation, I suppose. And he's worried about me being at the university even though he's proud of it, too."

"Worried you'll meet a horny atheist like me."

She laughed. "Oh, I know you, Allard! You're not an atheist at all!"

"I can see why he's nervous. I'm the leading character in his worst nightmare, and before you've been in college a year you've found me and invited me home."

"When he gets to know you . . ."

"I doubt that."

She stopped and turned toward him, serious, her clear eyes honest, lucid. "Do you really love me, Allard?" she said.

"Yes."

"Then I don't see . . ."

"Why it's not okay with your father?"

"Yes."

"You don't see it, really? Mary, what kind of daughter and Catholic are you?"

"I love my father and I'm a good Catholic. What I mean is that he loves me, too, Allard. Really. He's discouraged and afraid right now, but he does love Robert and me. I'm sorry about the way he acted, but he's never been a success in business or anything so you know how much our family meant to him. Maybe he wasn't respected much in the mill, but when he came home he was respected. He *deserved* it, too, and now our home is breaking up. Can you imagine how he feels?" There were tears in her eyes. "He's only fifty but he looks and feels about a hundred."

They resumed their walking, Mary a light presence beside him. He believed she would have liked him to take her hand. They walked together a little more separately than she would have preferred, maybe.

She showed him St. Agnes', a square, depressingly barren brick building where she had gone to school through the eighth grade. They went to Mass every day at St. Agnes', she said. The four-story building stood in the middle of an asphalt plain, an acre of asphalt. The elms around the edges of the lot were worn to eye level as if by scuffling feet; then they soared upward as if trying to escape the barrenness below, flourishing as living trees only in their upper reaches, in a green stratosphere all their own. Down the street was St. Joseph's, a large church built of the same burned dark brick, where he would go with them to Mass tomorrow.

"I guess we'd better go back," Mary said. "I've got to keep an eye on my roast."

He envisioned burning meat and blue flames. They returned to the house and entered its darkness. Mr. Tolliver, still upstairs resting, was a heavy presence.

The kitchen was too small to have a table or chairs in it, so Allard brought a dining room chair into the doorway and sat watching as Mary prepared dinner. Her flowered apron was coming untied and he tied it in a neat bow for her, then put his hands around her waist to measure it, feeling her bones' perfect and complicated movements within her. He watched her competently manipulate steaming pots and pans, her domestic art efficient as ritual. He volunteered to work the potato ricer, a hinged piston and cylinder that extruded mealy white worms from its perforated bottom.

"That's a help," Mary said. "I'd better wake Daddy now. We're about ready. Would you tell Robert?"

He descended the narrow stairs into the cellar, careful not to hit his head on a floor joist that crossed at eye level.

From somewhere in the dank spaces below came cracklings of blue light and the smell of ozone.

"Robert?" he said. "Hey, Robert?"

Robert stood in the far corner of the cellar before a lighted console, his narrow face illuminated from below by the dials and rheostats. The oil furnace stood behind him, a somnolent monster with its round arms raised into the gloom of the ceiling. Allard crossed the gritty cement floor and stopped at what he hoped was a safe distance from the crackling wormy yellow and blue energy he had never managed to understand. Robert nodded and kept turning his dials, gazing sternly at his quivering indicators. A metal globe as big as a basketball above the console grew bright blue hairs of light that forked and shredded off into the atmosphere like the pure hysterical essence of fright. The very air was ripped and fragmented by the demonic power Robert controlled. He glanced once at Allard, acknowledging his presence, but the narrow face, as stern as a helmsman's, turned back to its command. The blue crackling lessened, replaced by a deep, ominous hum.

"That looks dangerous," Allard said.

"Only if you're ignorant of its nature."

"Do you understand it?"

"I probably understand as much of it as anyone. But no one really understands; we just control it and use it."

"Then it sounds even more dangerous," Allard said.

Robert looked at him for the first time with some interest. "Yes. We make up terms for things and sometimes they make us think we know more than we do. Ohms, watts, volts, amperes, kilohertz, megahertz—but we don't know what the real power is."

"Sort of like religion," Allard ventured.

Again the look of interest. Robert thought this over for a moment, then said, "Indeed," with the dry, matter-of-fact dignity—perhaps stuffiness—of the M.I.T. professor he would quite likely someday be. "But of course all this is more tangible in its results. It works or it doesn't work. Its force is immediate and measurable." He made some notations on a clipboard, hung the clipboard back on the wall, and turned down the transformer hum of the infernal machine until all was silent. "I'm interested in electrostatic induction. Do you know what that is?"

"I'm afraid not," Allard said.

"Well, I won't go into the details, but it has to do with the transfer of electrical forces from one conductor to another, and the exact nature of the repulsion of similar charges. The blue lightning you saw was the result of electrons becoming so concentrated that they were actually sprayed through the air. There are certain phenomena here we don't yet understand. We know they happen, but not quite why. Sooner or later I'll explain them."

"To the world?"

"To the world."

"You mean you'll get the Nobel Prize and stuff like that?"

"Quite possibly, although 'all that' is of little importance."

In the wan light of the bare bulb Robert looked no longer the stern commander, the Prince of Technology, but the somewhat sallow sixteen-year-old he was, glands slightly out of whack, a pimple on his nostril. But Robert's knowledge was real, making, by comparison, whatever force or hardness there was in Allard's consciousness seem of doubtful value. Vagueness seemed his own lot. And the hardness, or sureness, of Robert's opinions, his lack of self-conscious modesty, was in such contrast to Mary's compliance, her submissiveness, even though some of her features were recognizable in his facial bones beneath the waxy adolescent flesh. Allard had to look up at him as they turned toward the stairs, the narrow head on its stalklike neck so firmly vertical it might have contained a gyroscope. It seemed quite certain Robert would do as he said he would, day by day, year by year, until he reached whatever heights of scientific glory he envisioned for himself. As if he were on a track.

"I've read some science fiction," Allard said, "and that

certainly didn't help my understanding much."

"Huh. Venus shuttles run by Portuguese. Time warp and jalopy spaceships."

"Yeah. As I said, I didn't get much out of it—except a sort of depressing general prediction that the earth's a goner."

"That's relative," Robert said. "Presumably, everything's a goner." They went up the cellar stairs, leaving the atmosphere of ozone, entering the more earthly one of roast beef.

"That's what I can't understand," Allard said. "How you scientists seem to get comfort out of relativity."

"It's logical. It's *clean.*" Robert turned to him almost with exasperation. "Listen, you're the one who ought to be Catholic."

They entered the small dining room, where there was so little space around the set and prepared central table that they stood on either side of it.

"I don't mean to dump on your ohms and ergs," Allard said. "Actually, I believe in them."

"That's what I mean. You take them on faith."

"Do you take your Catholicism on faith?"

"What else can I take it on?" He motioned toward a small crucifix on the wall, a bronzed Christ mounted on a wooden cross. "I manage to compartmentalize all sorts of conceptions. Science, religion, sex, vanity, love, mortality. Let's say I know the difference between evidence and conviction."

"Jesus!" Allard said. "You're a wonder, Robert. You know that?"

Robert flinched slightly at Jesus' name used as an expletive, then smiled a little out of vanity. Allard's admiration had been plain.

Mr. Tolliver came in then, Mary behind him, the delicate nurse. He sat down with a fragile lurch, and Mary pointed Allard to his chair. She went to the kitchen and brought back small bowls of soup, then returned for the dishes of vegetables and the roast on its platter. When all the food was present, there was a moment of grave silence. Mr. Tolliver bowed his head and said in a ceremonial voice, "Bless us, O Lord, and these gifts which we are about to receive from Thy bounty through Christ Our Lord. Amen."

Heads rose. Mr. Tolliver stood up and began to carve the roast. "This is a fancy dinner for Saturday," he said sternly, not looking at Allard. "What's the matter with baked beans?"

This time Allard saw that Mr. Tolliver was joking, in his fashion. He understood too that it was not a matter of give-and-take, that all such sallies would originate from one source. He tried to smile, but his facial muscles had cramped; then he reached for his water glass and nearly knocked it over. Somehow he would get through this meal. Time had to pass, whether one wanted it to or not. Robert hadn't said a word since his father had entered the room, this small dark room crowded with furniture like the tall, glass-fronted cabinet that contained fancier dishes than they were using. All the furniture seemed to have been bought originally for some other room in better times.

Bless us, O Lord . . . Occasionally he had eaten at tables where grace was said. That strange silence in which one was embarrassed and stunned by a sudden gravity. Somewhat like madness. *The Lord is great, the Lord is good; thank Thee, Lord, for this food.* For this fudd? What rhymed with good? Or the mocking other side of that madness: *Bless this soup and bless this meat; Jesus Baldheaded Christ, let's eat!* But now were they eating this food with Catholic mouths—this food blessed, as though flavored lightly with God sauce?

"When I was a boy," Mr. Tolliver said, "we had bread and milk on Saturday nights. The bread that had gone stale during the week. Not store-bought bread, either."

So how do I answer that? Allard said to himself so clearly he could feel his tongue moving in his mouth.

"I like to make bread," Mary said. "But of course I can't if I'm at school."

"Yes, everybody's going off to college," Mr. Tolliver said.

Silence.

"And what do you learn in college these days, Mr. Benson?"

"That's a hard question," Allard said. Suddenly he thought of Naomi lying naked on his poncho. "We read a lot of books."

"Most of which tell you God doesn't exist?"

"Some of them might imply that. Yes."

"And still we scrimp and save in order to send our sons and daughters to such places."

"Well, I'm glad you sent Mary there or I wouldn't have met her."

Mr. Tolliver visibly shuddered. "Would you like some more meat, Mr. Benson?"

"Yes, please." He passed his plate, and the long yellow hands manipulated the carving set. Allard also had more potatoes and carrots. His nervousness made him hungry, which was strange. He could have taken Mary's roast, that consecrated meat, in his two hands and wolfed at it, bloody juices running down his wrists to his elbows. The cheap flannel suit he wore bound him across the shoulders and under his arms. He glanced at Mary, his eyes feeling avid and dangerous. Asked, he explained between mouthfuls that his father ran a weekly newspaper, the *Leah Free Press*, that he had no brothers or sisters, that he had spent two and one-half years in the army, ending up as a corporal in the Tokyo-Kanagawa Military Government. Though Mr. Tolliver had asked these questions, he listened with impatience, frowning.

"Did you see Hiroshima?" Robert asked suddenly.

"Are we nearly ready for dessert?" Mr. Tolliver asked.

"No, I never went there."

"Do you think we should have dropped the bomb?"

"No."

Mr. Tolliver was consulting with Mary about the dessert. "Jello," she said.

"What flavor?"

"And then there was Nagasaki," Robert said.

"A center of Roman Catholicism," Allard said before he thought.

Mr. Tolliver was staring at him. "What did you say? Roman Catholicism?"

"Very many Catholics in Nagasaki, I understand."

"Japanese?"

"Japanese Catholics, yes."

"Don't you think the bomb helped end the war?" Robert asked.

"Maybe, but mostly you get a scientific toy like that and you want to see how it works."

Robert smiled for the second time. "I'm interested in more theoretical problems. Though I suppose you're right—theory transmutes into action."

"You said it again, Robert."

"What? What?" Mr. Tolliver said, looking from Allard to Robert and back again. He didn't like surprises such as this sudden familiar conversation. He reacted as though he had been physically shoved, wincing and then leaning forward again as if to regain his balance.

"We were talking about Robert's attitudes toward science," Allard said. He found himself enunciating the words carefully, speaking, he supposed, to a kind of senility.

"Hum!"

While Mary, with Robert's help, removed the dishes and brought in the jello—raspberry, with whipped cream on top—Mr. Tolliver said nothing and Allard could think of nothing to say. He fully understood by now that he was not supposed to initiate conversation in Mr. Tolliver's presence. While they ate their jello he thought of things he might say, things he honestly believed; but what he honestly believed would enrage Mr. Tolliver and hurt Mary, so he sat dishonestly among these people, himself unreal, not able to give Mr. Tolliver real answers. He knew the real questions in Mr. Tolliver's mind, all right, and he could answer them, saying to Mr. Tolliver that, yes, he was leading Mary into sin. The power was love, one we use though we don't understand it.

And yes, she would suffer, and if by any chance there was such a thing as hell, poor Mary would have to go there. But don't worry about it.

Words and phrases, tinnitus in his head. The pronouncements of a sage of twenty-one. Perhaps he had no control at all, and it was Mary herself who was the real manipulator here. Maybe she had enticed him to this dark place and trapped him, her green eye-fleck the only mortal warning of her power. He followed the sweetly agonizing promises he felt she contained, was dazed by her beauty, his dream of possession ridiculously presumptuous. And the Catholic religion he so easily patronized, with all its squirting blood, its thorns, rapes, burnings and nailings—was it that alien to his own experience? Baal, Antichrist, the Black Mass, nuns copulating in incensed inner sanctums. All of it a plot of the Powers of Darkness. But he had come here to rescue the beautiful part-human sorceress, to free her from her thralldom. The Knight of Reason and Lust (that perfectly reasonable emotion), come upon his Indian Pony . . .

Later, after the dishes were done—Allard wiping the warm plates he took from Mary's hand—and Mr. Tolliver had again retired and Robert gone to his room to study, she leaned into his arms in the dark living room.

"You put your hands on me in funny places," she said. "You seem to have a right. I never saw anything like it, but you just seem to have a right."

"It's that I don't think touching you is a sin." His leg trembled when he put weight on it. She jumped slightly, then stood looking off toward a corner. "What's the matter?" he said, knowing what it was she'd felt. That thing of the nether regions had grown, and she had suddenly identified it.

"I'm confused," she said.

"Why? What's so strange?"

"I don't know what you want."

"I want you."

"I don't know."

"I do."

"How can you be so sure of everything?"

"I'm not sure of everything." He put his hands lightly around her neck and pulled her, smooth as smoke, back against him.

"It's a sin. It is."

He wondered if she ever spoke to other women about such things. "What's a sin?" he asked.

"The carnal things you do to me."

"Really?" He had to laugh, partly out of nervousness.

"Yes."

"But I haven't done anything except touch you here and there, and kiss you rather chastely on the lips."

"That's carnal."

"We're both made of flesh, Mary, so whatever we do has got to be pretty carnal, wouldn't you say?"

"All my life I've been told not to. Not to *feel* this way. 'Purity of body'—that's what we were always told. It was always the Sixth and Ninth Commandments. 'Avoid the occasions of sin,' they always told us. We had retreats where that was about all that was said."

"What's an 'occasion of sin'?"

"Like, 'putting yourself in the position of being alone with a person of the opposite sex.' I can hear the words."

"And yet here you are in that position."

"You may think it's silly, Allard, but it's very real to me."

"What's it like down there? In hell, I mean."

"You can joke about it but I can't. It's fire. You burn. Forever."

"And so you go and confess out of fear?"

"I know I'll want you to touch me again. I'm not sincere in my contrition."

"So you confess just to assuage this voodoo shit?"

"Allard." She was frightened and sad. "I don't understand you."

The Catholic room seemed to darken around him. He knew no logic could free her from a lifetime of madness. He would have to enter her consciousness through her nerves.

"You sit over there, Allard," she said, pointing to one end of the davenport. "And I'll sit here."

They sat, but soon he reached over and pulled her toward him. She seemed weightless. Then he turned her so that he held her across his lap. So deliberately that it seemed almost natural even to him, his hand moved to her breast and she began to breathe quickly. She seemed to be trying to remove his hand, but her hand was weak. She was substantial to him yet light. He leaned down and kissed her on the mouth, her lips fluttering in little spasms against his.

"No, no. Take your hand away, Allard." She spoke into his lips and he breathed the small gusts of her breath.

"All right," he said, moving his hand slowly down. She was an instrument he must play, a perfect and even dangerous instrument because if he made an error she would have to take herself away from him. Yet he must play upon her senses with the exactly permissible intensity. He must be aware of all vital signs, even of the technicalities of inches, radii of muscles, bones, tendons, glands, hollows, straps, hems, plackets, the elasticities of flesh and fabric, of pulse and breath. And he was used by his own intensities; golden moilings, like felt clouds of gas, moved deliciously near pain through his body and his vision. He was aware exactly of the calm he must personify to her, and of course of the impropriety of passion in this crowded room haunted by death, Jesus, hellfire and angels. How far he must go—and what a strange word, *far*. As if moving toward the act of love were a going-away. But you had to move toward it and when you were spent of all of its beautiful violence you did move beyond and away, for a time at least, into the sadness that sooner or later, in the proper place and time, he would cause Mary to endure.

Later it was a painful, sweet good night at the door of the small room he would sleep in. They whispered to each other. As long as they were standing she let herself be open to all his dangerous knobs and projections, as she really wanted to be. She whispered how she loved him; he whispered how he wished she would come to bed with him, which brought no answer. It was a theoretical question; the answer was of course, *yes*—when their union was blessed with official documents and ceremonies. His testicles were full of molten lead. Mary was precious to him. Why, he thought in his pain, did he want so much to arouse her delicacy, to reveal the lustful animal in it? He wanted to hear Mary growl like a beast.

Someone stirred in a room down the narrow hallway and he let her go. She walked quickly, with soft guilty steps, and silently shut the door to her room.

Alone in the rather insubstantial, twangy bed he arrived again at the conclusion that he had no moral hesitations about seducing Mary except that he might hurt her, and since, at that moment, he considered his intentions honorable, he had none at all. Even he could see the subjective flaw in this system. The dull ache in his genitals was a remorseless crush. With Mary's heat, her scent, her willing body filling his head and hovering against him, his hand lovingly imitated her center. In a few moments came the relief of diffusion, the contented sadness; then, sometime or other without his awareness, as it had to be, he must have gone to sleep.

He woke up damp, chilly, immediately nervous. Yellow daylight, a tarnished, city daylight, entered his small window. He wanted a cigarette. He hadn't smoked the evening before because he had seen no evidence of smoking in the house—no ashtrays at all, though he had examined various small decorative objects looking for meaningful depressions in them. He waited, as though trapped in the small room, listening for his chance at the bathroom, then abruptly surprised Mr. Tolliver in the hallway, the man's skinny shins below a plaid bathrobe, his offended face above. Allard pulled his shirt together and said good morning. "Um. Yes," Mr. Tolliver said.

In the bathroom, now illuminated by the tired morning light, a tight, bluish old man's stink faded in the morning air. The short bathtub on claw-ball feet crowded a small wash basin, which in turn crowded the toilet with its narrow seat of varnished wood. Medicines stood behind the glass of the cabinet. He thought of Mrs. Tolliver in that tub, one-sided after her mastectomy, a woman bleakly sitting in tepid water. He took two nerve-melting drags on a cigarette and threw it into the toilet, where it gasped its last. Soon they would all go to church, the real God place, in which he would become, because of his appearance there with the family, semiofficially Mary's suitor, her fiancé, her intended. He emptied the bladder of her intended, washed the face of her intended, washed the crusty seed of her intended off her intended's belly and chest.

Downstairs he was still chilly. He couldn't speak unless spoken to. Mary smiled at him so warmly it seemed she had forgiven herself for their kisses and caresses the night before and now loved him even more because of a sweet memory. He grimaced back at her. Robert was quiet, neutral, businesslike, while Mr. Tolliver exuded illness and disapproval.

Time passed and soon they filed out past the Infant of Prague, who was too old to be an infant in his dusty finery, with his older figure and face. Mary wore a navy blue dress edged at the cuffs with white lace, and a navy blue hat edged with the same lace, the small hat changing the shape of her face so that she looked older, like a wife. Robert, who had only recently gotten his driving licence, backed the Tollivers' 1940 Chevrolet out of the narrow garage. Mary and her father got in back and Allard sat in front next to Robert, his feet manipulating ghostly dual controls as the car bucked and stalled before Robert got it down the driveway, up the street, then up the hill Allard and Mary had walked the afternoon before. Soon they arrived at the burnt-brick church, parked and walked slowly, as though stiff, toward the wide doors. Other Catholics converged here in their Sunday clothes, the young boys strangled by collars and ties, smaller children fresh and solemn. Allard felt fresh, too, against the constraints of this solemnity; he could, if he wanted, jump over everybodys' heads, a vivid jack-jumper among these ceremony-bound people who were all strangers, tranced by their religion. All the men seemed solemn yet bored, not aware of their boredom. Sunday duty: he saw it in their rugged faces. Only their fingernails and deepest pores retained the grime of their work. They were not large men. They were pale, small in the shoulders, large only in their wrists and hands. The coming ceremonies seemed the property of the women.

Entering the wide dim church with these people he observed with half-knowledge their familiarity with its crannies and receptacles. Fountains, or fonts, of water, odd closets, alcoves, candles guttering behind colored glass somewhere down there toward the holier places, the high, stained-glass-illuminated reaches of the ceilings no one but he examined with a measuring eye. Though Mary had shown him how to genuflect before entering the row of benches, he could only duck down a little. To him sacrilege was not disbelief but the show of honoring unbelieved rituals. Down at the front of the holy barn was the wide altar with its sconces, symbol-woven altar cloth, shrines in miniature and strangely kitchen-like utensils. Soon a priest and a small boy entered, with much sign-making, and against his conscience Allard imitated the hunched general movement of kneeling that surged throughout the church.

In Nomine Patris, et Filii, et Spiritus Sancti. Amen.

From the priest's chanting mouth the words were self-justifying, said with no emotion, needing no human inflections.

Introibo ad altare Dei.

Then a mumbled response, varied among the worshipers but general throughout the church: *Ad Deum qui laetificat juventutem meam.* The mumblings were like a tired groan.

Judica me, Deus, et discerne causam meam de gente non sancta: ab homine iniquo et doloso erue me . . .

As the voices made answer, Allard's mind turned half away from the words, not understanding most of them but feeling that nobody among these believers was really listening to their meanings, that the words that once must have meant something very specific no longer had to mean. The priest in his antique uniform, and the small boy who helped him, might have been wax models in a museum smelling of dust, the dusty armpits and crotches of ancient uniforms worn five hundred years ago now resurrected and mounted upon pale dummies whose skeletons were sticks of wood. They moved mechanically and chanted inaudible words. But words had to mean, and these words did not mean. You did not mindlessly repeat what had been previously said because that was rote, a kind of cheating, the death of reality which was life. You never said again what you had said before because that was the sore wounding of truth. He had no idea where he had acquired these strictures, but he knew that he believed them utterly and they seemed to apply here. In this place he could not feel the vibrations of faith, nor its always saddening nostalgic appeal.

Next to him knelt Mary Tolliver, a changed person here at the stifling godhead of her faith. A grown woman, clever and warm yet believing all of it, wearing that fancy hat for some lost crazy senseless reason, her senses and organs unnaturally stilled by this syrup of grave incantative madness, not functioning swiftly for him. This was the place for thinking about dust and dying. Here you were told to yearn for death, a lie masquerading as balm for despair. And it was interminable. That all these dark-clothed, crouching people allowed themselves to be thus punished was degrading. He could smell the sour odors of fear and sanctimony, the effluvium of the church.

Ah, but in spite of all this what if there was a God? Was there any permissible evidence revealed here in the church's hollowness, its vast dim spaces?

Confiteor Deo omnipotenti, beatae Mariae semper Virgini, beato Michaeli Archangelo, beato Joanni Baptistae, sanctis Apostolis Petro et Paulo, omnibus Sanctis, et tibi, Pater: quia peccavi nimis cogitatione, verbo, et opere . . .

Amidst the chanting many of the people struck themselves upon the chest three times. Mary, Mary, do not hurt your tender virgin breast.

. . . *mea culpa, mea culpa, mea maxima culpa. Ideo precor beatam Mariam semper Virginem* . . .

It went on and on. He was aware of his body, his person there observing, taking punishment. The priest and his server took their turns, their steps. It reminded him of one of those European tower clocks where, upon the hour, animated figures appear and move across upon a track. Observer, victim of these stimuli, he knew the only ceremonies he could ever enter into would be those of his own making. If only he could create a Mass for presentation upon this stage, for this stunned receptive audience. The church slowly rolled like an ocean liner—slow, slow, and then the return, none of the other passengers aware. Later the priest spoke in English, extolling the supreme worth, the magnificent glory, of motherhood, as all the mothers listened. Allard furtively looked around. Mr. Tolliver seemed bruised about the eyes by these sentiments, clenched with emotion. His yellowed eye sockets were squeezed shut behind his tinted glasses.

And somehow, after a convincing sample of eternity, it was over and they could stand, turn and follow the slowly moving people out into daylight. He had survived another of the stations of his self-imposed duty and felt light in the head. The sounds and rhythms of Latin had entered, without his consent, some deep organ of mimesis: *Prohibitum meam nolens volens introibo corpus Mariae non semper virgini. Mea maximus lascivus libidinosus, maxima magnus et paratus intrare puella, maxima non culpa si solum beato tuus meato* . . .

The sun was a heavy yellow on this windless day, the first always startling hot humid day of spring that changes the world completely. Immediately he began to sweat, to itch to get away. He had told Mary a small (duly noted) lie—that he had to visit his parents in Leah before going back to school. That had been the reason for the fancy Saturday night dinner, because he was to leave right after church. And he would; within a few minutes he would be escaping upon his Indian

Pony, pushing through the heavy air and making his own fresh wind as he rushed away.

Back at the Tollivers' he went to the guest room and took off his suit. It was too hot to wear it under his fatigues, so he folded it to fit in his saddlebags and wore only the baggy green fatigues, which seemed wrong with the white shirt underneath and his thin dress shoes. When he said goodbye to Mr. Tolliver it was as if they had already said goodbye. Everything necessary had been indicated between them.

"Goodbye, sir, and thank you."

"Goodbye."

"Good luck in college, Robert."

"Thanks," Robert answered with a smile that acknowledged their moments of understanding.

Then he was left alone with Mary, standing next to the raffish, oily Indian Pony. She had removed her church-going hat, but still wore her fancy church dress. She was pretty and immensely valuable, but in these clothes she seemed not to belong to him. Nylon stockings, slip, garter belt, panties, bra —those feminine things, official as badges, had an erotic effect upon him that felt puerile, as though she were an object to strip. It was not the way he wanted her; he wanted her light and free, companionable, riding behind him on his motorcycle, not a victim but part of a mutual joy. She looked at him as if he were a wonder, with the half-smile of love, and kissed him awkwardly as he stood there in the limbo before going. His hands came around her automatically and he felt the strap that ran across her back, with its hooks he would undo like Houdini when the time came.

Her joy in him seemed to take too many things for granted—either that or he couldn't understand it at all. In a way it was nice that she thought they sinned when they petted, but again that was not what he really wanted. He was depressed by the hopeless task of changing her. No, of course it was not hopeless. It was a dangerous and terrible responsibility because he would have to create an alternate world for Mary: ceremonies, rituals to contain and control all the dark powers of her past. He kissed her and said he would see her Monday evening; then, with the sense of emotion postponed, he mounted his Indian Pony and rode away, feeling relief in the sudden wind caused by his speed. He rode one block north in celebration of his lie to her, then turned east back toward the university. Out of the small city, on the highway again, he wondered why he had had to come along and complicate Mary Tolliver's life. She should marry a nice Catholic boy and have many bambinos. Then her father, that gaunt, tragic stalk of a man, would at least not have been betrayed by both of his children. It was the man's clenched face Allard retained most vividly from the Mass, the yellowed face weeping for a wife who had died horribly and young.

He pushed the old motorcycle up to the limit he had decided was the very edge of danger. Stone walls, trees, farms, hills, rushed at their varying speeds backward into his past. So we don't understand, he thought as his hard body cleaved the wind. Never mind; we are compelled to use those powers we have the power to use.

Aaron gets up from his desk and walks through his house, going nowhere, knowing that he will only turn around at a wall or the end of a hallway and come back to his study. But in the kitchen he sees his crash helmet on the shelf. Now what? he asks himself as he puts on his helmet and windbreaker. It would be safer right now if he left the motorcycle alone, entirely alone. But, in the garage, the Honda starts at the first kick and he is off, gravel flying, relaxed, boring on through the heavy pressure of the air. Soon he is on a narrow country road, leaning into curves, taking the curves with no movement of his handlebars. The engine hums beneath him, air whistles past his ears, the globe turns below him. He seems to know where he is going, yet he is not prepared to name that destination. The time is not now. There must be a corridor through these beautiful trees, a different voice speaking.

My name is Allard Benson, and I here confess that I have been in love with a certain kind of machine for most of my life. Love is love, and is not cured by the disapproval of love's object. I disapprove of all machines. Filthy, dangerous, what they do is remove us from our true lives, speed us loose from what we would be content to be—walking animals upon the slow and beautiful earth. But we are cursed with presumption, and never rest from creating false new worlds.

My first two-wheeled machine, which I possessed at the age of four, was a strange sort of bike with pedals on the front axle—a tricycle-like thing with only one wheel on the back. Remember that I don't use the word "love" lightly; even though I find the word impossible to define, neither can I define in any logical way my continuing relationship with machines that have caused me to break bones and lose skin. It's not reasonable at all. In airplanes, for instance, which have been proven as safe as our general lives, safer than the bathroom, the basement or the bed, I'm in anxiety, as nervous as a cat—that animal who, like me, feels control to be safety in a world of dangers that must be deftly avoided. Who controls those great silver monsters? But then one's control over a two-wheeled vehicle is pretty nominal at best, and when that modicum of control decides to disappear, nothing could be less visible. I once rolled a measured hundred feet down East Orange Grove Avenue in Pasadena—an unforgettable experience in non-control. One second I was riding, and the next I was six to eight feet in the air, watching my motorcycle's taillight pass beneath me. A rather classic wing-ding. Both the headlight and the taillight were broken in that accident. I tucked (a witness later told me that I resembled an oversized basketball). In that accident I lost some skin, blood, and the position of one kneecap, but not this weird and continuing fascination.

It is not for me to analyze this fascination. What I will do is remember one warm spring night when this love ran true, a night of no particular significance except that I have never forgotten it.

I was twenty-one, an undergraduate who hadn't the slightest idea what he wanted to do in life except that someday it must change into meaning—become heroic, dedicated, disciplined by style. I was on the GI Bill, drifting from one school to another and finding them more or less the same. At the time I was at the University of New Hampshire; next year I'd be at the University of Chicago. An aimless time, remembered without much nostalgia at all. There were girls to whom, I'm afraid, I could be attentive and then turn cruelly indifferent. I was writing my first novel, but hadn't yet come to believe it might be publishable, so even that possibility of a future seemed as unrealistic as any other daydream.

My motorcycle was an ancient Indian Pony, 1937 model, a two-cylinder four-stroke with a small frame, for its time, but quite heavy compared to modern motorcycles. It had the old, wide, longhorn handlebars, and the saddle was farther back and lower than modern ones, so that you had the feeling of being down in, of driving a beast whose knobs and dials rose up around you. The clutch was foot-operated and the gearshift was manual—a knob on a stick, as in a car. Your left hand controlled the accelerator, and your right, the spark. Anyone who rides a motorcycle now will understand how archaic this arrangement was.

My main problem was tires. These were clincher rims, and this kind of tire was extremely scarce. My rear tire was smooth but the casing was fairly healthy; my front tire was just plain weary and sick. It may have been on the wheel for more than ten years. The rubber was so tacky my fingers would stick to it and come away with a kissing noise, and every few miles the tire would lean sideways somehow, so that it actually rubbed against the fork. When this happened I'd stop, get off, and kick it back into shape again. Needless to say, I hadn't driven the motorcycle very fast.

But this warm evening a friend came into my dormitory room and said that he'd heard two guys saying that a dealer in Sanford, Maine, had two of these tires, and they were going up to buy them. At the moment, however, they were in a poker game, so I'd have a head start. It was a Friday night. I'd thought of going home for the weekend only because I hadn't been home for months and knew my parents would feel the world more in order if they could lay their eyes on me once in a while. Not that they were insistent at all; their child, though in their eyes in inevitable ways still a child, was a veteran who had been on the other side of the world in the aftermath of a great war. Within ten minutes I'd strapped my gear on the Indian Pony and taken off for Sanford.

It was one of those evenings when the air is so balmy, so benevolent, especially after a New Hampshire winter, that one feels perhaps the human metabolism evolved correctly for this planet after all. And yet this benevolence of nature usually presages some violent reminder—a "weather breeder," it's called. Huge altocumulus clouds rose up along the horizon against the warm blue, and in the distance what looked like a continuation of clear sky would flash pink, all in ominous silence, and that deceptive blue would turn out to be the vast canyon side of another cloud.

I had thirty miles to go, with stops to reshape my front tire. I wasn't at all sure that the dealer in Sanford would sell me the tires—if he really had them—or if my sick tire would get me there in the first place. I had enough money to buy the tires, but very little more.

So I headed for Dover, five miles away, past the new

green of the maples alongside the blacktop road, then to Rochester, nine more miles, and then into Maine, being very attentive to my front tire, riding carefully, with a brittle, nervous attention to bumps in the road. Sixteen miles on Maine 202, and I came into Sanford just at dusk. Before I'd even stopped to ask for directions, there was the place—a small shop attached to the owner's house. He was there in his shop, even at this hour, and yes, he did have the tires. He even helped me change the front one, a terrible job which took us over an hour. The old tire came apart along the bead when we pried it off. We marveled. "Must have been going on habit," the dealer said. He was a young man, skinny, a motorcycle lover. He charged me nothing for helping me change the tire.

And since everything here is true, I have to say that the two poker players did turn up, before I left, just as we were roping the other new tire over my saddlebags. They were disappointed, but knew of no collusion. "First come, first served," said the skinny mechanic. And then I was off, the new front tire crisp and solid. It was ten o'clock, and I was headed for my home in Leah, New Hampshire, about a hundred miles away, all on winding blacktop roads, through valleys and wild places, through towns that would soon be going dark, heat lightning and the balmy spring night. The danger of my machine had suddenly lessened a degree, so I could play with a little speed, lean like a flier into the long turns and let the earth tilt. I don't remember sound except for the hiss of the wind, and even that was gentle, controllable by a movement of my left wrist.

I passed through the country towns of Northwood, Epsom, Gossville, Chichester, and then on the heights above Concord I came upon a scene in the road that worked perversely toward that night's pleasure—I don't know how. Several people stood in the road, and a policeman swung a red flashlight. I'd slowed down, and was directed on past. But not before I'd seen beneath the weak headlights of an old car—a Hudson Terraplane with pre-Sealed Beam headlights—an old woman, flat on her back on the road as if laid out for her funeral. Her hair and face were gray as stone, and her hat, a round black thing, sat as solid as a pot beside her head. Then I had passed, on down the long hill into Concord, across the treacherous bridge over the Merrimack River. That was a bridge to make any rider shudder; if you fell on the metal gridwork of its roadway it would shred you like a carrot on a cheese grater.

In Concord I stopped at the all-night diner for coffee and a hamburger. No, I had a fried egg sandwich, which reveals itself into memory because of the big black grains in the pepper shaker; I see them scattered across the white.

In Penacook I found an all-night gas station and filled my tank. The old man who ran it at night turned out to be another motorcycle lover, who told me how he rode belt-driven Indians in 1926, on roads that were mostly gravel. "How far you riding tonight?" he asked. It was past midnight. "Leah," I said, conscious of envy. "That's a long ride. Hope the rain don't catch you," he said. Still those thunderheads moved along the horizon, flashing with no sound. I did have an army poncho in my duffel bag, but that wouldn't help much. "You got a chance," he said, and I kicked down the starter, set the spark to its smoothest rumble and went on north.

In Boscawen, by the big white church, I bore left, following Route 4 into the hills below Kearsarge, through Salisbury and Salisbury Heights—towns of a few old houses, dark now. Few cars were out. Then Andover and Potter Place, small settlements along what was mostly woods, with the branches of the trees flicking, mile after mile, over my head. The emptiness of the woods is always close on a motorcycle, because if you slow or stop you are alone and naked, already in the dark and part of it. Not like in a car, which is a room. Only your speed and the wavery hole your headlight cuts ahead of you gives some slight edge of independence from the night. It's risky; the trees seem to reach toward you as you pass.

Between South Danbury and Danbury a car followed me

for several miles, and with this audience I was more conscious of my graceful lean into the curves, what a daring figure I must seem as I pierced the darkness. At that age everything is referential; all lights are eyes. Perhaps a lovely girl drove that car, and measured the breadth of my shoulders. But at Danbury the car turned off toward Bristol, to the east, and I was alone again, at speed. Grafton, Canaan, Enfield, the long, curving descent into Mascoma by the lake, then the long hills above Leah.

Sometime in the morning I pulled up, stiffened by the wind but still hearing its rhythms in my ears, at the Welkum Diner in Leah, no more than a few blocks from my home. Home was a place I didn't especially want to be—a destination too much like a starting place, unworthy of my journey. As I had a cup of coffee in the diner, my Indian Pony waited upon its kickstand at the curb. Dark red, oily and warm, it had freed for me all those deserted miles, and carried me across a whole state. I didn't want to stop, but I had nowhere else to go that night.

And of course I thought then that my real life hadn't yet begun—if there ever was to be such a beginning. GI Bill bum that I was, I wasn't sure at all, then. But there is that one spring night my Indian Pony, imperfect yet faithful, carried me past certain borders I cannot forget—small triumphs and real dangers. If all the going of one's life could reverberate like that down through the years.

Aaron has just frightened himself badly. On loose gravel he approached a turn and found that he was not going to make it. First he moved into his lean with dreamy assurance, the machine sliding out, drifting out under the illusion of control, but then it went too far and he knew all at once, his mind calculating forces and vectors and coming to the bad conclusion that this was all real and final. He is now lying in a ditch, a tarnished beer can beneath his shoulder, another between his legs, taking stock of his wounds. His left knee will be heard from later. He nearly vomits from pain and shock, then slowly organizes his legs and arms. He has plenty of time, so he moves slowly, taking stock of synapses, the roots of muscles, the articulations of bones. He has just missed a small white maple, which would have been the end of him. Someday, he knows very well, the small maple in whatever final form it takes will not be avoidable, but as for now he has again missed the immovable object and must continue. He gets up, his knee causing some nausea still, and examines his Honda.

Gasoline is leaking from the tank, but he turns off the ignition and somehow manages to drag the machine around to a more vertical position and the gas stops leaking. The clutch cable is broken, torn out probably by the rock that kissed his knee, but since all the gears are synchromesh that doesn't matter too much, and he won't be stranded out here in the country somewhere north of town, on this gravel road among grown-up fields and woods. He limps up and down for a while, speaking to his knee and to his wrist in familiar terms, gruffly but with the familiarity one has toward old friends, old fellow campaigners. It seems that he had some idea of where he was going and the accident should somehow change that murky intention. The road does seem familiar. For the moment he hasn't the strength to drag his Honda out of the ditch, but that will come back as soon as the shock lessens. At least he is certain that none of his bones are broken this time. It is hard to light a cigarette with his trembling hands, but he manages, then sits with his back against the small maple God has fortunately commanded to have grown two feet south of Aaron Benham's appointment with death.

He can hear a car coming along the road, so he removes his white helmet and moves a few feet into the brush, becoming invisible. The Honda is deep enough in the ditch to be mostly out of sight. He'll lick his wounds in private.

The car is an old pickup truck, its springs weak, the bulbous metal of its front bumper and hood shimmying relaxedly over the bumps. Though it is several years older than when he last saw it he recognizes it as Forneau's old truck, and now he knows exactly where he is. Therese is driving it, alone in the faded cab, her face stern at the task of driving. She too is older. There is the same drabness of skin, the same good facial bones beneath, but several years have laid themselves upon her in their tiring ways. He thinks that as she is now, given himself then, he would think it strange to want to make love to her.

Fifty yards down the road she turns into her driveway. He hears the last rattle and squeak of the truck, then the cab door slamming, then slamming twice again, the last more solidly. So. He may have intended to come by here. At least this is where he is. With some wonder in his mind he walks, limping, down the road to the old house, his helmet swinging from his hand.

THERESE'S BEAUTY SHOP

says the old sign, more faintly now, muffled by the rains and winds of the last six years. No, it is more like seven years since he's been by this way. What should his welcome be? He limps to the door and knocks, noticing that the knob and lock have been replaced. The door opens and she is looking at him. She has to look through time, down through the tunnel of all those years. Then her face turns strange.

"You've hurt yourself," she says, and takes his arm. He lets her pull him inside the kitchen and sit him down at a chrome and Formica table that is also new. The room has changed. It is less cluttered, more colorful with orange-red curtains and frills over the cupboards. The battered old hair drier is nowhere in sight. A white-enameled gas range has replaced the wood-kerosene stove. Therese looks at him once, her expression nothing he can decipher, goes into what must be a bathroom, also new, and returns with a washcloth and towel. At the sink she fills a basin with warm water. Her body is still slim beneath the remorseless gravity of the years. Perhaps her neck has bowed almost imperceptibly. She must be thirty-five or thirty-six now. There is a certain graininess about the skin of her elbows, but again he is impressed by the good bones; the girl and this woman come together so clearly that it might be another time. But then she turns, and her face is more powerful than it once was. It has lived with itself for a long time now. She is no longer shy, or pretty in a young animal way. She is not about to smile at him, but firmly moves his chin so she can wash his face.

"It's been a long time, Therese. Are you mad at me?"

She squeezes the washcloth over the basin, the water turning pink. "I don't know what I am," she says. Her voice is louder than it once was, but not through anger. "You're too old to ride a motorcycle. Lean forward." She unzips his windbreaker and unbuttons his shirt, then follows the blood with the warm cloth.

"Have you got a drink in the house?" he asks.

"So that's it," she says. "You a drunkard now? All there is is some home-brew Forneau left down cellar. You want some of that?"

"Sure," he says.

Her hands move competently over his chest, doing nothing but wash him, as if he is a piece of furniture. "What'd you do, run off the road? Did you mean to come here or was it just accidental?"

"I don't know. I think I meant to ride on by, but I guess I did mean to ride on by here."

"Been a long time." There is grimness in her voice. Her brown eyes are harder, glittery where they were not glittery at all before, but soft and almost furry in their depths. "You never showed yourself around here."

"You've changed your hair," he says. "It used to be browner."

"It's been like this for three years." There are streaks of gold, or maybe platinum in it, and he prefers it the way it once was, drab and innocent. It's none of his business, her face declares. She has a vertical wrinkle between her brows, caused, he supposes, by many frowns. Life has gone on without him, which makes him sad. But it has to, after all, if he isn't there. If he never shows up.

"How's your family?" she asks. She removes the basin and wipes him dry.

"Okay, I guess," he says.

She looks at him wryly, quizzically, as she applies a Band-Aid to his jaw. "You guess?"

"They're away. They're down in Wellesley with Agnes' folks."

"Humph. When the cat's away the mice will play. That why you're half drunk, running around on your motorcycle?"

"May be."

"You still want some home-brew?"

"Will you have a glass with me, Therese?"

"I hate it. I don't know why I never threw it out." She goes down cellar and returns with a dusty brown bottle, then carefully, seeming to resent the necessary carefulness, decants it into a glass pitcher. Her resentfulness is probably from having to do this for Forneau so many times in the past, under pain of violence if she stirred up the yeast in the bottom of the bottle. She brings the pitcher and two tumblers to the table.

"Button your shirt up," she says, pouring him a full glass and herself two inches of the amber beer. His left hand, it becomes obvious, is still stiff, so she comes over him and buttons his shirt, her warmth over him, her breasts that are larger, softer now, close to him. She smells of the cellar, of potato peels, and of the warm soapy water.

"Oh, I'm not angry," she says. "I never was, much. By the time I thought to get angry too much time went by. I ended up maybe thinking you were some kind of a coward."

"How true," he says, his nose full of the effervescent ticks of the beer, its familiar acid and molasses on his tongue.

"You weren't scared of Forneau. You were mainly scared of your wife."

"That may be a simple way to put it, but you're mainly right."

She is her own property now. Her dress is in the current style, almost. She is wearing nylon stockings and red shoes. She takes a sip of the beer, grimaces, and gets up to put away the groceries she brought from town. "Life goes on," she says, with a sigh.

"I never see you around town," he says.

"I work in the shoeshop in Litchwood, so I do about everything there."

"I'm in a weird mood," he says.

"You must be if you come out here after all these years."

"You've fixed the place up. You going to stay here now?"

"I don't know. It's easy. I mean it's cheap. That old truck's about rusted out and the doors are falling off of it. I don't know much about things but I make eighty-five dollars a week as a stitcher and maybe I can get a real car if I don't go spending all my money on rent. I make maybe ten dollars Saturdays and Sundays out of the beauty shop. Got my regular customers."

"Do you have a boyfriend?"

"Maybe that used to be your business."

"Sorry."

"I don't harbor no hard feelings, Aaron. I was such a dumb goose in those days, though. I should of left Forneau and found a boy my own age. I was scared half to death Forneau would catch us but as long as you were around it was the only sweetness in my life."

She has turned softer. She has come back to sit across from him at the table, and toys with her glass, turning it around on the blue Formica. "You meant a lot to me, Aaron." Her use of his name means that she is remembering without resentment. "It sure didn't last long, though, did it."

"No," he says.

"Well, it's water over the dam. Life goes on. I got a boyfriend, all right, but he's married. They all are, the ones that want to keep a girl company. Get to be my age and they're all married with six kids. Fred, he works in the office. His wife's a real ugly bitch he can't even talk to her, he says.

I seen her in the Stop and Shop yelling at her youngest kid you'd think the kid was a criminal or something. Poor Fred. He's overweight, he's got a heart condition and he has to take little white pills. He's a nice, nice man." She shakes her head, the chromatic hair flying on its tethers with an abandon that seems for a moment youthful. "I put the beauty shop in the other room there. It looks real good. Professional. You want to see it?"

"Sure," he says, carefully testing his knee as he rises. It works, though the joint seems to be packed with sludge.

"I got a new Sears drier so now I can have two customers at a time. They like that better, some of them. They can gossip better, you know."

The gluey smell of the hair-setting chemicals brings him back to those other times. He remembers her drab brown hair with sadness and affection. In those days he thought her neither young nor old. She was such a tender animal, unused to receiving tenderness.

He has to admit that the beauty shop does look more professional without the kitchen paraphernalia mixed in among its own chairs, trays and racks of curlers. A fluorescent lighting bar, in peach tones, completes the look of an operating room when Therese proprietorially turns it on. "Very nice," he says. "It's a lot different."

"I'm my own boss now," she says.

He goes back to the kitchen table and pours himself some more home-brew.

"You sure you need that?" she says.

"I'm sure I don't need it," he says, and takes a drink.

"You all right, Aaron?"

"I can't help wishing it was seven years ago and Forneau was at Camp Drum with the National Guard."

"Never mind, Aaron. A lot of things've changed."

"That's right, Therese."

"Fred says he's going to get a divorce, but sometimes I don't believe it. That's life, huh?"

"That's right." He moves toward the door, taking a small detour to leave his glass on the sink counter. "Thanks for the first aid."

"That's all right, Aaron."

"Goodbye, Therese."

"Nice to of seen you again, Aaron."

He manages to drag his Honda back up to the road. Harboring no hard feelings, it starts on the first kick. With only a small gnashing of gears he gets it into low and he is off, up through the gears with no clutch. His eyes are bleary, his joints sticky and old. He is not afraid of the curves that he still takes at speed, but his energy has run low, and the only place he can think of, the only destination he can think of at all, is home.

It was during those cruelly beautiful days of final exams, in warm May, when all the young animals, including Allard Benson, found some strange trouble they hadn't had in February in appreciating the fine dry civilized voices of Addison and Steele, Dryden, Pope, etc. Though still fond of those voices, Allard seemed to be governed these days more by his skin than by his mind. He liked to look at Naomi, who wasn't speaking to him but did consent to give him smoky, murderous looks whenever they met—looks he interpreted correctly, his mysterious power making him thoughtful. And at Mary, fair beautiful Mary who said, now, beneath the barely trembling green of the maple leaves, "What's the matter with Naomi? She won't even say hello to you."

"We had a political argument," he said, a statement that might hold up in court.

They were in front of Mary's dormitory, she sitting on the steps, he astride his creaking, cooling Indian Pony. They had been invited that afternoon, through Harold, to visit Liliputown and have dinner with Colonel Immingham and his "lady," as Harold gravely put it. The problem was transportation. Nathan had taken Angela to Boston and Harold's Matilda was in the garage, having slipped a link or two of her timing chain.

"It's only five miles. I suppose we could walk," Allard said. "Or hitchhike, but that's a pain. So what we have left is Tonto, the flying red oilstorm."

"You know I promised my father . . ."

"Look, Mary, I gave Harold a ride back from the garage and didn't even blow his wig off. I mean old Tonto can be *sedate.* I'll go slow, enjoying your arms around me, holding me tight in abject guilt and terror."

She laughed, shaking her head, her fair hair following softly.

But she wanted to go. She wanted to ride behind him with her arms around him. She wanted to see Lilliputown with Harold and Allard, her admirers, and to have dinner with the strange old Colonel and his lady. This was what she wanted to do; there was nothing else in the world she wanted to do more, so he knew she was going to break her promise to her father. He saw her looking at the Indian Pony and began to try to see it through her eyes.

"I really promised, Allard. I can't break my promise."

The long, red, rangy machine was misty and faded in places, in other places worn to the bright steel, in others a luminous blood color where oil shone. In deeper cracks and depressions the blood dimmed to the black of oil and grease, where the engine did its revolutions. A brutally strong chain was just visible beneath its worn steel guard. Wires and cables, uncovered and nakedly functional, proceeded from one dangerous mechanical place to another. The double saddle was shaped into concave human buttocks, where hers would fit the polished, used leather.

"I have the feeling it will be a suit-and-tie sort of dinner," he said, "with candlelight and wine. Something out of Harold's novel. He'd be terribly disappointed if Allyson Turnbridge wasn't there."

Mary's face grew unamused, so he hesitated. He didn't

really want to make fun of Harold, either, though it was hard to resist. "Harold was upset about the unavailability of Matilda," he said, hearing the flippant tones enter his words again. "He really wants us to come, Mary. He says the Colonel and his lady are 'charming eccentrics.' "

She got up and touched the headlight of the Indian Pony, her hand sliding over it for a moment before she drew it away, as if the metal were hot. "You know I want to go, Allard."

"This *is* sort of an emergency, isn't it?" he said. "Doesn't your promise have any contingency clauses somewhere in the fine print?"

"My promises don't have any fine print. At least they never used to."

Ah, that was better. Better, but a little sad to see desire sneaking its way into the intentions, as it always did. He could see that Mary felt this sadness, too. He put his arm around her and drew her up against him. "We'll declare this an emergency," he said. She leaned against him, her hands on his waist, her fawn-colored skirt touching the nether parts of the machine.

"All right," she said.

"I'll pick you up in an hour."

"Now that I've said I'll go, I think I am really a little afraid of your motorcycle."

"It is but a servant to me, and obeys my every command."

"Don't have too much pride," she said, smiling and turning away. He watched her graceful calves and ankles as she climbed the steps. They seemed to glow with an inner light that of course was in his eyes.

Back at Parker Hall he prepared for this strange visit. In his short life, "charming eccentrics" had more often been pains in the ass—on the order of, say, Gordon Robert Westinghouse, who stood gangling beside his desk when he returned from the shower, a single piece of typewriter paper clutched in damp, bluish hands.

"I have worked forty-one hours on this verse," Gordon Robert Westinghouse said. "*Forty-one hours.*"

Allard found a clean pair of shorts, the olive-drab army-issue kind that tied with little olive-drab strings, and put them on. He thought, pleased, that he was no longer in the army.

"Forty-one hours of concentration unbroken except for certain prosaic human necessities."

Presented with the piece of limp paper, Allard read:

Melifulous Aponatatus, wind spun,
Grieves Our Silver Lady
Of the briny Moon;
She sails on velvet o'er the wrack
Of trees and sere eye-hollows
Once fair men, now bones bleached white,
Caught at a sad attention.

"Who's this 'Melifulous Aponatatus'?"

" 'Mellifluous' is an adjective. 'Aponatatus' is, so to speak, my *persona*, my alter ego."

"Well, you spelled it 'melifulous.' "

"Puh," Gordon Robert Westinghouse said, brushing such a technicality away with a long arm that seemed to have an extra joint in it.

"I mean you might have taken two minutes out of those forty-one hours and looked it up," Allard said.

"Why don't you write it down that you said that to me?" Gordon Robert Westinghouse said. "It will show the difference in quality between the creative and the ordinary, or merely assimilative, consciousness."

"Yeah," Allard said, putting on a white shirt. When he turned around again, Gordon Robert Westinghouse was gone, having ambulated out on his strange joints, taking his worn page with him. Again Allard wondered what Boom Maloumian had in store for The Poet. Maybe he was so strange even Boom Maloumian's creative consciousness couldn't conceive of a proper reward for him.

The business of the choice of a tie faced him. He had three: one a mauve gift he had never worn, another somberly maroon, the third his old school tie. The Dexter-Benham orange, blue and black stripes seemed a trifle gaudy, but perhaps the Colonel would go for that sort of thing. Harold certainly would. The cheap gray suit and brown army dress shoes completed his costume, the disguise in which he would go to Lilliputown. This visit seemed a digression from the present direction of his life—as did final exams, for that matter. What he really wanted to do was to create in Mary Tolliver the perfect receptor of himself. *The perfect receptor of himself;* that had a sort of ring to it. He went to his desk and wrote it down, not without his traitorous inner eye's ironic squint at whatever gods observed this pretentious popinjay. The perfect receptor of himself, huh? Yes. First chaos, the total destruction of certain deeply held beliefs, followed by calm sadness and then the careful, loving (yet stern) reconstruction. Of course.

When he picked her up at her dormitory she was pretty and sophisticated-looking in a dark blue dress she had made herself. He noticed that once she had made up her mind to violate her promise to her father she didn't hesitate, but with his help in arranging her dress so it wouldn't touch the dirtier parts of the Indian Pony, and with some conquered apprehension, she mounted the beast and put her arms firmly around him.

He rode slowly through the warm afternoon, not over thirty-five miles an hour, and soon she indicated by the reduced pressure of her arms that she was getting used to the earth's tilting. She didn't say a word until the five miles had passed and he had stopped, carefully, in front of Lilliputown Town Hall, across the narrow-gauge railroad tracks from the station. As he helped her off, his eyes were struck by a flash of smooth thigh and white silk. She turned to him as she arranged her hair with her hands. She had seen and wondered at the perfectly miniature buildings, but first she said, looking at him as though he had done something wonderful, "I loved riding. I really loved it!"

That gaze of admiration and gratitude made him feel as

though he were full of virulent microorganisms that would somehow cure, or fulfill, or raise up both of them when he entered her by the glimmering path of the smooth thigh, the immaculate silk. But wait, wait. Lilliputown, the old Colonel and his lady, however irritating and digressive they might be, must now be suffered. Down, he said to his mindless intensities. Be patient. This dangerous project he was entering upon was too important to risk because of impatience. He must wait. Remember that, and walk coolly with Mary toward Harold Roux, who now appeared like a giant before the opened, startling, wall-sized door of the Town Hall.

Behind Harold a tall man appeared. He was over six feet tall, and the first impression of him was of a nearly voracious pleasure. He smiled using all of his head, even the rigid gray bristles of his cropped hair. All of the lean, wrinkled flesh of his face and neck smiled. His ears seemed to cup forward into that smile. Each of his tanned ivory teeth expressed hungry pleasure.

"Colonel Immingham, may I present Mary Tolliver and Allard Benson," Harold said with high seriousness.

"Oh, how do you do!" Colonel Immingham said. He took Mary's hand as if to kiss it, but merely patted it with his other hand. "Charming!" he said. He reached for Allard's hand and gripped it with the sudden rigidity of a wooden vise—not hard, but with the firmness of great strength. "Young people!" he said. "How nice to have young people about! But now come inside and meet my Lady!" He bent from the waist, a welcoming half-bow. His ancient brown tweed suit looked if it it had been worn at grouse shoots before the First World War.

Inside the building they went down three unexpected steps and found themselves in a house of ordinary dimensions, the foyer a small office with a desk and the sort of upholstered chairs that are obviously for public use. Beyond the foyer, through a draped portal, was a cluttered, comfortable living room, with fireplace, bookshelves, bridge lamps and chintz-covered furniture. Installed in a rattan peacock chair, its flared back a frame for her, was a lady of fifty or so with the body of a child. She too smiled intensely, and held out her delicate little hands. Her hair was dyed a frizzled reddish orange, and on each little cheek was a spot of red rouge.

"Such a pleasure!" she said, her voice strangely loud coming from such a small person. Allard had half expected her to squeak like a Munchkin. "I am Morgana Immingham. And what a handsome couple you are, Miss Tolliver and Mr. Benson! Won't you all sit down for a moment before Hamilcar takes you on his tour? His *inevitable* tour," she added, beaming at her husband, who beamed back at her from his height. Mary, Harold and Allard sat in the deep chintz chairs, while the Colonel leaned against the mantel. "So nice of Harold to get you to come out for a visit," she said. "We do enjoy young people, yet we hardly ever see them. Nearly everyone we know has grown up and turned old! But, as Hamilcar says, I never have grown old at all, possibly because, as you can see, I'm only four feet, five inches tall!"

"And perfect in every detail," the Colonel said.

She squirmed with pleasure beneath his prideful regard. "Now, Hamilcar, I know how much you want to show these attractive young people your work, so I won't keep you." She turned to the young people. "I'd join you, but actually I haven't been feeling up to snuff lately, so I'll just sit here and read my magazine. Now go along and have a good time!"

The Colonel told them to meet him on the platform of the Lilliputown Railroad Station. Being guests of the Lilliputown Railroad they wouldn't need tickets: "But you might look into the ticket window and say hello to the Stationmaster for me!" His enthusiasm was at a level just above their wondering response, his grins and suppressed laughter demanding more awe than Allard thought he could quite manage, yet the Colonel didn't seem to mind this, if he noticed it. He went quickly out another door, and Mary and Allard followed Harold back out through the foyer.

"He's so excited," Mary said. "It *is* exciting."

"He loves to show people what he's done," Harold said. Harold seemed fondly proud of the Colonel and his creations. "Be sure to look into the ticket window."

They crossed the tracks, stepping over the shining rails and the little two-by-four ties with their perfect spikes the size of twenty-penny nails. Allard bent down to look at these and Harold said the Colonel made the spikes in his workshop. "You like tools, Allard. You've got to see his workshop."

They walked up the properly gritty ramp to the station platform. In the late afternoon sun the perspectives of platform, dark red arches, rounded windows with their clean glass, seemed to waver in Allard's eyes between the real and the created. Was that a one-foot drop to the roadbed or a four-foot drop? Only his enormous shoe at the edge confirmed the smaller dimension. The wooden arches were high enough so there was no danger of hitting their heads, yet they still seemed in scale.

"The man's a wonder," he said. "There's a principle here I can't understand."

"He'll want to talk about that," Harold said.

Bending over, they looked into the ticket window to be startled by the Colonel's grinning, vivid face. Because the small face looked up at them instead of levelly at a person of its own height, it almost seemed, for one frozen second before immobility proved the figure a model, that the Colonel had tricked them by turning himself miniature and scooting around ahead of them to install himself as Stationmaster.

"That's a little frightening," Mary said.

"He's got himself in that face. Christ, look at his grin," Allard said. He didn't understand how a man could be that much aware of his own strange facial paroxysms. Could he grin into a mirror and copy himself? As he turned away from the ticket window it seemed an ungracious thing to ignore the avid attention still beamed upward at his back.

Soon the earth gave the faintest tremble. From somewhere behind the Lombardy poplars came the high call of a steam whistle, then the whoosh-puff of a locomotive. They looked down the track to see a green semaphore on a pole move up to the horizontal, yet no train appeared. Squeaks and grinding noises could be heard beneath the huffing of the engine—the secondary clamor of a train—but the train did not appear. A small apprehension, then the startling appearance of the train behind them, coming the other way, having circled around back of the station. There it was, ponderously swaying on the narrow curve. Smoke and black iron, bright steel and brass, it came toward them, bell clanging, with the slow momentum and harsh clatter of a real train. The engine's wheels seemed too close together to keep the bulk of the machine from tipping over. It swayed, huffing dark smoke from a flared chimney as tall as the Mad Hatter's top hat. Three brass lanterns on its front end didn't assume to stare like eyes, but the brass valve in the very center of the boiler did, so that the engine seemed to peer straight ahead with the powerful yet slightly moronic, clownish intensity of a cyclops. Other hatlike protuberances and odd tanks connected by pipes were bolted and banded along the short barrel of the engine. It stopped with a metallic shriek from the brakes—locomotive, tender, two passenger cars and a red caboose. The Colonel wasn't there at all; in the cab of the engine a ruddy, weathered-faced railroad man in a striped denim uniform stared forward into the distance, his head no bigger than an apple. Then the whole top of the tender rose up, its imitation coal not spilling, and the Colonel clambered out, chuckling and grinning at their obvious appreciation.

"It's unbelievable!" Mary said.

The engine steamed and rumbled, waiting.

"This is an approximately one-sixth model of a Prussian State Railways 0–4–2T, the original made in the early 1880's," the Colonel said. " 'O' means it doesn't have any lead dolly wheels in front of the four driving wheels, the '2' meaning it does have the two smaller supporting wheels below the cab. The 'T' means it's a tank engine and carries its water alongside the firebox and boiler instead of in the tender. Notice the large diameters of the driving wheels, which show this machine to have been originally designed for the higher speeds of passenger work. The builders of the model, in their efforts to be accurate to scale, unfortunately retained the large wheels, which gives the locomotive a tendency for speed the Lilliputown roadbeds can hardly afford! I must apologize for a rather odd combination of stock," the Colonel added. "An American caboose on what is essentially a European passenger train, for instance; but my trackage is rather short and I don't have unlimited resources."

"Did you *make* it?" Mary said.

"Oh no, my dear. I've improved it in certain ways, and added certain small details, but of course the manufacture of a steam locomotive is beyond my capabilities. No, the locomotive and the passenger cars were made by Sepp Gerhardt *Aktiengesellshaft* of Erfurt, in 1910. They were meant to be the toys of a Hohenzollern prince, but here they are—the toys of a retired colonel of the United States Army! Stranger things have happened, I assure you!"

Allard was down on one knee looking at the silver piston rods and the sturdy driving wheels of the engine. Its steamy heat was real, oil and vapor leaking from its live, breathing vents.

"The locomotive alone weighs over three thousand pounds, so you can see, Mr. Benson, that it's quite a toy."

"It is," Allard said. "It is, indeed."

"But now you must be the guests of the Lilliputown Railroad for the journey beyond the poplars!"

The Colonel opened the three side doors of the first passenger car, revealing a single seat behind each door. Roof panels slid open, allowing the passengers' heads to look out over the top of the car. Gallantly helping Mary into one compartment, the Colonel then checked the closing of all the doors before resuming his place in the tender—this time his head visible above the imitation coal. The bell rang and his head turned around toward them. "All aboard!" he shouted, and with a huff, a skid and a lurch they progressed toward Lilliputown itself.

Allard had time to turn around once toward Mary, who had been given the rearmost seat, probably because of the smoke from the engine. Her eyes were wide and a little apprehensive. She smiled quickly and made a funny, mock-horrified face, as if to ask what their heads were doing sitting in a row on top of a railroad car, and then the train took them between the tall, yellow-green portals of the town proper.

It was evident at once that this was someone's ideal place, that a segment of another world had been created here. Buildings were arranged around a park through which a brook, a river within this scale, flowed quietly between stone embankments, below gracefully arched bridges. The trees, mostly elms, were too large, perhaps, yet they could have been great patriarchal trees. The air itself was somehow in scale, distances seeming longer than they could possibly be. It was the quality of shade, the way the shadows fell across this acre or two of tended landscape. The buildings were arranged around the park in an order that was neither uniform nor an obvious attempt to be random. On its own lot, with funereal-looking clipped hedges, was a little brown church, and then a bank in the Greek style (First National of Lilliputown), then a barbershop with its red and white striped pole. The scale, again, was hallucinatory in an unsettling way that kept the town from seeming midgetlike or cute.

The train, swaying on its narrow tracks, wove in and out among the buildings, each of which had a landing area before its disguised entrance. Finally, with bell ringing and steam hissing, the train stopped so they could get out. The Colonel took an iron rod from the side of the cab and turned it in a switch in the tracks, then ran the whole train out of sight in what looked to be a stone-arched tunnel. Soon he came back, grinning, wiping his hands on a large red bandanna.

He led them along a graveled path to the church, with its brown clapboards and high-peaked roof, its wooden Gothic windows. The building and its plantings had the somnolent, kept, Sunday-only look of all churches. A small arched signboard, glass-covered, stood near the broad doors. In tasteful white letters the legend said:

THE LITTLE BROWN CHURCH
IN THE VALE

Rev. John Shuttlesworth
Sunday Sermon: "They who have
eyes, yet do not see."

"Now, come with me," the Colonel said. He took them up the walk to the church. "Look inside," he said, pointing to a little square peephole in one of the doors.

Mary looked first, looked for a long time before she turned around, shaking her head, perplexed. "But this isn't . . ." she said. "But aren't all these . . . ?"

The Colonel grinned so hard his scalp wrinkled. "Before you say anything, let Mr. Benson look too!"

Allard put his eye to the dark little hole and saw a long aisle, rows of pews full of people, a stained-glass window down at the altar end, and a minister standing beneath the large window with his head bowed in silence. Light, the dusty beams of church light, fell from the high window onto the cross, the candlesticks, the pulpit with its opened Bible. Nearer, all the heads were bowed, various in their tilts toward reverence. A balding man, his wife, their small tow-headed child, an old woman with a frilly lace collar—all were bent toward the long perspective to the altar.

"You saw it!" the Colonel said. "Didn't you see it? Didn't you see it, Miss Tolliver, with your own eyes?"

"I saw a church full of people," Mary said. "But I thought these were all . . ."

"Now look again!" the Colonel said, and opened the church doors with a magician's flourish, his arms still outstretched as he turned triumphantly toward them.

Behind him, in a rather pleasant small room, were two single beds, an easy chair, a writing table with its Gideon Bible and ashtray, a straight chair, a floor lamp, a wastebasket, a casement window with a pretty view of trees, and a door which presumably led to a closet or bathroom. Allard found himself documenting these things as they slowly blotted out the quiet scene of worship he had known was there.

"But you saw them!" the Colonel said. "You saw the altar, the people, the minister bent over the Good Book!"

They looked at him.

"Ah! Is it magic, my dear young people, or is it art? Perhaps the sermon should read, 'They who do not have eyes, but see,' because you saw what was not (or was it?) and real eyes cannot see what is not (or is it?)!"

Allard noticed, on the inside of one of the church doors, at about the level of the peephole, a small cube about as big as a letter box. The Colonel saw him look at it. "Mr. Benson is beginning to see," he said. "You are interested in real possibilities, isn't that so? In how to do things? The difference between observer and maker, isn't that right?"

"You mean it's all in the box?" Allard said.

"It's all in the box! Yes, all in the box! This is called *trompe l'oeil*, which means 'fooling the eye.' I don't think I like that name. Because, you see, the eye is so skillful, such an efficient, magnificent organ, sifting out what is irrelevant to its purposes, focusing exactly over such a wide range, changing, letting in more light or less according to what it must see or wants to see. And we use these very talents of the eye, not to fool it—no, I don't like that word—but to reveal new dimensions. That is to say, we must understand it before we can show it new realities. Do you understand? What you saw, if my skill was great enough, was a church full of people, as Miss Tolliver said. A church full of people! Can you remember if you heard an occasional cough, a clearing of the throat, the shuffle of feet, perhaps the last dying chord of the organ? The congregation is at this moment quietly meditating, some of them even upon God. 'Let us bow our heads for a moment in silent prayer,' the Reverend Shuttlesworth has just said, and the church is almost silent." The Colonel took a ring of keys from his pocket and selected a small brass one, with which he unlocked the little box on the door. "Look inside and you'll see something entirely different!"

They looked into the box to see rows of little cutouts, two-dimensional. A small bit of color at one end showed itself to be the stained-glass window. The top of the box was set with thin, arched pieces of wood to make it the ceiling of the church. A light bulb the size and shape of a Christmas-tree bulb gave light to what they had seen and believed.

"Cardboard, cellophane and balsa wood, put together with glue," the Colonel said. He shut the box and locked it. "To keep out curious little fingers. Children, especially, want to find out things. Who can blame them?" Again with the flourish of a magician, though now more subdued, he reverentially closed the church doors upon the small bedroom. "And now I'll show you, if you'd like, some more of the minor wonders of Lilliputown."

They followed him on a tour of his marvels, the sun slanting dustily through the giant elms, printing on their eyes the eaves, walls and cornices of his buildings. At the barbershop they peered through another *trompe l'oeil* peephole to see the bald barber with his comb and scissors at the hair of a small boy who did not seem to be enjoying it at all. In the shop were the waiting customers, posters on the wall, a mirrored side that reflected everything in the plausible room. The saloon's box was still in the process of being made, the Colonel said. It would, he thought, be his best so far, a period piece with Wild Bill Hickok and Calamity Jane drinking at a round table center left, with a magnificent rococo bar of brass and mahogany and a painting of a voluptuous semi-nude on the wall behind it. Yes, he admitted to an unasked question, he did tend to mix periods and styles. His enthusiasms wandered, but never far from Lilliputown.

They examined the Greek-revival First National Bank of Lilliputown, the City Jail, the Post Office, the General Store. He was planning little boxes for these too, but they took time to plan and make, and the mere maintenance of the landscape and the exteriors was time-consuming.

As they strolled through the central park, where the clear brook ran quietly in its channel, the Colonel talked happily, looking around as eagerly as a tourist, observing his blessings with constantly renewed wonder. After a while he pulled out his gold pocket watch and said that it was time for him to attend to the details of their dinner, and would Harold be so kind as to entertain their guests for a while? He'd be ready for them at six-thirty. With a small bow and a bright nod, he was off.

Harold took them up the path along the brook, climbing away from the village proper up a long rill of white water, through the trees, until they came to a deep pool filled by a narrow, three-foot falls at one end. Gray rock descended into the clear water, which must have been six or seven feet deep in its deepest places. The bottom was smooth, quartz-streaked granite smoothed by water, with patches of pebbly sand here and there. On one side of the pool was a grassy area and a small outdoor fireplace built of stone. The surrounding ledges were sun-warm even where they finally sat down in the shade of a young hemlock.

"He's slightly crazy," Allard said. "But in a nice way, I suppose."

"He *is* a charming eccentric," Mary said.

"Who is he, anyway?" Allard asked Harold. "How'd your uncle get to know him? And his 'Lady'!"

"My uncle was his 'batman,' as he calls it, in France in the First World War. They always kept in touch."

"His wife's a strange little bird."

"They're both strange, I guess," Harold said. "He doesn't want her to do anything and she's perfectly happy doing nothing."

"Nothing?"

"She reads a lot."

"She doesn't even help with the dishes?" Mary said.

"No, he does everything. During the summer he hires someone to mow the grass, and a woman comes in to change the linen and do washing and things like that, but he does everything else. He's quite a chef, too. I think even I'm gaining weight out here. But he's the happiest person I think I've ever met. He *worships* Morgana." Harold looked at Allard. "He thinks she's the most wonderful object God ever made. 'Perfect in every detail.' "

"She looks sort of like a doll," Mary said.

"Especially with that hair and the clown spots on her cheeks," Allard said.

Harold shrugged. "She's over fifty. Anyway, he thinks she's beautiful."

"That's *nice*," Mary said.

"But crazy."

" 'Beauty is in the eye of the beholder,' " Harold said.

"Yeah, but it's nice not to have to work too hard at it." They both looked at Mary, who blushed and looked away.

"The water's beautiful," she said. "We should have brought our swimming suits. Wouldn't it be nice to dive in there? It's so clear."

"You could come out tomorrow," Harold said.

"Or we could go skinny-dipping right now," Allard said. "We've got over half an hour."

"Oh, sure," Harold said, looking away from Mary in the wake of this scandalous suggestion. She laughed, believing, no doubt, that this idea was too strange even to contemplate, as Allard now very seriously contemplated how this very thing could and would ultimately be arranged. Smooth Mary, silver-pink in the cool moonlight, sliding in the easy friction of water into his welcoming arms. That lovely cold. Just the two of them, of course. No shivering lonesome Harold Roux sitting on the rocks under his dry, inviolate wig, observing. Again he wondered how Harold Roux came by the authority to make him feel guilty, to make him spend any thought at all on the morality of his choices. There Harold sat, looking too neatly fragile to be sitting on anything as crude as a granite ledge, with that obviously fake wig on, and yet there was in him the iron of judgment.

"But what do you do here, Harold?" Mary asked.

Harold looked at her and then again away, flustered by her direct gaze. He half stuttered. "I . . . I'm sort of bookkeeper, clerk, errand boy, I guess. Also maybe an audience. I like them, I really do. They live as if they were very important. They are. I think I'll stay on this summer."

"Important?" Allard said.

"Their lives are formal. I don't know. They live as if they were very glamorous people. Everything they do is important to them. It's like they live every minute."

"It sounds exhausting," Allard said.

Harold disapproved of this tone. "They have the best of everything. Not the most expensive, but the best. Once the Colonel told me that life was too short not to have married the most beautiful lady in the world, and to take her for drives in a 1926 Bentley. You'll have to see his car. It looks like it once belonged to a rajah or something."

"But, Harold, the little lady is more or less ugly."

"You'll never understand. Never." Harold was close to anger. He looked at Mary and then at Allard, shivering with disapproval, as though it were all too much to bear.

"Are they rich?" Mary said.

"I think they have some money, yes. This place is more like a hobby. I mean more than a hobby. They don't advertise for customers, you know. There's only the one little sign on the road. I think the Colonel wants people to be shocked—or maybe surprised is better. It all has to be unexpected. It's such an out-of-the-way place. Anyway, he's got his pension, too. They never seem to think about money at all." Harold seemed breathless, nervous, as though he were giving away secrets, or being slightly disloyal.

The little falls at the end of the pool splashed quietly, the sun slanted down over the rocks. A little brook trout, as if he had just noticed them, sped from one dark crack to another, where he disappeared after his wild underwater flight. Allard lit a cigarette and put the burnt match in his pocket. Smoke moved across the water without changing shape, then, still unchanging, moved like ectoplasm through the softwood needles. "I like it here," he said.

The statement was more important to him than it must have seemed to them. Mary was here, undangerous, friendly, waiting for him to be the maker of events, yet somewhat frightened of him and of her feelings. And here was honest Harold Roux (honest except for that one unmentionable flaw) to keep him somewhat in line with reality. Suddenly he felt so much energy in his legs he had to run up the side of the ledge, jumping from one shelf to another in his slippery leather-soled shoes until he reached the top. All around were nothing but trees, the soft green of pines and hemlocks, the harsher sunlighted green of maples and birch.

"You could dive from here," he said. They watched him, Mary smiling, Harold a little apprehensive. Instead of diving he came lightly stepping back down the ledge. He field-stripped his cigarette butt and put the little ball of paper in his shirt pocket with the match. "Tomorrow we'll come out here and go swimming," he announced. "Mary will wear her yellow bathing suit. When's your next final?"

"Thursday at eight," she said.

"All right, it's settled. If it doesn't rain. Two o'clock. All right, Harold?"

"Yes," Harold said. "I've got a final tomorrow morning and my car's supposed to be ready by noon, so I could bring Mary out with me."

Harold was aware of the promise to her father about the motorcycle. Allard looked at Mary and spied her guilt. A flush, a warmth of skin there. He admired the curve of her cheek, her lips in tension with her skin. He was impatient to begin, but for the moment he watched her metabolism heighten because of his observing eyes.

At twenty minutes after six they left the pool and went down the rill path to Lilliputown, now more in shadow, its imaginary people all within their real houses.

The Colonel, who had changed into less informal clothes,

though not quite a dinner jacket, led them into the dining room, helping Morgana and Mary with their chairs. Morgana's chair must have been raised, because once seated she seemed of normal height, though small in other dimensions. She wore a dark red brocaded dress now, with a yellow chiffon scarf to mask the softness of her neck. The table was lighted from above by a chandelier of bulbs no bigger or brighter than candle flames, and the soft glow was reflected by glass and silver, linen and china. Morgana's dyed hair had a reddish sheen caught here and there by the light. Compared to Mary, who was smooth and golden, she shone and twinkled with an ancient glitter. The Colonel was so pleased to be their host, to serve them "from my limited vocabulary of French cuisine, *escalope de veau viennoise,*" and a red wine he had decanted into small clear pitchers—"a California Burgundy I won't bother to name, but we like it." First each of them was served a small crab on a plate, its shell removed and the meat arranged again in the shape of a crab, with two sauces, one yellow and hot, the other red and sweet.

Harold was so satisfied and impressed by all this he could barely speak when spoken to. His novel must have come alive to him in these glamorous surroundings. When he looked at Mary his eyes grew misty and deep, as though he were creating story and dialogue. Allyson Turnbridge and Francis Ravendon, dining with the Colonel Imminghams. No Allard Benson with his crude and dangerous youth showing. How shyly Harold had presented his novel to Mary, one long romantic love letter she had found sad, resenting her desire to laugh at it. She still remembered with gratitude the real pleasure she used to get from reading novels not much better than *Glitter and Gold* by Harold Roux. And in one year at college under the tutelage of Allard Benson she had been alienated forever from those perfect people, their loves and fortunes.

But the Colonel did beam at his aging Lady with love and admiration. Though it was strange, Allard felt that it was real. *Trompe l'oeil.* The old artificer had to understand reality before he could reproduce it. Did he ever suggest to his Lady that those feverish blots of red might not be the perfect decorations for her little cheeks? Evidently he did not change people, only their images. Maybe one had to be fooled, to be a fool in order to fool.

His Lady, with the enthusiasm and equality of youth, was asking Mary about herself. "All about yourself! I'm ferociously inquisitive and I hope you'll forgive me, but such a beautiful young woman must be strange and interesting."

"But I'm not," Mary said.

"Oh, pooh! And why then are there two swains so much aware of you? And I assume there must be many another who wonders what you are doing at this very moment!"

"For instance Hilary David Edward St. George," Allard said.

Harold frowned.

"Is that one person or several?" Morgana said, laughing. "Surely, Mr. Benson, you must find Miss Tolliver fascinating?"

"Indeed I do," Allard said.

"She is talented. I know I'm right. I have ways of telling because I'm descended from a witch. The fleshy lobes of the little fingers say things, and just where the thumb bends is very, very important. And I suppose you don't think I've noticed the small jewel in her pretty eye? That is tourmaline, Mr. Benson, a gem of great beauty, but it must be cut ever so carefully before it is transparent."

"Morgana is never wrong," the Colonel said.

Mary was pleased and embarrassed by this flattery. Harold was somber, perhaps sad that his daydreams and reality came so close together here, with the real Allyson Turnbridge sitting across from him, her beauty in his eyes so vivid it must have hurt. Allard was impressed by these judgments, too, and thought of her arms around him on the ride back to town. It would be a calm, clear night. Even the cold of the stars would not bleed away the warmth of the air.

After dinner the Colonel served small glasses of brandy which they took into the living room. He was telling them of his affinity with others who had become enthralled by projects such as his—some magnificent, some absurd, some both. A man in a poor suburb of Los Angeles was constructing great colorful towers out of what was, simply, junk; yet the towers grew daily toward a statement of some magnificence. Another, near San Francisco, was carving an elaborate city in limestone, all beneath the surface of the earth—grottoes, shrines, staircases, rooms and underground vistas of somber and impressive beauty. Not far from here a retired farmer was filling his empty cow barn with murals upon plaster, frescoes almost terrifying in their primitive power. A man in Vermont, not nominally an artist, and never with the idea of selling his work, carved great humanlike figures from the boles of ancient pines. Another man, in Massachusetts, was constructing a gigantic machine out of old automobiles and farm machinery, washing machines and pumps, with gears and pulleys, revolving shafts and cams, all to no purpose except that it was a machine and ran only for its creator's aesthetic purposes. Others filled their basements or attics with models of idealized countryside through which model trains busily rushed upon command.

"The Lilliputown Railroad is of slightly larger gauge, of course, but everyone has his scale. I'm condemned to have less trackage, I suppose, but it's a matter, I'm convinced, of finding the right *scale.* I know a chap who prints books so small they'll fit into your watch pocket and you have to read them with a magnifying glass. He makes and sets his own type and he has a library larger than mine in a cabinet no bigger than an orange crate. Amazing!"

The Colonel had trouble sitting down for long. He got up, leaned against the mantel, walked to the end of the room and back. His bristly gray hairs looked as stiff as wicker. He seemed wiry, in perfect shape except for the veins and wrinkles on his hands and face that gave away his age. For the first time in his life Allard thought he too would probably get that old, and it wouldn't be so bad to look like Colonel Immingham at sixty, trim and spare in his lightweight summer suit, his body quick with energy. When the Colonel stood for a moment beside his wife's chair, she put out her small ringed hand and he took it between his wide brown ones, holding it as carefully as a tender young bird.

When the Colonel listened he stared, awed, totally unselfconscious about his bugging eyes or the play of expression running in waves and counter-waves across his face. This made Allard speak slowly, thinking about each word before releasing it to such intensity of reception. The Colonel had asked him what he intended to do with his life.

"I'm not sure," Allard answered, "but I want to make something."

"What do you make now?" The wide eager eyes stared into his.

"I write things. Nothing I like very much yet."

"But the time will come, eh? The time will come!"

"I hope so."

"Harold tells me you do interesting things. If this is true it's only a matter of persistence, a matter of persistence!"

"Hamilcar is the most persistent person I've ever known," Morgana said.

"I had to be persistent in my pursuit of this lady! Let me tell you, every junior officer in the United States Army came under her spell!"

"That's what you *thought*, Hamilcar, but you were always the one. Next to you most of the others seemed half alive."

Bowing, he kissed her hand.

At ten-thirty the Colonel and Morgana went with them to the columned portico of the Town Hall to say good night and to ask them to return whenever they wanted to, that they would always be welcome. Mary's enjoyment and excitement were so apparent in her thanks that they both seemed to gleam back at her. They held hands, the tall Colonel and his tiny lady who was almost in the scale of Lilliputown. After a final good night the Imminghams retired and Harold stayed out in the night air for a moment.

"Be careful on your way back, Allard," he said.

"Harold, it was just absolutely fascinating," Mary said. "I'm so grateful. I really had a wonderful time."

"The Imminghams," Harold said, and cleared his throat. "The Imminghams . . . are pearls of great price." He said this in a ministerial voice meant to cloak his emotion, but he was so moved by his own statement he was actually close to tears.

Mary saw it, and said, "They're charming people, Harold. I can see why you like them so much."

"Yes," Harold managed to say.

They left him there, pale and stern beneath the portico lights of Lilliputown Town Hall. The Indian Pony's forever interesting surge of power took them out into the wavering yellow beam of its old headlight, Mary's arms tight around Allard; her body, pressed against his back, sent needles of ice and molten metal through his nerves as he controlled his and his woman's passage through the dark.

Aaron Benham, forgetting that he cannot release his clutch, stalls his Honda in his garage. He turns off the switch and puts the machine on its stand, hearing immediately from his knee in the form of hammerlike pain and the feeling that something alien, something similar to a bubble in the throat, teeters beneath his kneecap.

"Idiot," he says to himself as he enters the kitchen. On the table is a pile of mail he now remembers putting there after his last trip to his office—familiar brown campus mail envelopes, shiny brochures from textbook publishers, various campus organization handouts, maybe even a legitimate letter or two. Since he seems to have little left in him but habit, he sits down (hello, knee!) and opens the first thing at hand, which turns out to be the announcement of a new freshman English text based upon "mass media" and intended to seduce recalcitrant minds by using materials as familiar as the television programs, comic strips, advertisements and movies they grew up on, thus enabling them to communicate without hang-ups. The next envelope contains the announcement of a meeting of the senior members of the English department for—he looks again—four o'clock this very afternoon. An hour and ten minutes from now.

He doesn't really have to go to this meeting because he is on leave. There are other reasons he might also find convincing: he doesn't feel good; he has just had a motorcycle accident and finds it painful to walk; his only means of transportation is stalled in gear in the garage; he is depressed because he has been unkind to his family. And there is the sadness and guilt of an ancient passion, and who needs a senior members' meeting when he is depressed already? But he knows that one of the items to be discussed in this meeting will be a possible extention of George Buck's dissertation deadline. George is probably unaware of this, but he isn't. What makes the whole thing intolerable is that in theory he is against such extensions. A man should never ask to be coddled unless sick or disabled in terrible and obvious ways. And even then he probably shouldn't ask. But this concerns his friend's livelihood, perhaps more than his livelihood. So, taking with him no definite attitude or plan, no comforting moral reserves whatever, Aaron must go to this meeting. His eyes ache, his pulse becomes audible in his ears, tangible in his wrist and knee. Maybe if he goes and soaks in a hot bath for a while he can let some of this anxiousness dissolve.

But why is this house so breathless and silent? Where are Agnes and his children? Not that they would be expected to comfort him; he is expected to be perfect, or at least to approach perfection, and anything that goes wrong is presumed to be his fault—which it often is. They all seem to love him in a kind of exasperated way. Intensely, but with this undertone of betrayed perfection. "What has he done now?" he can hear them thinking. "What has he forgotten now?" But it is unnatural not to have them here. It feels like falling—that breathless, anxious moment in an elevator that quickly passes, but now does not pass. He limps upstairs, no witnesses to see how painful his knee really is, and begins to pull off his clothes. If he gets into the bathtub at three in the afternoon the telephone is sure to ring. Somebody will come to the door. Why is he compelled to answer every ring, knock and question, no matter whose? And what is he going to say to Mark Rasmussen's mother, whose child is a man but still her child? Just as his children are still his, though growing into their strange independence.

He sits in the bathtub, the water rising, burning him slowly, its half-visible presence, this strange white-blue translucence, rising on him as slowly as the minute hand of a clock. It seems wrong to be alone in an empty house and in the bathtub. There is sin in this flowing liquid, this unfamilial solitariness.

There could be a winter night with the cold snow ticking at the windows, the two children in their cotton flannel pajamas, warm against his inner arms. Janie and Billy Benham, those soft-hard awarenesses, one on each side of him, waited for his voice. Agnes waited, too, for their story to continue, watching from across the room where the fire flickered in its black irons. The story would continue, immune to change because the children would not let it change. They would grow out of its magic someday and it would remain, whole, like an abandoned old friend, like Jonquil the teddy bear in the old tin trunk in the upstairs hall closet, fondly remembered if thought of at all.

Janie said, turning her intense, pale face to look up at him, "Come on, Dad. Where the little girl and the little boy saw the mountain and the waterfalls and the black clouds."

"In the old lady's eye," Billy said. "Right *inside* her eye."

"All right," Aaron said. He must tell the story but keep himself from the power of their involvement in it. It is so dangerous to him to have this power, so far beyond pleasure in the telling of the story. When his children squeeze his arms in happiness, or in anticipation or dread, he feels their lives moving beyond his fiction, beyond this warm house, into the real places of blood and death.

But he told the story as best he could, about Tim Hemlock the father, Eugenia the mother, Janie and Billy the children, and of the terrible winter when the Traveler never came, when the strange old lady who never spoke except with her hands sat every day and night on the bench before the fire. He told what they ate when their food began to run out and all the animals were gone from the forest. How they had to slaughter the pig, and how they did it, the pig's bright blood crimson on the snow, and all the lean pieces and parts of the pig.

Later Tim Hemlock grew weak and sick. That happened after the one-day thaw when the air turned summery and strange, then turned back to winter cold so deep the farm and the forest were encased in blue ice hard as iron. When, after that, Oka's milk began to dry up, Janie spent many hours in the animal-smelling richness of the barn. Sometimes she thought she could talk to Oka, but other times she wondered if she made up Oka's words in her own mind and Oka hadn't really said them at all. Brin, the ox, deep in the stall, sighed as if he never felt like saying anything, but Oka did seem to say things to her, to answer her questions in deep ruminant slow answers as heavy in themselves as Oka's great body and bones. "Oka knows how butter grows," the butter song went, and those seemed to be Oka's words, too.

"My father's sick, Oka," Janie said. "And you didn't give much milk this morning. Are you sick, too? I hope you aren't."

As Oka moved her head slowly, sighing, her jaw sliding slowly from side to side, Janie seemed to hear deep, echoing words. They were about a calf, a brown and white calf with long awkward legs and a handsome bony head, and how Oka's milk was rich with cream then, she turning in the warm air and sweet grass, clover grass, into richness and sustenance, the giver of life. But now she was sad, down through the hollow, four-chambered depths of her cowness, heavy, heavy with sadness for a place she had once been long ago, a wide meadow and a bony calf, sweet water and the green heat of the grass.

Janie was filled with sadness to hear of the deep yearning of her friend. She had always been so grateful for the milk and butter and cheese that Oka gave them. Oka was the giver of life, and now her sadness made Janie sorrow for the beautiful rich meadow and the bony, long-legged calf, as if she, too, had been happy and calm there long ago.

Janie Benham's fingers dug into Aaron's arm, both of her hands gripping him fiercely. He knew her feelings; he didn't dare look down at her face which would reveal her pure sympathy for the cow, the beloved beast. Those emotions were so pure and clear, not innocent—because a child could never afford to be innocent—but clear, with the naked clarity of a child's vision. He had stopped, and now he coughed to hide the uncertainty of his voice, that deep adult tonality that was the maker of this tale for them. Billy had taken hold of his other arm, pulling on it to hurry him up, to get him going again. His children, not by their own choice thrown into dependence upon him.

So he went on with the story, about how Tim Hemlock grew worse, until he lay by the fire on a pallet, breathing quick little breaths hardly longer than the breaths of a deer mouse, and how Eugenia and the children were near to despair. They were all hungry, and the wood was giving out so the room was so cold they could see their breaths. Death itself seemed to hover at the door and the frozen windows of the cabin.

And then came the time when Billy couldn't make himself eat the small crust of bread he was given for supper. It would not soften in his mouth. There was his father, so sick, and the bread seemed as hard as iron. Iron, he thought. And then he remembered. It was the old woman. They were all so worried and frightened about his father they hadn't thought of the old woman at all. She might have been a piece of wood sitting, sitting there on the bench all day long. She had said once in her hand language to Tim Hemlock, "The month of the iron ice will be the worst." And now, certainly, they were in the month of the iron ice. February. With these thoughts he was awakened again to the strangeness of the old woman, what she had brought with her as a gift when she first came to the cabin. Yes, there they were, all the little birch-bark boxes of powders up on the shelf, each with a picture cut into its top. He remembered some of the pictures of plants: goosefoot, arrowhead, roseroot, kinnikinnick, glasswort, purslane and dock. Others he didn't recognize. Suddenly he felt that it was time to open the boxes. For one thing, all of those plants he recognized were good to eat, and they were hungry. He got a stool and climbed up on it so he could reach the shelf.

"What are you doing?" Eugenia asked.

"We've got to eat," Billy said. "Here, Janie, take these as I pass them down."

"But we don't know what's in them!" Eugenia said.

"I do. Some of them, anyway." Somehow he knew he was right, that it was almost too late but not quite. Then he happened to see a movement out of the corner of his eye, a brown thing moving. He looked, and was shocked to see that the old woman stared brightly into his eyes. She was speaking to him! Her arm was raised, her hand limp at the end of her wrist, limply falling. Her hand reminded him of something, of the picture of a hand. Yes! He remembered that on the cover of one of the boxes was a hand delicately poised like that. It also reminded him of something else, something plantlike, but quickly he found the box with the hand on it and took it to the old woman.

She nodded, her polished, cracked old face unmoving but her eyes bright. She raised her arms and her hands began to move quickly, up and down, back and forth, her crippled old fingers moving, too. He couldn't understand anything of what she was trying to say, and he felt hopeless again. But a strange thing happened, little by little. He would never know how it happened, but he began to understand! Her gestures that a minute before were nothing but the meaningless twitches of an old woman's arms and hands suddenly began to mean water, box, powder, cup. Other movements suddenly meant open, heat, pour, stir, and finally all the different kinds of words—words for things and words for doing—came together just as easily as the words he had spoken all his life.

When the old woman stopped speaking she nodded three times and he nodded three times back, then began his preparations. Janie and Eugenia watched in wonderment as he put just so much of the brown powder from the box with the hand on it into a large cup. He added hot water from the water pot that hung over the fire, added a pinch of kinnikinnick and a pinch of glasswort and stirred the mixture with a wooden spoon. He got down from the shelf the two kinds of mushrooms they hadn't dared to eat before—the yellow ones and the red ones. They were dried out now, and he put them together in the mortar and with the pestle ground them into a fine powder.

"But what are you going to do with those things, Billy?" Eugenia said. "They may be dangerous!"

"I'm making medicine for Dad," Billy said, pouring the ground mushrooms into the steaming cup.

"No!" Eugenia said. "It might be poison! We don't know what those things are!"

"Are you *sure*, Billy?" Janie said.

"No, I'm not exactly *sure*," Billy said, "but I feel this is the right thing to do."

And so Billy propped his father's head up in his arm and held the strange steaming broth to his lips. Billy could see the orange-yellow steam enter his father's nose at each short breath. Soon the breaths became longer, longer and more easy, and then, still deep in sleep, his father drank the brownish broth. When he had drunk it all he still slept, far too deeply for their voices to follow him, but it was an easier sleep, and they all at once dared hope that he might live.

Now Billy Benham's hands pressed Aaron's arm, the small hands holding his father's thick forearm as if it had been in danger of going away. He would not be as demonstrative of his excitement and pride about the boy's brave cleverness, but his hands held tightly.

The story went on, as it had to. When they looked around to thank the old woman, she was gone. When they looked further they found that the barn door was open and that Oka was gone, too. Brin and the goats were there in the dim light of the barn, but Oka was gone. They couldn't tell which direction she had taken because no hoofprints would show in the ice. They tried to comfort Janie but she could not be comforted. Eugenia made a thick, nourishing soup for them from some of the powders in the birch-bark boxes, but Janie couldn't eat. "Oka will be hungry!" Janie cried. "Dear Oka! Where can she go on the ice with nowhere to sleep and nothing to eat?" Later, when she was in bed, all she could see was Oka, somewhere deep in the strange wilderness, hungry and alone. Oka, who had been so generous to them, all alone in a cruel land so different from the warm green fields she yearned for, with no one to help her. Even now the deadly cold might have her down on her side, awkward on the hard, slippery ice. Janie couldn't think of anything else. She couldn't sleep in her warm bed when Oka was in the cold, so when everyone else was asleep she got up, as quietly as she could, dressed herself in her warmest clothes—her fur parka with the fringed hood, her fur-backed mittens, boots with the fur inside and the iron crampons strapped to the soles—and stepped out into the moonlight where it was so clear she was in the cold zero chill of the moon itself. She didn't know where to go to look for Oka, but she had to go. And that was how she left her warm home and her family for the cruel shadows of the frozen forest.

His last words had that final sound. Janie Benham groaned, a noise that held, at its rising end, a question. Could the story go on? A little girl named Janie was going on her great adventure. What about that vision of dark mountain and falling water, and the black clouds rolling? How brave and kind she was! Because she loved a cow she would leave her home and go alone upon that deadly quest.

"It's time for bed," Aaron said.

"It's nine-thirty," Agnes said from across the room. "It's late and you both have to go to school tomorrow."

"Just till where the little girl . . ."

"No. Come on, now."

Billy stared quietly across the room at the fire, his cowlick standing up in a silken whorl on his head that was still balanced upon the slender neck of childhood. "*They* don't go to school," he said.

"It's a story," Aaron said. "Maybe they're taught at home. I just didn't get to their lessons."

"His father taught him to cut jerky and he helped his father all the time."

"Her mother taught her how to sew moccasins and make butter," Janie added.

"You're both procrastinating."

"I don't want to go to bed yet," Billy said in a calm, thoughtful voice, as if for the first time in his life that feeling deserved rational consideration.

But they had to go to bed because the father and the mother, who had the power, would make them go to bed. Not soon, not later, but now. Janie got up with a sulky swagger. It wasn't fair. Her look at him was resentful, glistening, her turned-down mouth almost ugly. He was about to call her ungrateful; wasn't the story a gift from him?

"I just want to talk about it for a little while," Billy said.

Janie immediately understood Billy's new method and joined it. "What's the matter with that?" she asked.

His children's brilliant sly reasonableness made Aaron's heart turn with love and admiration.

Aaron has been dissolved. He wakes bodiless, his soul at the specific gravity of tepid water. What used to be his legs and arms feel little more cohesive than gelatin. But there is something he has to do. All he knows is that it is something he doesn't want to do, but of course that condition is so usual it doesn't help him remember. Then he does remember and reaches a gelatinous arm for his watch, where he left it on the bathroom scales. Four o'clock: he must go right now. He'd rather be a sinuous body of kelp, his head a hollow flotation chamber swirling gently in the warm tides of a timeless sea. But like an awkward, transitional monster he heaves himself from the brine. His knee no longer hurts quite so much but it does not want to be bent; certain valves within that complex joint are plugged with grease. His wrist will do nearly anything for him except be leaned upon. In the mirror he sees a Band-Aid melting from his jaw, a bloodless blue cut showing. He talks to the parts of his faithful body as he dries and gets dressed, reminding them of all their shared experiences. The captain may be crazy but they owe him a certain loyalty and he is certain they will do their utmost. Besides, they are far from port and they'd better make the best of it.

He finds a clean cotton shirt and some untorn pants, cleans the unfortunate squashed bugs from the lenses of his glasses. Soon he is beneath his humid crash helmet in the garage, trying to find neutral—any of the three possible places where the Honda will be in neutral and will start. Finally, with a lugging and a crunch of the delicate gears, he is off down his driveway, numb here and there but in general feeling that his articulate minions, his good crew, will get him through the campus to the somewhat decaying building, moldering sedately beneath its ivy, that is the dark center from which the English Department, whatever that is, insidiously spreads its tentacles around the tender, overly receptive brains of what was once our pride and our hope, our youth. Perhaps he shouldn't go; the water has got to his flotation chamber after all—that gray, soapy water mildly chemicaled by some of Agnes' bath oil beads. Is that why he feels so slippery?

It is not that he dislikes his fellow senior members, those who have been graced with tenure, those eminences beginning to gray or wholly gray or white (strangely, none are bald) who can without any mnemonic devices tell immediately whether the sixteenth century is actually the fifteen hundreds, the sixteen hundreds or the seventeen hundreds.

When he arrives they are there behind the closed door of the chairman's office. The two and one-half secretaries smile at him, the one-half secretary referred to this way because she works half time. There are one-half assistant professors who are there full time, he always has to think when he looks at the one-half secretary, who is actually a pretty girl, as bilaterally symmetrical as one could wish. He takes his mail in with him to read during lulls. Not lulls of talk, for his colleagues can talk forever, but lulls of emotional tension. He is nodded to, an eyebrow is raised (he is on leave, is he not?) and he finds a chair.

Forty-five minutes later the subject of George Buck comes up. It is not that Aaron hasn't been listening; these men are really no more digressively verbose than any others, nor do they enjoy the sounds of their own voices more than men of any station. They are, if anything, more precise, more intelligent than most, and their ambitions are no more nakedly egocentric. Perhaps a certain intensity of moral fervor can at times make them ruthless or cruel, but often the same fervor causes them to make judgments that are moral. Why expect from professors an Olympian objectivity beyond that of ordinary men when one has, no doubt, once taken a course in ancient Greek mythology in which one found out all about Zeus? And, after all, these men have reached their august positions through competition—grinding, eye-blearing competition—with other ambitious and intelligent men.

Well, this isn't exactly true in all cases, but what is? Aaron is listening. Perhaps the most fervently moral, those whose standards of teaching and scholarship are impeccably rigid, are those whose work hasn't progressed very well for the last ten years or so. But he won't generalize in this area, either.

There are ten men sitting in the chairman's spacious office. Their styles of clothes and hair vary according to their (comparative) youth, their convictions concerning fashion, politics, student *Gemütlichkeit*, or having to get along with local, nonuniversity artisans and officials. He notices that the student representative, who has been duly elected to this body, is absent. And there are no women, but several female junior members look promising enough so that this sexist segregation will most likely be broken soon. There are also two junior member blacks, one of whom is definitely on his way in unless he is grabbed by Harvard.

But this tone, Aaron has to think, is not exactly fair. How easy it is to caricature these colleagues of his, to feel superior. Professors are either revered or despised, according to the age. But there is X's strange involuntary smirk, Y's sly attempt to sound like an honest, candid, good old country boy, Z's Rhodes scholar accent which is entangled glottally with the Down Maine inflections of his childhood, W's slightly off renditions of not quite current student jargon ("Outasight!"), V's prissy, pursed lips and bow ties, U's ostentatious annotating of a Latin text all during the meeting, S's constant complaints that the students don't work any more, have no standards, don't care about anything (who, during the Cambodia–Kent State spring was so frightened by their caring about that issue he was pale and speechless for several weeks). A strange set of perfectly normal, ordinary men, as honest as most, most of them Aaron's friends, none of whom he really dislikes.

The arguments over George Buck's case will proceed along certain lines. Those to whom published scholarship is not and never has been their strong suit, who in fact sometimes sneer at the value of the Ph.D., including their own, will support George wholeheartedly, citing student evaluations of his classes, his personality, his fairness, his "feedback" and so on. Those, on the other hand, who have the glory of the departmental Ph.D. degree in mind, will point out that even if George does manage to get his degree he will probably never do scholarship—visible, published scholarship, that is —and so will never be a candidate for tenure. If, in effect, we give him more time, all we are doing is putting off an inevitable and much more traumatic firing of the man two years hence.

Are we going to reward good teaching at this institution or not? asks group number one.

We should reward good teaching, of course, answers group number two, but good teaching along with good scholarship.

Publish or Perish! a member of group number one says, and suggests that what with all the wordy, irrelevant, feather-splitting nonsense the scholarly publications are full of today we should pay these young scholars *not* to publish.

While the argument runs its predictable course, Aaron is silent. His heartbeat seems to him erratic, his palms are sweating. He has descended into that terrible internal place that is too close to the center of the organism. It is the control center, and he's there with no plan, no directions from the captain. He *is* the captain, and he doesn't know what to do. So he inhales eighteen cubic feet of poisonous cigarette smoke in one drag, thinking that a better method of suicide would be to open the window of his study that overlooks a blackberry patch, take his shotgun, put the muzzle in his mouth and carefully blow his brains out the window so as not to mess up the house and cause his wife to see unnecessary gore. A gentle summer rain or two and everything will be fine. Having gone over this familiar recipe for immediate, painless, sure-fire extinction, he comes back to George Buck, Helga Buck, and Edward Buck. The fact is that in his own screwed-up, ambivalent way he loves these people, and they, in their much more human and sincere fashion, love him. God knows why.

Group number two is probably right, but it might very well kill George to have to sell his beloved house, to leave his beloved students and move away. And what will that do to Helga and Edward? Their unhappiness is so inevitable. Of course, all this is George's fault; George is no revolutionary, either, who might have a crusade or such against the present form of the university. He entered upon his job willingly, knowing what was expected of him. He worked himself to exhaustion at Brown in order to finish his residency requirements, his written and oral examinations. All he has to do is write his dissertation, God damn it! And be interested enough and curious enough and original enough to discover new ideas and share them with his peers via the printed word, God damn it all to hell!

Ah, but these arguments are mere procrastination. All Aaron's life he has known people, one here, one there, who have given him the supreme gift, the highest, most valuable gift of all, and that is to have redeemed in his eyes the human race. Certainly he cannot find in himself much evidence for the possibility of such grace. Again he thinks that it has always been his role to be stronger and morally inferior to these chosen few.

He has been asked a question. It is Z, the chairman: "Addon, praps you have news of Jawge's pro-gress tawd the complation of his dis-tation?"

If he could only say how happy he is to report that it will be published by Columbia University Press this fall; that they also plan a series of monographs in pamphlet form on Henry Troy, George to be the general editor of the series, followed by *The Complete Works.* Columbia is also *very* much interested in George's as yet unfinished book-length manuscript, *Troyism as an Aspect of the Age,* and they hope to publish it toward the beginning of next year.

"He says it's coming along," Aaron says.

"Ah, but is it?"

"I really don't know," he lies.

He thinks: screw this university. Screw all institutions. It is the seed of murder when a man is loyal to anything but another man. But what arguments can you now muster that will change anything? And listen, you compulsive survivor, how much exactly do you need this system, not to mention the check in the warm little green envelope that comes every two weeks? Yes, you are one of the lucky few and could probably live on your writing, but do you feel that you have all that energy? No, he would not want to take on that nervous risk—not at the moment, anyway.

Aaron, who rarely gets headaches, now has a red-hot ball bearing just under the skin at the back of his head. Or maybe it's a crunching, vise-turning sort of thing, not heat so much as pressure, so there probably isn't a column of smoke rising from the back of his head. Whatever it is, it's real pain.

He remains silent; he does nothing to help his friend. This is the moment a man with any greatness in him would seize. He should speak, jolting them with his emotion, shaping their beliefs with his brilliant clarity and logic, outlining for them a whole new philosophy of their stewardship. He is silent because he has none of these ideas and probably wouldn't agree with them even if he could get his golden tongue around their invincible sonorities. So he tries to think that, after all, in the end, it will probably be best for George, a favor, really, to . . .

He is presented with a small blank piece of paper, upon which he will write "yes" if he wants the department to recommend to the dean that George's deadline be moved forward to January 30, and "no" if he wants it to remain August 30. Of course he will write . . . what? Why doesn't he write "yes" and be done with it? He almost writes "no." Might he write "abstain"? Finally he writes "yes." The vote is counted and the "noes" win by two votes, a result he exactly knew beforehand.

After a few announcements that Aaron's on-leave mind safely evades, the meeting is over. W wants him to play squash for an hour but Aaron explains that he fell off his motorcycle and his knee doesn't work very well today. Maybe in a few days.

He takes his mail down the hall to his office, unlocks the door and dumps the envelopes and brochures on his desk, then quickly sorts them out and puts most of them in the wastebasket. Through his two windows he sees the graceful branches of a heroically surviving elm, an expanse of green lawn and the stone legend over the library arch: YOU SHALL KNOW THE TRUTH AND THE TRUTH SHALL MAKE YOU FREE. You shall know the truth and the truth shall drive you up the wall. He doesn't want to see George. He doesn't want to see anybody who might want to discuss George's case, so he leaves.

At home he stalls the Honda again. When he comes out of the garage the cat, across ten yards of grass, stares at him. It has a live, thinking, bright-eyed chipmunk in its teeth. The cat always takes its prey to an open place where it can play out its torture with little chance of the victim's escape. The cat is wary because at times Aaron, perceiving a common look, a fellow look in the victim's eyes, goes charging and roaring after the cat, who then grabs the victim and finds another more distant arena. These pleasures must be taken slowly.

This chipmunk has already lost the skin and fur of its tail, the bare red bone naked to the air, each small vertebra plain to the eye. Seeing that it isn't one of Aaron's days to charge, the cat lets the chipmunk go. It turns, knowing it can't get away, and assays a fearsome front by chattering and trying to fluff its skinless tail into a threat. The cat growls and turns away. The chipmunk gets six feet toward an apple tree before a hook enters its abdomen and jerks it back to the delicate teeth that are so careful not to extinguish life, which is what is all the fun. With birds the cat kills more quickly—say after ten minutes of this. Perhaps birds are more delicate, or the cat can't tell if they are as yet too sick to fly. For its fellow mammals it reserves the longest, most thoughtful deaths.

Janie loves this cat, or this cat wouldn't be. It is an affectionate, cuddly, nose-touching cat, as endearing as the devil can make himself. That Janie must love this killer, even though she knows its cruelty, hurts Aaron. He can take such truths about life—God knows he has to. But a child? Don't be so bloody sentimental, he tells himself; it's as if you can't remember childhood as it really was. Or anything as it really is. He has found a stone half as big as his fist, and he throws it with all his strength as if to kill the cat he cannot kill. The stone of course misses the cat, who jumps, takes its live plaything and departs.

Mary and Allard were at Lilliputown. They had come in the afternoon to swim in the rocky pool above the little village. One at a time they had changed into their swimming suits in the nearest cabin—a miniature bungalow on the outside, a room with double bed and bathroom on the inside. Harold decided he had too much paper work to do, so he couldn't swim with them, but he opened the bungalow and gave them towels before he went back to the Town Hall.

Mary and Allard sat on the ledges in the sun, warming up after their first plunge into the cold pool.

"I wonder if Harold can't swim because of his wig," Allard said.

"It's too bad," Mary said. "I wonder if he'd be what he's like now if he didn't wear it."

"I wonder what he looks like without it."

"I don't think girls care so much about that sort of thing."

"Well, it's hard not to feel proud that you've got your own real hair," Allard said, pulling on his.

They hadn't touched each other. Allard shivered, feeling himself to be a tensely vibrating system of muscle and bone, every part connected just right, nothing slack or extra. Mary, in her yellow one-piece bathing suit, looked the same to him, except that she had a tan from sunbathing on an upper porch of her dormitory. She was dusky blonde, gold on brown. His own whiteness seemed to him bony, rangy, ready for some violent act or other. He followed when she dove in again, and caught her slim ankle under water, then followed her legs with his hands, to her hips, her waist, her breasts, her arms, and kissed her on the lips as they stood together. "Allard!" she said. For him the cold no longer existed. He held her against the length of him, his hands on the small of her back. She was gleaming, fresh, her hair darkened by the water. She loved to have him kiss her; she wanted to melt into him, it seemed, even letting his leg move forward between her thighs.

"Let's take our suits off," he said.

She laughed. "Don't be silly, Allard."

"I'm not silly. I want to see all of you."

"No, we can't do that. It's dangerous enough as it is."

"What's dangerous?" Her thighs slipped along his leg.

"You're dangerous."

"I'm not dangerous to you, Mary."

"Yes, you are."

"I swear I'm not dangerous."

"Yes, you are."

They argued this point as they held each other, her hands moving over his back, the most definite immobile contact between his leg and her small mound down there, his hands on her lower back exploring delicate muscles and hollows here and there, some of them out of bounds if it weren't for the covering innocent water and of course her bathing suit which was like armor to him. She must feel his gross bulge against her but she chose not to be skittish about it now. She must have thought about that part of him, and he wondered what she made of this so obvious thing she caused: *His body changes shape when he touches me. I do that to him, make him grow enormous.* Did she think that? Or maybe she thought it was some uncouth thing he did to himself.

He put his hands on her shoulders and slipped the straps of her suit down her arms. She looked at once entirely different, lusher, more fleshly, older even. He kissed her between her breasts before he let her raise her arms to replace the straps upon their white lines.

"Oh!" she said, and swam away from him. She climbed with a woman's pelvic grace up onto the ledge and wrung some water out of her hair, staring at him, staring with a dark, worried, wondering intensity at him as he swam toward her. He climbed up beside her and she glanced once at, and quickly away from, the long ridge that was like a piece of wood beneath the cloth of his trunks.

"Are you afraid of me?" he asked.

"I'm afraid, yes."

"You don't have to be afraid of me."

"I'm not really afraid of you, Allard."

He thought it marvelous that he could actually talk to this beautiful creature, that in spite of the difference between them that was changing him into what was essentially a beast they could still talk to one another.

Two nights later they lay on his poncho in College Woods looking up at the few stars they could see through the sighing branches of the pines. He had sensed in Mary what was, for her, a rather reckless mood. If Mary could ever be reckless, she had seemed that way when he picked her up on the Indian Pony at her dormitory. There had been no hesitation, no hint of the broken promise to her father.

"It's a crazy night," she said now in the starlight. "Or maybe I'm going crazy."

"Why?" He opened a can of beer and handed it to her. She felt for and found it in the dim light.

"This, for one thing."

"You were surprised when you liked it."

"I didn't like the first taste. Too sour or something. But now I really think I like it."

"My promise makes you feel safe with me now?"

"Yes. Yes, Allard."

She was troubled by having had to exact the promise from him that he would not "take advantage of her." Before they had gone swimming alone at the rocky pool, he was certain, she never would have felt such a promise necessary. But now their true love was more than merely haunted by this other thing. Supposedly, though she wouldn't want, ever, to have to be in any way *legal* about the question, his promise had now removed the danger. Yes, but even though she was incredibly innocent about the actual process, she knew what he wanted, and whatever he wanted her love wanted to grant to him. She didn't know that throughout the whole steamy history of mankind this promise had always been not so much a pure lie as a contract made by parties who hadn't the real authority to make it.

Soon they put down their cans of beer and moved into each other's arms, breathing, soft, gauzy about the edges, warm, sighing. The pines sighed too in the warm wind. The earth beneath them was firm below its forgiving coverlet of aromatic needles. No one would come to startle them because they were deep in the quiet woods. The stars, seen through the pines, were distant and discrete, as coolly eternal as if their orbits took them far beyond God.

Aaron Benham, abandoned by his family, sits at his desk wondering how much Mary Tolliver did know, wondering how much he knows, wondering about everything. Here is a moment, deep in the distant past, the distant half-past, or non-past, or ever-present past which, it has been said, is (still) the single most traumatic event in a girl's college life. Mary is six months past her eighteenth birthday, just finishing her freshman year in college. All vital signs normal. Her period is due in about a week, give or take a day. She is lying on a boy's poncho that has been spread over the long soft needles of white pines, on a balmy, starlit night in June, having a beer, which she has just recently decided she likes. It has been a dry spring and the mosquitoes and black flies are few, a prosaic consideration that could be quite important. She cannot but believe that she is deeply in love with this boy (man, really, for he is twenty-one, a veteran of the recent war). She is a very pretty girl and no boy has ever been able to talk straight to her before, to talk without blushes, awkward pauses, strange glandular twitches and obstructions of vision. But this boy seems unaffected by those adolescent spasms altogether. His palms are dry, his gaze intense but unembarrassed, his sense of humor unwounded by her beauty.

So he fucks her.

No! Jesus God, how did that tonality burst in?

All tonalities are possible to lustful, cruel, fickle, various, faithless humankind. Remember, too, that something mechanical is about to happen, and there is the question of proper documentation. The crude mechanics themselves are basely stimulating, mostly to men, as though any woman will do as long as she has the usual functioning parts. He must ask himself what, exactly, are the proper uses of the word in rendering such activity, providing it should be rendered at all.

He held her gently, carefully, in his arms. He was aware of dimensions, borders, the exact anatomical tensions and vectors of the two trembling bodies, one his. And of belts and buttons, zippers, elastic, silken forbidden places. These were not to be undone and opened to him by skill alone. His ally was love; she loved him. They kissed, tongues touching, and she pushed him away with a little moan.

"Is it wrong for me to kiss you?" he asked.

"I don't know," she said. His arm lay lightly across her waist.

"Even if I put my hand on your breast?" he said, putting his hand lightly on her breast. He could feel the seams of her little harnesses. She put his hand back on her waist. Her blouse, of a glowing, slippery material, was coming out of the waistband of her skirt. His fingers touched silken skin.

When he kissed her again his body leaned over hers, the tentative beginning of its move toward where it would go. He was careful not to let her feel the presence of his erection; that subject, that thing, must be kept hidden.

Time passed, an ooze of time they hardly noticed while she took what was to her too much pleasure and while he moved in an excruciating slowness toward what he would have. She had allowed his hands the neutral though bare skin of her sides, the tight young skin of her ribs. His knee had traveled cautiously, pretending honesty—an honest stretch—

across her thigh, and soon he lay mostly on top of her.

"Allard, I think we'd better go," she said, truly out of breath.

Time passed, and she would raise her lips to his to be kissed. He wondered through a haze of pleasure how she could be unaware that her skirt had worked up her thighs. She must know that she held her legs together against a gentle insistence, his firm yet somehow innocent insistence of pressure that it would be more comfortable for them both if he could just lie between them.

"Why don't you let me put my hands on your breasts?" he asked.

"No, no, Allard. This is too . . ."

"How can that hurt you?" he asked rationally, gently. "I wouldn't hurt you, Mary."

"I don't know," she said.

"I wouldn't hurt you, Mary."

"I love you, Allard."

"I love you, Mary."

"You won't do anything? You won't take advantage of me?" She spoke in a small voice. "Oh, we'd better go. This is too much. I almost feel sick."

"I could never hurt you," he said.

"Promise?" she asked in a little girl's voice. "Promise you won't do anything more?"

"I promise, Mary."

In time she let him unbutton her blouse, undo her brassiere and touch her naked breasts. When he kissed her hard little nipples she shuddered and squirmed beneath him and her legs opened.

"Stop now," she said. "Now you must stop, Allard."

"All right," he said. He covered her breasts with her blouse, covered them against the night air and the stars. Then, pretending a kink in his leg, stretched and at the same time opened his pants and with quick fingers freed his erection. The air burned it. He kept its touch from her. They kissed, and she moaned.

"Oh, my goodness," she said. "Oh, oh. I almost feel sick."

He kissed her nipple, gently sucking its rubbery little button, and she squirmed again. He pulled the crotch band of her panties aside, opened her easily in the gentle watery oil and went in. A hardly felt ring of resistance, then he was all inside her and she knew what he was doing.

"Oh, God! Oh, God!" she said. "What are you *doing?*" She struggled to get away. "My God! You're *doing* it to me!" He held her down, and when her voice grew too loud, as if to keep it from offending the deep woods, he put his mouth over hers. She struggled against him and her love for him, how he was defining her, but after a while that melting, that love, was all that she was. She let him move upon her, moving with him, though real tears came from her eyes and wet her cheeks and hair. As he felt himself changing toward orgasm she moaned. She was all sweetness, all women yet this one woman here in the private night, receiving him. She was more complete than all the rest of the earth and its objects, complete with him, as though they were one beast breathing and moaning in the forest, having one bloodstream, connected forever at their deepest places. Then all his flesh began its changes. For one moment he thought of danger, but he was beyond all that and he loved her. He saw white light as his body gave her what it had to give to her. As the light burst and waned he slowly lost his strength, as if the beast's heart slowed and grew thick.

After a while he slipped from her, kissed her with affection and lay on his back, open to the cool air, cool and empty.

At first she lay as if stunned, then freed herself from his arm and got up on her knees. She returned from the golden heat of their oneness slowly, cooling, full of wonder and fright. She cried bitterly. She loved him and he had broken his promise. Now she had left herself behind, left behind her the friendliness, the purity, the openness; she had turned into something else, an alien creature, defiled, guilty of it all. She loved him, but now that love was sordid, infected by the flesh, illicit in the eyes of God.

She cried, "I trusted you!" She seemed to be trying to organize herself so she could run away. When she bent down, feeling for a part of her clothes, he pulled her down next to him. "Ugh!" she said, fighting him. "I know you now! You're a liar! You said you loved me but you never meant to keep your promise!"

Then she lay passively beside him, weeping silently. After a while she let him kiss her gently, and rub her back. Her lips were soft as down from crying. "I do love you, Mary," he said. "I just couldn't help it. Do you understand?"

"Yes." Then, thinking: "No! What you *did!*" She let him kiss her and responded, for a moment softening toward him, then remembered: "It *can't* have happened! I *trusted* you!"

Though he loved her and pitied her unhappiness at the moment, he felt that she was, perhaps, a little too hysterical, or that these instantaneous changes of feeling were just a little too irrational. Ah, but how she had responded, finally. Her body had responded to his with such beauty the memory of it caused him to begin to rise again. Careful now, he thought. You have in your arms something of so much value you can't appraise it. She could be hurt, damaged or lost. Be careful. It was time for rational discussion now, using the words that would reshape the usual world. He would like to take her again, right now. But first would come a form of rational equality. Talk.

"When was your last period?" he asked her.

"What? My last what?"

"You know what I mean, Mary. The last time you menstruated."

She took the question thoughtfully. He understood the great revolution of delicacy, of taboo, that she must now begin to experience. But they would talk, and she would find a way to tell him the unmentionable.

He found their beers and offered one to her. For a moment she lay still, thinking her long thoughts, then sat up and took it. He touched her breast and she recoiled.

"Well?" he said. "Can you remember? It makes a difference about whether or not you'll get pregnant."

She shuddered and turned away from him, her light blouse a vague gleam in the starlight.

"Because we didn't use anything, you know."

"No, I don't know. I don't know anything," she said bitterly. "I'm due to have my period in about a week, I think. I don't keep track of it that carefully."

"It's probably all right then," he said.

"I wouldn't know. I don't know anything except what you did to me."

"What we did together," he said.

"I can't *believe* it," she said, but he detected a small amount of wonder that was not despair. Perhaps there was room for some wonder about growing up and having such experiences.

It was getting late and she had to sign in at eleven. He got her back to her dormitory with ten minutes to spare, but she wouldn't speak or let him kiss her good night. She turned away, thoughtful, almost grim as she walked up the steps in the lights of the portico.

At eleven-thirty his name was called while he was in the showers. He wrapped a towel around himself and went down the hall to the telephone.

"Hello?" he said to the telephone.

"It's me," she said.

"Hi."

"I don't know what I want to say to you," she said.

"You know I love you," he said.

"I just had to talk to you."

"Okay."

"I can't talk to anybody about it and it never happened to me before."

"It wasn't that horrible, was it?"

"I wish I could touch you."

"Tomorrow."

"All right."

A week later they were in the miniature bungalow,

where they were supposed to be changing their clothes before going to swim. On his knees, holding her calves in his hands, he tasted her feet. He looked down between her legs at that part of her she didn't think pretty, and in fact didn't know much about at all. She saw him looking at her, where no one should look. She saw him looking at her there and her face grew bothered and dark. He spread her legs wider, watching her look at his strange face looking at her wound. She had no places forbidden to him. Nothing was forbidden to him and her life had changed so much she could hardly remember what it was like to have honor and to tell the truth. She would go to hell, where she would burn. As for confession and contrition, she would never speak of her lover to anyone and she was much too intelligent to fake contrition when she knew he would call for her and she would do whatever he wanted her to do. She lied to her father, to her priest, to God. Strangely, the knowledge that she was damned had grown easier to bear. At first she needed her lover's presence and was sane only when he was there to touch—the tangible, convincing reason for her fall. When he was not there she was in agony. She couldn't eat, she couldn't study, she couldn't sleep. In a week she grew so thin her clothes became baggy on her, her nylons loose on her calves and thighs. She missed two final exams, and if it hadn't been for her A averages and her puzzled but sympathetic professors she would have failed both courses. Dark places appeared beneath her eyes. She looked older, an experienced woman, a divorcee, making that tragic, half-humorous grimace in the mirror. She tried to think of herself as one of those women who have been ruined for love, used and ruined—the Sorority of Deflowered Virgins. Ex-virgins. But she got no relief from communion with all those teary fallen angels. It had really happened to her. She knew he was lying. She was known by this man. She received him. She was his slave. She knew that she was his slave because she had no right not to do whatever he wanted whenever he wanted. She lied to the housemother; Naomi signed her in when she was not in. The dormitory and the university had no meaning any more. She existed to be with him. She had nothing left of her own, nothing. If he didn't call for her, she died. Sometimes, when she was riding behind him on his motorcycle, her arms around him, she hoped for the worst, the blackest sin of all—that they would crash and both die instantly, the dead hearts touching. But then that night he would take her and she didn't know her pleasure from agony. She didn't know if the moans she couldn't stop making were moans of pleasure or of terrible fear of the pleasure that came up out of her and became him and burned herself out of herself. It was a stranger to her, a vile corrupted sinner who did it. Far away now were the years when she was at peace.

And then, in the afternoon in the bungalow, he was empty and she was full. She touched his face that was miraculously pure and clean. He slept and she wanted to bear him like a baby, feed him from her breasts, hold him and protect him. His breath was sweet on her lips. She touched his little nipple as he slept.

For a minute or two he did drop off to sleep, awaking to find Mary kissing his chest. "Have we swum enough?" he said.

She laughed, a short laugh that was new to her, as was the ironic twist it gave to her lips. "We ought to be getting back, I suppose," she said.

In one week she had changed so much. He had noticed the small bluish places beneath her eyes. For some reason her worries had turned her beautiful, as though she had lost baby fat. Her face had more angles, more character.

She moved her hand down his belly to his pubic hair and his soft penis, taking it in her fingers. "I can't believe what I do with you," she said. She pulled the soft thing up straight and watched it begin to fill, then quickly put it down. "Harold will wonder what happened to us. We'd better go on down."

"I imagine he'd disapprove a bit," he said.

"I almost feel like laughing but I don't know what's so funny," she said, a grimace twisting her lips.

"Are you that unhappy?"

"Yes. I want to be honest."

"We're honest with each other," he said.

"Are we? Anyway, come on, get dressed. We'll go have a glass of Harold's sherry and pretend I'm a virgin."

"Harold *is* a virgin," he said as he began to put his clothes on.

"I'll tell you something I don't like. I felt I had to wet our bathing suits in the bathroom so if Harold saw them he'd think we went swimming."

"Fuck Harold, Mary. What do you care what he thinks?"

"Because, whether he wears a wig or not, he's honest."

"He's a good Catholic," he said, watching her carefully.

She was not ready to discuss this. "He's kind and gentle," she said.

"That I've got to admit. He's also a little prissy and fussy."

Mary took a breath. "Also," she said, "there's something you'll be relieved to hear. I just found out in the bathroom I'm not going to have a baby."

"I wondered why you brought so much luggage today." She'd brought a wide leather shoulder bag with her.

"Sometimes your sophistication makes me sick," she said. He was buttoning his shirt. He turned toward her to find that her eyes were shiny with tears, so he put his arms around her and she leaned into him, snuffing her nose. Her fingernails dug into his back with a fierceness that was just this side of doing real damage.

"Harold will be expecting us," he said. She hiccupped within his hands as he lifted her off the floor. "Look, Mary, we are not sinners, you are not a ruined woman. In fact you're twice as pretty as you were last week. You are definitely not a virgin any longer, true, but who in hell wants to be a virgin?"

"Impure," she said.

"And thank God for that."

"You don't understand."

* * *

Harold met them at the Town Hall. His style of clothes had changed, probably in imitation of Colonel Immingham's. Gone were the rickety thin-soled shoes and the white or light blue socks with clocks, the printed argyles, the peaked-shouldered suit coats and especially that constricted, trussed and pointed area about the throat that used to be Harold's center of formality. Today he wore a soft shirt open at the collar and a sweater. Only his usual burden was the same—his crown of fake hair balanced upon his careful head.

"Did you have a good swim?" Harold asked them.

Mary said nothing so Allard said, "Marvelous, Harold! Marvelous!"

"The Imminghams have invited us to have sherry with them," Harold said. He was looking at Mary, frowning a little, a concerned look.

"Harold," Allard said, "you ought to get some sun. All that paper work is making you too pale."

Harold smiled as he usually did at Allard's brashness, and ushered them through the foyer and into the Imminghams' cluttered, comfortable living room. Morgana sat stiff as a doll in her thronelike peacock fan chair, the rouge spots vivid as little rising suns on her cheeks, her hennaed hair a nest of copper. The Colonel looked up from his decanters and smiled with all his muscles, showing his teeth like a dog. Delighted, formal greetings seemed to clash in the air, glinting and rebounding upon smiles as both the Colonel and his Lady issued them simultaneously.

"My dear, you look absolutely stunning," Morgana said to Mary. "And you look *different.*" She cocked her little head, bright as a bird, and gave Mary a smiling, speculative look, her eyes flickering to Allard and back. He looked at Mary more closely himself. She was wearing shorts and blouse and a white cardigan sweater, pure white against her light, even tan. She was stunning; he had a surge of proprietary warmth, tempered or made more immediate by the memory of the almost ludicrous bands of whiter skin he had just seen, where her body was not tanned. Those masked areas had made her seem either not quite naked or even more naked, he couldn't decide which. But here, in her crisp clothing, sipping a glass of the Colonel's Dry Sack, she did look expensive and stunning. It was pride he felt. This was his woman and he would decide upon the right course for them both. No hurry. During the long summer they would be apart; he had not discussed this with her, but of course there was little to discuss. She had told him several weeks ago she had a summer job as a waitress in a hotel in the White Mountains, and he had decided recently to ride his Indian Pony to Pasadena—a three-thousand-mile trip—where his uncle would get him a municipal laboring job for the summer. Meanwhile, the school year was ending; the dormitories would close in a week.

It was at that moment he got the idea for the party, a sort of farewell-to-the-school-year party, very nice and sedate but cheery. They would have to get a date for Harold. Naomi? That was an interesting idea. There would be Nathan and Angela, Knuck and his date—which was also a problem because Knuck tended to go out with demimondaines from Litchwood. Oh, well. And maybe even Hilary David Edward St. George and date. The Colonel and his Lady would put in an appearance early in the evening, of course, then leave the young people to their younger boisterousness or whatever. And what better place to have the party than up at the rocky pool, with a cookout at the little stone fireplace and blankets on the ground, beer and wine and maybe a moonlight dip or two?

He would always remember that the idea for the party was his.

The Colonel was speaking to Allard in such an animated fashion he spilled a drop of his sherry. "Tools!" the Colonel was saying. "Harold tells me you enjoy good tools." Allard had once shown Harold his rather complete set of chromium-plated wrenches, gauges and screwdrivers for the Indian

Pony. He did take care of them pretty well, keeping the sockets and drives clean and in place in their enameled boxes.

"Yes, I guess I do," he said.

"Then you must see my workshop! Come, I'll show it to you."

Allard followed him to the basement. At the foot of the stairs the Colonel paused. "I'm quite proud of my workshop," he said, and flicked a wall switch. Before them a long room flickered into bright fluorescent white. The white ceiling and walls reflected so much light there seemed to be no shadows anywhere. The Colonel's machines on their pedestals or tables were arranged down one wall like exhibits of sculpture in a museum, each one oily clean, some on casters and some sturdily grouted into the cement floor. Allard recognized a bench saw, a lathe of some kind and a drill press, but the functions of others escaped him.

"Now," the Colonel said. "Here are my major tools. I'm just as fond of the smaller ones, the hand tools in the steel cases there. A well-balanced hammer, for example, is a thing of great beauty. A set of socket wrenches, clean and in their places, is more beautiful to me than a chest of jewels. For one thing, the proper tool gives us a Godlike gift, doesn't it? The gift of leverage, of power. And power that never damages the object it is used upon! *That* is the gift!

"In the cases upon the left are my inch, or standard wrenches; on the right are my metric ones. The Lilliputown Railroad, for instance, is all metric except for the caboose."

The Colonel took two clean white mechanics' smocks from a wardrobe and handed one to Allard. The workshop was so immaculate Allard supposed these uniforms to be purely ceremonial.

"Now," the Colonel said when they were both buttoned properly into their smocks, "first we have a twelve-inch radial arm saw. You see how it can move in any direction, even tilt?" He pulled the saw, which was mounted above its table on a gallows-like moving arm, forward and back, from side to side, the circular blade gleaming silently, teeth just skimming over the table. "With this instrument I can do nearly everything I want to do with wood. I can crosscut, rip, bevel, miter, dado, rabbet, tenon and shape. With certain attachments I could even rout, plane and sand with it, but I have more specialized tools for those purposes. However, as you can see, it is a machine created by men with a real love of craftsmanship. The electric motor developes more than three horsepower. Behind it you will see an industrial drum vacuum cleaner which will pick up three bushels of shavings or sawdust, or eighteen gallons of wet material. I don't like to kick around in sawdust when using such precise and also potentially dangerous machinery."

Next in line was an eighteen-inch bandsaw-sander with, the Colonel excitedly explained, a ball-bearing-gear reduction unit and four speeds, 118 to 3,550 feet per minute, that would cut wood up to twelve inches thick. Then a wood lathe for turning dowels, chair and table legs, banister posts, etc., then a six and one-eighth inch jointer-planer. On its iron pedestal was a fifteen and one-half inch drill press, then a double-wheeled bench grinder with aluminum oxide grinding wheels, its own lamp and safety-glass eye shields. Next was a metal-turning lathe that seemed to sprout cranks, wheels, levers and gauges all over it—accurate, the Colonel said, to one one-thousandth of an inch. A power hacksaw, next, would cut sixty strokes to the minute. The last of the major shop tools were the 295-amp AC arc welder, a big gray steel box, vented on its sides, with huge cables and clamps, and an oxyacetylene welding and cutting outfit, its tall gas cylinders chained into a two-wheeled dolly, the gooseneck torches polished and at attention in their racks.

"There is almost nothing I can't do with the equipment in this room," the Colonel said, waving at the big oily machines, the steel cabinets housing other tools, the racks across the room of wood and metal stock.

"It's a beautiful workshop," Allard said. Memories of childhood's frustrations and lack of power haunted him in this room full of machines that could actually do things. To be able to weld, for instance, had always been miraculous to him, far beyond his resources. To take two pieces of steel, the seemingly God-shaped hardness of the metal, and to join them together as one unit, as you wanted them to be—a miracle. Or to have any machine with those magical horses inside harnessed and working for you, so that all you had to do was conceive of the design and with calm, unstrained hands guide that power into your service.

He felt the Colonel's sense of completeness, of place here. To have everything you wanted in one neat, known place was appealing. But of course he still had to travel. Places called to him, new and strange places where there would be adventures not related to property at all. Later, when he had been everywhere, perhaps. He thought of the apartment he and Mary would share, the calm work he would do. It all seemed now on a far shore, waiting for him warmly and patiently, but it would be some time before he arrived there.

After a few moments of admiring silence they hung up their white smocks in the wardrobe, took their sherry glasses from the bench where they had put them upon entering the workshop (alcohol and machines don't mix, Allard seemed to hear) and went back upstairs to rejoin Harold and the ladies.

Mary was smiling as she listened to Morgana's loud voice. Allard thought of a parrot, but Morgana's voice hadn't that metallic tonelessness; it was just that the voice was too large for the small person it came from.

". . . of course not a thing Hamilcar would have anything to do with," she was saying.

"Did I hear my name?" the Colonel said.

"Can't I talk about you, Hamilcar?"

"As long as you don't bore our visitors, my dear."

Morgana laughed at the absurdity of this idea.

Harold, quite serious all of a sudden, said in an aside to Allard, "I'd like to talk to you."

"Okay."

"Not now. Can you come back?"

"You mean without Mary."

"Yes, exactly."

This was high seriousness indeed. A little guilty-feeling, but being lectured to by Harold was for some reason interesting all the same. And then there was the idea of the party, which he would have to broach to Harold with some care.

"All right. After supper? Say about seven-thirty or eight?"

Harold seemed surprised that he didn't ask what their talk would be about.

When he left Mary off at her dormitory Allard said, "I won't be seeing you tonight. Harold wants to talk to me."

"What about?" She frowned, worried.

"I don't know. I didn't ask. But I imagine it will be Harold the Protector of Catholic Virgins night."

"Very funny."

"That's the spirit, Mary. You know, I think you're getting over the awfulnesses."

"I don't know why I love you."

"Because I don't treat you like the Virgin Mary?"

"You don't know anything about the Virgin Mary."

"I'm sorry, Mary, but you know I've got to convert you to my religion!" He laughed, the sounds coming up unbidden, a kind of mild hysteria.

He was in nearly the same mood when Harold met him back at Lilliputown that evening. He put the Indian Pony on its stand next to Harold's Matilda and followed Harold to his room off the foyer of the Town Hall, a comfortable room much larger than Harold's former room in Parker Hall. Here was his easy chair, a long wooden desk, his books in a bookcase, even a well-worn leather davenport and a glass-topped coffee table. Harold, or someone, had decorated the dark, brownish room with old sporting prints and a Currier and Ives. It might have been a room in Harold's novel, say a reading alcove off the Ravendon library.

Harold poured them beers in tall, narrow pilsner glasses.

"Hey. Fancy," Allard said. "Cheers!"

"I wanted to talk to you," Harold began.

"Don't you have a bed? Or is this just your sitting room?"

"It's in the wall. It's a Murphy bed."

"Like in Charlie Chaplin?"

"Yes," Harold said, annoyed.

"Harold, I'm sorry. I'm in a strange mood. End of semester and all that sort of rot, eh?"

"I wish you'd be serious for once. I'm worried about Mary and I want to talk seriously with you. Did you know she missed two finals?"

"Yes, but it's all right. With a 4.0 average you can do nothing wrong in college. You know that."

"I'm not worried about her flunking out, I'm desperately worried about *her*."

"Well, what am I supposed to do?"

He listened as Harold spoke about his and Mary's basic incompatibility because of upbringing, religion, and especially because of (said with a certain hesitant delicacy) Allard's being essentially not right for her because, er, well, he didn't, couldn't, appreciate a lady of Mary's delicacy and refinement—spiritual refinement—and in fact when one came right down to it Allard was too much of a different kind of person entirely for Mary. He listened, but in flashes his mind was off, thinking of Mary, of Naomi, of women and what in God's name they found so powerfully fascinating in men. Compared to their loveliness a man seemed to have very little to offer. Perhaps a strange fusion happened in a woman's mind (tenderness as he thought of a woman's mind thinking of a man) concerning the wideness of shoulders, the narrow buttocks of a man that were more tensely vigorous than the misty, acquiescent tenderness of a woman. That, and possibly the increment of a child only a man could set swimming toward her womb. Maybe. But no, we use powers we don't understand, can't understand. He did know that Mary now wanted to exist in his shadow, to have him dominant and near, and he had known this would happen. She trembled, she hummed within her nerves, she had become too intensely a mirror for each of his thoughts and attitudes. She waited for him, always waiting, he knew. She considered him a real man, the man, and most of the time he didn't quite recognize that quality in himself. He was twenty-one, a veteran of many things in the past, and the future seemed full of reality, but the present was less definable. Actually he was only a student, that gelding state in the eyes of the real world. What he would do later would be real and substantial. Now was limbo, a sort of limbo, but he felt that it wasn't any sort of limbo to Mary. Yes, and a darker side was that he thought himself an uncrowned prince who would come into his inheritance someday; would Mary Tolliver be the consort of the future prince?

"Oh, you're probably right, Harold," he said. "But love conquers all, doesn't it?"

"Do you love Mary?" Harold asked slowly, as though Allard were about to take an oath.

"I swear on the shop manual of my Indian Pony I love Mary."

"Will you be *serious*?" Harold was really angry now, willing to endanger their friendship. Allard was fond of Harold; he did recognize the differences between people like Harold and Mary and people like himself.

"I'm sorry, Harold."

Harold took a deep breath and a little color came into his face, emerging in his skin as a delicate shade of olive. "Because," he said. "Because I'm really afraid that without really knowing it, without being responsible, you two might fall into something that neither of you will foresee . . ."

Allard waited, wanting to laugh but at the same time embarrassed for Harold, who was trembling with nervousness now.

"Because you're both very young and won't know what you're doing until it's too late . . ."

"Yes?"

"I mean that in a moment of passion you might go all the way. *That's* what I mean. I happen to know how much Mary is infatuated with you, Allard!"

"I'll try not to hurt her, Harold."

"Don't joke, Allard. You won't know how powerful the sins of the flesh can be until it's too late."

Ah, Harold, Harold, he thought. What a sweet gentle naïve prince you are. Once Harold had told him about a girl friend he'd had in the army, a WAAC private first-class named Mary Ann Waltzel, and had even shown him a letter he'd received from her after she had been transferred to Fort Benning, Georgia.

Dear Harold,

Well, here I am at Fort Benning and I don't know whether I am going to like this set up or not. My commanding officer I am told is a big bull dyke. She is from Alabama and looks like General Patton without the six shooters. I will sure be glad when I get out of this woman's Army.

How are you? I will never forget how nice you were to me, Harold. I think you are the nicest person that ever came into my whole stupid life.

Love ever,
Mary Ann

In spite of the chummy, companionable, even somewhat hard-bitten tone of Mary Ann's letter, Harold had been embarrassed and offended when Allard asked if he had slept with her. *Of course not!* They went to movies and played honeymoon bridge and talked. But didn't you even try? Allard asked. *No, and don't pretend you're so experienced either, Allard Benson. I know better!*

Well, Allard wasn't going to argue about it now because it was useless and it would endanger Harold's receptivity toward the party, which would have to be presented as a chaste, dignified affair all around.

Harold said, "Don't hurt her, Allard."

"Look, I do love Mary. What if I said I was going to marry her?"

"I'd be appalled. You aren't about to become a Catholic

and it would be a very unhappy situation for her. A tragic situation."

"You're right about the Catholic part. To tell you the truth I went to Mass with her family half expecting to be impressed, but I wasn't. It all seemed sort of mechanical. And the priest gave a talk about motherhood that was really creepy. I mean that priest was really strange."

"What that particular priest was like has nothing to do with it. It's deeper and has to do with the truth."

"The truth!"

"Yes, the truth. You may be young and proud and self-confident and think you don't need God, but you're wrong. I fear for your immortal soul."

"Oh, come on."

"You are not a complete man. Without God you are not complete. You cannot make your own sacraments."

"Well, I still don't think I'm a total shit, Harold."

"No, and that's the tragedy. You're really a very sweet person underneath."

Allard thought he wouldn't go quite so far as that, himself, but on that milder note he brought up the subject of the party, emphasizing its sedateness, its farewell-for-the-summer cheeriness and so on. "And we won't mess up the area, either. We'll police up the trash and leave the place as clean as ever. Just a small gathering of old friends havin' a brew or two and a hot dog, singin' some good old songs 'neath the spoony Juny moon . . ." Now stop that, damn it. Why couldn't he keep that tone down?

Harold considered the idea. "Well, I don't know. The Imminghams won't be here all next week. They'll be in Boston. But I don't know, it might be all right. It might be a nice idea, really. If we just have a few nice people. Yes, I can't see why anybody would object. All right, I'll ask the Imminghams if it's okay." Having come to this decision Harold drew a deep breath and let it out.

"Great, Harold. It's been sort of an odd year. And you

did manage to escape the clutches of Boom Maloumian, The Mean Armenian. I suppose that alone is worth celebrating."

"Getting out of that dormitory was the best thing that ever happened to me, Allard. I'm serious. I feel I have some dignity now." He looked around at his high-class digs. "And the Imminghams. I can't tell you how much they've meant to me." Harold was getting emotional, his eyes growing misty over the Imminghams. "They're so kind, so thoughtful, so *honorable*, Allard!"

He knew Harold had a final in the morning so he left early. As he rode back through the campus to the town square he noticed that the lights were on in Herbert Smythe's apartment over the pharmacy. Though Herbert might indeed be an ass, he was probably owed an apology. Also, Naomi might be there and he wanted to try to talk to her, to get all the bad feelings over and done with. She was Mary's roommate after all, and ought to be invited to the party. Yes, she should come to the party, bringing Herbert if she wanted to, or maybe she could be Harold's date. Poor frozen Harold; maybe she'd be good for him. But let's be honest, Allard, let's be honest now. All other considerations aside, Naomi is your burnished, beautiful animal, the dark one, the one with the unshaven armpits smelling of myrrh, and you haven't been with her a long time now. No, it was more complicated than that. It truly was more complicated than that.

Still wondering what he was doing, he parked the Indian Pony at the curb and climbed the dentist-smelling stairs toward Herbert's apartment, thinking that he ought to be ashamed to show his face there after the scandalous way he had behaved last time. But he wasn't. None of the people he might find there seemed totally real to him—the men, that is. Naomi and Ilse Haendler seemed real people infected by their crazy, unreasonable Stalinism, but the men all seemed to have been dissolved by their beliefs into shadows and cutouts. Several of Herbert's male troops were physically bigger than Allard, but it was impossible to think of them as threats to him no matter how bloody the situation.

When he knocked on the door the room behind it immediately grew silent. Suspicion was so palpable he could almost smell it over the medicinal fumes of the hallway. The door was opened, finally, by the deprived boy in the steel-rimmed GI glasses, whose shin Allard had damaged on his last visit. The deprived boy stepped back, his small face defensive, suspicious, and Allard confronted all of them, the same deep disapproval on all their faces. Most of Herbert's group was there—Herbert himself, Naomi, Ilse, a small girl in a dirndl dress whose name Allard had forgotten but who was the new mimeograph girl, and several men or boys. Their faces were like cold walls, all defining him, walls people were stood against to be shot. He was the enemy, he supposed, the real enemy: not a mere misled fascist dupe who might be converted, but a nasty ironist, a creature of no faith.

"I came to apologize for previous violent behavior," he said. The very words his brain chose for him were unforgivable; "previous," "violent"—this was style, not substance. He wanted to tell them that he truly wished them no ill, that though he was strangely immune to faith, in its presence he felt, always, a vague nostalgia. As if they would be interested in his subjective psychological innards.

None of them spoke or changed expression. Their pens, papers and inky fingers were still. "I apologize," he said, "not only for my violence but for my patronizing attitude, which is probably twice as unforgivable."

"So get out of here, you son of a bitch," said one of the male troops.

Allard looked at him with an inner coolness, a clear, frosty coolness that was almost pleasant. It was a pleasantness he had to resist, however, since he had come here to apologize and not to revert to the beast, however refreshing that might be. "Naomi," he said, "may I talk to you for a little while? We can sit on the bench across the street and I promise no more Tarzan stuff. Just a few civilized words."

"Don't go with him!" Herbert said.

And why, Allard asked himself, had he chosen the word "civilized," which was taboo to them? Naomi was thinking; there was a slight vertical indentation in her round forehead —a place that would in the distant future be a wrinkle.

"Don't go anywhere with the son of a bitch," said the same male troop who had spoken before. This time Allard heard a proprietary tone, and looked at the boy again. A glance showed him to be damp-palmed, palpitating, in love.

"Just a few words for old times' sake, Naomi. How about it?"

"Say what you want right here," she said angrily.

"And then shove off," said the male troop.

"Oh, all right!" Naomi said. "I'll talk to him!"

She walked coldly past him and he followed her down the stairs. She wore her usual Levis and a man's full shirt. Her hips moved beneath the shirttails in a complicated parabolic motion. Across the street they sat down on the cement bench, the lights of the store windows and neon signs across the way and an occasional car's lights outlining her face in profile, her straight Roman nose below the black band of eyebrows, her black hair absorbing all light in its shadow.

"So?" she said.

"So I want to make up. What's wrong with that? I'm sorry about the way I acted, which was sort of brutal."

"How true."

"So all I can do is apologize and humbly request a renewal of our friendship."

She turned to him, her pale eyes gleaming. "You're screwing Mary now, aren't you."

"Did she tell you that?"

"No, but I'm not exactly totally blind. You are, aren't you."

"Well. Yes."

"She cries a lot when she's alone and she doesn't sleep very well. Jesus, Allard, you don't know what you're getting into."

"Maybe not."

"She's awfully naïve and all that, but she's a sweet thing and you could really fuck her up, you know?"

"I don't want to do that. I want her to think about these things the way I do. And anyway, I think I'll marry her."

He saw random flashes of light because she hit him on the mouth. When the immediate numbness went away he tasted blood from the insides of his lips, which were already getting rubbery.

"I must admit I didn't see that one coming," he said.

Naomi still sat beside him, now looking at his mouth with concern. "Did I hurt you? Jesus, I'm sorry! But Allard, you are such a shit."

"It's refreshing to talk to you, Naomi."

She smiled. She smiled! For a moment he was disoriented in time. When was this? And it was not like her to find such a remark funny at all.

"Well, it's true," she said.

"No one has ever offended me by calling me a shit, so either I believe, deep down, that I'm not a shit, or I believe deep down that I am a shit. In any case the epithet never really comes as a surprise."

"Words, words, words, words," she said.

"So is the ultimate victory of the proletariat over the capitalist running dogs, et cetera."

"Strange," she said, leaning back and stretching her torso and her long legs, "I don't feel like fighting with you tonight."

His heart gave a vacuum-like pause and a thump. He leaned over and kissed her on the cheek; his lips made it feel as if he had a golf ball in his teeth.

She took his hand. "Allard, Allard, Allard," she said. "You stand for everything I find regressive and meaningless in this country."

"But you're willing to be friends with this enemy symbol?"

"All right."

He leaned back, safe and relaxed, at ease in the warm night with his woman beside him where she belonged.

"I've got to go back," she said. "I promised to finish a pamphlet tonight."

He liked the addition of the promise, but he remembered the proprietary tone of the male troop and felt jealousy. "Back to that damp character who told me to shove off?"

"Sexual jealousy is a typical bourgeois reflex," she said.

"But I fondly thought there was a little bourgeois reflex there when you gave me the shot in the mouth."

She took her hand away. "Nothing of the sort. You deserved it."

"This may sound irrational indeed," he said, "but my problem is that I don't want that creep to put his damp little hands on you."

"That's none of your business." She said the words so softly, however, that warmth returned to the cold places along his spine where jealousy had crept.

She got up. They walked back across the street where the Indian Pony leaned on its stand. Someone, perhaps the damp troop, was looking at them from Herbert's window.

"Good night, Allard."

"Good night, Naomi."

They shook hands firmly and she went up the stairs. He watched her bones move the outer surfaces of his dark woman until she reached the top of the stairs and went out of sight.

Nathan was alone in the room when he got back, Knuck being in Litchwood visiting a girl he always referred to as Vera Upstairs. He told Nathan about the possibility of a party at Lilliputown on Friday night. Nathan seemed to like the idea but he was obviously preoccupied with something else.

He sat at his desk in his Brooks Brothers shirt and slacks, his neat loafers tapping the terrazzo floor, his angular, beard-shadowed jaws tense, staring off through the wall.

"What's the matter?" Allard asked.

"I've made up my mind to do a fairly drastic thing."

"What? You and Angela getting hitched?"

"That I intend to do in any case, when the time comes. But I've got another problem."

"You got dosed up in Litchwood."

"No." Nathan smiled, where ordinarily he would have uttered his oogah laugh. "No, I've made up my mind to . . ." He was silent, thinking. He gave Allard a shy, worried look that was uncharacteristic of Nathan the man of the practical world.

"To what?"

"You might disapprove, but it's because you don't have the problem. Anyway, you know I'm a Unitarian, right? So what do you think of the name Weinstein? I mean what's the first thing you think of when you hear 'Weinstein'?"

"The first syllable rhymes with the last syllable."

"Come on, Allard! I'm serious. I'm deadly serious. If you laugh it'll make me feel bad."

"Okay. It doesn't sound Unitarian. Unless you're using 'unitarian' as a generic term meaning a belief in one Supreme Deity and in the mortality of Christ, in which case 'unitarian' could also apply to Judaism."

"That's right, Allard. But remember, I'm serious."

"I'm sorry, Nate. I've been running off at the mouth all night and I guess I can't stop."

"I'm changing it. I've made up my mind. It's a business liability, for one thing. I'm changing it to Winston."

"Nathan Winston. Well, that does have a ring to it."

"It's easy for you to be superior with a name like Allard Benson. But there's an awful lot of anti-Semitism around that you might never notice. Believe me, when most people hear the name Weinstein the first thing they think of is a hooknose, a skullcap and they wouldn't want their daughter to marry one."

Allard noticed that Nathan had filled a sheet of paper with his new signature. He said, " 'A rose by any other name, Nate. But you're sure you want to go through all the paper work and everything?"

"I've already looked into it. It's complicated but it's done every day. Nathan Winston," he said. "Nathan H. Winston." His eyes, big and sensitive in his small, bony face, were wondering and thoughtful. They reminded Allard of the eyes of a deer.

After a while Nathan did look over at him and actually focus on him. "Jesus, who gave you the thick lip?"

"Naomi."

"She's still pissed off, huh?"

"No, I think we made up, sort of. I got this when I told her I was thinking of marrying Mary."

"You deserved it, then. Jesus, you don't *tell* a girl you're jabbing you're going to marry her roommate!"

"Nate, you want to know the horrible truth? I want both of them. I want . . ."

But Nathan was laughing, his reverberant noises distorting his Adam's apple. "Oh, dear!" he said finally. "My Jesus, Allard! And you sure can pick 'em, too! An Irish Catholic and a Jewish Communist! I mean with a harem like that what else could you want?"

"I'm aware of the basic humor of the situation and fully forgive your boorish laughter, but the fact remains that I want both of them."

"I'm glad I've only got one," Nathan said. "She may be nearly as big as two, but she's only got one *head!*" And he broke into laughter again.

"You sit there laughing, Mr. Winston, while my poor heart burns with impossible love."

The name sobered Nathan. Suddenly he was thinking

about it again, how the magic of the name would change his life.

Aaron Benham, left alone by his ungrateful family, wanders through his house looking at things, looking out windows, thinking about the party at Lilliputown. It was so long ago and so different, really, from what he must make of it. He is thinking about the tawdry side of the human psyche, of the puerile, the banal. No, that time of youth when the body ruled in all its perfection, demanding worship, not really suffering from mistakes or consequences. He thinks that youth does not really live in its own time because there is always more time, more youth ahead. Work that is not being done is not lost forever because there is forever. Especially back then, when the problems that now beset the world were not visible wherever one turned one's eyes. The doom that breathes upon the world. The cruel and the nasty who have power. He stood at this very window in May of 1970 staring at that apple tree, grieving at its inevitable doom, fearing for the students he found so sweetly reasonable in their strike. Three times the town had been surrounded by the National Guard. Aaron knows guns; those who control guns want to use them. Perhaps his despair came in part because of the knowledge that those in power really wanted to kill the university. Of course he should have been aware all the time that he himself was an alien, only barely tolerated by any state, but he wasn't ready and was deeply shocked. Write anything you want, but do not get in the way of patriotism as defined by the gun. All right, he thinks, let's stop this thinking; these desperate issues cause an emotional death you cannot afford.

The telephone rings, startling him. "Hello?" he says to its black distance.

"It's Linda. Linda Einsperger. Mr. Benham, we just heard they're firing Mr. Buck!"

He sees her pale, intelligent face, her long body that

always suggests to him the dignity and grace of a giraffe. Two years ago there would have been anger in her voice, real anger, but now he hears the melting hesitations, hollow places where tears are possible.

"Not really," he says. "It's the business about a deadline for his dissertation. If he can get it finished . . ."

"He's the best teacher I've ever had. Even Frank thinks he's a great teacher! Don't they think he *knows* enough? I mean he knows as much as any professor!"

"It's not that. They all want to keep him here, really."

"I don't understand! It's because of Mr. Buck I became an English major! I mean what's writing a dissertation got to do with what he really is? He made it all come alive here! We *all* think so!"

"I know he's a good teacher."

"But is there anything we can do about it, Mr. Benham? Anything?"

"You could write letters, you could see all the senior members of the department, the chairman, the dean, the vice-president for academic affairs, maybe even the president if he's around. I just don't think it would do any good in the end. George has to finish his dissertation. It's part of the contract he made when he came here, Linda. According to the way things are he's got to be a scholar too. Eventually he'd have to teach in the graduate program and just as a starter he'd have to have the degree."

"The way things are," she says. "Frank's so down he's thinking of just dropping out again, and all he needs are three finals. It just makes it not worthwhile. After all that bullshit about rewarding good teaching we went through last year and the year before, here it is right back again."

"George is my friend," Aaron says. Is he George's friend? "But I have to see their point." Why that guilty *their* rather than *our?* "Maybe George will finish his dissertation."

"You don't think he will, though."

"I don't know."

"I don't know anything, either. This whole thing makes

me want to cry." There are tears in her voice, little echoes not quite voiced.

"Me too," Aaron says.

"It just makes the whole four years seem ugly in the end. Mr. Buck helped some of us in other ways, too. When Frank was crazy in 1970, and when Bradford was back on his heroin. And other people. But he was all business in class. I mean you did the work and you knew he cared about whether you did the work."

"I know all that."

"I mean I'm not upset just because Mr. Buck helped me in my personal life. I mean his classes, what I learned."

"Yes."

Linda hears the impotence in Aaron's voice. It is hopeless; she and Frank, Bradford and the rest, will get no real help from him.

When the call is over, when their voices have expired, Aaron walks away from the telephone table, down the hall to the front door, opens it and stares out into the world. He remembers an incident in which he had the choice of action or inaction, but it was less complicated then, perhaps like an earlier version of Hamlet. Being central in his life, he can at least in private do without the wry muck of false modesty. The hole he is in is the most important hole on the front. No one but he can even attempt to define his view of the world. Man of violence, death-dealer, inclined to protect the weak, ashamed of all dogma, believer in man's bestiality and in democracy, as afraid as anyone of death, not afraid of violence —a waking dream he has entered many times, often with joy —but afraid of the joy of violence.

A warm evening in May, lively with the odors of Tokyo that were then human, coming from the processes of life as it survived in the rubble. Hibachi smoke, fish, onions, *shoyu*, beer, piss, the warm odors of the ages. He had left the Nihon Yusen Kaisha building, gone up the short broad avenue past the Maru-no-uchi, through the busy, bombed-out shell of Tokyo Eki and was crossing a long wooden footbridge over the yards of railroad tracks below. People moved quickly, small, gentle-seeming defeated wraiths going home from work in the dusk, *geta* and shoes clattering softly on the wooden planks, mixtures of Western and Japanese clothes, muted tired people walking with the delicate economy of the partly hungry.

Ahead of him a big American soldier had something small trapped against the railing. Aaron approached this frantic center of energy, the Japanese who came toward him glancing fearfully at it, then setting their eyes ahead as they passed. The big shoulders of the soldier hunched forward in a rage Aaron saw was necessary to his task, created by desire but blown up by real sanctimony. Though his voice was strangled by his rage, the soldier seemed to be accusing a middle-aged Japanese man—an office worker, probably, in round spectacles, neat shabby Western coat and tie over the baggy cotton knickers of surplus Japanese army pants—of possessing American cigarettes. Possession was the soldier's legal term. *Possession.* An observer, Aaron stopped behind the soldier and watched him steal the man's wrist watch, discard his empty lunch box, rip his coat pocket in his search, all the time cursing out his one legalism, wanting to kill. The thin Japanese, in his terrible danger, of course said nothing. The people passed in their muted hurry, having to survive. Across the tracks, past a stone-lined canal, were the cracked buildings still standing, dim lights in windows, then the streets, stalls, the mounds of the city in the dusk.

Aaron looked up at the breadth of the soldier's thick neck from behind, feeling more than naked. Amputated. He felt made of air, a ghost. He had no weapons. It was not his business; it was always his business. He yearned for a gun, a knife, a two-by-four, anything to give him leverage beyond his thin bones. A bar of soap in a sock, which one soldier he knew carried in his back pocket, would have made a sap. But he had nothing, and after a while he walked on by. For a long time he daydreamed of his ideal duty, in a sick rage within himself. He might have reached down from behind and grabbed the soldier by the cuffs of his pants and heaved him up and over the railing, where he would have fallen twenty feet or more to the tracks below. Because of Aaron's weakness, death or terrible injury were the only choices he had. It was what the soldier would have done to him if he'd said a word. By then he knew murder's symptoms.

He could later tell his friends about it and gain some of the fraudulent relief of confession. Little Willy, a corporal, showed him the folding stiletto he carried—a mean-looking knife made in the Philippines. But even with such a weapon, acting on such a level, where would he have cut or stabbed the soldier? The blade, though five inches long and thick enough, didn't seem adequate for a mere threat. He might have hamstrung the soldier, or cut his Achilles tendons, but he didn't think he would be able to carry away the responsibility for the blood, the blue-white tendons drawing up along their ruptured sheaths into the leg muscles. In the absence of real power blood seemed the only alternative.

Though he could walk away, and had to walk away, he could not walk away with impunity. He could never be a mordantly amused or merely interested observer of the beast.

He acquired the Nambu later, but never carried it.

Dusk is falling in his yard, the apple trees fading into their night shapes in which one doesn't think of them as having mass, they are so quiet in the dark.

His wife and children will be returning soon, the headlights of the Chevrolet beaming down the gravel there, bringing the apple tree brightly out of its shadows for a moment before the lights are swallowed by the garage. And then from the garage, after the slamming slabs of the car doors, will come those closest to him, the ones bound to him so deeply he cannot function without them. This he knows because he tried it once and it was like trying to live without his heart or lungs. They are the forces that keep him alive, shocking him into his duty with the irritant voltage of pacemakers.

Embedded in him. Sometimes he doesn't like any of them. He feels misunderstood, taken for granted, attacked. He would rather be an Eskimo leaning over a seal's breathing hole waiting, waiting in the sub-zero wind for the meat and fat with which to feed a hungry and grateful family. All he wants is for them to smile and be happy when he feeds them. He can't remember everything! Don't they understand how much he tries to remember, has to remember?

He finds himself shaking with indignation and guilt. His eyeballs grate in their sockets, his brain dims, there is a short in the electronics of his spine caused by his bruised knee and wrist and the dying day's hangover. This wreck who peers bleakly across the falling darkness can't be him.

It was such a short time ago when he and Agnes moved into this house with the two young children, when the house's warmth was a wonder to them all as the snow swirled at the windows and the wind was beaten back up the chimney by the fire. He and Agnes saw through much younger eyes then, as though childhood were more translatable among them all than this later time.

But now it seems too late. He can speak to his children, who are growing up into their ironies, their humor that speaks to his, but he can seldom speak in that relaxed way with his wife. Of course they always had little to say outside of the tensions of their relationship—once good tensions, exciting ones. Still exciting, but now often wearisome, turned into accusation. When they are making love it is still the way it used to be. He would like to have a woman again with whom he can relax, admit things, be valued for the nonvalue that consists of merely being a man.

He thinks that he will never leave Agnes, but he can't predict what he will do. He isn't much different from any man, his years have slowly but surely taught him, and he sees so many of his friends and acquaintances breaking up, desperately looking for a remembered calm.

Agnes is the sort of woman who remembers everybody's children's names, and the full names and occupations of couples met once at parties. She has the talent to make him feel guilty that he does not. She has the talent to make him feel guilty most of the time, and it has always seemed to him a strange talent for a wife to cultivate. His colleagues think of him as a prodigy of industry. He is never sick and never misses classes or conferences or meetings. He is always available to his students and his colleagues. Though he thinks of himself as a fairly lazy writer, the statistics seem to disprove this. And so it is mainly through his work that he retains a sense of his worth, except for the negative indication of Agnes' possessiveness. He is wanted; he is demanded. It is demanded of him that he be prompt, courteous, efficient, etc. And if he is a writer, of course he writes; doesn't a doctor doctor, a plumber plumb? God, he hears the echoes of his self-belittling screams of rage.

Aw, shut up and get to work, says his other voice. You need a woman to tell you you're great all the time?

Yes! Yes!

Well, then why don't you and, say, Helga run away together? Take the old Vollendam to Havre and the train to Paris; there's still a fine little hotel with tall windows near the Luxembourg Gardens.

The two children, tender in their cotton flannel pajamas, snuggled on either side of him; across the room in the black interior of the fireplace dark orange flames silently flowed upward from the hardwood logs. He was the father, the large one who kept the cold away. In the deep chair Agnes was not reading her book but listening. It was a winter story Janie and Billy knew as deeply as experience, a story as frightening as they knew things really were. But they were allowed the hope, the slightest hope, that virtue and love would in the end surmount the most deadly tribulations.

And so he told them the story, how, that night, when everyone was asleep, Janie put on her warmest clothes and went to search for Oka under the frozen moon. She went to the barn first, the crampons her father had made squeaking on the blue ice. Maybe Brin, out of his warm, phlegmatic vastness, might have something to tell her. Or the clever goats, who seemed to know so much though they never seemed to care, their indifference as distant as the moon—what they must have seen through the black slots in their yellow eyes.

She stood in the breathing barn, slits of moonlight and the briny smell of hay and manure around her, saying, "Brin? Brin?"

He moved a gigantic part of him—brisket or flank, she couldn't see that well at first—and rumbled deep inside one of his stomach chambers: *I am only a beast and do not understand much. Oka was warm and could help to bear the noises. She could smell wolf and bear when they were hungry, but now she is gone and I am only an ox, strong but with few opinions.*

"But where did she go, Brin? Where did she go?"

She will follow the moon because how else could she see?

"But the moon goes over Mount Gloam!"

Why do you ask anything of an ox?

Behind her the goats, amused, tilted their heads at each other and stamped their feet.

Janie didn't know if she'd heard anything at all other than the movements of penned animals and the creaking of frozen timbers, but she had to go toward where the moon would set, toward where it was forbidden to go. Mount Gloam was dark, sacred to the Old People, Tim Hemlock had told them many times, and only the Old People, if there were any of them left, could go there. It was said that the gods of the Old People could never die, and without their people they had grown mean and vicious.

But Oka knew nothing of this. If only she could catch up with Oka before she got to the forbidden place, she could lead Oka home to the warm barn. With her crampons she could cross the ice better than Oka on her slippery hooves.

She took Oka's rope bridle from its peg and tied it over her shoulder. As she left the barn, carefully closing and latching the door upon its warmth, the frozen windless air came into her nose, into her chest. She knew she shouldn't go alone into the forest, across the crackless ice that was smooth as the ice on a pond yet frozen into hills and waves, but she must find Oka. Her crampons squeaked, complaining of the hardness, as she entered the frozen, silent trees.

"She didn't take the Timothy seeds," Janie Benham said. "She didn't take the Dandy Timothy seeds so she could drop them one by one and be able to find her way back."

"I didn't think she'd need them," Aaron said, "because Billy could see which way she went by the crampon marks in the ice. So could she."

"Oh."

"Suppose it gets warm and melts," Billy said.

"But you know it didn't *melt,*" Janie said. "Anyway, I liked the Timothy seeds."

"All right," Aaron said. "Before she left the barn she reached into the gunnysack and filled her pocket with Timothy seeds."

"The chickadees would eat them all up," Billy said.

"Do you want to hear the story or not?" Janie said. She turned to Aaron. "He's already heard about how smart Billy was to understand the hand language and make the medicine."

"He wants to hear about Janie, too," Aaron said. "Anyway, the birds had all gone, remember? Even the chickadees."

"So, smarty," Janie said.

"Maybe you both know the story too well," Aaron said.

"No! No!" they said at once. That wasn't the question; of course one knew a story, and the knowing of the story didn't hurt the story. They were answering his tiredness, the suspicion that he would just as soon not tell the story now. "No, Dad! Come on!"

"And don't change it," Janie added.

"Everything changes unless it's written down," Aaron said. "And even then it changes."

"No, you can't change it!" Janie was upset. She suspected

betrayal; tears were moistening her eyes. She didn't like paradoxical statements of any kind and refused to see any sense in them at all, just the cynical attitude behind them, which meant betrayal; was life so complicated one had to say what one didn't mean in order to mean what one meant? Janie's clear eyes, their wide pale look with all feelings there shining from inside would give the lie to all paradox if they could. On Billy's longer face paradox got its recognition less grudgingly, and for him the story would no doubt soon change, though its words might not.

"All right," Aaron said. The children grew quiet, vibrant, tensely silent while he told them how Janie searched through the frozen forest and came, at dawn, to the terrifying waterfall and cliffs they had both seen in the old lady's eye. Oka's and a deer's tracks led along a narrow trail in the sheer cliff, a trail no more than a foot wide in the cragged rock along the side of the cliff, and it led directly toward the thunder of the falling water.

At this point Janie Benham held his arm in both her hands, her blond head pushed against him, half-hidden, fearful, trembling, proud. This was the little girl's bravest moment. To go on because of love and duty, the terrible energy of the water on one side, the narrow path beneath her feet, the icy cliff at her small shoulder, ahead old stories of vicious gods and monsters. Had they taken Oka and killed her? Would she find Oka hung on a hook, her warm body turned into cold meat? Or was Oka now a battered wet cow-corpse tumbling over rocks in the chasm below?

Now Aaron took them back to Tim Hemlock's log cabin, back over the miles of iron-hard ice, through the frozen trees where no bird flew and no wind whispered. In the morning Billy and Eugenia discovered that Janie was gone. Billy found the crampon tracks like pricks made by needles in the ice, but Eugenia insisted that she herself follow Janie's trail while Billy took care of his still-unconscious father.

And so Eugenia made the long journey and came to the waterfall. She had always been afraid of heights, but it was her little daughter who was lost, and she made herself take the narrow trail along the misty cliff. She came to the end of the trail beneath the falling water and found nothing but a blank wall of stone. Convinced that Janie had fallen into the maelstrom and was dead, she wanted to let herself go, to die herself among the battered rocks far below. But Billy and Tim Hemlock still needed her, so gathering all her courage she returned home.

Then it was Billy's turn, in the night when his mother was asleep, to follow that hopeless trail himself. In the cold morning light he came to the falls and the dangerous trail along the cliff. He was tired and hungry, but he was nearly a man, the only man in his family now who was not sick, and he would go on until he saw for himself what had become of his little sister—or until what had happened to her happened to him. He had hurt himself before, and been hurt; he knew what happened to all living things: trees, animals, the tall grass cut down in summer and fall. But even so he found the tracks along the narrow ledge, read them as his father had taught him, and went on.

Billy Benham was now tense beside Aaron, his small hands clenched as he stared straight ahead toward the mountain he could surely see. The dangers a boy was about to face, alone, only his small life going toward the indifferent world.

When Eugenia awakened, back in the cabin, the fire was nearly out. Once again the gray light of dawn filtered wanly through the ice and the small windows. The cabin was cold—too cold, near to freezing. Immediately she felt its emptiness. Billy had gone while she slept; she had not taken care of her children. Her husband lay on his pallet, his breaths faint mists above his thin nostrils. She knew without looking or calling out that both of her children were gone, gone forever into the cold.

Now Agnes, too, dreamed of the story, her book in her lap. And how would you like it, Agnes, if your husband might never awaken (as he sometime won't) and your children were gone (as they will be)? Her eyes gathered them together this evening, in this warm enclosure.

Billy and Janie had heard, again, that ending tonality: And now to bed.

"We'll finish it tomorrow night," Aaron said.

"Dad! Please! Please!"

"No," he said.

"It's late," Agnes said. "School tomorrow."

"I want to hear when they're happy again!" Janie said.

"But you know they will be," Aaron said.

"No, I don't!"

Could he not believe her? Her wide face was flushed, dark with true feelings, the hurt of unfairness. About her compressed expression her light blond hair swirled almost weightlessly.

"Oh, all *right*," Billy said, disgusted—a beautiful simulation of utter disgust.

Aaron almost said, Look, do you want me *ever* to tell you a story? Why do you act this way? "You're both going to bed and that's that," he said.

They had to go, of course, but with those particularly eloquent grudgeries children do so well with their postures, thus robbing him of the nice feeling that they would both be so safe upstairs in this fine house he had provided for his family.

He would not look over at Agnes, who watched him, her eyes feeling out for him, showing her feelings. She always understood what was for that moment not to be understood, went toward levels of understanding that hurt him and ignored, as if willfully (but not willfully, he knew), the meanings he meant when he said what he didn't mean. Why of all women had he chosen this one whose mind he could never predict, as though its turns and counterturns were of another age—the dark conclusions of a midwife, medium, oracle or coven witch. Conclusions always wrong and never wrong. She could be fooled, and had been. But she could not be fooled, and hadn't been. She was a mystery, the only woman he had had to marry, whose central places he must enter but could never understand. Sometimes when they spoke to each other it was as if in a third language native to neither of them.

The tour of Lilliputown's wonders had been conducted by Harold for those who hadn't seen them, and now in the slanting sunlight at the rocky pool Allard, Mary, Harold, Naomi, Nathan, Angela, Knuck and his girl from Litchwood, Vera Upstairs, were gathered listening to Hilary David Edward St. George, who played his ukulele and sang in his boyish tenor.

"Let him go, let him tarry,
Let him sink or swim.
He doesn't care for me,
And I don't care for him!"

It had been the theme song of his flight during the Battle of Britain, he explained, and some daredevil types had sung it as they broke through formations of HE-lll's, the jaunty words coming through their radios along with the stutter of machine-gun fire.

"I'm going to marry
A far nicer boy!"

Plinkety-plunk went the little ukulele. Hilary next sang "Roll Out the Barrel." His flashing vaudeville smile was unaware that the others' enthusiasm was nowhere similar to his, but his blithe confidence in his talent was endearing.

Cold brown bottles of beer were stashed beneath the silvery falls at the head of the pool, and Knuck, in his undershorts, swam back and forth bringing bottles to everyone. Vera Upstairs sat primly on the ledge above him, refusing to get into the water.

"Come on, Vera," Knuck said, his politely wheedling tone false and out of character. "Come on in, the water's fine."

"I don't have a bathing suit," Vera said.

"Who needs a goddam bathing suit? Strip down to your goddam skivvies and come on in."

Vera looked to the heavens, her face set. She was a muscular, somewhat clay-colored girl whose thick calves were iron-gray above her white bobbysocks. Knuck's attitude, she seemed to indicate, was much too vulgar for a high-class party like this.

"Aw, come on, Vera, don't be so fuckin' prissy." Her face set harder. Knuck was a little drunk. In a loud aside to Allard he said, "Jesus, I can't understand this broad."

Harold, too, thought Knuck's behavior too crude for the party he had in mind. "Maybe we can fix Vera up with a bathing suit," he said. "There's a whole collection of odd clothes in the laundry room." Mary, Naomi and Angela were going down to change into their swimming suits and they took Vera along to see if they could find something for her.

Knuck surfaced, blowing spray. "I'll never understand that broad," he said. "She gimme a blowjob on the way over here and now she's scared somebody'll see her goddam knockers. Christ, I pull her out of a horseshit hogwrassle in Litchwood with Maloumian and all them crazy bastards and bring her to a high-class party like this and she gets all hoity-toity on me."

Harold shuddered at the name of Maloumian, and then said, "Knuck."

"What?"

"I mean I hope you won't get too . . ."

"Too what?"

"Well, embarrassing to people."

"Me?" Knuck shook his head as though to clear it for such a consideration. "Okay, Harold. From now on I'll be a perfect goddam gentleman." He retrieved his beer from the ledge and drank as he floated on his back. "If I get too bad just give me a kick in the ass. 'Course, me and Vera'll disappear into the boondocks from time to time. That all right?"

" 'Oh, my name it is Sam Hall, it is Sam Hall,' " Hilary sang, plinkety-plunk.

Harold, though proud to be host, was still worried; Knuck's white body displaced the dark water with the powerful nakedness, even obscenity, of a shark's rolling belly.

While the girls were away Allard and Nathan changed into their trunks. Harold built a fire in the stone outdoor fireplace and arranged the blankets around it on the sparse grass and pine needles. The sun sank lower, warm and friendly to the skin but with a just perceptible lessening. They were friends in a private place surrounded by permission and the masking woods.

Nathan's pelt of black chest hair gave him that evening's name, "The Otter." After an awkward dive he swam back to the steeper bank and pulled himself shivering out of the water, saying that though he shivered he wasn't cold—he always shivered. Allard watched him shiver from being alive and eager for events, for seeing great beautiful Angela, beautiful slim Mary, beautiful dark long-boned Naomi, even Vera Upstairs whose near-ugliness was the encapsulation of her selectively willing mouth, cunt—whatever the crude words were in the world of her men. Or maybe Allard was again investing himself in someone else's anticipations. When he dove into the water himself it was all cool light hands.

The girls came back and he stood facing them, hands on hips, the sun touching him with its warm distant regard on separately felt ridges of muscle. Angela in smooth white satin, the creamy giantess; he could understand Nathan's feeling of bonanza. All that healthy, spanking flesh, every pound alive. She and Nathan dove into the pool and swam together, an otter darting about a great white seal. Mary and Naomi stood on the ledge for a moment, day and night, Allard's light and dark Iseults. Vera appeared in a red bathing suit that must have been designed for a middle-aged woman, with a skirtlike apron in front meant to hide some kind of excess or other. She didn't want to go into the water but hesitatingly waded in from the shallower side, standing inhibited by the chill, the water just up to her knees, her arms folded across her heavy breasts until Knuck arose from the shallows, a sea monster within a nimbus of spray, and grappled her as she screamed in real terror and was taken down into his deadly element where she was at once seemingly drowned, raped and eaten.

Harold, kneeling carefully upon a blanket edge as he fed the fire, turned his face toward Mary and was visibly stunned by the slanting sun's celebration of her. She dove into the pool, smooth as a returning minnow, followed by Naomi, a dusky golden nymph in black, and then by Allard to whom the pool became them and they were both his at once.

Allard moved as though pulled through the water shadows toward where Mary flashed light gold and Naomi a darker gold, and came up next to them. He put his arms around them both and felt the immediate resistance, their backs tense but not really enough to be an overt signal to him; they wanted to pull apart from each other and from him. He couldn't have both of them. He was supposed to be with Mary tonight, or maybe forever. No, no, said those faint but deep signals.

Tonight Naomi was supposed to be with either Hilary or Harold—that would be decided politely, precisely, but later. As Naomi swam away from him he felt loss, even though Mary was here in his arms, her cool lips upon his collarbone. "You're pretty," he said. She said nothing and he was afraid she had read his mind. Not really afraid, for he felt that he had nothing, not one thing in the world, to be afraid of.

They sat on the blankets around the fire, the girls having so delicately ripped their rubber bathing caps from their heads and shaken down their young hair in the last of the sunlight. Vera's hair was wet because she hadn't had a bathing cap, and her soggy, slate-colored hair made her sullen. She drank her beer in gulps, offended because (again Allard's attention was perhaps going beyond its rights) she wanted to be here and wouldn't think of going away but she hated the way Knuck was treating her. Allard tried to think of a time in his life when he had given up so much just to be somewhere not alone. It seemed that he could remember the feeling but not the actual circumstances.

Hilary sang, urging them to join in.

> *"Roll me over in the clover,*
> *Roll me over, lay me down and do it again."*

In its comradely bawdiness the most innocent of songs.

Harold roasted hot dogs over the wire grill and they all tasted the bite of yellow mustard and the singed hot meat. There was plenty of light bitter beer and after a while an easy silence as the sun went behind the trees. Nathan, that mountaineering otter, held his great Angela or was held by her. Naomi and Harold sat Indian fashion on the blanket next to Mary and Allard, Naomi there because she had helped Harold serve the hot dogs. Hilary was the solitary, as so often happens, in the company of his ukulele. Though Knuck, beneath their folded blanket, had been trying to do something or other to Vera Upstairs that she found somewhat embarrassing, the easy silence had now come over them all. Harold was the agent responsible for their permission, whom they did not fear; only Knuck might act uncouth, but he was a friendly force not to be feared either. All of them were young enough to remember having been chased out of paradise.

Harold sighed contentedly and said, "What would you consider a good life, Allard? I was just thinking that here we all are, pretty young. What are we going to do with our lives?"

Allard wondered why Harold couldn't live his life right now, beginning with Naomi. He saw Harold's pale white nervousness as it might tremble under Naomi's tender care. If she wanted she could lead him into tremendous changes.

Harold said, "What do you see in your future, Allard?"

"When I grow up?"

"Yes, if you can be serious." Harold's voice meant *Don't break this fine moment with sarcasm.*

"All right, Harold. Let me think." He put his arm around

Mary, feeling her deep pleasure, deep enough so that it met her desperation about him—an intensity that might have been frightening, but he had no fear. "I'm looking into the future," he said, deciding to try not to be flippant. Why not reveal certain real daydreams now, silly and exciting as they might be? He was among friends and admirers, whether he deserved them or not. No, you never deserved such things; they came unquestioned, as rights. So he decided to tell them one of his fantasies: "I envision an apartment in Manhattan between 8th and 23rd Streets, not too many blocks east or west of Fifth Avenue. I see high ceilings, tall windows, many books, parchment yellow lampshades over comfortable chairs, some modern, some not, paintings and drawings of the same mixture on the walls, all interesting. It is a ground-floor room, and the plane tree, or maybe it's a fig tree, in the small back garden through the French doors has turned yellow and dropped most of its leaves on this fine October evening. There are maybe ten people in the spacious room, all of them interesting friends, and next to me stands a lovely and intelligent woman. Although it is quiet, the thick brownstone walls admit some of the vibrations of Manhattan—just enough to let us know that the world continues. Champagne has been chilled and poured because it is an occasion, a surprise arranged by my friends. On the coffee table is a novel with a handsome dust jacket; it is mine. It was just published today."

"Ah," Harold said. With his arms around his knees he stared into the fire. "Yes, that's good. I'd like to be there, Allard."

"And your novel, Harold, is to be published the next week."

Harold laughed softly. "May it all come true." His voice turned nervous as he said to Mary, "What about you, Mary? What would you like to see?"

"I'd like," Mary said. "I'd like . . . Why not say so? I'd like to be the woman standing next to Allard."

Allard felt pain he could not quite locate, as if he, not Mary, had been too much revealed by her candor. This made him thoughtful, a little cool, and they sat side by side quietly as the others took their turns at describing the future.

Knuck would be the head coach of the Chicago Bears, carried on the shoulders of his men across the field after their championship victory, the hoarse jock shouts sweet in his ears, his Cadillac and high-class broad waiting and the cold kiss of a shower to get the champagne out of his ears, his ass red from the smacking spanks of heroic giants. Fame, money, approval and good booze.

Hilary foresaw a gentle, ordered life as a partner in his stepfather's law firm, a fine house in dark brown tones, leather, tweed, very good wine, a beautiful wife, sailing his ketch off the Cape on summer days.

Nathan would be privy to affairs of state, he and his noble wife, Angela (Fitzgibbon) Winston, entertaining the great and near-great in their town house off Copley Square. Polite, suave, rich, clever, yet engagingly witty and erudite, Nathan would be known as the man who had gracefully turned down the Republican nomination for governor of Massachusetts in favor of a less visible yet more interesting position with the State Department in Washington, where he and Angela would host, from their town house in Georgetown, national and international luminaries. Surviving by talent, and as if by miracle, all party rises and defeats, perhaps in the middle of a distinguished career an appointment to the Supreme Court might beckon, but for now we will leave these glittering yet broadly cultured people of affluence and power . . .

"Bullshit," Naomi said in a friendly, almost dreamy voice. "You're talking about a fantasy, a doomed decadent anachronistic bunch of shit that never existed in the first place."

"Oh, something like that exists," Angela said. "Naomi, I swear it does exist because I've been fairly near to it, you know."

"Reality is the poor, the people . . ."

" 'Yearning to be free,' " Allard said. "Yearning to get rich and screw the rest of the masses."

"Oh Jesus, Allard," Naomi said. "Drink your beer."

" 'Revolution destroys the worst and the best in a society' —I. V. Lenin."

"So?"

"So how can I trust the dumb-ass masses, not to mention their commissars, when I can't even trust myself? That trust would be the biggest fantasy of all."

"Just because you're a shit . . ."

The others weren't listening to this exchange. Harold and Mary were talking to each other, Allard and Naomi having drawn closer together across the blankets behind them, in their shadows. The sky was bright, but the trees and rocks bled darkness all around the embers of the fire. The little falls splashed at the head of the pool. Naomi lay on her stomach, her face framed by her long hands, her long black hair gleaming, the dark gold of her shoulders cut by the narrow straps of her swimming suit. He reached over and freed the straps so they came down her arms. She looked at him steadily.

"Let's take a dip," he said.

"What about . . ." She nodded toward Harold and Mary.

"We're all friends here. Anyone for a dip?" he added in a louder voice.

"Mary and I are going for a walk," Harold said. "We've got some things to talk about. Do you mind, Allard?"

"Somehow I trust you, Harold," he said. Mary looked very serious, somber over the magnitude of their conversation. She put on her sneakers and arranged her towel around her shoulders. They strolled off down the path, Harold speaking to her in a low voice.

When they had gone, Naomi put on her bathing cap and she and Allard slipped into the cool water. Across at the ledges she took his hands in hers when he began to take her straps down again. "You must feel pretty important," she said.

"All I feel is that I want to go inside you."

"This is ridiculous."

He took off his trunks and put them on the ledge, feeling

the movement of the water displaced by her.

"Doesn't the cold affect you at all?" Naomi said. "No, I can see it doesn't." Her hand had touched him lightly before it fled away, quick as a fish.

"Just the opposite," he said.

"Jesus Christ," she said, letting him peel her suit down away from her beautiful freed flesh. He went underwater, down the long columns of her legs, and brought her black suit back up, shapeless now. She glowed through the water, cool and uninterrupted beneath his hands.

"It feels so strange," she said. "It feels so strange in the water. I feel so naked." Her hands came and examined him. "Your little scrotum feels like a couple of walnuts." Her hands drew quickly away, and she turned and swam away from him underwater.

They went the length of the pool, where he cornered her by the little falls, Naomi turning in the white water, the rising bubbles stinging his skin. She wouldn't let him hold her, but kept turning, moving her long legs across his body as he came at her. He reached for her in the foam, the bubbles like carbonation clinging to her skin that was smooth, grainy, slippery. Her breasts were moved by the water and by her defensive contortions. She was his, wasn't she? Some anger rose in him and he grabbed her roughly by untender places and entered her. She continued to struggle, meaning it, even hurting him, until it was too unreasonable to him and she turned victim, woman to be taken. For that moment he thought nothing else of her and let his seed explode deep inside her.

When he had finished grinding and pumping, she put her face close to his in order to see him more clearly in the dim light. "Well," she said. "I hadn't been raped lately."

He was quiet and sad.

"We might just get a baby from that bit of irresponsibility," she said.

He had come out from where he wondered why he had gone. Could she feel his sperm swimming up toward her center? Dark Naomi, the Jewess, daughter of a people leading back through ancient times in caravans, with herds of goats into the Old Testament and beyond. Dark blood, dark flesh, tribal oil and wine, sweat and genocide. And now his Anglo-Saxon sperm, pale and callow, moved into strangeness like tiny Vikings in a dark sea. Come back, he wanted to call to himself, but his mindless silver things could not be recalled. He shivered, the central warmth of her blood making him apprehensive and open to the cold of the water.

"Are you still going to marry Mary?" she asked.

"I don't know. I don't know anything."

He swam back toward their swimming suits, wanting to be covered. She followed, turning and gamboling in the water, enjoying her nudity. While he tried to put on his trunks she poked and tickled him.

"Cut it out!" he whispered.

"Cut it out! Cut it out!" she said, imitating him. "What's the matter? You sure wanted to play a minute ago."

"I don't know what I want to do."

He gave up trying to put on his trunks and just stood there in the water, his feet on the grainy ledge below. She circled around him, treading water, her knees coming up, her breasts pointing at him.

"Why didn't you say it was Mary you wanted next to you in that apartment in New York? Don't you know how unhappy it made her when you didn't say it was her?"

"No. I didn't think," he said.

"Do you ever think?" She grew quiet, standing on her tiptoes. Someone had put wood on the fire across the way and its distant light flickered across her high cheekbone. Hilary's ukukele tinkled, a lonely sound. The water between their bodies seemed to make them touch.

"Anyway," he said, "maybe in that daydream it's you, once you've lost all that Stalin crapperino and have your brains back again."

She didn't move for a moment. "Do you mean that?" she said.

"Yeah, Naomi. I don't think, I just say what I mean."

"You make me feel funny saying a thing like that." She had moved an inch closer to him and he took her nipples delicately between the tips of his fingers. "Allard, you know you may have made me pregnant."

"Yes, there's millions of me swimming inside you. Can you feel them?"

"I don't mind."

His cautious brain was again severed from the sources of power. She kissed him and put her chin across his shoulder. This time it was with consent, and in the strange element that made her buoyant and firm, they made small, slow waves, her legs around him. The pond moved with them. The water seemed to give slowly, then push them back into each other with a slow volition of its own. He seemed slow yards long.

Later, when they came dreamily out of the water, their suits properly back on, Nathan got up and came over to Allard as he toweled himself off by the fire. "Harold and Mary came back, Allard. I'm afraid they saw you and Naomi and then they went away again."

"They saw us?"

"Yeah. I hadn't noticed what you were doing until I saw them looking. I guess they had a better view, standing up, you know. Anyway, it was pretty obvious."

Knuck and Vera had gone, taking their blanket. Hilary had drunk too much beer and was asleep next to his ukulele, someone having put an extra blanket over him.

"What do you think we ought to do?" Angela said.

"It's my fault, but I feel sorry for Mary," Naomi said, looking accusingly at Allard.

He did not like to think of Mary seeing their urgent rhythms in the water, she perhaps thinking at first that the shoulders she saw were not his, then having to know that they were. He went to his clothes and found a cigarette.

"Should we go find them?" Angela asked. "I suppose the party's fairly well over."

"I feel awful. I feel like a bitch," Naomi said.

"Well, I'd better find them," Allard said, though he wondered what the proper talents might be. While the girls turned away, he and Nathan changed into their clothes.

They walked unhappily, or at least uncertainly, down the path to Lilliputown. Because he was the agent of Mary's and Harold's unhappiness, Allard found it hard to consider the moment truly tragic. And if he were the cause, he might somehow undo the unhappiness. Naomi was keeping away from him, walking upon her handsome legs on the other side of Nathan and Angela, her graceful hips encompassing (a painful sweet thought) part of him. A nearly full moon had risen over the trees. He moved to her side.

"Are you going to marry her?" Naomi said.

"Do you think I should?"

"Have you told her you would?"

"I can't exactly remember if I did or not."

"Have you told her you loved her?"

"Yes, I guess so."

"Well, do you?"

"I guess so."

"Christ!"

Like giants, aware of their heavy footsteps, they came down among the silent streetlights and the elms of the village.

Somewhere in this happy complex of miniatures, the Colonel's work of art, Mary was probably crying, Harold holding her hand. How sad, how serious their thoughts would be. Mary would know now that Allard had lied to her for mere lust of the flesh, destroyed her honor just to toy with her, sent her to eternal damnation with no more thought than he might give to flicking away a cigarette. She had loved him more than she loved God. What a stupid fool she'd been! To him she was nothing more than a vessel, a . . . *cunt.* That was what he must think of her, what he'd thought of her from the very beginning. And Naomi, who'd pretended to be so friendly and nice. And all the time . . .

"What will you say to her?" Naomi asked.

"I was going to ask you the same question."

He and Nathan waited by the laundry room, which was disguised as a livery stable for dog-sized horses, while the girls dressed. Nathan squeezed his shoulder. "Maybe it's worse finding out something you wouldn't let yourself think about," he said.

"Yeah."

When Angela and Naomi came out, they all stood looking at each other for an indecisive moment. Allard wondered if it was absolutely necessary to have this confrontation. Evidently it was. He knew he had to find Mary and say what he could. If he got her alone he might patch things up somewhat. How, he didn't know. There would be a certain amount of lying involved. He felt tenderness for Mary, and pity for her. She should not have had to see him and Naomi in the water; that was wrong. He had caused that. And there would be Harold's parent-like, moral outrage to listen to.

They walked across a miniature stone bridge, single file, and came through the poplars by the walk along the railroad track. The Town Hall showed a light here and there; the Railroad Station was all dark. Without speaking they entered the small foyer, or lobby, of the Town Hall. The door to Harold's quarters was open, light coming into the dim foyer. Nathan tapped on the doorframe and they all stepped into the room. Mary sat in the davenport, small, smudged around the eyes when she gave Allard a look and looked down again. She still wore her bright yellow bathing suit, her white towel over her shoulders. Her hair, slightly damp, was darkened by the moisture and curled at its ends into pathetic little ringlets.

Harold sat beside her, holding her hand. He gave it back to her and stood up, pale and stern. Anger did his homely face no justice; his nose was sharp and bloodless around the nostrils, and his eyes, in spite of their brightness, were gummy and moist.

"Well!" he said. His pinched, vibrating anger seemed to constitute a danger to his toupee, that perfectly parted cloud of darkness above his white forehead.

"Well," Nathan said, "we sort of figured the party was

over so we wanted to thank you and all that, Harold. We'll go back and collect Hilary and clean up all the bottles and stuff."

Harold wouldn't look at Naomi or Allard, but seemed to direct all his outrage toward Nathan. "The party! What a joke! It's all over as far as I'm concerned!"

Naomi suddenly went to Mary and sat down next to her. "Mary?" she said. "Mary? We all love you, honey. You know that, don't you?"

Allard was stunned by that speech. It seemed entirely out of his league.

"Love!" Harold shouted. "*Love!*"

"Yes, love," Naomi said. "So why don't you calm down and shut up, Harold?" She turned back to Mary.

"*I want you to get out of here!*"

"Aw, come on, Harold," Nathan said, embarrassed.

"Yes, Harold," Angela said. "There's really not enough reason for all this shouting and anger, is there?" She looked down upon him from her smooth, somewhat monumental height. "After all, Naomi and Allard are old friends, you know, and in a moment of passion who knows what can happen? What I mean to say is that such incidents are not terribly unexpected or unforgivable."

"*Unexpected!*" Harold was truly startled, breathless for a moment. "*Old friends!*" He choked. His trachea did not seem up to these heights of emotion.

"Don't blither, Harold," Angela said sternly. "Let us discuss this, if we must, in calm voices."

"You! I can't understand any of you! Mary found it *very* unexpected! She was in *love* with this monster. In spite of her faith she was willing to marry him, and then, at a party, she finds them—her roommate, her so-called friend, and the man she loves—naked, fornicating! Do all of you think this is just something casual? A joke? Do you have any idea how Mary felt? Is this the way you treat other people, the way you'd like to be treated? You're monsters! All of you are *monsters!*" Harold hit his hands on his thighs and choked again. "Practically *betrothed*, and promises, and I can't understand . . ."

Mary said, "No, Harold."

"What?"

"I was never sure about that."

"The bastard! The complete, utter bastard!" This time Harold's standards had been so unforgivingly violated he was through with friendship, with all of that. All of that was over.

"Yeah, well, okay, Harold," Allard said.

"You shut *up!* Who asked you anything? And why don't you just get out of here?"

Allard saw with sadness Mary's narrow, delicate fingers, her pale knuckles each a little jewel of bone beneath the clear skin. Her wrists were so slim yet squarish, with such tidy sturdiness. He looked from Mary to Naomi, at Naomi's long fingers, the dark gold of her skin, a hazy fuzz of fur on her long arms. Black silky hair next to Mary's finer dark blond silk. Mary's eyes were bothered, dingy from crying but beautiful inside the lids—and there, she looked up for a second and he caught that green fleck of jade. She wouldn't look at Naomi, who leaned over her to comfort her. Naomi, who'd had sex with Allard, just as Mary had. He wondered what images Mary had of that sex, or if she even thought of organs and lengths and diameters. Maybe not. A man did because certain of his dimensions actually had to change. Maybe Harold didn't think of it that way, either. Poor Harold.

Mary looked up again, her mouth trembling at one corner, but turning down, then, toward irony. A little pucker came and went on the exact point of her chin. He didn't mind this caught feeling of already being married to her because he did love her, as far as he could tell. He cared about how she felt right now, which was pretty awful and embarrassed. Her swift, ironic scowl-pout now told him that. He knew, too, that she hadn't done any real confessing to Harold, and that caused a wave of love for her, for her real dignity. And for Naomi, who'd said, "We all love you, honey." Honey! Where did Naomi get that word?

"My feelings were hurt," Mary said in a weak, breathy

voice. "I felt sorry for myself. That's all. Nobody has to marry me or anything like that."

Saying that, she was so beautiful his eyes dimmed. He felt that he was the only alien here, a nonhuman observer among real people who could say the truth about themselves, while he watched from a position of strength that was really coldness, selfishness. He wanted Mary and Naomi. It was as if they were so much meat and bone, hair and skin. Their female complexities, their womanness, their givingness, even the dark differences of uterus and womb—the mere youth that he was, all of whose history was open and known to him, had no right to claim these others whenever he chose, for his own gratification. He could make either of them unhappy with a word or a glance. He should not be allowed that power.

"Of course your feelings were hurt," Naomi said. "He should have kept his hands off you in the first place."

"But what about you, Naomi?" Mary asked, meaning *Aren't you hurt, too?*

"Mary, dear, I have a different attitude about sex than you do."

"Sex?" Harold said, staring at Mary. "Sex?" His face went through the strange focusing effect caused by a new conception.

"Yes, Harold," Mary said. They could hardly hear her voice. "I'm sorry but I'm not going to lie about anything any more."

What happened then his eyes observed, Allard's eyes that were accustomed to detecting quick motions, centers of possible violence, burning fuses, etc., so that his catlike self could triumph either by attack or escape. Now they merely watched as Harold's thin arm drew back into the classical, or seven-year-old boy's bent-elbowed, aimed, telegraphed haymaker, the thin white fist diminishing as it clenched. He observed the hatred on Harold's usually gentle face, also the fragile fist as it came toward his mouth. But how could it be Harold Roux who was doing this? It was Allard Benson's unmoving, non-ducking head that was being grossly punched by Harold, gentle Harold of the delicately balanced cranium. The white fist was surprisingly hard and painful, painful several times, in fact, as was the other thin fist.

He spoke to Harold, asking him to stop. He could not think of hitting him back, to stop him that way. The pain increased, Harold evidently being one of those thin people who possess surprising strength, as though their wheyish flesh were part metal. Everyone in the room thought this horror should stop, but before any concerted effort could be arranged Harold had hit him many times in the face, neck, forehead, chest, until he put out his hands to protect himself, to push Harold away. He couldn't see very well through the blows that stung him as if he were being whipped with a stick. He was being thrashed, demeaned, humiliated not so much by this punishment but by whatever he must have done, whatever inconceivably shameful thing he must have done to cause Harold to turn so violent. He tried to grab Harold's fists, to still them, though he could hardly see, and suddenly there was quiet in the room; even Harold's sobbing breaths stopped for the moment, and Allard realized that he had something soft, something crinkly but soft and furry, in his hand.

They were all looking at Harold, who stood frozen, staring at Allard's hand and what it held. They looked too, then, at what Allard had in his hand. Then back at Harold, who was not Harold but a slight, forty-year-old man with a head pale as the belly of a fish, blotched by an even paler patchwork, a strange design of unearthed, unentombed skin. That person was not Harold, and Allard saw in shock how much that pad of hair, this pad of hair he now held in his hand, had been Harold's youth. It did matter, so much more than the before-and-after photographs in magazines could ever show. He held part of Harold in his hand, wondering if he should give the part back.

Harold fell back into the davenport and sat with his hands over his face, hiding the room from himself. They soon realized that he was crying. Heavy wet tears appeared below his hands and gathered on his chin. Shudders and hiccups made him tremble, his arms and sharp shoulder points trembling beneath the weave of his light sweater. Allard considered whether or not he might put the hair back on that naked head, turning the thing around straight and placing it gently back on. He could not have been more surprised and horrified if he held one of Harold's fists in his hand, the bloody stump in the air for everyone to see. It did not seem an act he could say he was sorry for.

Mary put her arms around Harold and hugged him, moving his frail shoulders around toward her. He tried to pull away from her, his hands still pressed tightly against his eyes, but she wouldn't let him. She pulled his naked head next to hers, the fringes of real hair at his ears and around the back of his ears mussed, upset, wilder than they had ever expected to see any part of Harold. Allard still held the wig, its severed human hair glossy in his hand, a forbidden feeling against his fingers. He felt like a dissectionist. This human part was weighty, corpselike, and belonged back on the rest of its body. But of course it was too late. Harold's bruised hands seemed much younger, pale and reddish as a child's, than his blotched naked pate. He wondered if it were glue, or psoriasis, on that head.

Angela and Nathan drew chairs up before Harold's knees and sat down, which seemed planned, ceremonially odd. Naomi came around and sat on the arm of the davenport on Harold's other side, her long arm reaching down so she could squeeze the back of Harold's neck. Allard couldn't understand all this touching, all this squeezing and patting and touching, as if Harold were a little puppy. He couldn't understand how that could comfort a man. But he did know, and again he felt himself an alien here. Each of the others had made an instant and proper diagnosis of Harold's state. Angela and Nathan were patting Harold's knees, their voices saying it was all right, it was all right, Harold.

"Don't cry, Harold," Mary said. "Don't be so upset."

Allard observed, since he was useless here, his observing.

Evidently, in some terribly accidental, coincidental way, he had destroyed Harold's ability to look at his friends. The destroyed person seemed battered, savaged beyond salvation. To remove anyone's dignity in this fashion was not what Allard wanted to do, or thought himself capable of doing, and this was Harold, who had more than once nominated Allard to be his best friend, his only confidant. Allard did not think of himself as being brutal, or as a betrayer, and yet here he was and something awful had happened. He put the crumpled wig down on Harold's coffee table; then, still having to watch his victim, took out his handkerchief and blew a small amount of blood out of his nose. His lips were swelling too, but the only bad place was where Naomi had hit him the other evening. Of course his little bruises were nothing compared to Harold's paralysis, which suggested to him the grief of bereavement, all the worst terrors of grief that could ever happen to a person. Men and women had gone into that denying, crouching position from the beginnings of the race, covering their eyes from the viciousness of their fellows.

Harold's friends, those other people, still touched him, still moved their hands over him. Allard felt shame, or anger at his shame, or maybe anger at Harold's shame. "Harold!" he said sharply. "Hey, Harold!" He could not agree with all this demeaning patting and cuddling. In similar circumstances, if they could be imagined, he would find it intolerable to be petted like a baby. "Harold!" he said again.

"Shush, Allard!" Naomi said.

Shush! Another word he hadn't known Naomi could ever use. Did these women have all those childhood words ready at any moment? He felt a lack of control; those were not the words he had chosen for his maturity, or for Harold's, or for anybody's. He wanted to leave but he couldn't leave Harold in this condition, in these hands. So he stood, agonized in some more complicated way than even this complicated situation seemed to demand.

Harold had contracted into this shivering thing dressed in human clothes but not really there. His face and head seemed out of shape, as if squeezed lopsided by his own fingers.

"We've got to get him to talk to us," Mary said.

"Come on, Harold," Naomi said. She massaged the back of Harold's neck, leaning over him now with both hands massaging his neck and shoulders. He held his head rigid, although it must have been an effort. Pink areas that changed slowly, like clouds, had appeared on the skin of his head. He was surrounded and couldn't get away.

Mary, who was no longer the consoled but the one to console, spoke to Harold. "I know how you must feel," she said. Part irony there, but she spoke softly, with a confessional dryness Harold surely listened to. "Allard didn't mean to pull off your hair, I'm sure of that. He doesn't know what he's doing sometimes." She gave a short laugh that was worldly and sad, then continued in a soft, barely ironic voice. "I know how bad you feel. I do. I didn't tell you I was a fallen woman, Harold, did I. I'm sorry you felt the way you did about me and then you had to find out, but I'm through lying about anything. We all knew you wore that false hair anyway, you know, and if it made you feel better not to look bald none of us held it against you. I know I didn't. I don't think anyone did. Maybe Allard, I don't know. But he didn't want you to wear it because he thought it would be better for you not to wear it. I know he didn't mean to pull it off, though. That was an accident. Do you want to put it back on now? Do you want to put it back on?"

Harold wouldn't answer, even by moving his head one way or another. It seemed so strange that Mary, in her yellow bathing suit, was ministering to Harold, hugging him now to show her affection toward this somehow partially decapitated person. The frivolous yellow bathing suit and Mary's young smoothness, the perfection of her skin. She was only eighteen, and though Allard had once thought eighteen an advanced age for women he was twenty-one now and she seemed young. Harold was twenty-four, even if he did look middle-aged with all that bare pate showing. Twenty-four did seem adult, and it seemed to him that age, that proper gauge of developement that had always meant so much in childhood, was going undependable and wrong. All of these people had resources hidden from him, or weaknesses hidden from him. They had tenderness and consolation hidden from his knowledge. They were all larger continents than he had suspected, dangerous and enveloping. He could not reach for Mary and Naomi; his reach was not great enough. Angela and Nathan and Harold all had depths he hadn't considered, maybe didn't have himself. Even Knuck and Hilary, and Vera Upstairs, that poor creature, maybe she was also too deep for him.

And yet, he thought, *I* caused all this. He was the stranger who had caused all of this emotion, these screams and tears and the evocation of all this sympathy that was probably love, whatever that might be.

So could an assassin have caused all of it.

His Indian Pony could take him three thousand miles away from these complicated lives. He traveled light. He could be packed and on the moolit highway headed west in less than an hour. He could leave his footlocker with the housemother to be sent home, pack his saddlebags and roll the other things he might need in his poncho, roping the tight bundle neatly across his saddlebags—balanced, comforting, ready for speed. His new tires were crisp and round.

"Go ahead, Harold," Nathan said. "Put it back on if you want. It's not going to shock us or anything. If I was bald at your age I'd wear a hairpiece, too. It's nothing to be ashamed of." Nathan retrieved the wig from the coffee table and put it on Harold's lap, where it sat, a furry hemisphere Harold wouldn't acknowledge.

"Look, Harold," Naomi said, "somebody's got to straighten you out. You can't just go into a cataleptic fit or something just because you found out a few things about life."

"I'm worried about him," Mary said. "We can't just leave him all torn apart like this."

"We won't leave him like this," Naomi said, "but we don't seem to be getting through to him very well."

"What can we do?" Angela said.

They were all so grave, these strange women who had revealed their flaming harlotry to poor Harold and now wouldn't let him go. Allard felt hysteria, or something near it, rise in him. He might suggest shock treatment: they could have a Black Mass, right now. Naomi would be the Christ-killing Altar Witch, playing the skin flute. *Amen. Sancti Spiritus et Filii.* Mary would be the virgin deflowered by Beelzebub upon the altar. *Jesus womb thy of fruit!* Allard would play Beelzebub with mad relish. Then they would strip Harold naked and paint him blue, using that bottle of Quink right there on his desk, to prepare him for Angela, great naked spanking Angela, thighs like a wild mare, who would ponderously rape him while his slobbering friends chanted a High Mass backwards.

He didn't suggest this; it barely flickered through his criminal mind, followed by pity. Shocking things were still happening to Harold, if Harold was listening.

Angela said, "I don't suppose it would do anything to try to explain to Harold that Mary is not a 'fallen woman' just because she and Allard have had sexual intercourse. Personally, and I'm sure Nathan will agree, I think the act of physical love is a beautiful and natural thing, but I do think it wasn't very nice of Allard and Naomi to have done it in front of Mary and Harold, even if by accident, considering Harold's religious sensitivity and his protective feelings toward Mary. And poor Mary must have felt betrayed because Allard is, or was, or had strongly suggested that he might be, her intended husband."

Allard looked around Harold's room, at his sedate furniture, his framed Currier and Ives prints against the rich wallpaper, his books safe and orderly behind glassed cabinet doors. His friends had followed Harold here to Lilliputown, his sanctuary, even to this room he had made into a place of calm and dignity—and proceeded to violate all of his sensibilities, even tearing the very scalp off his head. With friends like these, who needed Boom Maloumian?

Angela, with her good clear patrician eyes, had already seen the first ominous sign. Just after they crossed the narrow bridge on the way to the Town Hall, she had seen a tall person standing in the moonlight across the park. The figure was dark-clothed above the waist, but below were long, moonlit bare legs. This tall creature, caught in that bemused, half-hunched posture that is never mistaken for anything else, looked down at what it was doing, or at what part of its body was doing. And yes, there was the glittering, pencil-thin arc connecting a man to the earth.

She had thought it must be Hilary, who had probably awakened and followed them, and of course it wouldn't have been good form to point him out at that moment. In any case, thinking that he would be along presently, she hadn't mentioned it.

Aaron finds himself in his small study, standing there looking down at his notebooks. His desk light prints a warm yellow circle on the place where all of his thoughts should be directed. He should be working right now, but his family will be home soon and he has a sense of the preciousness of time, much like the last few hours of a furlough. Time is running out, including these last minutes before they all get home and demand his attention, guilt and acceptance.

But he is too tired, and where is his family? Where is the crunch of gravel, the slamming of the car doors, those voices that fill him with dread and love, that make his skin bunch up in knots and his eyes hurt? There has been an accident; they have all been killed and he is free. Free! And then the true meaning of that freedom comes over him like a wind from across the Arctic ice, a continent empty of all but white ice.

Maybe he'd better call Wellesley and find out when they left. A perfectly useless thing to do which would only make John and Cynthia worry. If they have been in an accident he will be notified. Along the ugly and murderous highway speeds a police car, blue lights frantic, siren screaming panic, guilt, death, and in the blood and oil and broken glass the number of this very telephone, the ugly black telephone in the hall, will be found.

The telephone screams. It screams out of his vision of its squatness so that at first it is only hallucination. But it is not hallucination and he is frightened into nausea; it is shock, that same coldness and vertigo. His body, still knowing how to function under adversity, moves toward the hallway and the screaming.

"Hello?"

"Hello, Dad?" It is Bill, who is fifteen, the deep voice still new.

"Bill! Where are you? What's the matter?" He sees the strobic blue lights, the grotesque immobility of the wreckage.

"We're going to stay over tonight. It seems you forgot to get the headlights adjusted and everybody was blinking their lights at us. Mom got blinded so we turned around and came back."

"Oh."

"We'll start in the morning, okay?"

"Okay. Let me speak to Agnes. Is she there?"

"Hey, Mom?" The voice of his son is fainter yet louder to itself, directed into another room in another place. There is the feeling of depth over that distance, perspective through sound, dimming to the vanishing point.

"Hello?" Agnes' voice is suddenly there, hard, mature, yet beneath is the echoing sweet sound of a girl. She has grown up no more than he has.

"How are you?" he says, feeling love for her.

"I was surprised you'd be home."

No, no. His soul wilts at this short circuit, sickened by the old pattern of their discontents. It is so familiar and it never fails to make him angry or despairing and it is unanswerable.

"I thought you'd probably be out comforting Helga," she says.

Helga! But he hasn't . . . It was George he was to comfort! But of course Agnes knows because it is her only business to know. He hasn't and wouldn't, but that is never enough, never enough. His most suppressed inclinations are as guilty as flagrant acts. So why not act, then? asks his anger.

"That makes me unhappy," he says.

"Well, good night," Agnes says, and hangs up.

He wants to speak to Janie, and to say more to Bill. Her hostages? No, not that simple. She has as hostages all those years with their moments, her joy that can be unalloyed, her duty toward her children that is born of love and can't be faulted. For richer or for poorer, in sickness and in health. History as hostage. He wants to break down a wall. He could drive his fist right through this wall, but it is too late to do that because he has already located the two-by-four studs and would aim in between them, so his rage is not pure, is it?

Allard would not have had it end this way. Perhaps as an allegory, purer and simpler, evil against good—that would have been nicer to be in, provided it ended well and he was neither maimed nor killed. More like the Second World War, for instance. And here was Lilliputown, the very name suggesting allegory.

Whom had Angela seen?

And if it were Robert Gordon Westinghouse, the Poet of the Lady of the Orbiting Moon, Mellifulous Aponatatus, who always let down his pants to urinate, how did he get there? They had seen no extra cars in the parking spaces in front of the Town Hall—only Harold's Matilda, Nathan's Ford, Knuck's newly acquired ancient Plymouth rumble-seat coupe and Allard's motorcycle. Was the Poet a highly improbable scout? A spy?

In Harold's room they still surrounded Harold with their earnest care for him, touching him, loving him back to life. Little by little Harold overcame the conviction that his life had been ruined by their betrayals. Naomi turned in his mind from harlot to doubtful person, just as Mary, in time that heals all, or nearly all, resumed something of the status of angel. Fallen angel. She, after all, had been betrayed by Allard—seduced and then again betrayed. Angela, whom Harold had always admired for her class, seemed to have lost none of it despite her shocking admission. As for Allard and Nathan, they were the brutal seducers of innocence—men, their filthy minds in the sewer. Yet they had been kind to him in the past and were trying to be kind even now. A great gray curtain seemed to descend between him and their force, their ability to threaten him. All right, they were all merely men and women, imperfect sinners. What matter that they had torn away his faith in them as well as the secret from his head? He would quit school and spend a calm life here at Lilliputown with Colonel Immingham and Morgana, who did live with grace and dignity. He would read, yes, great books that spoke with gravity and honor. Goodbye to these false friends who had once seemed so charming and good. Goodbye, goodbye; he no longer needed any of them.

He was very calm now. He took his toupee from his lap and placed it back on his head, smoothing it down as best he could without comb and mirror.

"I'm all right now," he said. He got up and went to the door. "I just don't want to see any of you again." His mouth trembled at this momentous declaration, but he meant it.

"I'm so sorry, Harold!" Mary said. She was crying.

Harold said nothing. He stood at the door waiting for them to leave, his gray face set by pride and justification, his hair slightly askew.

They walked quietly out of Harold's room, through the foyer and out into the night, where they stood looking at each other in the moonlight. "Do you think he's okay now?" Nathan asked no one in particular.

"I don't know," Mary said. She still wanted to cry and Allard put his arm around her. She moved her shoulders and stepped away from him.

"We'd better go collect Hilary and the bottles," Nathan said. "God knows about Knuck and Vera."

"You've got to change out of your bathing suit," Naomi said to Mary, who didn't answer but started walking up the path along the railroad tracks. They followed.

When they passed through the line of Lombardy poplars they became aware, one by one, of a muted sense of motion within Lilliputown, as if the town were a ship moving at anchor, its timbers making deep, half-heard noises. Small creaks, a shutting door, muffled laughter? A clink. People moved among the small buildings—people or animals or things, but they could not pick out, in the elm-shaded moonlight, any single entity. They stopped, close together, watching and listening.

"What the hell is it?" Nathan said in a hushed voice.

"Lilliputians?" Allard said.

"I saw someone earlier," Angela whispered. "I thought it might have been Hilary."

"Weren't the streetlights on when we came down?" Naomi said. Now the town was dark between islands of moonlight. Across the park and the brook with its narrow bridges, somewhere near the Little Brown Church in the Vale, a bottle smashed, the secondary noise of its shards proving its reality as they sprayed along the cement sidewalk.

"I doubt if it's Knuck or Hilary," Allard said.

"We ought to tell Harold," Mary said.

"What did you see earlier?" Allard said to Angela.

"A tall man without any pants on, urinating."

"You thought it was Hilary?"

"Yes, but now I don't think it was Hilary. There was something peculiar about his neck, the way he was looking down at himself."

"Peculiar?"

"Freaky, rather. Anyway, I didn't mention it because I

thought at first it was Hilary and I didn't want to embarrass him."

Allard looked at Nathan, who was looking back at Allard —the same odd surmise. Nathan said, "Were his pants off, or just down around his ankles?"

"What? I don't know. He was standing way over by the First National Bank or whatever it is. A long way, you know."

"If it was the Piss Poet I suspect the fine Armenian hand of Boom Maloumian," Allard said.

"Did he know about the party?" Nathan said.

"God knows. Knuck was in Litchwood with Maloumian tonight. Maybe he let out where he was going."

The girls were frightened. Allard and Nathan were not too calm either, and the girls had heard it in their voices.

"If it is him, he's after Harold," Nathan said.

"But what will we *do?*" Mary said, her voice breaking. "Poor Harold! Should we call the police?"

Allard thought they should find out a little more about the situation first, suggesting that the bluecoats, for Harold's sake, be avoided if possible. Anything of that sort might offend the Imminghams and hurt Harold's position here. They decided that Nathan would take the girls to the Livery Stable and get Mary's clothes, then get Hilary and try to find Knuck and Vera. The girls, following Nathan, walked away with quick, fearful steps.

Allard would scout out the noises over by the Little Brown Church in the Vale. He waited until the others were out of sight and hearing. He stood quietly for a while, listening, trying to see across the park in the pale light that was deceptively bright but could hardly penetrate the blue-black shadows. Lilliputown was not his creation but it was a creation, another's idea of perfection, or near perfection. And of course Harold, having renounced his friends, had nowhere to be but here.

He wished, thinking it dangerous and stupid and yet still wishing it, that he had his Nambu. He seemed such a frail instrument to try to stop whatever evil menaced Lilliputown. And it was evil; the sound of the bottle when it smashed over there, the glass cascading, was evil. He experienced in the center of his body fear of Maloumian, and the fear brought anger. What would happen would be too complicated for that fear and anger. There would have to be words, arguments and threats. He thought with nostalgia of the war, when he was in the infantry in Georgia, how the pop-up silhouettes of German soldiers were driven violently back on their hinges at each jump of his Garand. He might go back to the Colonel's workshop and pick out a well balanced open-end wrench, or a ball-peen hammer, or maybe the Colonel had a gun . . . Maybe it wasn't Maloumian over there after all. Except for the smashed bottle. How evil was Maloumian, really?

His cold center told him very evil, very big. He needed troops. Even if Knuck could be found and apprised of the situation, he didn't know if Knuck would oppose Maloumian; they were in their separate ways both such heavy men, and they always seemed to have an agreement, or treaty, between themselves in which Maloumian was to Knuck a clown whose japes and escapades should not be taken too seriously. Nathan would fight but he was so small. Hilary seemed in his bland good nature made of paper-mâché. And poor Harold had been destroyed once already on this disastrous evening. If only he had Nathan with him and they were both armed.

He knew he had to go over toward the Little Brown Church in the Vale no matter what waited for him, so he moved as quietly as he could through the shadows, keeping the trunks of elms between himself and whatever unknown watchers might be there. Partly on his hands and toes he went through the park to the brook, where he could make a transverse approach in its depression, crossing it on stones and moving along its bank. When he thought he was across the railroad track from the Little Brown Church in the Vale he rose up, a barberry hedge identifying itself painfully to his fingers. He raised his head slowly, hearing stifled laughter and giggles from quite close by. Many bodies—too many of them, at least eight or nine—sat or lay on the lawn of the church, large forms some of which passed bottles or drank, glass glinting sharply in the moonlight, followed by coughs and throat-clearings. "Quiet!" someone whispered. Was it Short Round? "Quiet! You want to queer it?" It was Short Round, from somewhere near the door of the church.

The church door opened upon glaring light which, after whispered curses, was turned off from inside, but Allard had seen a man standing next to a bureau zipping up his fly—a large jock he knew slightly whose specialties were football and lacrosse. Whalen, his name was, a mediocre athlete who made very professional-looking moves, gestures and remarks on the field.

"Okay, who's next?" Short Round was exasperated. "Come on, damn it, and get your goddam money out!" One of the lounging figures got up, unsteadily it seemed to Allard, while the others laughed into their hands. The bulk that must have been Whalen collapsed into the general shadow of the lawn and asked for a drink. "Hoo, boy," he said.

"Keep it down!" Short Round said from the doorway. "Jesus Christ, will you?"

A cloud, crossing the moon, turned silver at its edges while the town went dark. No sign of Maloumian, who might be inside the church. He must be here somewhere, standing or moving, maybe moving through the darkness. Allard shivered, as though eyes observed him from behind, and tried to tell himself that this was not, after all, a deadly situation. Though all of these men had been in the war they were now civilians, college students, not authorized to wound or kill. But he knew that even though the war had ended the animal was the same, and this engagement was the one he was in. His anger grew reckless and frightening; one always had the option to introduce violence, but he must forsake that seductive fantasy and think.

He took advantage of the cloud to move back down the brook, crossing back over the way he'd come. Just before he reached the open glades of the park, where he would be exposed to the moonlight, from straight ahead of him, from the direction of the poplars and the Town Hall, came a scream that in its hoarseness was identifiably male, though it shrilled in its high ranges like the voice of a caught rabbit.

It was prey in the teeth of its hunter, that scream of useless terror, and it struck him through his own hunting memories as well as through dreams of having been pursued and caught. He wanted to hide and also to charge with the right of a hunter toward the place of the kill. Listening so intently he was not aware of himself in either role, he didn't move, then heard a distant scuffling, drumming sound, like the hooves of horses. It was not coming toward him, but going off to his right along the poplars. Somewhere over there, near the Barbershop and the Saloon, glass shattered, not a bottle this time but the xylophonic chords of window glass.

He ran back past the poplars to the Town Hall. The front door was open, the foyer empty. Harold's lights were on but he was not there. He thought of a weapon but couldn't think of anything short of a gun that would be effective at all. A quick look into the Imminghams' living room, peacefully quiet, waiting in its comfortable chintzy clutter, revealed no weapons. The door to the Colonel's shop was locked. He turned off a bridge lamp, nearly knocking it over, steadying its parchment shade, and ran back out of the building, up the path again. He had thought of the police but couldn't make himself call them. It would not be right, not understood by them. This microcosmic war was between known adversaries, and his own guilt might make him guilty of everything in their stern distant eyes. Of course he should have called the police. But what police? He wasn't even sure what town this was. The operator, of course, could have told him. When he was just about out of breath he nearly tripped over a body whose long legs stuck out into the path, its thin trunk propped against an elm. Bare ankles in sneakers, baggy dress pants with cuffs: Gordon Robert Westinghouse. In a rage, Allard hauled him to his feet and banged his bony back against the tree.

"All right, you useless son of a bitch, tell me all."

All! Would he ever have rage or any intensity of emotion in which he did not hear strange words, odd insincere constructions?

Melifulous Aponatatus smiled and drooled. "Erk," he said.

No amount of banging him against the tree changed his expression toward awareness, and Allard saw that though he was actually drunk he was going beyond that and playing glorious, romantic drunk, letting himself descend under the pale eye of the moon into magnificent dissipation.

"You can't act, you shit-for-brains," Allard said. "The likes of you can't act. Come out of it or I'll break your ass."

"Balaforuh. Narpaluff."

Allard let him fall.

"Allard! Allard!" Naomi called as she came running up to him. Mary, Angela and Nathan followed, Hilary stumbling along behind.

"So it was the Piss Poet," Nathan said.

The poet lay on his side trying to breathe.

Allard sensed some disapproval of his violence and said, "He's being drunk and won't talk. I think Maloumian's got Harold. Did you hear the scream?"

"Yeah, we heard it," Nathan said.

"What are we going to *do?*" Mary said.

"He's got a bunch of frat jocks over by the church, about eight or nine of them, and Short Round's charging them for whatever attraction he's got inside there."

"Like what?" Naomi said.

"Like a whore, I suppose." His anger and fear made him go on. "Or a chicken or a Chinaman or eighteen queer midgets or his hairy grandmother or whatever his joke is for tonight."

"But what's he going to do with Harold?" Mary said.

In the silence following this unanswerable question they heard the growing intensity of the sounds of invasion. Laughter and thumping, even growls and barks, as if wolves prowled through Lilliputown. They thought one screaming voice must be Harold's, and its pathetic desperation came from somewhere near the Little Brown Church in the Vale.

Allard asked if they'd found Knuck and Vera. They hadn't.

"You don't suppose it's Vera he's got in the church?" Nathan said.

"I doubt it, unless Knuck's unconscious or something."

"What are you *talking* about?" Mary cried. "What do you mean? That's Harold *crying.* I can hear him!"

"I say," Hilary said groggily, "what's going on?"

"They're killing Harold!" Mary cried.

"Oh, I say! That's too violent," Hilary said, alarmed. He peered down at Gordon Robert Westinghouse, fast asleep at their feet. "Oh," he said, "is it Maloumian then?"

"I haven't seen him yet, but Short Round's over there so there's not much doubt," Allard said.

"Why are we just talking?" Mary said. "We've got to get Harold!"

"I think maybe you girls ought to go home," Allard said. Nathan and Hilary agreed. Angela could take them back in Nathan's car.

"I'm not going anywhere until I find Harold," Mary said, and began to run through the moonlight toward the church, her light skirt fading into the dark. Allard ran and caught her around the waist. She fought him, crying and still trying to run. Her sobs were voiced, frantic; she mewed like a cat.

"Mary!" he said, pulling her against him so hard she had trouble breathing.

"Let me *oh!* Let me go!"

He had to pin her arms under his. "Mary! Listen! Those drunken bastards are dangerous! Listen to me! We'll try to get Harold! I'll kill that bastard Maloumian . . ."

"Let go of me!"

She would go directly to Harold no matter what lay before her. He couldn't let her go; he had to hold her still in order to think.

The others came up. Naomi put her arms around Mary, too, so that she and Allard had her captured between them, surrounded by arms, the three bodies locked together. Mary could not be calmed; she struggled, her bones and flesh harder than Allard had ever found them in his arms before. He and Naomi hushed her and spoke to her, trying with their voices to soothe her though they had nothing helpful to say except please be calm and everything will be all right. Her head, small and angular, turned against Allard's chest. Her hair, because it was tangled and compressed, wet in places, was thinner, the silky growth common to the heads of children. He found that his arms, his voice, the bulk of his body, all of his presence was useless against her determination. She cried, "Harold, Harold," and soon they had all come under what seemed then the invincible logic of her desires and were walking with her toward the Little Brown Church in the Vale.

Unarmed, they would also lose all the advantages of knowledge and surprise. He was being led into a position of weakness by this woman's logic and he asked himself how it could be happening. She heard Harold's cries and must go to him, though Boom Maloumian would most certainly be there. Not to mention Whalen and his probable companions whose thug values were so cruel it had always seemed odd to Allard that those animals had human names. Whalen, Morrow, Gilman, McLeod, Likas, Schurz, Harorba, Manolo, O'Brien. He had played in their games—poker, pickup football—and knew how their crude superiorities were exacerbated by constant closeness and mutual agreement. Meanwhile he walked with his eccentric, vulnerable friends toward evil, believing that he was the only one who recognized its real dangers.

The streetlights flickered and came on again, each above its little amphitheater of light. Scattered cheers, grunts and shouts of wonder or approval came from here and there across the town. They could see movement, the flicker of a broad, white-shirted back as a running figure appeared and disappeared down by the First National Bank, near the tunnel where the Colonel kept his train. Dark figures crossed between trees and buildings with seemingly aimless energy. From their left as they approached the church came a quick flurry like a dogfight—breathless snarling and a scraping of earth or wood that might have been done by frantic claws.

The Little Brown Church in the Vale was softly illuminated by its own streetlight as if in a suburban evening, its brown gables and stained glass, its square bell tower giving it a look of staunch inviolability until, as they approached, it shrank into its real dimensions. Leaves whispered above their heads in a new wind. Then the raucous voices of men overcame all the natural sounds of the night. The men stood in a half circle in front of the church, one of them unable to stand without his arm around another's neck and falling to his knees as his support turned with the others, seven of them, to see the strange group approaching. Little Nathan, stately Angela, pale Mary, dark Naomi and gawky Hilary—Allard's odd forces of flawed righteousness walking straight into the hands of their enemies.

Vague, fierce, shiny, the faces turned toward them, some with wonder. O'Brien, Harorba, Morrow, Gilman—he knew most of them and they all had certain common characteristics, such as slightly humped backs from holding up their freakishly thick arms and the weight of their menacing struts, the forward lean of their manliness. They had imitated each other for so long, in so many ways, that only minor differences in shape or texture indicated their separateness; somewhat as with identical twins, Allard always found himself examining each of them carefully for a shorter brow or a barely different cast to the eyes.

"Hey! Broads!"

"White meat!"

"Shaddup, dumbhead!"

"Don't step in the puke!" Advice, laughter. "Don't step in the gism—it's coming out the scuppers!"

"At ease! At ease!"

The last said by Boom Maloumian, his black slits wet with laughter as he appeared at the church door. In an excess of hilarity he had to put his head down upon the wrought-iron railing for a moment as all turned to watch him. The men turned their appreciative faces toward this larger exemplar of themselves as if they were his devotaries, created smaller, like commoners surrounding royalty in a primitive painting. Maloumian (Moloch—the word came into Allard's mind) had all the time he wanted, command of time for his ponderous dance of amusement. At first he did not notice the newcomers, or seem to hear Mary's shrilling voice.

"Where is Harold?" she cried. "Where is Harold?"

"Where is Harold?" answered several falsetto voices. "Where, oh where, is Harold? Have you seen Harold? No! Have you? Who the fuck *is* Harold? Harold? Harold? Are you there, Harold? Oh, Harold, where *are* you?" In their falsetto voices had been an accidental harmony that sent them into laughter—even, from one of them, a near-hysterical, effeminate shriek.

It was all a question, now, of how much collusion, or loyalty, there was between Maloumian and these morally stunted jocks, and how much they wanted what was going on to go on. This sort of calculation kept working in Allard's mind, though it seemed hopeless. At least Whalen wasn't here, although he might be inside the church. There was something he ought to remember about Whalen that was either dangerous or merely irritating, but he couldn't bring whatever it was to mind.

Maloumian, who now deigned to recognize them, took all of Allard's attention. The massive head, iron-colored shiny skin, hair like wires bent into place by pliers and painted black—all turned on the invisible neck. The hilarity, which Allard had recognized as if he had been coldly informed of it, changed now into amazed, voracious delight.

"Aha!" Maloumian said with the expansive joviality of power. "The party! We all came to the party but we couldn't find the party." Deep disappointment: the assumed expression fit Maloumian very well, as if it were that easy to change all that muscle into the configurations of a child's hurt face.

"So we decided to have our own party! While we waited, so to speak!" He looked at Angela, imitating her upper-class diction. "You see, ladies and gentlemen, we all felt rather left out. Our *feelings* were hurt. But never mind, we decided to make the best of it even though we *did* think to bring Harold a present and it seemed so . . . so rather . . . *not nice* of him not to welcome us!"

"Where is Harold?" Mary cried.

Maloumian ignored her and went on speaking words Allard couldn't understand because the terror in the voice of this girl he himself had hurt was sending him beyond, where the cold white-out would make him forget his helplessness, ignore all the possible legal and argumentative powers they might have left to use. Now he was sliding over toward rage. He and Maloumian were now at the place where expression became the length of exposed fang, the constriction of eyelids and the laying back of ears, and Maloumian of course saw it at once.

"Now, now, Benson," he said, comfortably safe, interested.

"Hey, Allard," Nathan said. "Wait a minute."

Words were not really words. They meant nothing, even though Allard found them coming from his own head. But he had always been a fountain of words. He listened to his own sounds, but the combinations, though familiar, meant nothing but intent. Yet he was full of distant thoughts, an odd detachment, as he moved up the steps toward Maloumian.

He had been given the thesis constantly, ever since he could begin to understand, that he must think the best of mankind, believe in an essential goodness that should never be violated. Of course he knew how innocently ridiculous this thesis was, but perhaps it was responsible for his rage against those who did not conform to his expectations, as he didn't himself. *Sen gurt dúrn ful lama sinis:* You were born out of your mother's asshole. In other words, fight me as your grandmother, who was raped and dismembered, would have called upon you to do with her last scream. He always meant the unforgivable, invited his enemy to go for his jugular, and yet he himself had never quite killed. It all seemed exceedingly dangerous that he was ultimately deficient in this motivation. But maybe he was not this time.

Perhaps he hadn't said the Turkish curse out loud, or hadn't remembered it right.

He didn't know whether Maloumian was here to make money, essentially, or for research—to amass additional raw data for one of his great tales. Whatever the reason, this evening was Maloumian's creation. Allard might alter events somewhat but he knew that Boom Maloumian would be the master of the coming ceremonies.

Words still came out of his mouth; he was no doubt telling Maloumian all sorts of things. Something physical but insubstantial kept getting in his way and it was Nathan, probably, whom he pushed aside. Then it was Naomi, and Hilary was there, too, and then not there. Then some brilliant strategical center of his lower brain pointed him not directly at Maloumian but toward the door of the church. This threw Maloumian off just a little—power can be fooled, but not for long—and Maloumian instead of hitting him grabbed his arm. That contact at once gave Allard power; the moment Maloumian's fingers encircled his arm he did what he could never do through empty air. He had to be touched before he could fight, as though he were blind and knew the other's anatomy only through touch, seeing clearly now in his mind all levers, lengths, vessels and nerves. Maloumian fell back down the steps, his fingers or knuckles playing a dull, harp-like thrum along the metal columns of the railing. Now was the time to shoot Maloumian with the Nambu, but he didn't have the Nambu so Maloumian would be back very soon. Meanwhile, since he had little else to do, Allard opened the church door. He had time to see two men—Short Round and another he didn't know—holding Harold's arms behind his back. From the bed rose a black figure which turned white, a dark bird with white wings now seen as a chenille bedspread enfolding the dark body. Then he was taken from behind and hit so many times on his head he began to count the blows, as though he'd been asked to count his way into anesthesia. Nothing hurt, but it took too long before the blows, or his knowledge of them, stopped, and he was again at the bottom of the steps, on his knees, feeling the loss of a short but totally unaccounted for passage of time.

He was weak, partly through delayed fear; while his head was being hammered by fists—on the back, sides, top, front, anywhere—he had wondered if they knew enough not to kill him. His scalp was bruised, pulpy. His arms felt as if they had been removed. The two men who held him seemed to be doing something they didn't have to do. He still observed this place, shaking away a tendency toward diplopia. He had acted perhaps honorably, if stupidly—what was the difference? Mary's crying, now that he had lost his strength, made him distantly sad. Angela had her arm around Nathan, her square hand gently wanting to support, but not quite daring to touch, his jaw.

"You've broken his face," she said to Maloumian, "and I'll see that you pay for it." She was not fazed by these unruly peasants, and for a moment her dignified outrage seemed to be having an effect.

Naomi then said the wrong thing: "You miserable *pricks!*"

Oh, Naomi, Allard thought. Laughter, whiskey fumes and a hint of distant urine surrounded him. To them that was the language of a whore, an outlaw, and one of them began to wrestle with her, laughing and blocking her fists with his shoulders. References were made to kosher meat. Mary cried out for all this to stop, while Hilary tried to comfort her.

"You're in trouble, Maloumian," Allard said.

"Benson?" Maloumian's voice stilled them, not so much because of its deepness but because of its sad forgiveness, almost plaintiveness. "Benson? Why'd you have to come up here and get all feisty like that? You ought to know we don't mean no harm. We're good boys, just havin' a little fun. Just funnin' around now."

Just a folksy fella, a good old boy, trying to comprehend. So it was a movie now, a Western, and they would wait, knowing the coming turn to nightmare: the rope slithers up and over the cottonwood branch, and suddenly the mask of friendliness is removed.

Angela spoke of the police, and Maloumian laughed good-naturedly. "We're all friends here," he said. "We just came to the party. Just a little beer-and-whiskey bust among old school friends. All this talk about the cops seems mighty unfriendly, in fact downright inhospitable. Ain't that right, boys?"

Assenting laughter. Then, except for desperate retching off in the shrubbery somewhere, came an expectant silence as the church door opened and the white chenille bedspread appeared like bodiless wings. It was occupied by a Negro woman with a young, battered-looking face—black eyes, tan in the whites, swollen lids, thick, blue-black lips inverted as if pushed out from inside the mouth, mussed straightened hair as slick in places as polished onyx or grease.

"Ladies and gentlemen," Boom Maloumian said, bowing with a barker's flourish, "may I present *Miss Betty Bebop!*"

Applause, which she did not bother to acknowledge.

"Gimme my money," she said to Maloumian, holding out a palm that shone flower-pink above her hand's smoky black, its demanding surface bright in the streetlight.

Harold Roux, no longer held from behind, came out then, followed by Short Round and the other one Allard now recognized as McLeod. Harold's stiff back and pursed lips revealed that he was trying to assume a posture of unassailable dignity. Maloumian looked down upon him, ignoring the outstretched hand of Betty Bebop. Harold looked defiantly up at Maloumian's breadth of muscle that was thinly encapsulated by a university T-shirt, black hair curling at his chest and along the thick forearms. Maloumian grinned down at him. At a gesture Short Round handed Maloumian a pint bottle from which he took a swig and then offered it to Harold, who made no answer.

"Sixty dollah," Betty Bebop said.

Maloumian continued to ignore her. "Harold, Harold," he sighed. "Sometimes I get the feeling you're *so* unfriendly. And after all the trouble and expense I've gone to! At great trouble and expense I've brought you this dusky maiden as a gift, free, just for you, and now I'm informed that you cannot be induced to partake of her voluptuous charms!" His virtuosity overcame him and he laughed, hitting his chest with the sloshing pint bottle, roars of helpless hoarse laughter reverberating among the trees. "Perhaps . . ." He laughed some more and then gained control, sighing at his wit. "Perchance one of these nice young fellows over here would be more to your taste? How about Allard Benson, there? I'm positively certain he'd be more than willing to let you have your way with him. Hmm?"

Harold spoke, his voice unsteady but his dignity still pathetically wracking his body, making him look like a toy soldier at attention. "Is this what you want?" he said. He put his hand to his head, pulled off the toupee whole, revealing the naked bone of his skull, and tossed it at Maloumian's feet. Suddenly he was old, adult, deathlike.

Maloumian was, for an unforgivable moment, astounded. Something had gone wrong; the tale was out of control. His eyes retreated into their muscular slits as if into the embrasures of a turret, and he began to chew the gristle on the inside of his cheek. Whoops of pleased amazement from the jocks did not alleviate his disappointment. He drank from the bottle again, still scowling at Harold, looking at him all the time he drank.

"Sixty dollah," said Betty Bebop.

"Take down his pants," Maloumian ordered Short Round, who stepped forward to obey.

"Sixty dollah!" Betty Bebop said.

"You ain't finished yet," Maloumian said, slapping her hand away.

"I is *finish!*"

"You is finish when I *say* you is finish!"

"That boy crine! I ain' gon do nothin' with that boy."

Short Round had undone Harold's roller belt buckle and pulled his pants and shorts down around his ankles. His skinny white legs were hairless. He had a little pot, pale as a honeydew melon, pure above the sudden dark smear of his pubic hair, where his genitalia hung shyly, raped by this exposure yet revealed to be the same as any man's.

"Sixty dollah!" Betty Bebop said.

Maloumian ripped the bedspread away from her and she stood naked, shaking a broken fingernail in pain. A tiny bulb of red blood grew on it and she sucked it. Her body was rich chocolate, too large an expanse of warm brown, yet almost not naked under all that smooth creamy pigment. They all looked and looked at her, at her black bush, at the shadings of brown where at armpit or groin the brown grew condensed, gummy, grayish black, then stretched to near amber on the tight skin of her belly and breasts. Her thighs gleamed of water or slime. When she turned back toward the doorway her buttocks stood out from her body like heavy balloons, round repositories of power and energy. Maloumian scooped his hand up into her from behind, his thumb and fingers entering her body with a thrusting solidity that justified her scream of pain and rage.

"Oh, my God!" Mary cried. "Oh, my God! My God!"

With his other hand Maloumian grasped Betty Bebop's brown neck from behind and held her up in the air. "Now, you nigger bitch, I got you in the bowlin' ball grip, hear? You do jus' what I say or I'll *tear out the partition!*" His laughter, strained by effort, boomed out over her screams of impalement. Her brown legs ran in the air.

Then they heard the steam whistle, and after a bronchial huff, huff, chug, chug, the slowly increasing rumble and iron clatter of wheels. At that moment Allard knew what it was about Whalen he had tried to remember earlier. Engine Whalen, he was sometimes called. Submerged within the synthetic toughness Whalen had assumed as a member of his group was an odd, uncharacteristic interest, something held over from his boyhood, and it had to do with steam locomotives; before he'd gone into the Navy he'd worked summers on the Mt. Washington Cog Railway.

Winding out of the dark at the end of the village came the train, backwards, the red caboose jerking back and forth on the narrow tracks. It came up Main Street between the Saloon and the First National Bank of Lilliputown, across from the Barbershop. Turning between the Jail and the Pharmacy, it fed itself out of sight behind trees and buildings, then came out again toward them and rumbled past the Little Brown Church in the Vale. Everyone paused to watch it except Betty Bebop who, freed from Boom Maloumian's thick fingers, had run back into the church. The Prussian State Railways 0–4–2T locomotive came last, backwards, gleaming brass and oily spurts of steam and smoke, alive and moving. Whalen, if it were Whalen, could be seen as a smudged blond head within the tender, staring into bright light. The apple-sized head of the permanent engineer grinned his fixed, forward-looking grin, now back toward where he had come from, as the train turned and departed for the poplars and the Lilliputown Railroad Station. The whistle screamed again, with a departing swoop of sound, as the train disappeared into the darkness and shadow of the trees. But they could hear it and feel its real weight through the ground beneath their feet, its mass thumping and moving even if out of sight. Shortly it appeared again, going faster, the huff-chuff blending into one panting breath, the red caboose jarring back into their sight with the frantic vibrations of a child's model train on a curve—too fast, yet still huge, as though the picture in their eyes had been speeded up by the camera. No one thought to try to correct what was happening; they could only watch it on the long curve across the park, again feeding itself out of sight down behind the Barbershop and around the shorter curve by the roundhouse-tunnel and then coming at them again, the red caboose lightly jumping from side to side, tilting, its trucks hammering against the tracks as it disappeared again between the Jail and the Pharmacy, only to shoot into sight again and go by the Little Brown Church in the Vale too fast, seeming closer this time, the clickety-clack part of a rumble that even contained the sound of wind. Too fast, iron wheels clanking and jumping, the caboose and passenger cars turned across the viaduct over the brook followed by the steady frantic breathing of the engine. The engineer still grinned at where he had been, but Whalen's head was not visible this time. Smoke fell over them, its oily richness dimming the brass of the departing engine as the train rolled on toward the Lilliputown Railroad Station and its curve that had too small a radius for such speed.

They could only wait, hearing the distant busy sounds of wheels and tracks and the thumping breath of the engine. Muted but not made less momentous by distance, first came the tearing of sheet metal, the ferrous squeal of iron on iron, then various crunches logical in their orchestration, a fugue of deep and falsetto bangs and shrieks followed by one last more wooden-sounding crash that was somehow climactically satisfying—the end of a nightmare of momentum. Flames somewhere over there grew quickly until they outlined the narrow tops of the Lombardy poplars. Allard ran toward the crash, choking with apprehension, out of breath before he had even started. If Whalen were in the tender he might well be dead, and immediately he resented having to pull Whalen's burned, broken and possibly dismembered body from the wreck. Others ran alongside him; he could hear feet pounding across the bridge and on the turf behind. Everybody ran to see the extent of the disaster, and the run seemed to last forever. Down along the tracks that had lately held the train on its course Allard ran and ran, running out of breathless terror and resentment toward what he didn't want to see or touch.

". . . toward what he didn't want to see or touch." Aaron Benham, it seems, is also running as fast as he can toward what he doesn't want to see or touch. Running as time runs, no matter what you do, toward the bad news. But that is obvious to everyone. His problem is always doubled, however, because there is his life and there is also that thing that is of his life, the thing he is making, whatever it happens to be at the moment, and he never knows what it happens to be.

It is dark outside now. He feels vaguely hungry—it must be ten o'clock and he hasn't eaten since Helga's big breakfast, her slim green wrist and hand moving the spatula, her morning smell of sheets and woman's moisture he caught as he leaned down past her shoulder to smell the frying bacon.

Right now could come a knock at the door of this very house. Right now. A tentative, worried, Helga knock. An emotionally confused, wanting-to-talk knock.

"Helga! Come on in!"

"I just felt so peculiar, Aaron. I'm on my way back from the hearing on the trailer court . . ."

To go to the hearing on zoning at the junior high auditorium she has dressed up a little bit, and in her knit vest, skirt and panty hose she is sweetly delicate of body yet worried around the eyes—a smoky look of experience that is pathetic and makes her his equal, nearly his contemporary; there is that look of sithared years.

"Come in. I'll make you a drink."

"Where's your family?" she says as she puts her leather handbag on the counter.

"They're coming back tomorrow. Billy called and informed me that I'd forgotten to have the headlights adjusted and they didn't want to drive at night."

She stands leaning her hip against the counter, her arms crossed on her chest, while he makes them both a drink. It is all a little nervous because they are both married and here they are alone in this house. His hand wants to tremble, and so does hers as he hands her her drink, the moisture-cool glass and the ice cubes tinkling together in the amber. Their eyes meet and shyly look away.

Yes, how plausible, but it didn't happen; Helga did not stop by. He stares from his study window at the leaf-shaken lights of nearby houses. Our adventures, after a time, are mostly fantasies, and his are worse because of those minor but convincing details that are his curse and his talent. The little silver stretch marks, the musky taste of cigarettes in her mouth. Speaking in low voices to each other, saying funny things, afterwards. He misses all of his strange women, the women of his youth, yet he doesn't want them to be strange any more. He wants to fill them and to fill their eyes with that look that says I am alive and where I am, there is no time but this, there is no past, I have survived nothing, there is nothing that need happen next.

Allard was the first to reach the wreck. It was the overturned locomotive that burned, the dark orange flames of kerosene baking the oil and paint from its bent metal, spreading themselves along the gravel driveway. The train had nearly made it around the corner by the station, but then followed the lighter caboose when it jumped the tracks and crossed the path. The caboose had entered the Town Hall through the wall of Harold's room; the passenger cars were jackknifed, one on its side, and he had to jump across a coupling to get near the flaming engine. Whalen was not there, at least at first glance. He ran for the large carbon dioxide fire extinguisher in the lobby of the Town Hall, and with it quickly put out the flames. The engine creaked and hissed, steam, fuel and water leaking from the ruptured tanks and boiler.

Boom Maloumian's troops tended to take one impressed glance and leave. They had sneakily parked their cars out along the highway, and now they walked soberly, not quite running, toward escape. Whalen, too; Allard saw him across the parking lot, his white face staring for a moment before he disappeared. Knuck's car was gone; he and Vera must have left quite a bit earlier, and Allard wondered how much, if anything, they had observed before they left. Only later did it occur to him that they must have seen all the cars parked out on the highway. Or maybe Knuck was too beered up to notice much at all.

Angela and Nathan, Hilary, Mary and Naomi stood looking at the wreckage of the train that now seemed monstrously cataclysmic in its frozen writhings between the Lilliputown Railroad Station and the Town Hall. The engine hissed and creaked, slowly dying as its last pressures ran out.

Boom Maloumian, followed by Short Round and Betty Bebop, walked past without speaking. Betty Bebop, wearing a short jacket over a red satin formal dress, didn't even look over at the train, or at anyone, but scuffled awkwardly along on high wedgies, her battered face staring ahead. Short Round looked once, quickly, and Boom Maloumian strolled along humming to himself as the three of them faded into a darkness now suddenly split by the headlights of those who were leaving.

Angela and Naomi first noticed that Mary was no longer able to cope with the events of the evening. They exchanged glances and converged upon her. Her teeth chattered; her eyes focused upon nothing. Nathan gave Angela the keys to his car. "We'll try to find Harold," he said through closed teeth. "Get her to Brock House and see if you can pry a sedative out of the night nurse."

"We will," Angela said. "Don't worry." Mary let herself be led to the car.

"Barbaric," Hilary said. "It's barbaric." Since the only remaining transportation would be the motorcycle, he left with the girls.

Allard and Nathan, both wounded and a little dizzy still, searched Lilliputown for Harold. Allard found the sleeping poet, that bird of ill omen, but let him lay. Calling out Harold's name, they split up and covered the town. At the stone pool Allard was afraid he might find Harold floating the dead man's float, his white scalp dim in the dark water. But he was not anywhere. Finally they returned to the parking lot to find that Harold's car was gone.

"I wonder where he went," Nathan said, really worried.

In the wreckage of his rooms, under a ceiling light that still worked above all the plasterboard and broken studding buckled over the equally buckled caboose, they found signs of some hasty packing. He had taken his clothes from the undamaged closet and his toilet kit from the bathroom. The drawers of his bureau were mostly empty. He had taken none of his beloved books; those that weren't spilled across the floor were still evenly aligned on their shelves. His notebooks and manuscripts were still there, too; powdered softly with plaster dust, they lay neatly arranged upon his desk.

Allard turned over the top sheet of a deep pile of manuscript pages.

GLITTER AND GOLD
a novel
by
HAROLD ROUX

"Have you read it?" Nathan asked.

"He let me read some of it once."

"If he took his clothes he probably won't do anything drastic, huh? What do you think?"

Allard looked down at the solid pile of manuscript pages Harold had amassed with such love and care, that lovely story Harold had told himself to believe. Within those pages, in the kindly warm light of sincerity, Allyson Turnbridge is drawn through danger and terror toward Francis Ravendon, toward the culmination of their true and perfectly mutual love.

Nathan stood beside him, with his thin face, his wide, delicate mouth, his tremor of worry and life. Beneath the pale skin of his forehead was the angular bone that gave it shape. Nathan, unendowed with Allard's natural gristle, had behaved through it all with impeccable awareness and bravery. His speech to Harold, saying that he would wear a hairpiece too if he were bald at twenty-three, contained dimensions Allard hadn't been aware of.

Harold, too, grew rounder, deeper in his regard, so that

his degradation was unbearable. He had thrown his fantasy hair like a gage at Maloumian's feet, and stood there naked in Mary's presence. Harold hadn't been destroyed by any of that. But he had been left in charge of the Colonel's masterpiece and couldn't face its defilement, so he had run away. For a moment of real crisis, Allard felt all of Harold's responsibility but could not contain it. He was frightened for Harold's life. All these lives grew round, as though his vision had been flat and now grew painfully into color and depth. His eyes hurt. He had no way to repair anything that had been done.

"I found this on the church steps," Nathan said, pulling a crumpled hairy thing from his back pocket. "It's kind of yucky but I couldn't just leave it lying there. It's sort of like part of Harold." He put it on the desk, its brown human hair glinting, the body of the thing wanting to spring back into the roundness of a human skull.

They turned off all the lights of Lilliputown and shut the door of the Town Hall before they left on the Indian Pony. It was the time of the year for leaving. The next day the dormitories would close and Nathan and Angela would drive to her home in Connecticut for a confrontation Nathan Winston would handle all right, although a few years later he would find that his new name denoted a popular cigarette. Naomi would leave for her home in the Bronx, Mary for her home in Concord, Allard for his home in Leah. No matter what else happened, those departures would occur as inevitably as the changing of a season. When the place you lived in was closed and locked, you had to leave, and nothing could change that.

In the morning Allard woke unrested, his head swollen in places, his ears hot. Before he had gone to sleep he could not stop seeing Harold Roux driving his old car on and on through the night with no destination, his pale head shining, his eyes emitting a viscous liquid that might have been tears or blood. Now he saw that vision into a dreary daylight. The pain in his head seemed both an excuse for and a reminder of what he didn't want to remember, and as he walked down the hall to the telephone he let himself limp, though his bruises were not really that bad. They were healing already; he felt his body curing itself, as it always did.

He called Naomi because he had to. He thought it might help, hoping to hear that everything was not as bad as it seemed.

"Hello?" said Naomi's complicated voice that proved she was all there, right at his ear.

"It's Allard," he said hopefully.

"So what are you selling?"

"Please, Naomi. I just wanted to know how you and Mary were."

"We're getting ready to leave, like everybody else."

"So is she all right?"

"She says she's not coming back to school in the fall."

Silence, in which he unsuccessfully tried to assess his guilt. "We never found Harold," he said finally. "He took his clothes and left while we were looking around Lilliputown for him."

Silence.

"Say something, Naomi."

"I don't know why I came to your stupid party in the first place."

Her enmity hurt him so badly he spoke without thinking. "Well, that's something you'll have to figure out for yourself."

"I won't bother."

Now he turned toward anger, a shift to flippancy, an oscillation he hated himself for. "You think you're knocked up?"

"Possibly. I'll know in a couple of weeks."

"What'll we name it?"

"Allard B. Abortion."

"You know, you're kind of funny when you're not being a Stalinist."

"Go fuck yourself."

"Why do people hate me so much?"

"Allard, it would be no great loss to mankind if you started fizzing and steaming and melting until all there was left of Allard Benson was a soft white thing lying there like a segmented worm."

"Everybody goes around hitting me all the time, too."

"You may be interested in knowing that Mary's brother is picking her up around ten this morning."

"Listen, Naomi. Maybe I'm just hysterical. I don't want to talk like this, really. I'm worried about Harold and Mary and you."

"Don't worry about me. I'm not Mary or Harold."

"But what if you're pregnant, really?"

"I'll take care of it."

"How will you take care of it?"

"Daddy's money will take care of it. Look, Allard, it's bye-bye time, when all the little butterflies leave the flowers and flit off on their little male vacations, so don't let a thing bother you." She hung up.

It was nine-thirty so he got dressed and went up to the dormitory to say goodbye to Mary. He felt terrible, didn't know what to say to her to make her reasonably happy except that he . . . what? He could ask her please to wait and see what the summer might do, and to come back to school in the fall and they'd be together again, and maybe Harold would be back, too. Along the curb in front of the dormitory were girls and their trunks and suitcases. Fathers and brothers loaded the cars while the girls smiled and were teary and said Goodbye, goodbye, have a good summer and we'll see you in September. But Mary wasn't there. He asked in the lobby and was told that she had gone. Robert had come a little early and she had gone.

He walked back in the warm spring air, beneath the leaves, feeling free and at the same time depressed, as though he were falling. He couldn't even find in himself enough energy to feel hatred for Maloumian, Whalen, Short Round or any of that bunch. They seemed not individual men but the same universal force he always recognized and that recognized him and his kinship with them and eventually smashed him in the mouth. Shape up, Benson—are you one of us, or not? Today Colonel Immingham would return to find that the Vandals had found his paradise.

Back in the room, Nathan was about all packed but Knuck hadn't yet returned from wherever he'd gone last night. A little nest of dirty clothes lay in its circle on his bed.

Then Allard and Nathan were both startled by the appearance in the room of Paul Hickett. There he was, in the flesh. Allard could not at first believe that the excited, wizened face of Short Round was right there within reach of his hands.

"You got to hear what happened!" Short Round said breathlessly.

"You've got some kind of crust coming in here," Nathan said.

"Wait a minute! Wait a minute! You got to hear what happened, for Chrissakes! Cut it out! Listen, I got to tell you what happened!"

They both looked at him coldly while he explained that last night they took Betty Bebop back to Boston in Harorba's car and Boom wouldn't give her all the money she thought she was supposed to get and she hit him with her pocketbook and he hit her back, *wham!* Man, the car was going thirty anyway and Boom pushed her right out into the street. Down in Roxbury someplace. She went ass over teakettle into a bunch of garbage cans and they kept right on going, man! Boom said what's one beat up dinge whore, more or less. Even if she croaks it won't even be in the papers.

"Honest to Jesus, that's what happened! Can you beat that? I was scared shitless, man! But Boom! Cool as a cucumber! Even Harorba was scared shitless! Can you beat that? So she didn't get a goddam plugged nickel, not a Christly nickel!"

Short Round went on, even when Knuck Gillis lurched into the room and stood looking down at him, vaguely knotting his hairless eyebrows at Short Round's dance of joy and hysteria. Short Round finally left, screeching with desperate laughter. He was afraid, badly frightened by it all, and he would not be able to stop talking about it.

"Do you believe it?" Nathan said.

"I'm afraid I do."

Knuck merely sighed and lay face down on his bed.

"We ought to call the cops," Nathan said.

"Yeah, but I bet we don't."

They didn't, because nothing could continue after that day. The year was over, the exams were over and the marks were in.

Allard left that afternoon for his home in Leah, where he stayed a few days before heading west.

Aaron, sitting at his desk in front of the yellow circle of light, the only light in the dark empty house, tries to remember the name of the girl he went out with that summer in Pasadena. She went to Occidental College, she could always borrow her father's Packard, she always wanted him to drive, she lived in Monrovia . . . Other things about her are as clear as if they had happened yesterday. The powdery texture of her thigh as it moved over his, a favorite phrase of hers: "What a kick!" Her hair that was so black and glossy it was almost Oriental, her uptilted narrow nose. And also a general warmth of feeling about her presence. But her name is gone, gone out of his memory altogether. It is another of those failures, smallnesses. He hasn't in his life been an avid or compulsive collector of women; there weren't all that many and he should remember. He wonders where they all went, what happened to them. He doesn't like to think how old they must be now, how their lives ran on through other people and other places, small satisfactions and the probable tragedies that loom for everyone.

His own children are at that threshold now. Bill will get his driving license in the fall, and will take his chances in that unending lottery, those blinding oncoming lights. Janie is developing breasts even though she isn't yet fully grown. In her there is the vulnerability of kindness. She loves without a certain clarity he would wish her to have; she loves that murderous cat for its moments of purring, avaricious softness. She will be too generous, unwary, forgiving. The amateurs will be after her with their needful smiles, their callow wit. Some selfish young blade will casually break her heart.

He is alone in his house, but then he is used to being alone, to having at his work nothing really tangible for company—no good paint or canvas, no solid clay or stone, no musical instrument to carve real sensual impingements out of the air. He is alone with uncontrollable, freakish, perversely willful images. Better to be like Boom Maloumian (dead in an automobile accident in 1950) and act out one's myths (but not that last one, not yet) than to be condemned to this constant fantasy state, ever alone when the activity is most frantic.

There is always booze, with its paradox of revelation and impotence, but he chooses not to go there; life is getting so much shorter in these latter days, so much shorter it even seems an indulgence to worry about any of George Buck's public nightmares. But he does, he does.

What future there is is the work he will do, the chaos of the past he will somehow make into form, all the fragments now swirling just out of reach, the excitement inside him somewhere like an itch he can't scratch, a pain he can't locate. Pain is one of the necessary functions, however.

The circle of yellow light on his desk seems to contract and grow brighter. The only light in the whole dark house is directed here.

Fragments. He's got to get everything together, first, then discard what must be discarded. And he must tell the truth—that all of us were once immature and stupid, oscillating between the banal and the sublime (or in some range between those polarities), and that the banal is also true. Allard Benson, once flip, facetious, to whose golden youth other bodies were sometimes felicitous tools, must learn and be touched. We perceive depth slowly. When a man tries himself he constructs a scaffold and a throne.

There is a letter, a document he hasn't read for a long time. He never deliberately looks for it, but every once in a while he comes across it and reads it again. It is surprising that he still has it around here somewhere—in a drawer or folder or stuck in a book. Where is it now? Most things from those times have worn out, been discarded or lost in his travels.

In the semi-dark outside of the circle of light his hand goes to a drawer below a cupboard, to an old manila folder, straight to the letter. His act of keeping it all these years is vaguely shameful, as though he has kept it as a souvenir, something as untoward as the polished wristbone of a corpse. The letter was written to him out of a sadness that was too close to self-hatred. It was a sadness he caused, though everyone grows sad and who knows whether this or any unhappiness would have been less if he had never been born. But he has kept these sheets of scalloped-edged, buff-colored stationery, this document, because even from the beginning it has always suggested to him use, a colder use. The handwriting is round, generous but not unformed, the hand of a girl who did her lessons and was bright. It is neat, spaced, incapable of lying, written in liquid blue ink with a fountain pen. That alone proves this document to be of historical interest, yet he must remember her as the young girl she was, so much of her unused, untouched, unworn. Eighteen, and adult life just beginning for her.

Mary, he thinks, but is then startled; her name, of course, was not Mary, and again he is troubled by the uses he must make of past reality. Once this beautiful, complex being did exist upon a real Earth, but the Earth has changed and any recalling of it will be shaped, changed again.

Dear Aaron,

You don't sound like you in your letters, you sound like an old philosopher or something, so I don't know who's writing to me. Am I reading the truth or some sort of fictional treatment of a letter? Do you enjoy writing them or is it painful to get around to saying what you mean? I know I never criticized you like this, but I know it doesn't really make any difference anymore.

I get this terrible feeling that you're the only boy I'll ever love. I sometimes think—maybe all the time when I'm not trying to think of something else—that when I let you make love to me I was marrying you and I was a stupid little fool because you weren't going to marry me so I threw it all away. I mean the whole possibility, ever, of marrying a boy I could really love. Because there will always be you back there smiling about it all and composing those sophisticated letters with all the long sentences and subtle little twists in the middle of them that mean you'd like to make love to me but you don't love me enough to marry me. I know.

In July my period came about six days late and that was a scare. But it's all right now—you didn't leave any tracks behind you.

Don't worry about going to the University of Chicago in the fall. I'm not going back to school anyway. I couldn't walk around there and see all those places again. Dad isn't any better so I'm going to stay here and take care of him. Richard will be gone, you know. Dad looks so bad we're really worried about him. He's even more yellow-colored now. The whites of his eyes and his fingernails are yellow. He has trouble getting around and spends most of the time in bed. It's sad because even if he's grateful he can't show it because he resents being like he is so much. He's only fifty and there was Mother's death and now he's so sick I guess it all just doesn't seem fair.

Natalie wrote me a long letter trying to explain everything and cheer me up at the same time. She is very angry at you. Sometimes I feel like a baby or a feeble-minded child everybody is trying to reassure. But I guess I do feel different from the rest of you. You were always trying to convince me that all the things we did weren't sins and all that. But I know they were, even if it's just how empty I feel now. I never used to feel empty. I don't feel complete anymore. Why should I believe Natalie doesn't feel that way too?

She's thinking of transferring to Hunter College beginning in the spring semester next year. Anyway, we sign our letters "love."

Sometimes I resent the way nothing really matters to you, so you can just jump on your motorcycle and you're away, free as a bird. But I don't think it's your fault. That's the way you are and always will be. Maybe it was that about you made me love you. But no, it wasn't. You're really a very kind person, Aaron, I know. You can be a little sarcastic sometimes but you don't go out of your way to hurt people. It's just that you're not really mature yet and you don't want to be tied down. You've got a wonderful career ahead of you, Aaron, I know it, I'm sure of it. I guess I can't blame you even if like a little idiot I wanted to be with you always. Well, don't let my self-pity spoil your summer.

Sincerely,
Maura

But now it is the present, timeless time, tense; only we pass, and that is some of the meaning, he supposes, of every story, even of that other, unchanging one, in which Billy Hemlock gained strength and knowledge from the powders, especially from the powder of the graceful hand, which he finally recognized as the outermost frond of the hemlock tree. And so he did enter, as a descendant of the Old People, the passage into the mountain denied to Eugenia, and after many adventures found Janie and Oka in that strangely warm interior valley. The old lady was the Lady of the Deer, one of the ancient gods herself, her feet delicate deer hooves. Then, refreshed by grateful gods in the form of wheat, sweet grasses, the very bodies of the animals who were conscious only as long generations, generous in the timeless knowing that they would always survive, Billy and Janie came home with Oka, bearing sustenance, to wake Eugenia and Tim Hemlock from their long sleep of despair. How the children loved that loving reunion.

But that was the children's story, and they are not here, in fact are no longer children. When they return tomorrow they will bring to him lives that are their own, that are growing away from him. All lives move beyond his ken. George Buck will have to leave after next year, George and Edward and Helga vanished from their beautiful house. You can't write another man's story for him. You can't raise Mark Rasmussen out of the despair of his years. But this is only reality with all its collisions and coincidences.

It is deep in the fathomless but temporary night. Aaron has gone to bed, alone into the fresh sliding of the sheets of his and his wife's bed. Soon he is washed under, where the currents, themselves not in control, control him. He dreams that a strange woman watches him. He is twenty-six years old, ageless, having had all of his experiences yet inhabiting the quick, observing body that is never conscious of its perfection. He is sitting on a couch, in an old brownstone garden apartment, in a gray city of the 1950's. The air is the air of the city, not dirty but busy, moving, only a trifle gritty. The towers of the city are gray stone and crystal glass, having meaning and dignity, as have the trees in its parks, its arcades, avenues, squares. All have the somber dignity of the city. Windows are clean, all of its interiors are clean, polished, glittering with care. He half reclines on the couch in the high-ceilinged apartment, the strange woman standing across the room next to the French doors, watching him. She is not strange, she is in part every girl he has loved; she is Agnes, a mystery. She is twenty-four—old, experienced, wryly humorous, her light hair floating around her thoughtful face in undisciplined yet deliberate small fronds. She does not smile as she looks at him. The brave, eternal angle of her hip as she stands, in a light dress, melts his heart and he holds out his arms to her.

ABOUT THE AUTHOR

THOMAS WILLIAMS was born in Duluth, Minnesota, in 1926, went to New Hampshire when he entered high school and, except for army service in Japan and graduate work at the Universities of Chicago, Iowa and Paris, has been living there ever since. His short stories have appeared in *Esquire*, *The New Yorker*, and *The Saturday Evening Post*. One was awarded an O. Henry Prize; others have been included in *Best American Short Stories*. His novel *Town Burning* was nominated for the National Book Award in 1960, and his volume of short stories, *A High New House*, received the Dial Fellowship for Fiction and the Roos/Atkins Literary Award in 1963. His most recent novel, *Whipple's Castle*, was called "a masterpiece—a book for other times as well as our own." He is also a Guggenheim fellow and was awarded a Rockefeller grant for 1968–69. He now lives in Durham with his wife and two children and is at work on several projects as well as a new novel, *The Followed Man*.